NO SUCH THING AS WEREWOLVES

DEATHLESS BOOK 1

CHRIS FOX

CHRIS FOX WRITES LLC

For Lisa. The most imaginative part of O.W.L. yet...

PROLOGUE

"How the hell did we end up in Peru? And not even the good part, down in Lima where the locals think we're marines," Jordan asked, shading his eyes from the sun's relentless glare as he peered over the helicopter's console at the wide valley below. It was flanked by high peaks, some of the tallest in the Andes. At eleven thousand feet, it was a place none of the locals ever came willingly.

"Is shit," Yuri agreed, the Russian's face hidden behind a large pair of aviator glasses and a thick black goatee. The wiry pilot eased the yoke, tilting the copter forward to afford a better view of the scrubby hillsides. "Should be in jungle. Is pretty there. Birds. I like birds."

Why *were* they here? The team had been put together with incredible haste, dispatched from a dozen different countries to the Peruvian city of Cajamarca where they'd been given one day to acclimate to each other. They'd been dispatched here, given four old Boeing AH-64 Apache helicopters—the type that had been mothballed back in the 1980s after serving since Iran Contra.

"Commander, are you seeing this?" a female voice crackled over the com. It was either Savinsky or Jewel, but having just met them Jordan couldn't readily identify which was speaking.

A massive chunk of stone broke loose from the southern face of one of the mountains, plummeting to the valley floor with a crash so loud he could hear it over the rotors.

"Pretty tough to miss," Jordan replied, studying the cloud of dust curling skyward. A smaller piece broke loose from a neighboring peak. Boulders began jouncing all over the place, bucking about like Mexican jumping beans. "Carter, this place isn't seismically active, is it?"

"Not even slightly," Carter's nasally voice echoed back over the com. "We're nowhere near a fault line."

"Holy shit," another voice broke onto the com. That one was definitely Jewel.

A black spike bored out of the earth like the tip of some gigantic drill. It was nearly as large as the peaks surrounding it, a jet-black pyramid unlike anything he'd ever seen. Jordan's eyes widened as the structure approached. "Pull up. Pull up."

Yuri yanked back on the stick, guiding the Apache up and away from the approaching structure. Savinsky wasn't so lucky. Evidently she'd been distracted or maybe just surprised by the structure's momentum. The pyramid slammed into the Apache, unleashing a fireball of flaming wreckage as it continued its ascent.

"Get clear," Jordan roared. The other three copters veered safely away, hovering around the strange pyramid like angry wasps. Up and up it went, until it towered over their comparatively tiny copters. He turned to Yuri. "What's our current elevation?"

"Nine hundred seventy-five feet above valley floor," Yuri said, jaw still hanging open as he gaped at the pyramid. "Is taller, so structure eleven hundred feet. Give or take."

The pyramid finally stopped moving, its jet-black slopes covered in patches of dark soil. Jordan had a million questions. How old was it? Who'd built it? Most troubling, how had their employer known it was going to appear? That they'd been dispatched to such a remote location at the precise moment this thing had appeared was no accident.

"Carter, are you getting any readings from that thing?" he asked, tightening his sunglasses. The structure seemed to drink in the light around it, reflecting none of the midday glare.

"Nothing," Carter's voice crackled back. "And when I say nothing, I mean nothing. It's not sending back radar. It just absorbs the ping. It's eating the signal somehow. Never seen anything like it."

Something like a heat shimmer appeared around the structure. At first Jordan wasn't sure what he was seeing, but eventually his eyes widened. The entire thing was vibrating. The dirt clinging to the sides slid off, like butter on Teflon, falling away until the structure was as pristine as it was on the day it was built, whenever that was. Great piles accumulated around the base of the structure. They surrounded the entire thing except one place where the dirt was conspicuously absent.

"Carter, check out the center of the western face. What do you make of it?"

"There's definitely something strange there, sir," Carter said, a rare note of uncertainty in his voice. "There's an area in the exact center of the wall that's devoid of debris. If you use magnification, you can see that there are poplar trees scattered all about, but their branches stop at the edge of the clearing as if they were sheared through with a really sharp plane. I don't know what to make of it."

"All units, make your approach. Prepare for field recon," Jordan ordered, filling his voice with authority and confidence he didn't feel. What the hell had they been sent into?

Yuri eased back on the yoke, and the whirring of the rotors slowed. The craft descended smoothly, drifting to the edge of the ring of dirt now surrounding the pyramid. The copter set down just beyond, between a still-standing poplar tree and a cluster of boulders.

A hawk wheeled overhead, screeching a challenge as the whir of the rotors finally died. Jordan pushed open the canopy over the craft's rear seat. Intended more for combat than transport, it was just large enough to hold two people. An intimidating machine gun had been bolted under each stubby little wing, along with a boxy missile launcher on the right. Hardly the sort of hardware you'd send to scout unless you were expecting serious trouble.

Jordan slid from the cockpit, dropping to the dry earth with a puff of dust. The high desert made his eyes water beneath his sunglasses even though the wind was bitterly cold at this elevation. He withdrew his pack from the boot, the harness jingling as he buckled it at his waist and chest. The black nylon was compact enough to not restrict movement and still contain the basic supplies they might need on such an op.

"We're going in hot. No sense in taking chances," he said into the sub-dermal microphone that Mohn Corp. had so graciously provided. It was state of the art, picking up words people right next to him would miss. Jordan buckled his sidearm, an M-411 smart pistol, into place. The weapon fed targeting data to his goggles, making combat nearly as easy as your average video game.

"Is very strange," Yuri said, dropping to the dirt beside Jordan. His gaze was fixed on the pyramid, or more specifically, the clear space in front of the wall some fifty yards from where they'd set down. He could tell the break in debris was clearly something the builders had intended, because it lay directly outside a gap in the structure. It was as if a square section had been cut away, allowing visitors to enter a tunnel that led inside.

"Carter, what can you tell me?" Jordan said, turning toward the third helicopter as the short, sandy-haired tech fell awkwardly to the ground. He got up quickly, dusting off his pants and trying to act like he wasn't as clumsy as they all knew him to be.

The tech trotted over, taking a sip of water from the blue hose leading into his pack. "I ran a full scan on the valley. We use sonar imaging to build maps, which the satellites confirm. Only there's gaps in my model, gaps caused by that thing. It's eating the signal, sir. That shouldn't be possible."

"Yeah, you mentioned that in the air. What else can you tell me?"

"Not much," Carter admitted, turning to face the structure. He withdrew a bulky black box from his belt and aimed it at the tunnel. It beeped and hummed for several seconds before Carter turned back to face him. "Sir, this is damn odd. That tunnel is emitting ELF."

"Ee el eff?" Jordan asked. Carter would speak in nothing but obscure abbreviations and acronyms if allowed to do so.

"Extremely low frequency waves, sir. A very special type of signal we used back in World War II to transmit codes. It's slower than most signals, so you don't see it much today," Carter explained, adjusting his goggles as he watched the pyramid. "They're also given off by power plants. Nuclear power plants, for the most part. It's possible there's a power source inside, or maybe whoever built this place is using them for communication. No way to know without checking it out, sir."

"Then that's exactly what we'll do. Yuri, take Carter down that tunnel to see if you can find a way inside. If there isn't one, then make it. No chances. If you run into anything, topside. If you have a question you can't answer, topside. Back in ten minutes," he ordered. Jordan could have sent a larger team, but with Savinsky's team gone there were only six of them and he didn't want to risk any more personnel than he had to—one tech and one experienced soldier to keep him alive.

Yuri fished his M4 rifle from the cockpit, the smooth-bored weapon menacing as he propped the barrel up over his shoulder. The weapon was standard issue, but in the hands of a crack shot like Yuri, it could devastate a battlefield.

The Russian trotted toward the pyramid, bringing the stock of his rifle to his shoulder as he scanned the oppressive darkness that so neatly blended with the structure's dark surface. Carter trotted a little ways behind, replacing his bulky black box with a smaller green gizmo. Jordan was good with technology, but he had no idea what either device did. He doubted anyone other than Carter could tell him. The tech was always tinkering, and the gadgets were both things he'd cobbled together in his spare time.

The pair began to disappear into the darkness, though Jordan could still make out their shapes. They stopped perhaps ten feet into the strange tunnel, a perfect square that could have been bored with a laser. Jordan shaded his eyes, watching as Yuri leaned a shoulder into the massive stone door and shoved. To the Russian's apparent surprise, it gave easily, spilling him to the ground as the door slid soundlessly open. Damn. That kind of engineering could barely be accomplished today. How many tons did that door weigh?

Jordan began to pace, his right hand settling on the grip of his pistol. Ten minutes. Such a short span of time, but it crept by. What was happening inside? Something echoed from within. Gunshots. He resisted the urge to order another pair inside, instead gesturing at both sides of the entrance. The squad moved to flank it, each soldier leveling an M4 at the opening. Long seconds passed.

At nine minutes, sixteen seconds they heard the slaps of booted feet on stone as something approached. Yuri's form emerged first, bent low, arms pumping as he hauled ass back into the sunlight. There was no sign of his rifle. Carter's form trailed behind, the lanky tech clutching his side as if he had a cramp. Only it wasn't a cramp. His black uniform was soaked with blood, and his face was ashen as he limped forward.

"Jewel, get the medical kit," Jordan bellowed, jerking the stock of his rifle to his shoulder as he scanned the darkness. The rest of the squad did the same, including Jewel. The weapon suited the tiny blond, despite the fact that it was nearly as large as she was. She lowered it reluctantly, trotting back toward the helicopter. She was the closest they had to a medic.

Carter stumbled, sprawling to the ground just past the thick shadow provided by the tunnel. Yuri didn't even stop to help. What the hell had spooked him so badly he didn't stop to help a wounded squad mate?

A third figure moved in the darkness. It was tall. Too tall. Maybe seven or eight feet, if the glittering amber eyes served as indicators. Then it stepped into the thinner shadow near the end of the tunnel, providing Jordan with far more detail than he'd ever wanted to see.

The creature looked like some sort of dark-furred Egyptian god, with a head that clearly belonged on a wolf. Sharp white fangs bared over black gums, and the long claws on one massive hand still dripped blood—Carter's blood. The creature wore some sort of golden necklace, a torque, Jordan thought it was called. Its clothing was cut from shimmering white cloth, something like a Roman toga.

"End that thing," Jordan roared, aligning the crosshairs in his goggles with the thing's chest. He squeezed off three rounds, the gun bucking in his hands as it belched gouts of flame. Echoing fire came from all around him as the squad reacted instantly, every last member a veteran of one war or another.

The thing didn't move. In one moment, it was standing in the center of the corridor. In the next, it stood next to Carter. The rounds they'd fired found nothing but stone, ricocheting down the tunnel. The beast knelt, savaging the back of Carter's neck with those wicked teeth.

Jordan adjusted his aim, firing again. So did the others. This time the thing jerked backward, raising a hand to its shoulder. Its amber gaze touched Jordan's for an instant; then the beast disappeared.

"Behind us," Jewel roared. Jordan spun to see her drop the med kit. She jerked her rifle up, but it was too late. The beast raked its claws across her throat, showering the dusty earth with her blood.

"No," Jordan roared, sprinting toward the downed soldier as he squeezed off several rounds. None hit, but they did draw the beast's attention. It blurred across the space between them, looming over Jordan like a linebacker over a toddler. Its claws descended, death's embrace plummeting toward Jordan's face with impossible speed. Jordan dropped to his back, bringing his rifle into alignment with the thing's midsection. He didn't take time to aim, just squeezed the trigger.

The beast stumbled backward under a withering hail of fire, face twisting into an all-too-human expression of frustration. Then it simply vanished. Jordan scrambled to his feet, spinning around as he scanned for a target. Nothing. How did it move so swiftly? It defied reason. Yuri approached, offering Jordan a hand. The big Russian helped him to his feet.

"Is crazy. Not paid enough to fight fucking werewolves," Yuri said, shaking his head. He was staring at Carter's corpse. There was no way the tech had survived.

Jordan wanted to correct him. There was no such thing as werewolves. But he'd just seen one. How the hell was he going to explain this to Mohn? Maybe he wouldn't have to. Perhaps this is exactly what they'd expected.

1

A BIGGER BULLET

Commander Jordan eyed the hangar thoughtfully. The silver dome was out of place, nicer than either of its neighbors. That didn't fit Mohn's low profile imperative, so who'd authorized this place? He'd never met the woman in charge of the Panama facility, though he'd seen her at a distance when he deployed to Cajamarca just a few weeks ago.

Taxis and buses flowed down the road behind him, ferrying passengers to one of the busiest airports in Central America. He slipped through the gap in the fence, walking briskly to the door near the south corner. Jordan withdrew his cell phone, speed dialing the Director. The phone clicked several times and then rang once before it was picked up. He recognized the commanding voice immediately.

"Have you arrived?"

"Yes, sir," Jordan replied. Director Phillips was all protocol, and even though they weren't officially military they wore the same trappings.

"Good. Review the weaponry and ensure that it will meet your needs," the voice on the other end said. The words were clipped, efficient.

"With respect, sir, I don't know what our needs are. That thing took everything we had to throw and kept on coming," Jordan said. He didn't want to be insubordinate, but command needed to know what they were facing.

"I realize that, Commander, but your own reports said that you hurt it. That was with more conventional ordnance. The weapons we've prepared should be considerably more effective," the Director said.

Jordan watched traffic rumble by, so damn normal.

"Sir, we're fighting a god-damned werewolf that crawled out of a pyramid with no right to exist. We don't know *what* will be effective. I'll take the added firepower, but what I really need is more men. That thing carved through my squad like a Thanksgiving turkey," he said, trying unsuccessfully to keep the heat from his voice.

"That takes time, and you damned well know it," the Director snapped. Jordan was shocked. He'd never heard the Director lose his composure before. "We're working on replacements, but they've only had two weeks training. If I send them in now, I'm as good as pulling the trigger myself."

"What about mercs, sir? There has to be an off-the-books option," he offered. Mohn Corp. had ties with a number of black ops organizations that specialized in wet work.

"That could bring unwanted attention," the Director said, sighing heavily. "I just got off a call with the Peruvian president. They want to know what the hell we're doing up there and why we're bringing in so much hardware. I can't afford any more scrutiny, and that's exactly what sending in cowboy mercs will do. You're just going to have to make do with the personnel you have. Review the weapons and get your ass back to Peru."

"Yes, si—" Jordan began, but the phone beeped as the call ended.

He wiped sweat from his forehead with the back of his hand. Damn, this place was hot. Such a contrast to the frigid Andes. He resisted the urge to see if anyone was watching, and instead pounded the hangar's door three times with his fist. The hollow booms were swallowed by the road noise, but the door opened almost immediately. A hard-eyed man in full Kevlar opened the door. He carried an unfamiliar rifle, front hand resting on the underside of the barrel, with the other over the trigger guard. In one fluid motion he could snap it to his shoulder to fire. His face screamed drill sergeant, though he bore no insignia except Mohn's standard green triangle on his shoulder. The guy could have been R. Lee Ermey's shorter, angrier brother.

"Jordan?" he barked, leathery face set in what Jordan guessed must have been a permanent scowl. "Get your ass inside. This isn't the goddamn shopping mall."

He opened the door just wide enough for Jordan to slip through, slamming it behind them the instant they were clear. The place was pitch black except for a pair of stand lamps overlooking narrow tables lined with weapons. Behind them stood a skinny, nerdy-looking guy with a thick mustache and small tinted glasses. He wore a flannel shirt under a polyester vest, not exactly standard-issue gear. The guy reminded him of Carter, summoning a memory of the dead tech's lifeless eyes. Jordan had seen a lot in his time, but that memory was one of the worst.

"You're here to get some real firepower," Sarge said. A made-up name helped because it was the only one Jordan was likely to get. Mohn ops were anonymous. You never knew more than you had to about the people you were working with.

Sarge walked over to the tables, gesturing at one of the rifles. "Your last op used the M4, right?"

"Yeah. Lacked stopping power though," Jordan replied, crossing to stand next to the table.

"The M4 is great," the skinny guy broke in. Jordan decided to call him Lester, after a character from a video game he'd played back in the '90s. "It's one of the most ubiquitous military firearms on the modern battlefield. Definitely the most familiar rifle to your mercs... er...soldiers."

"A lot of *operatives*," Sarge corrected, "use the Russkies' AK. Cheaper than the M4."

"Yeah, uh, operatives. Anyway, the AK's great too, but I like the M4, and that's what we've got here, a typical M4," Lester said, patting the stock lovingly. "The locking bolt gives a more stable ballistic chamber and, thus, a more accurate shot than an AK." He picked up the rifle, thumbing the switch near the trigger to full-auto. "Even fully automatic, your first three or four shots are dead on."

"Yeah, and that's why we love it," Jordan agreed. He knew the rifle's internals intimately. "But, like I said, it didn't have enough stopping power. The 5.56 round just isn't enough." He picked up a long brass bullet from the table to illustrate.

"Yeah, I'm not surprised," Lester said, grin spreading. "The round is only twenty-two caliber, even if it is high velocity. You'll core soft targets, but it doesn't do squat against anything with armor. Even a car windshield will stop a round. The bullet just punches through your target without much expansion. That's why it lacks the stopping power you're after."

Jordan folded his arms. "I didn't come here to talk about what didn't work. I came here to get something that will. If we're going to take down my target, I'm going to need…"

"…A bigger bullet," Sarge and Lester finished in unison.

"Not just any bigger bullet. Something special I invented," Lester said. Jordan hadn't thought the kid could get any more perky, but somehow he did. He patted a sleek black rifle a little larger than the M4. "I modified the M4 to fire a thirty-caliber Blackout AAC. You keep the same shell base, thus same bolt carrier group, magazine, etc. All that is needed is a barrel and chamber change, and voilà: stopping power and penetration of a heavier bullet without changing the familiarity of your weapon. I call it the XN8."

"That might give us the edge we need. How many can I have, and when will they be ready?" Jordan asked.

"We have a demonstration ready and—"

"That's not necessary. You've explained how the gun and the round work. This is what I need. Can I leave here with a case? I need to get back on-site for my op," Jordan replied, cutting Lester off. The kid clearly wanted to say more but gave a heavy sigh instead.

"All right. We can skip the demo. I guess the pig would appreciate that, if no one else," Lester said, offering Jordan the XN8. "You can take this one with you now. I've got another crate of eight I can have loaded on your departing flight. Was there anything else you needed?"

"Yeah, some luck," Jordan replied, accepting the rifle. He set it gently in the rectangular case, settling the weapon into the foam before snapping the case shut. "Thanks, guys. These weapons are going to save lives."

Jordan hoped that was true. He'd never seen anything like the monster in Peru. M4s hadn't even slowed it down, though they had driven the creature off. That meant it feared pain and could probably be killed through conventional means. Guess Jordan was about to find out, assuming the thing came back to the pyramid. He walked back to the door, case in hand.

Jordan withdrew his smartphone and called the Director. "It's done."

2

PREHISTORIC ALIENS, MY ASS

2,600 BCE. Blair wrote the words out laboriously, fingers cramping around the tiny nub of chalk. He underlined the date, turning to face rows of disengaged freshmen. Santa Rosa JC's finest. The back rows shot clandestine gazes at smartphones under their desks, either not knowing or not caring that Blair could see. If today's lesson didn't grab them, they'd be the ones who dropped.

"Why is that year significant?" He asked, pausing for a full three seconds as he scanned the room. Curiosity lurked in a few corners, but no one ventured a hand.

"That's the approximate date the Great Pyramid of Giza was built," Blair said, taking a step toward the front row. He began to pace. "You've seen it in movies. It's the most well-known wonder of the ancient world, a masterpiece that has endured for millennia. It's visible from space, forty-five stories tall, and has fascinated every culture from ancient Greece through the United States. Today you're going to learn how and why Pharaoh Khufu built it."

Several hands shot up, the most enthusiastic in the front row. It belonged to an Asian girl with long, black hair and a pink backpack. Jesus, these kids were young.

"Yes, Miss..."

"Samantha. You can call me Sam," The girl said, all but bouncing in her seat. Probably her first semester. The boys were just as bad, worse if their voices cracked during questions. "You said it was built by a pharaoh, but how do we know that? I saw this show, and it said that the Pyramids were built by aliens. It makes sense. I mean, how did cave men move those giant stones? They would have needed, like, cranes and stuff."

Every semester, it was the same. A misguided student, or six, parroted the drivel they'd read on Google or seen on Netflix. Not that he could blame them. If the Internet said it, it must be true, right?

"Was it the one with the guy's hair that gets crazier every season? Looks like a bird that got on the wrong side of a hurricane," Blair said, fanning his fingers out in parody of the host's incredible hair.

"Yes," she said, eyes widening as she straightened in her seat. "That's the one. That guy is crazy, but like, brilliant, too."

"Yeah. Here's the problem with that show. It's bullshit," Blair said, crossing his arms. Had he just gotten chalk on his sleeve? Damn it. "We know who built the Pyramids. We know when. We even know how. That's what—"

A cell phone went off, obnoxiously loud. He seriously doubted anyone else was using the *Game of Thrones* ringtone, which meant he'd just broken his own phone rule in class. He glanced at the desk drawer. If he answered it that would legitimize students doing the same for the whole semester. He ignored it.

"That's what we're going to discuss today. I promise by the end you'll agree the only thing alien on that show is that guy's hair," he said, pausing for a few polite chuckles. The phone stopped. Thank God. "I'll begin by passing out—"

There it went again, somehow more obnoxious. Snickers rippled through the class. He was losing them. "You know what, guys? I don't know about you but I could use some coffee. Let's take a fifteen-minute break. Go grab a Starbucks and get back in here." The stampede began.

Blair walked over the desk, jerking the drawer open and fishing out his phone. He almost dropped it when he saw the caller. It was Bridget. He was paralyzed, a deer about to be run down by a careless driver. Fuck. He sagged into his worn leather chair.

"Hello," he said. Somehow the phone had found his ear.

"Blair?" a trembling voice asked. He recognized it immediately. How could he not? "Listen, I know this is out of the blue, but my God, you've got to see what we've found. It's enormous, bigger than Giza, older than Göbekli Tepe, at least thirteen thousand years from the sediment covering the structure. How soon can you be here?"

"Bridget?" he asked, chair creaking as he leaned back. He removed his wire-frame glasses and set them on the desk. He'd need his full attention or she'd have him agreeing to some crazy plan before he even knew what she was talking about. "I haven't heard from you in almost three years, and our last conversation wasn't exactly friendly. I don't even know what country you're in. Slow down and explain."

"Peru. Blair, we've found a pyramid unlike anything ever discovered. It's *at least* thirteen thousand years old. Thirteen, Blair," she said, pausing long enough for the implications to sink in. "The hieroglyphs don't match any recorded style. They're not Incan, and they're more advanced than the Mayans'. Steve is completely baffled."

"Ahh," he replied, surprised by the depth of his bitterness. Blair rose from his chair, pacing back and forth as he watched the last student trickle from the room. "So that's why you called. Steve ran into more than he could handle, and you need me to bail him out. Then, assuming I can somehow help, he takes all the credit. Again. Is that it?"

"He doesn't even know I'm calling. Leave him out of it, just for a moment. Don't you want to be a part of this?" she asked, plunging forward with the conversation like an implacable wave, as always. "Think of it. This could completely redefine our understanding of—"

"Let me stop you there," he interrupted, cradling the phone with his ear while he shoved the day's quizzes into his briefcase. "I'm not interested, Bridget. I have tenure. I live in Wine Country. Things are good for me here. Besides, I don't want to play Indiana Jones anymore. The pay is shit and the hours suck. I like sleeping in a real bed. You know what I like even better? Not having to see you on a daily basis."

"I deserved that," she said after a long pause.

Her contrite tone didn't *seem* feigned. She must need his help badly. "Blair, you're too young to be a stuffy professor. Don't cheat yourself out of this because you're angry at me. This could make your career. Think of what we could learn. This could be your chance to—"

"I mean it, Bridget. I'm not budging on this one," he said as firmly as he could manage. It was difficult to deter her once she had decided she wanted something.

"I understand your reservations. I get that. Things didn't end well, but please don't let my mistakes make you miss this. You'll never forgive yourself once you understand what we've found. It's beyond amazing," She said, tone suffused with her usual passion.

There was a long pause that stretched until he thought maybe she'd hung up. "Besides...I'm scared. I've never seen Steve like this. He's obsessed, more than usual. He won't eat, and he barely sleeps. All his time is spent down in the temple's central chamber."

"I'm sorry to hear that. Really," Blair answered dryly, grabbing his keys and trotting up the stairs to the door. He almost flicked off the lights before remembering the students would be returning in a few minutes. He left them on, slipping into the cool evening. "If you want to send me some pictures, I'll take a look. That's the best I can do. I'm not flying six thousand miles to bail Steve's ass out. Again. I have forty tests to grade."

"All right, all right. I'll leave you be, for now. Just remember that I don't fight fair," Bridget replied, giving one of those throaty little laughs he'd so loved when they first met. It sliced through the intervening years.

The phone beeped its melancholy disconnect. Blair threaded past clusters of students as he crossed the lawn, toward the south lot. A handful of cars still dotted the parking lot. At least he wasn't the only one desperate enough to teach night classes. The extra pittance mattered more than he'd like to admit.

He fumbled in his pocket for his keys, opening his Ford's door with a reluctant groan. Blair tossed his briefcase in the back, dropping onto the sheepskin seat cover he'd added to hide the battle scars. If only he could do the same to this thing's tragic paint job.

Damn Bridget for knowing him so well. The oldest known pyramids in the Americas had been built, what, 2,600 years before Christ? Around the same time as the Egyptian ones, though the ones at Norte Chico were little more than large mounds. In both cases, the structures had been the center point of an entire culture. The implications of one existing six millennia earlier were monumental. That meant that there had been an older culture that had left almost no trace of its existence.

Who were they? Why had they disappeared? What had knocked their descendants down so hard that recovering even a fragment of their culture had taken eighty centuries? It was just the sort of mystery he'd always dreamed of solving. Discovering a common parent culture meant leaving a legacy that would endure as long as mankind continued to record knowledge. More than that, it might answer his own questions. What had come before the Egyptians and the Sumerians? Who built Göbekli Tepe? Why was it buried?

He smothered his enthusiasm. Was it worth leaving Santa Rosa, knowing he'd have to deal with Bridget and Steve? No, no it wasn't. He turned the key, and the Ford revved to life. "Fuck her and fuck Steve."

His phone buzzed in his jeans pocket. Blair fished it out, thumbing the home button and checking the notification. He swiped the screen and peered at the image that sprang up. It had been taken from the bottom of a ravine and angled steeply upwards along the slope of a jet-black pyramid. Calling it massive was like calling a Siberian tiger a kitty cat.

Blair turned off the car. Nothing in the Americas—hell, nothing in the world—rivaled it. From the context, he guessed the height at more than three hundred meters, over twice as large as the Great

Pyramid of Giza. The structure was carved from obsidian or maybe polished slate. Did they even have obsidian in the Andes? Even if they did, how had they gotten it there? The seams between the blocks must be incredibly fine for them to not show up in the photo.

"Clever Bridget," he said, slouching into his seat. She definitely *wasn't* fighting fair, but he wouldn't take her bait. It was an amazing discovery, but not amazing enough to deal with her cheating ass again.

His phone vibrated. This time the picture was darker, probably a shot of an interior wall. It showed highly stylized hieroglyphs with more complexity than anything ever exhibited by a Mesoamerican culture—or African, for that matter. That wasn't what caught his eye, though. The glyphs could have been painted yesterday. They were a riot of colors the equal of anything Photoshop might churn out.

The dense script contained thousands of symbols. That would make deciphering their alphabet impossible. Blair couldn't even hope for a Rosetta stone. Modern societies shared no common language with a culture this old. No wonder Steve was baffled. Blair opened his recent calls and tapped Bridget's name. The first ring hadn't even finished when she picked up.

"How soon can you be here?" she purred.

"I can't just walk out on my job, Bridget. I have rent," he replied.

"If that's the hang-up, I think we can reach an agreement. How does a hundred and fifty thousand dollars for eight weeks of work sound?" She said. He could practically hear the smile.

"That kind of money is too good to be true. Way too good," he replied, but he'd already made his choice. Sometimes, you walked into the trap even though you knew it was there.

"I know, but it's true. If you're in, I can have the funds wired as soon as you sign your NDA and contract," she said. "We'll even arrange for a call from the president of Peru to arrange a leave of absence. So what do you say?"

"If you're on the level? I'd say I'm in," he replied, turning the car back on. This was going to be the most memorable mistake he'd ever made.

3

RUNAWAY BRIDE

Liz's hand shook as she tamped out the cigarette in the chipped ashtray. She stood up, eyeing the phone on the table like a black widow that might attack at any moment. The bamboo floor creaked as she paced the short length of the drafty cottage, threatening to give way beneath her at any moment.

Why was she so afraid? Trevor was her brother. He'd never judged her. Quite the opposite. He'd always been supportive. Maybe she was just afraid of disappointing him. He'd always thought so highly of her, and she was about to cop to the most chicken-shit thing she had ever done.

She darted over to the table, seizing the phone and swiping the screen. A moment later, the phone was ringing as it clicked past Peru's local network and winged its way all the way to sunny San Diego. Trevor picked up on the first ring.

"Yeah?" he said, distracted. She could hear fingers flying across a keyboard.

"Trevor, it's Liz," she replied.

There was a pause. "Wow. Okay. Hold on a sec, Liz. I'll be right back."

Sound ceased. She'd been put on mute. She waited, almost as

terrified about him coming back as she was about the fact that he might not.

"I'm back. I just had to tell David to watch something for me. We've discovered a solar flare—a big one. Maybe the biggest anyone's seen in our lifetime," Trevor said, reverting to the excited kid Liz had grown up with. He was always dreaming.

"That's awesome, Trevor. Tell David I said 'hey,'" she said, relieved to talk about another topic, any other topic.

"I will," he said. His tone was different now, more somber. Uh oh. Here came serious Trevor. "Liz, you know Ernesto's been calling me, right? Like six times a day. The guy's in a complete panic. He thinks you've been kidnapped. Where are you?"

"I'm in Peru. I left him a note," Liz said, maybe more defensively than she'd intended.

"A note? Liz, it says 'I can't do this.' That's it. Not even goodbye or a signature. He's not even sure it's your handwriting."

"Yeah, I know it was shitty," Liz said, walking to the window. She opened the shutters, staring out at the muddy road leading up the mountain. It was going to rain again soon.

"Don't you think he deserves at least a phone call?" Trevor asked. The question was harsh, but the tone sympathetic.

"Yes, but I can't, Trev. He'll push me and push me until I tell him where I am, then he'll fly down here," she explained, horrified because she knew it was true. "I can't deal with him. It's like kicking a puppy, Trev. He's a great guy, but I needed to get out of there. To breathe."

"To breathe? Liz, you flew all the way to Peru. You could breathe in California. Mom and Dad would be happy to see you. You flew down there for that woo-woo bullshit, didn't you?"

"It's not bullshit, Trevor. Shamans have used Ayahuasca for millennia to help people. It's a psychological aide. Besides, the village needs someone to run the clinic. I—"

"Liz, I get it. I really do. This is important to you, and clearly Ernesto isn't the one," Trevor said. That floored her. She thought he'd liked Ernesto. "The thing is, you can't just let him twist like this. He's got to get closure. You owe him that."

She knew he was right. It was the fair thing to do. "I'll tell you what. I will write him a real letter. When he calls you next, tell him that."

"Will you actually write it?"

She hesitated. How important was this? Could she make it a priority, or was she going to agree only to let herself and her brother down?

"I'll do it today. I promise, Trevor," she said, the words as close to a vow as she was willing to make.

"Awesome. Liz, listen. I gotta go. What we've discovered is big. I have to get my report ready for the dean. Call me in a few days?"

"Yeah, I'll do that. Thanks, bro," she said, smiling. She hung up, turning back to the window.

She'd been dreading that call for days, putting it off as if doing so would make it easier. Calling had only gotten harder as her awkward silence had stretched. But in the end, she'd laid the issue to rest with a single phone call and an hour with a pen. She could finally move on.

Liz turned back to the desk in the corner, fully intending to sit down that instant. She hesitated as a shrill horn shattered the sleepy morning. She peered out the window, gawking as a trio of mottled green jeeps rumbled into view. They didn't look like the Peruvian National Police, but the black-clad men inside each vehicle carried what appeared to be assault rifles.

That would have been unusual in the U.S. Here, it was unheard of. There was nothing resembling an organized military force in the area—not that she knew of, anyway.

The trio of jeeps rumbled past the clinic. As the third one passed, she spotted a pair that stood out almost as badly as she had at her prom: a man and a woman, late twenties, maybe early thirties. He was handsome, with wind-tousled hair and a pair of wire-frame glasses. She was on the shorter side, even sitting down. A stunning brunette with wavy hair. Both Americans. Liz was sure of it.

Liz opened the door and stepped onto the porch. She shaded her eyes, studying the cloud of dust as the caravan made its way up the narrow path the locals insisted was a road. There was nothing up there, just barren mountain peaks and a village even smaller than this one. So where the hell were they going?

4

MEMORIES

Blair seized the leather seat ahead of him as the jeep bounced up a narrow trail that no sane person would call a road. They were in the last vehicle in the caravan, which helped lessen the terror. He could see the two jeeps ahead making the same trek, and the logical part of his mind said that if they made it, then he would too. At least he wasn't driving.

That fell to the beefy soldier with the Russian accent. Yuri, he'd introduced himself as. His silver sunglasses made him look like some emotionless android, the pistol strapped to his thigh making it very clear that he was the threat in most situations. Blair had never seen anyone like him anywhere near a dig. People like that with equipment like this were expensive. Nobody spent that on science. Nobody.

"Towns like this are so small they don't even have names," Bridget said, resting a hand on his forearm to get his attention. He resisted the urge to pull away. Blair would be damned if he was going to let her know how much she still affected him. "They might have a car that the whole village uses, or a few motorcars."

"They're farmers," he said, realizing it as he spoke the words. Fields of corn covered most of the ground where the few buildings did not. The stalks were shorter than the ones back home. "All the way up here. I can't even imagine how much work that must be at this altitude."

"It's amazing what they get by with." Bridget gave him a warm smile. She hadn't removed her hand. "They're extremely self-sufficient. In fact, they export food into Cajamarca. They live below the poverty line, but the whole community helps ensure no one goes hungry. It's remarkable."

A flock of sun-darkened children sprinted alongside the vehicles, laughing. They waved enthusiastically, one boy with a crooked smile meeting Blair's gaze. He found himself waving back, smiling in spite of himself. He really did have a lot of be grateful for, not the least of which was the massive deposit that had shown up in his bank account the night before. He'd paid off twelve thousand dollars in credit card debt this morning, finally freeing himself from years of not quite making ends meet.

"How much further to the site?" Blair asked. He didn't want to admit it, but the three-hour trek from Cajamarca had been devastating to his back. If he never saw another road like this, it would be too soon.

"About a half hour to base camp," Bridget answered, finally removing her hand. She gave a softer smile, a child who'd gotten away with something. "The jeeps will stop at the camp. Then we need to hike down into the ravine where the pyramid was discovered."

"That's not too far from this village," Blair said, pointing up at the ramshackle structures perched even higher up the hillside, "or the smaller one I can see up that way." The place was about half the size of the village they'd just driven through. "How do these people not already know about the pyramid? I can't imagine word not leaking out if it's as large as the pictures indicate. Everyone should know about it."

"Steve made me promise not to tell you specifics. He wants to see if you can determine why this place was never discovered until now," Bridget said, her smile becoming more of a smirk. She'd always known exactly how to play to his ego, and that he wasn't going to let Steve show him up yet again.

"Okay, keep your secrets for now. I guess I'll just have to figure it out for myself," Blair replied, shifting his gaze out the window. The foliage had thinned as they gained elevation, but stunted trees still dotted the roadside. Like the corn, they were smaller than they would have been near sea level. Flocks of bright-green parrots perched in many of them, as numerous as the pigeons back in the states. That, too, surprised him. He'd expected them near Cajamarca, but he didn't think they'd be tenacious enough to live up here.

The sky was an unrelieved grey. Those clouds almost felt close enough to touch, which made sense. He'd bet the high peaks of the Andes trapped them in the same way the Sierras did back in California. Unwilling to glance at Bridget, he stretched the silence as he studied the terrain.

"Blair," Bridget finally said, dropping her gaze as he turned to face her. "Listen. I know it isn't fair asking you to help Steve. I know how you feel about him and his role in how things...ended. But I didn't know who else to turn to. I'm scared. You've always been so dependable—"

"Dependable? Seriously?" Blair snorted, breaking into laugher. It felt good. He wiped a trickle of sweat from his forehead. "I can't believe you led with the reliable friend card. You're a shitty salesman, Bridget. Steve was my friend way before I introduced the two of you, and while he might be the world's biggest ass, he's also brilliant. He's contributed a lot to our understanding of Mayan culture, and he might do even more at this site. I want to be a part of it because I think you're right when you say we're about to make history. *That's* why I came. Not for you, and certainly not for him. So drop the whole remorseful ex thing. You've got more class than that."

"You're right. I didn't realize how bad that sounded until the words were out. I know you didn't come for me. I'm sorry," she said. Her shoulders slumped and hair screened her face. It was possible she even meant it.

"Don't apologize. I don't want to hear it. If this is going to work, it needs to be strictly professional. Why don't we start with you telling me what the hell is going on? How about some details instead of cryptic hints? What's wrong with Steve?" he asked, dropping his voice as he glanced at the soldiers in the front seat. Neither seemed aware of them.

"I'll start at the beginning," she began, finally meeting his gaze as the jeep labored up a particularly steep incline. Blair's stomach lurched, but he stubbornly ignored it. "We were approached by the Peruvian government. They sought out Steve because of his work at Tikal and Norte Chico. They figured he was the best qualified to lead a team and gave him a blank check. We were told we could bring whoever we wanted as long as we got them here within three days."

"How long ago was that?"

"Just under a month," Bridget admitted, eyeing him sidelong from under the protective screen of hair.

"You waited a month to bring me in?" Blair asked, suppressing the surge of heat in his gut.

"Steve wasn't willing, at least at first," Bridget said. Finally, she looked directly at him. "He still respects you, but he doesn't think very highly of your current career path. He wasn't sure we'd need you."

"So he thinks I've lost my edge. What changed his mind?" Blair asked, eyes narrowing.

"I did," Bridget replied. She waved her hand to dispel some of the dust wafting through the window. "I reminded him that the three of us worked better together, that you think of things everyone else misses. Steve is stubborn, but when he realized he wasn't ever going to be able to open the room in the central chamber, he finally admitted he needed your help."

"Central chamber?" Blair asked, straightening in his seat. "What have you found in there? Is there writing, or is it purely utilitarian like the Great Pyramid at Giza?"

"There are symbols everywhere, Blair. The kind left by an advanced culture, one which knew more than anything else in the ancient world, despite predating it by millennia. Hell, they may even know more than we do. We don't know why they disappeared, much less what they knew at the height of their culture. All that remains is this one structure," she said, eyes shining with the same wonder she'd had whenever *they'd* discovered something. It drove a knife through his innards. Damn. He missed this part of her.

"On the phone, you said Steve was acting strangely," Blair said, shifting the topic. He couldn't handle the old Bridget, not right now. He needed to focus on business. Stay professional.

"I'm getting there. We spent several days exploring the outer structure before we descended to the central chamber. Like you pointed out, the pyramids at Giza are completely barren on the inside, no writing of any kind. This one couldn't be more different. Every wall is covered in elaborate hieroglyphs like nothing we've ever seen. They're more Egyptian than Mayan but don't really belong to either. Steve thinks this is the history of their entire culture. Though, of course, we can't be sure until we translate it. If his theory is correct, we may have just found the parent culture that could have given rise to legends of Atlantis. They could have inspired the Egyptians, or might be responsible for Angkor Wat."

"He may be right, at least about this being a record. If the glyphs from the pictures you sent cover the interior, we could be looking at centuries of their recorded history," Blair agreed, grabbing the seat again as the jeep lurched over a rock that would have broken the axle on his Ford. "It's too soon to theorize about them being a parent culture though. This isn't the X-Files, Bridget. I seriously doubt aliens are behind this...any more than they are the construction of the Egyptian pyramids."

"You're only saying that because you haven't seen it," she teased, shooting him a wink. "This place is going to blow your mind."

"I'm sure it will," he said, still off balance, and from more than the bouncy ride. How was it that she could still affect him like this? Anger and sadness boiled up, but he pushed the awful mix right back down into his stomach. Stay. Professional. "You were telling me about Steve."

"Sorry. I got distracted. Anyway, Steve became convinced the key to understanding it all lay in the central chamber," Bridget continued, the leather seat creaking as she shifted. "He started spending entire days down there, hours and hours. That's when I first noticed the strange behavior. Steve has always been very...attentive. But he started ignoring me. Unless I went down to that chamber, I didn't see him at all. Even then, he barely even looked at me."

"You didn't consider that he might just be excited about a monumental discovery?" Blair asked. Was she that narcissistic? He remembered her being better than that.

"It's more than that, Blair. I know it sounds like I'm overreacting, but I promise you, I'm not," she protested. Her gaze rose to meet his as her mouth tightened. "He was excited, sure. Especially in the beginning. Who wouldn't be? But he barely eats or sleeps. Or bathes. All he's done for weeks is work. His mood has deteriorated to the point that he snaps at anyone who interrupts him. That isn't like Steve and you know it. I've seen him driven, but this? It's obsession on a level I can't even begin to understand. I know this is going to sound odd, but it feels...unnatural...like he's a drug addict or something."

"Unnatural? Bridget, I don't understand the problem *or* what you think I can do about it. Steve and I aren't exactly on good terms, and even if we were, what do you want me to do? Offer therapy?"

"You're taking this lightly, but you haven't seen him. You'll understand when we get there," she said, face going pale. She crossed her arms over her chest, huddling down into her seat as she stared out the window.

5

ARRIVAL

"Holy mother of God," Blair wheezed. It was the only appropriate reaction when confronted with, well *this*, regardless of his lack of religious beliefs. The structure dominating the valley below was otherworldly, a stately matron next to the uncouth mountain peaks that flanked it. The pictures had failed to capture the majesty, the foreboding. This place had been the center point for an entire civilization. He was certain of it. It was a focal point that must have taken generations to construct.

The smooth black slopes dipped down at a precise angle, absolutely perfect. Each jet-black slab was unbroken. There were no visible cracks or seams. Hell, the entire thing might have been carved from a single block of stone. The jet black had a mirrored sheen, kind of like the banks of solar cells springing up on houses all over California. The thing drank in the late afternoon sun, a gaping black hole in the center of the ravine below.

He took a cautious step closer to the edge, the frigid updraft almost mocking. It was such a long way down—a two-thousand-foot drop to the valley floor, itself nine thousand feet in elevation. Its effects were palpable, and not just the vertigo or the animal inside of him screaming to flee. The trembling of his legs and the rapid shallow breaths that just couldn't quite get enough oxygen were constant reminders both of the altitude and his fear of it.

None of that mattered now. He slid forward another foot, kicking a puff of dust over the edge. "I just can't believe it. That has to be, what, a thousand feet tall?"

"Eleven hundred," Bridget corrected with a smile, joining him at the ledge. She threaded her ponytail through the back of her cap, donned a pair of sunglasses, and then turned back to their escort. Two of the three jeeps had already moved off to the base camp erected on the south ridge, but the third idled nearby. "Thanks for the ride, Yuri. You can head back to camp. I'll bring Blair down to the site and introduce him to everyone."

"Is good," the beefy Russian said with a nod. He romped on the gas, and the jeep shot away in a cloud of dust, leaving the two of them at the mouth of a very narrow trail threading down into the valley. It ended near the base of the pyramid. Bridget was right. The structure was more advanced than anything in premodern culture; yet, if the dating from the sediment was correct, it had been constructed in the Mesolithic. Before man had learned to farm or write. Before they'd formed anything beyond primitive tribes. Its existence destroyed everything modern anthropology took for granted. The accepted theory of Egyptians being the world's first pyramid builders had been shattered. The whole field would be in chaos for years.

"What is it made out of? The Egyptians used limestone, but that's too dark to be any variety I know. Shale? No, that would be too soft. The rain would have eroded it. Obsidian, maybe? No, that would have flaked off," Blair muttered, shaking his head. He removed his sunglasses and cleaned them on his shirt.

"The outer surface is solid marble. Black marble is rare, but it exists in a few corners of the world. We've just never seen something of this size," Bridget said. She waved away some of the dust left in the wake of the jeep.

"The weight must be incredible. How would they have gotten it this far up into the Andes? There's no source of marble for fifteen hundred miles. Even if there were, how could they have moved it?" he asked, glancing at her.

"Let's see how long it takes you to figure it out. Steve got it right away," Bridget taunted, elbowing him in the side with a playful grin. He was too awed by the pyramid to be baited.

"They must have quarried it from one solid block—a piece that was already here. *That's* why it's built in such a remote location. They just carved it where they found it. It's the only possibility that makes any sense," Blair said, grinning in spite of himself. It was good being back in the field. He'd missed the wonder of exploration, of seeing the remnants of ancient peoples and trying to piece together their lives.

"First try. That's why you're so amazing," she said, kneeling to tighten the laces on her hiking boots. He glanced down the trail, skin turning to gooseflesh. He knew he needed to go down, but did it have to be right this second?

"I still think the location is odd, if we use any other pyramid-building culture as a template," he said, caught up by the majesty of the gleaming structure below. "The mountains around the ravine shield it. It could only be seen from the air or by pilgrims who could handle the hike up here. Every other pyramid was built as a monument. Kings wanted them to be found. Why hide this one?"

"Maybe they feared equally impressive tomb robbers, or maybe this was the only chunk of black marble they could find. Perhaps that material was important for some reason. In either case, the culture that constructed this place was clearly advanced," Bridget said. She hefted her pack from the rock where Yuri had left their luggage, the wind tugging at her loose cotton shirt, exposing a simple black strap over her shoulder. Didn't she feel the cold?

"Advanced? In what ways?" he asked, prying his gaze from the pyramid and dragging it back to Bridget. He grabbed his pack, grunting as he fit the straps over his shoulders. Why had be brought so many books? He had a damn tablet on his desk at home.

"The structure is in perfect alignment with the cardinal directions, just like those at Giza. There are pictographs on the lowest part of the base that perfectly mimic our solar system. They're just like those at Teotihuacan, and they include all eight planets," Bridget explained, approaching the mouth of the trail.

"That's incredible. We didn't even find Saturn until Galileo in the sixteen hundreds. How the hell did they look that deep into space? They must have had an advanced telescope," Blair theorized. The question was maddening because, barring the discovery of such a device in the structure below, they might never know how the ancients had observed the night sky.

Astronomy was the hallmark of every ancient culture. The more advanced their astronomy, the better their math. Every advanced culture mankind had discovered had been fascinated by the cosmos. This culture was as far removed from predynastic Egypt as Egypt was from the present, and yet they'd shared that same love of the cosmos, passing it on to their descendants for over thirteen millennia.

He had to get down there and see it, so he took a step down the trail. The rational part of his mind knew it was a good three feet across, but the terrified kid still remembered the episode in the Grand Canyon. "Jesus, you didn't tell me I was going to have to climb down a goat trail to get there. How many people did you lose on the way in?"

"Take my hand and stay close to the wall. I know you don't do well with heights, but you've been through worse. Remember China? That little cliff we had to jump? This isn't nearly so bad," Bridget said, offering an encouraging smile. That smiled dimmed when he ignored her proffered hand.

"I can handle it," he replied, pushing past her with all the resolve he could muster. He would be damned if he'd trail after her like some wayward puppy. He had too much self-respect for that.

"Fair enough. So the pyramid raises a lot of questions, don't you think?" Bridget asked, trotting after him as if they were strolling through a park rather than picking their way over a granite face that straddled the trail. "It could represent a common ancestor to both Egypt and Mesoamerica. If that's true, it will change the world's understanding of history forever. Hell, this culture might have even been responsible for Cambodia, too."

"It's possible, but that's a little too *alien conspiracy* to me. Clearly, this thing is advanced, but that doesn't mean that this was a global empire. It could have been localized to Peru or maybe South America," Blair countered, trailing his left hand along the granite wall and avoiding any step that took him too close to the edge.

"Skeptic," she teased. She was wielding her throaty laugh like a weapon.

"Scientist, you mean. What are the mounds of dirt around the structure's perimeter?" Blair asked, finally taking in the area surrounding the structure. It resembled a gopher mound with the pyramid at the center.

"There was a seismic event here that we're guessing revealed the structure. That's how this place was originally discovered. The university in Cajamarca catalogued the event," Bridget explained, pushing back the brim of the battered cap. "The pyramid was somehow entombed under layers of sediment. Either the earthquake pushed it to the surface—"

"—Or the pyramid pushed *itself* to the surface, triggering the quake," he finished dryly.

"Don't be so dismissive," she said, rolling her eyes. "The pyramid is at the epicenter for the quake. The *exact* epicenter."

"That's one hell of a coincidence," Blair admitted. He glanced into the ravine. "If this thing was buried, why aren't the slopes covered in dirt? Did you spend time cleaning it?"

"We found it like this—pristine—like it was constructed yesterday. No erosion, no discoloration. No damage of any kind," she said. Blair winced as his foot landed within inches of the trail's edge.

Before they'd made it a hundred yards down the trail, Blair regretted wearing such a thin cotton shirt. His teeth chattered as he struggled for breath. The seasons were reversed on this side of the equator, but summer hadn't reached this elevation. Bridget seemed unfazed by the chill, her khaki shorts bouncing in time with her ponytail as she ducked past to his right.

"Are you crazy?" he asked. His voice rose at least half an octave as a stone bounced down the trail.

"You know I am," she shot back with a grin, pace increasing.

Blair yanked his gaze from her, like a child touching a hot stove, and instead turned it to the trio of pavilions below. They'd been erected on the pyramid's south face, just a simple work camp. They would never erect a full base camp anywhere near the pyramid since it was impossible to know how far underground the site extended. There could be more structures right under the camp.

Several figures congregated around a collapsible table. He couldn't make out much detail from this distance, but he thought he recognized one of them.

"Bridget, is that Sheila?" he asked, steadying himself against the rock wall as he navigated a particularly terrifying stretch of trail.

"Yep," Bridget replied, pausing to beam a radiant smile over her shoulder. "We were lucky to land her, especially on such short notice. She just finished a dig down in Norte Chico."

"I thought she was an Incan scholar. What was she doing all the way down there? Norte Chico predates the Incans by at least two millennia."

"She thinks that there's a connection between the ancestors of the Inca and the tribes that built Norte Chico," Bridget replied. A spray of dirt tumbled down the cliff as she continued her daunting pace. He was starting to lag behind. "Given what we've discovered thus far, I'm betting she's right."

"Who are the other two?" Blair asked, focusing on his footing as they continued. The cliff was harrowing, but—thankfully—their elevation was dropping as they approached the valley floor.

"Dr. Roberts is a geologist from Cal Berkeley. He's handling the quake investigation, obviously. The man with the curly hair is Alejandro Rodriguez. He's an artist from Mexico City who did some amazing sketches of what Mayan culture at Teotihuacan might have looked like. We're hoping he can do something similar here."

"That's a pretty impressive roster, especially on such short notice. How did you pull it off?" Blair asked. They both knew exactly what he meant by "pull it off." An operation like this took months or even years to get funding, and when it did, they weren't paying anthropologists six figures to excavate.

"Steve was approached by a representative of the Peruvian government and asked to investigate the pyramid. They let us put together a dream team, though we were all required to sign the same NDA you did," Bridget answered with a simple shrug. Her eyebrows knitted together though, a sure sign that something about this made her less comfortable than she was willing to admit.

"Why do we need soldiers, especially ones that well armed? I counted at least six at base camp."

"They mostly keep to themselves, and we're happy to let them. The only one we talk to is their leader, Commander Jordan. He's the type of guy that can kill you with his bare hands, and just uses guns as a courtesy," she said over her shoulder, still moving confidently down the trail. At least they were nearing the bottom.

"You sound like you're happy they're here," Blair said, more than a little surprised. There was a longstanding feud between the military and almost every group of scientists. If they were funding a dig, it *always* meant strings were attached.

"The government's worried that someone else will find the site, and they want to be able to protect their interests."

Bridget's words were practiced, as if she were parroting back a message she'd been taught.

"You have to admit this place is pretty unique. What we find inside could be very valuable to them," she continued.

"Makes sense, I guess," he conceded, though not without reservations. "They paid me enough that I probably should just leave well enough alone. Am I the last one to arrive? Or did you manage to get Connors on board?"

"With you here, I didn't think we'd need him," she said, pausing at the base of the trail. She lowered her cap to shade her eyes, face growing somber. "Besides, Steve refused to even consider it. He got... violent when I suggested it."

"Steve?" Blair asked, finally catching up to her. A hundred pounds of stress melted away now that he was on more or less flat ground. "There's no way. Steve's the most non-confrontational person I know. He'll avoid you for weeks just to prevent a minor argument. Violent?"

"I know. Completely out of character, right?" She turned back to the trail, setting a dogged pace.

Blair let the silence stretch as they approached the pavilions. He didn't like all the cryptic hints about Steve, but now wasn't the time to interrogate Bridget. The people at the makeshift camp had spotted them, and Sheila was moving in their direction. She wore her self-created uniform: khaki pants with a flannel shirt covered by bright-blue suspenders. A wide-brimmed leather hat that covered a shock of black hair worked with a pair of thick glasses to complete the outfit. He doubted he would even recognize her without it.

"Blair Smith, is that you?" Sheila said, dipping backward in mock shock. Her exaggerated southern drawl made him smile. Sheila had been born in Los Angeles. She'd never been near the south. "I haven't seen you in ages. I heard a nasty rumor that you took a job as a professor. I must have heard wrong. Though I guess that would explain the beer belly…"

"Wine belly. It happens when you live in Wine Country. That zin isn't going to drink itself." Blair hefted her tiny frame in a fierce hug. "I missed you too, by the way. Even if you did get old. What are you, like forty now?"

"Forty? I'll show you forty. God, it's good to see you, Blair." She returned the hug just as fiercely.

She leaned in close and whispered the rest. "We should talk in private when you have a minute."

What didn't she want the rest of them to know?

Blair set her down, giving her a quizzical look. She shook her head slightly and resumed her smile as she led him and Bridget toward the pavilions. Neither woman acknowledged the other. Guess he shouldn't be surprised, given their history.

He was thankful the moment he stepped beneath the blue canvas, because someone had the foresight to set a large space heater near the center. A pair of men stood next to the collapsible table, a black plastic top with aluminum legs. The map atop it was an aerial survey.

"When was this taken?" Blair asked, stabbing the center of the map with a finger.

"Boy, you get right to work." The shorter of the two men laughed. He had a dark complexion and an easy smile. His accent had probably landed the man a lot of tourist girls. "I'm Alejandro, and this dour fellow behind me is Dr. Roberts. That's his first name, Doctor. I'm convinced of it."

"Ignore the artist. He doesn't appreciate the rigors of science," the taller man droned, glancing up from a thick textbook. *Seismic Wonders* was emblazoned on the cover in blocky red letters. The man placed an arm over the cover when he realized Blair was staring. His face sported a bristly black beard badly in need of shearing. "I'm Dr. Roberts and prefer to be addressed as such. To answer your question, that survey was done three months ago. It's a Google Earth satellite image, and as you've deduced it shows no trace of the structure behind me. That's why I'm here. To determine where it came from and how it appeared. If I understand correctly, *you're* here to tell us who built it."

"Let's hope so," Blair said, offering Dr. Roberts a hand. The man's grip was surprisingly firm. "It's a pleasure to meet you."

Blair offered Alejandro his hand, but the man swept him up in a hug.

"We are beyond handshakes, my friend. Together, we will unlock a world not glimpsed in thousands of years. We are more than friends. We are family."

"Uh, nice to meet you too. So where's Steve?" Blair asked, disengaging from the strange little Latino. There was no sign of his former friend among the makeshift pavilions. He scanned the area around the pyramid but saw nothing else of note. Perhaps there was another set of pavilions on the far side?

Everyone looked pointedly at Bridget, who dropped her gaze. Jesus. Given how uncomfortable everyone looked, Blair thought maybe she wasn't being melodramatic about Steve's condition.

"Blair, why don't I show you your tent?" Sheila said, trying to fill the lengthening silence.

"I'd appreciate that. It would be good to drop this pack and get settled in. Afterwards, maybe you can show me the site."

Bridget raised a hand as if about to say something, and then she let it fall limply to her side. She turned to examine the aerial photo, though he seriously doubted she saw any part of that map. He'd seen that expression before. She wasn't concerned. She was terrified.

6
___

AHIGA

Crouching atop the tree's limb many feet over the jungle floor, Ahiga knew despair. The strangely armored warriors with their deafening armaments had driven him from the Ark. The fight had been brief but bloody, and he had fled when his energy waned. True, he could have stayed and likely slain them all, but at what cost had he failed? His role was vital. If he did not wake the Mother, this new world would be naked before the coming storm.

He kicked off the limb of a capirona, vaulting from the arboreal crown to a perch in a neighboring tree no unblooded could have climbed. The sounds of the jungle washed over him, an island of familiarity amidst all the strangeness of this new world. The harsh cry of the macaw and the chattering of monkeys were familiar things, a precious remembrance of what had once been. These things had drawn him here, a place to contemplate, to plan, several days from the Ark.

If the Mother's predictions were correct he'd slept for time beyond counting. Two full ages, nearly half the longest count. It was long enough for time to scour away all knowledge of his people. What had survived? Was there some fragment? Everything depended on the seeds they had planted.

Ahiga leapt again, seizing a thick limb and using it to renew his momentum. He lost himself in the rhythm, leaping from tree to tree as he traversed the jungle. His people had used the dense foliage to harry the ancient enemy whenever they were foolish enough to invade these shores. Champions could ride swiftly through the jungle even in their human forms, as he was now. The shelter of the trees allowed them to fall upon the unsuspecting deathless wherever they were found.

The jungle thinned to mighty kapok trees, so distant from each other that each leap taxed even his abilities. There. A great river, dark with mud and vegetation. Its course had shifted from his day, but it was unmistakable. The River of Life bisected much of the continent and had been thick with the unblooded in their ungainly canoes during his time. If man had survived, they would be near the river, still drawing from its bounty.

Many leaps later he paused atop a sprawling root tree near the shore, its tendrils disappearing into the dark waters. In the distance a single plume of smoke wound skyward, all but disappearing into the thick grey clouds clotting the sky. He studied the area beneath the plume, though most of it was blocked by a knot of trees on the far side of the river. Several crude structures crouched near the water's edge, each cut from weathered planks. Only one figure moved amidst them.

Ahiga channeled a quick pulse of energy, infusing his eyes with far greater clarity than they normally possessed. The dark-skinned man knelt on the edge of a dock, tying off a frayed rope that led to a small boat cut from the same timbers used in the buildings. An odd bulky box was affixed to the rear of the boat. What purpose might it serve?

Ahiga leapt skyward, angling his flight high above the river. He dove into the muddy depths, the force of his flight propelling him through the water. He channeled another spark, this time into his limbs. It gave him far greater strength than any man had, allowing him to traverse the water more quickly. He swam toward the structures, careful not to break the surface lest the figure see him. The brief glimpse had certainly been less intimidating than the strangely armored warriors, but there was no way of knowing if this man possessed abilities he'd never encountered. It was best to be cautious.

He burst from the river near the dock, landing with a hollow thud just behind the man. The stranger spun, uttering what Ahiga took for a curse. His clothing was odd, a dark pair of breeches cut just over the knee and a white shirt with colorful red markings. He reached for a long knife sheathed at his belt, but Ahiga gave him no chance to defend himself. He seized the man's wrist in a vice-like grip, forcing the stranger to his knees, where he belonged.

"Quien es?" the man sputtered, but the words were gibberish to Ahiga. He would correct that.

His second hand shot out, locking around the man's neck. Ahiga stared deep into the man's eyes, activating his dwindling supply of energy. The world around him disappeared, replaced by a swirling vortex of memories. He sifted through them, gathering information as he journeyed through the unblooded's mind. He absorbed many things, more than he could process quickly.

The language was called Spanish and was spoken by many of the natives in this land. The land itself was Peru, though he was near the border of another land known as Ecuador. Beyond that was a more massive nation called Brazil. Through the man's mind, Ahiga glimpsed vast cities, cities of millions, and they weren't the only ones. There were other lands on other continents. The most powerful were on the continent to the north, the continent of his birth. He continued his exploration, dimly aware of the man's trapped consciousness fluttering like a caged bird in his iron grip.

Interesting. The world contained scattered myths with grains of truth. Werewolves, a crude but accurate description for champions. Though much of what they knew was wrong, they even remembered the ancient enemy. The man's knowledge painted a romantic picture of the deathless. Was that the enemy's doing? Perhaps they had modified the genetic memory of their unblooded just as the Mother had done. If so, it did not bode well.

Shock shivered through Ahiga's mind as he discovered the root of the technology the people of this world had employed. They used signals indiscriminately, blanketing the world to deliver messages to their communications devices. They did so in ignorance, unaware of the tremendous abuse such a network could allow. Of how it could be employed to shape their minds and even their bodies.

Ahiga retreated back to his own mind, releasing the unblooded. Miguel, he called himself.

"What did you do to me?" Miguel rasped, rubbing at his neck with a calloused hand. He no longer reached for the knife.

"Such information is useless to you," Ahiga explained in the tongue he had stolen from the man. He released Miguel's wrist and took a step closer to shore.

"Why?" Miguel asked, clearly still dazed from the experience.

Ahiga wasn't surprised. Sifting a mind disoriented the target.

"Because you are about to die. All who draw breath in this village are about to die," he answered calmly. He channeled a spark of energy into his right hand, extending the claws that were his birthright. They gleamed wickedly as they flashed for the man's throat. Miguel collapsed in a spray of blood, and his body toppled into the water with a muddy splash. He didn't even have time to give alarm to his fellows.

Ahiga turned toward the village, making his way between the ramshackle huts. There was grisly work to be about. Important work.

7

THE ARK

"Wait till you see the inside of this place," Sheila said, boisterous enough that even coming from her the words sounded a bit forced.

Maybe Blair was just being paranoid, but he wasn't so sure. He paused a moment as she unzipped a tall domed tent and ducked inside the white canvas. Blair followed and was surprised to find that he could stand at full height. Despite how thin it was, the fabric warded the worst of the chill.

"You guys have some great friends," Blair said. "We never had anything like this on any of the digs you and I were involved with. You remember the debris huts we had to make ourselves? This place is paradise."

"Yeah, and that's what I want to talk to you about." Sheila lowered her voice. Her dark eyebrows furrowed. "Listen, I don't know what we've gotten ourselves into here, but I don't like it. The way the Peruvian government found us is too convenient, and they *definitely* have more resources than any government I've seen, *especially* Peru. Take Jordan, for example. He's the bully they left to babysit. You know what? I don't think he's military at all. He reeks of corporate money. No military I've seen has access to so many high-tech toys. Like this little satellite dish he sets up every morning. And the pair of little black drones that circle camp."

"Who cares about the funding? We're diggers, Sheila. We're here for the knowledge, and if we have to kiss a little corporate ass to get it, that's part of the gig. You were the one who taught me that. There's no way I'm looking this gift horse in the mouth, not when we get to both be part of history and line our wallets for once. I just paid off my house."

"*I* care and you should too. They know something about this place they aren't telling us. They put together the team in an awful hurry, and they're not sparing any expense. No one does that for science," Sheila countered, biting her lip as she stared in the direction of the pavilions. She knelt and zipped the tent shut in one smooth arc.

"So they sell off all the artifacts and make a tidy profit. Isn't that always the case? Pure research is dead. Besides, our names will still be in the history books even if we don't make another dime."

"Keep your voice down. This goes much deeper than profit," she whispered, locking gazes with Blair. "Commander Jordan drove Steve to get into the central chamber as soon as possible. He hounded him to work long hours down there. Here's the really scary part. He didn't seem concerned or surprised when Steve's behavior began to deteriorate."

"Deteriorate? What the hell does that mean?" Blair whispered, finally catching a bit of her paranoia. If Bridget and Sheila were both worried, there was genuine cause for alarm. They disagreed about everything on general principal.

Sheila's jaw snapped shut, trapping the unspoken words he could read in her gaze. Footsteps crunched outside.

"Knock, knock." Bridget's voice came from outside the tent flap. She unzipped it, revealing a tentative smile. She looked ready to bolt, especially when she saw Sheila. "I hope I'm not interrupting. Blair, I figured you'd be eager to see the pyramid. Do you want a tour of the site? I can come back if this is a bad time."

Sheila bristled, eyes narrowing as she sucked in a breath. It would soon birth one of her legendary tirades, sending Bridget packing and raising tension for days. As much as Blair shared Sheila's anger he wanted them focused on solving this thing.

"Sheila was just telling me a bit about the site," he interjected, rising to block Sheila's view of Bridget. "I'd love a tour, though. Sheila, do you want to join us?"

Both Bridget and Sheila stiffened, but neither objected. The two had been inseparable once, just like he and Steve had been. It seemed like a lifetime ago.

"Of course I'll come. Bridget can barely tell the New Kingdom from the Old. You need a proper guide, not a jumped-up grad student. She can tag along though. Might even learn something instead of riding her boyfriend's coattails."

Bridget replied as if Sheila hadn't spoken. "We should start with the lowest level. There are stunning passages of hieroglyphs. The colors are mind boggling."

This was going to be a very awkward tour.

"It could take years to decipher their script, but the sheer volume of symbols will yield the key. It has to be here somewhere. I simply cannot wait to find out what they've been waiting so many millennia to tell us," Sheila said, clapping Blair on the back with one of her calloused hands.

"We've got the best team in the world," Bridget agreed, beaming one of *those* smiles his way. It stung, but having seen several similar ones so recently dulled the impact. "There's a Rosetta stone in there somewhere. There has to be."

"It took five different scientists a half century to unlock the Mayan language. I seriously doubt they left *Ancient Peruvians for Dummies*," he said. It was far more likely they'd merely catalogue everything here, and that the translation, if it ever came, would be made by someone decades from now.

"They didn't have Google. Or image analysis. Our benefactors provided a computer that can read images and find common sequences," Bridget said, with a bit less enthusiasm. She was short enough that there was no way he could miss her cleavage. Was the low-cut top for his benefit, or was he reading too much into things? "Steve has already done a lot of work with it, so you've got an incredible foundation to work with."

Blair slipped passed her, ducking through the flap and back into the keening wind. Apparently, Northern California's warm winters had softened him more than he'd thought. Hopefully he'd adjust quickly.

Bridget and Sheila ducked through after him, still glaring at each other. Blair stifled a sigh, wondering who'd thought it a good idea to have the pair on the same dig. Things were worse between them than he'd ever imagined. It was disconcerting to see the pair at each other's throats. Their words were friendly enough, but the underlying tone had been nasty. When Bridget and Blair had been together, they were like mismatched school girls, always gossiping and whispering. He knew why that had changed, but it still saddened him.

"We've excavated a small portion of the wall on the northern slope and another on the southern," Bridget explained, adjusting her ball cap to provide a bit more shade for her eyes. She wore sunglasses as well, but the glare of the sun was intense. "We wanted to see if the symbols along the lowest part of the face extended all the way around. We're not positive they do, but we've found them everywhere we've cleared."

"Can you show me?" Blair asked, intensely curious. "The Mayans carved symbols into their pyramids, but the Egyptians left the outside blank."

"These symbols aren't carved," Sheila broke in, starting toward the pyramid. She threaded through a neighboring group of tents, plunging past the pavilions and toward the structure itself.

"Not carved? How did they get there, then? If they were painted, they would have flaked off millennia ago, especially if the pyramid was covered by soil. The acid would have eaten away at the ink," Blair said, hurrying after her. He peered up at the massive structure, such a baffling enigma.

The trio picked their way around the mound of dirt, the pyramid filling the sky above. Its gleaming ebony surface was blinding under the sun, a beacon that could have been seen for hundreds of miles if not sheltered by the peaks forming the ravine it rested in.

Sheila plunged ahead, making for a break in the wall of dirt. The team had excavated a twenty-foot section of the pyramid's base, revealing incredibly detailed hieroglyphs. The multicolored symbols covered a six-foot swathe, but it was neither their complexity nor their beauty that caused Blair's jaw to drop. The symbols could have been laser etched. They were absolutely pristine. Whatever dye had been used caught the sunlight, causing the hieroglyphs to glitter and flow as if alive.

The glyphs had similarities to both Mayan and Egyptian writings. They used clear logarithmic symbols to represent words. That brown one was clearly a mountain. The white, clearly a cloud. Animals of all sorts dotted the panels. Most were recognizable, though some were long-extinct species or fantastical imaginings of the glyphs' creators.

"What do you think?" Bridget asked, sidling up next to him. She seemed amused, though he'd bet she'd had a similar reaction when she'd first seen this.

"I can see what you mean about the builders being incredibly advanced. I'm not sure we could replicate this today," he admitted, moving closer to the wall. The symbols were even more impressive up close. Though he couldn't read them, he was left with the impression that they were not mere symbols but rather whole words, much like Japanese Kanji.

"I think the scope is what gets me," Sheila added, touching a vibrant red fox. "The entire interior is covered in symbols like these, and it seems likely the whole base is as well. How long must that have taken, and how did they do it? We tried scraping off a sample, but steel didn't so much as scratch it. We've placed an order for a diamond-tipped drill."

Something caught Blair's eye. He wasn't sure what he found to be wrong, but something was definitely there. He scanned the area they'd excavated, particularly the place where the pyramid disappeared into the dirt.

"Have you dug down to find the base? I don't see the bottom of the marble here. What if it goes deeper?" Blair asked, kneeling in the dirt to scrape some of it away from the marble. The stone radiated heat from the blistering sun.

"Commander Jordan de-prioritized it," Bridget said, kneeling next to him. She rested her hands on her knees, watching as he scooped away dirt. "We were curious, but he insisted we focus on the symbols in the central chamber."

"What are you thinking, Blair? You've got that look," Sheila asked, resting her back against the hot stone.

"The structure could be even larger than what we've uncovered so far. There's no way to know how deep it goes," he said, finally giving up on shoveling dirt with his hands. "We'd need better equipment."

"You'll have anything you need, Dr. Smith. Just get a requisition form from Dr. Roberts, and I'll see that it's taken care of." A deep voice startled Blair from behind. He spun to face the speaker.

The man towered over Blair. His tree-trunk arms were bare to the sun, and a form-fitting black t-shirt covered his chest. Dirty-blond stubble and a shaved head made him look very much like a pit bull— an angry one. The dark sunglasses and black cap added to the effect. The man himself was far more intimidating than the holstered pistol at his side.

"And you are?" Blair asked, already suspecting the answer. He thought he'd spied the man over at the soldiers' camp.

"Commander Jordan. You can call me Jordan if that's easier. I'm a representative of the Peruvian government, empowered to look after their interests here. We've invested a great deal in this operation, and we want to make sure everything is handled according to...policy." He delivered his speech smoothly, too-white teeth glinting as a predatory smile slid into place. "We're eager to see your collaboration with Dr. Galk. You should consider heading down to the central chamber rather than wasting time up here. I think you'll want to examine your colleague's findings. I'm told they're quite revolutionary."

"I'll get to it after I've mapped all the exposed panels along the outer surface. I want to see if there are any discernible patterns or if there are any stylistic differences between these and the ones inside,"

Blair replied. He immediately distrusted the man, and not just because Jordan had probably beat up kids like Blair for their lunch money. This man held secrets like Fort Knox held gold.

"I really must insist, Dr. Smith."

"Just Mister. I never finished my doctorate."

"Mr. Smith, then. Time is very much of the essence. We've paid you a considerable sum and expect prompt results," the commander said. He flexed his hands as a subtle reminder that he could break Blair in half.

"What's the rush? This place has been here for thousands of years. Another day or two isn't going to make much difference. We'll do this faster with less interference," Blair argued, tensing as the man clenched his fists. Despite the casualness of the gesture, Jordan looked a hairbreadth from violence.

"It's unlikely that we are the only interested party in such a discovery." Jordan's smile was frigid as his right hand wrapped around the hilt of a very large knife strapped to his thigh. It had the look of a reflexive gesture, but it was damn unsettling. "We need to gather all the data we can before the media circus begins. That's all. I regret intruding on your methodology, but time is the one resource we cannot provide you."

"Yeah, sure...I'm eager to see Steve," Blair agreed with a nod. He turned to the two women. "Maybe we can tour the rest of the outer structure later? Most of what I'm going to need is in the central chamber. Besides, I want to talk to Steve about his initial findings."

"If you're going to head down, I think I might see about some dinner," Sheila said, a look of distaste flitting across her tanned face. "Why don't you drop by my tent after you come back up? I'd love to brainstorm some of the glyphs with you."

"I'll do that," Blair said, turning to Bridget. "Will you show me to the central chamber?"

"We may as well get that out of the way," she said, with the reluctant determination of a soldier girding for war. "It's this way. The tunnel entrance is on the western slope."

"I'll leave you to it, then," Jordan said, giving another one of those dangerous smiles as he turned to leave. "It was a pleasure meeting you, Mr. Smith."

"We'll catch up over dinner, Blair," Sheila said, giving his shoulder a squeeze. She delivered a pointed look as she walked off, though he wasn't certain what it meant. It felt like a warning, but of what?

"Shall we?" Bridget asked. Her smile was back in full force.

"Lead the way," Blair said, falling into step beside her as she headed around the northern face of the structure. Commander Jordan watched them go, a predator studying its next meal. Blair waited until the man was well out of earshot before continuing. "So, why was that guy so insistent that I head inside? I got here less than an hour ago."

"Because this stuff is just window dressing. What you've seen so far? That's nothing," Bridget explained as they rounded the corner of the massive structure. He could see the gaping darkness of the tunnel mouth, wide enough for ten men abreast.

8

STEVE

Blair was surprised to find a familiar black-clad soldier waiting just inside the massive marble doors. The hulking man had been their driver on the way from Cajamarca. The Russian. Yuri, his name had been. He bore a decidedly lethal-looking rifle, and his eyes were still obscured by those silver sunglasses, despite the fact that he stood in the shaded entryway.

"Taking Smith to central chamber, Bridget? Is expected," he rumbled. His face was an impassive mask, especially behind those sunglasses.

"I'm bringing Blair to review Dr. Galk's findings," she explained, gesturing in Blair's direction. She beamed one of her best smiles, one that Blair had fallen prey to many times, but the Russian seemed unmoved. Carved from stone, apparently.

"I'm Blair. We weren't introduced earlier," he said, stopping before the man and offering a hand. The soldier stirred, accepting the handshake with a half smile shaded by a few days' stubble. His grip was firm but not painful, though Blair was sure it could have been.

"Yuri," he rumbled, releasing Blair's hand. The name sounded like *yoo-ree*. "Is very much pleasure. Be careful on stairs. Slick." He gestured down the hallway.

Stepping through the towering doors was entirely too much like entering the throat of some great beast. Blair was immediately conscious of the tens of thousands of tons of stone above. The fear that they might suddenly come crashing down wouldn't be banished. He wasn't claustrophobic, but the scope of this place was unnerving.

"It's a straight shot for a while," Bridget said, her voice echoing dully from the walls. Her form was difficult to make out in the thin shadows of the headlamps. "It's about three hundred meters to the central chamber. Most of it involves gradual descent through corridors that switch back on themselves. Some are filled with statues that strongly resemble the Egyptian pantheon. We'll see those later."

Bridget set a brisk pace that he had trouble matching, not due to elevation but to the hieroglyphs covering the walls. Every inch of them. He knew he could study them later, but it was impossible not to spend at least a little time examining them. The passage was wide enough for three people to walk side by side and tall enough that he couldn't reach the ceiling even when he jumped.

"Bridget," he called, hurrying after her. "Does Steve have any theories on why the tunnel is so large? I could see making it wide, but why so tall? That has to be nine or ten feet up."

"No idea. The hieroglyphs go all the way up. They even cover the ceiling. That's a lot of extra space just to add a little more room to write. I'm guessing there was some sort of religious significance to the size, though damned if I know what it is."

"I hadn't considered that. Religion drives a lot of strange customs," he replied.

The passage sloped upwards, eventually ending at a set of broad stairs that descended back into the darkness. Each was just a little too tall for a man to comfortably step up.

"Do you think the builders were just taller than we are? Australian aborigines are shorter. Maybe these people were extremely tall." Blair used his hands to assist himself down the stairs.

"That's a possibility, though the people of the Americas aren't really known for their height. I find it hard to believe their descendants would have changed so dramatically in height, even over that many centuries. We're only as tall as we are today because we have such an abundance of food. If this place was built when we assume, it would have been during the final glaciation of the last ice age. Food would have been scarce," Bridget said, pausing on the stairs to examine a hieroglyph-covered wall. "Anyway, take a look at this section. What do you make of them? Steve was absolutely baffled by the imagery, and I haven't the faintest idea either. It's the first time they break from their more traditional glyphs, which are largely uniform in size. This imagery includes larger figures."

"Hmm," Blair said. He removed his glasses and cleaned them with his shirt before examining the pictographs in the light provided by their lamps. "This is interesting. See these red figures here? They're lying down as if sleeping or dead. But then in this next pictograph, they rise and begin fighting. These brown figures are driven back to what I'm guessing is this pyramid. Maybe the dead represent a foe they thought they'd defeated?"

"Or a foe that can't be killed," Bridget added, leaning closer to examine the next panel. "What we don't get is this next part. Take a look."

The next panel was odd. The red figures, the ones that had risen, had surrounded the pyramid. A few of the brown figures stood at the very top, and on the stairs loomed a prominent silver figure that Blair could only describe as a monster. It had elongated claws, was covered in what he guessed was meant to be fur, and had a mouth full of vicious fangs.

"I think this is some sort of champion or war god," he said, dropping to a crouch and shining his lamp on it. There was something maddeningly familiar about the figure. "I think I've seen it before, or something very much like it."

"Really?" Bridget asked, crouching next to him. "Who, or what, does it remind you of?"

He considered for a long moment, taking in the wolf-headed figure. "If it was male, I'd say it was an exact likeness of Wepwawet, one of the sons of Anubis. He was worshipped in Lycopolis, the

Egyptian city of wolves. The ruins are still there, though they're in a bad enough state that we aren't sure what the place was used for."

"Interesting that the gender is different," Bridget replied, pressing against his side as she leaned closer to the image. "It is clearly female, though."

"Gender aside, our wolf-headed friend here appears to be protecting the people from the red figures," Blair interpreted, touching the figure with his index finger. Like the pictographs outside, it had no texture and a much higher level of detail than anything he'd ever encountered. The archeologist in him railed at the idea of marring the ink with the oils in his skin, but he couldn't help himself. "I want to study these in detail before offering a hypothesis, but I'm betting this figure is central to their culture. Perhaps the best warrior was dressed in special trappings that make her appear to be a beast? It might be similar to the Mayans and their belief that warriors could channel the power of the jaguar. It would have terrified their enemies."

"That's a connection we hadn't thought of," Bridget admitted, resting her arm on his shoulder. "See? I'm already glad we called you in."

He rose stiffly, letting her arm drop as he took a step back and turned his lamp on the other wall.

"Look at this," Blair said. His momentary irritation was quickly forgotten. "The champion is standing at the apex of the pyramid, these brown figures being led up to her. It looks like she's sacrificing them. But why?"

"We're not sure. It could be some sort of cultural ritual. The Mayans would sacrifice their enemies to gain their strength," Bridget offered, shining her headlamp on the same panel Blair was examining. "That was Steve's theory, anyway. I'm not sure I agree, but I didn't have a better one. What do you think?"

"The Mayan connection is a good one, but I don't think that's what we're seeing here." Blair leaned so close that the beast's claws felt almost life sized. Each was tipped with a dab of red, and a victim lay prone at its feet. Its mouth was awash with blood as well. The figures were stunningly detailed. "These don't appear to be enemies she's sacrificing. They appear to be the same citizens from the first panel. If they were enemies, I'm guessing they'd have been bound in some way. I think she's killing her own people. They're going to their deaths willingly."

"That's bizarre. Take a look at the next panel. I'm curious what you think."

Blair did as he was asked, shining his lamp on the panel closest to the doorway. The champion was helping one of the figures who'd been sacrificed to his feet. The victim was now silver as well.

"It seems to be a ritual," Blair mused, scratching absently at the hair at the base of his neck. It was thick with sweat. "Perhaps this champion isn't killing the citizens. Maybe she's putting them through a test that wounds them, and if they pass, they are elevated to champion. It could have symbolized some rite of passage men underwent at a certain age."

"Or women," Bridget corrected, accidentally blinding him with her lamp. He blinked away spots as she continued. "I guess we should head down to see Steve. He'll want to hear your theories. Listen, when we get down there...well, you'll understand."

She began to descend, and Blair trailed after, his vision still recovering. He moved slowly, glancing at either side of the hallway to see what the pictographs contained. He wanted to stop for closer examination, but that would come later. For now he needed to focus on Steve. Besides, it would be worth skipping this for a look at the central chamber.

"Watch your footing," Bridget cautioned, pausing to shine her light in his direction. "The stones are remarkably well preserved, but some of them are slick. Alejandro twisted his ankle a few days back."

"Wouldn't *that* be embarrassing?" Blair said, imagining tumbling to the bottom with a broken leg.

"You've always been clumsy, but not *that* bad. Alejandro can trip on flat ground," Bridget said with a too-quick laugh. He knew her well enough to know when she was preoccupied.

They climbed in silence up perhaps another hundred steps

before the hallway leveled off. The floor now sloped downwards, but the decline was very difficult to notice unless you'd spent a lot of time underground. Fortunately, Blair had.

"The central chamber is just around the corner." Bridget's voice echoed off the stone.

A faint sliver of light splashed the floor ahead, proving the truth of her words. They quickened their pace, eventually reaching the light and rounding the corner. Blair could do nothing but stop and stare. The hallway continued for about fifteen feet, but what lay beyond was what had captured his attention so completely. He'd seen the inner chambers in nearly every pyramid on this continent, but nothing rivaled the room ahead.

The light from his headlamp barely touched a ceiling that had to be at least a hundred feet above. At each cardinal direction rested an enormous obelisk, like miniature versions of the one in Washington DC. Each probably weighed forty or fifty tons.

A fifth, larger one sat in the very center of the chamber. Blair guessed its height to be fifty feet, and it looked to be solid, black stone. Obsidian perhaps?

There was only one other feature of note, a perfectly carved replica of the wolf-headed goddess from the first panel. It stood against the far wall, palm raised in what appeared to be a gesture of friendship. It had nobility to it, majesty even. Every strand of fur was sculpted to perfection.

"It's tough to make out unless we turn on the generators, but the walls are covered in hieroglyphs. The ones near the obelisks are the most exquisite in the entire structure. You're going to wet your pants when you see them," Bridget teased, though he could tell the behavior was forced.

"Blair?" a voice called, cracked from disuse. A figure hobbled into the light of Blair's headlamp; apparently Steve had been resting in the shadow of the central obelisk. "Blair, is that you? You've come at last. I need you, my old friend. We must find the way down. *She's* in there, waiting. She needs us. Blair, we have to get *in*."

Blair's eyes burned from a sharp odor when his old friend

emerged fully from the shadows. Steve had always been muscular, the athlete all the girls loved. That was gone. Soiled khakis and a polo shirt hung from his emaciated form. His dark hair was disheveled, and his skin peeled in patches, as if it had been subjected to bad sunburn. The glasses were familiar, but the man who wore them couldn't possibly be Steve. His eyes held a feverish glint that made Blair tense defensively.

"Steve?" he asked, aware of Bridget's hesitant form on the step behind him.

"Yes," his friend answered, voice wavering. It was a bit more steady than it had been a moment ago. "I'm so glad you've come. The rest of these fools don't understand, but you do. You can help me get in. You can, can't you? Promise me. Promise!"

The last was delivered in a shriek that echoed through the cavernous chamber. Spittle flew from Steve's mouth, and his eyes leaked hatred. He lurched forward, seizing Blair's shoulders. The madman's gaze locked with his, and to his horror, Blair could find no humanity lurking there. Not a shred.

"Of course, Steve. I promise. I'll help however I can. It's going to take some time though. I'll need access to your notes," he said, speaking slowly and calmly like he would to a wild dog.

"Notes? Yes. Yes, you'll need those," he said, releasing Blair and scurrying to a folding table that had been erected in the shadow of one of the obelisks. He began grabbing loose sheets of paper and arranging them into a ragged stack. "Here, you can study these, but you must hurry. The end is coming. We must get inside before it's too late. We *must*, or the world will burn."

9

DECISIONS

B lair shivered as he left the sun's thin embrace for the shadowed pavilion. A fistful of now-familiar faces clustered around the portable heater next to the folding table. Blair set his coffee cup down, thankful for the gloves Bridget had insisted he bring. They had conductive fingertips, so he could use his smartphone without braving the cold.

"Good, Blair's here. We can get started," Sheila said, nodding at him from across the room. Her southern drawl was so faint it threatened to disappear entirely. This must be serious for that kind of lapse. Sheila prided herself on her Georgian heritage, though her family hadn't lived there since she was three.

Blair followed her gaze to the pair of guards on the ridge and then watched as it roamed the lot of them.

What was going on? Everyone else looked as mystified as he felt.

"I called you all here because I want to address what we're all thinking. Whatever we're all too afraid to say. Something dangerous is going on in that pyramid. In the central chamber, specifically."

Silence reigned. Bridget stared fixedly at the map on the table while Alejandro splayed his hands over the heater. The only sound was the wind as it tugged at the pavilion's blue canvas. Blair had only been on the team three days. Should he speak up? No, it wasn't his place.

"You're not wrong," Dr. Roberts finally said. He crossed his arms, eyes staring out from the bushy beard that covered his face. "I've compiled the seismic data from three separate sources. The pyramid caused the earthquake; I'm certain now. It *chose* to reveal itself...for reasons we can't begin to guess. But that's not the terrifying part. My data strongly suggests that what we're seeing is, quite literally, the tip of the iceberg. The structure goes deep into the earth possibly a mile or more."

"That dovetails with Steve's notes," Blair said, taking a step closer to the table. All eyes were on him now. "He believes we've only discovered the entryway to this place. What we assume is the central chamber might be nothing more than an antechamber at the top."

"It doesn't surprise me. Not one bit," Sheila said, drawl back to full strength. She leaned into the table as she speared them with her gaze. "Why else would they spend millions of dollars to explore this place? We have an escort that's three times as large as the science team. I don't know much about guns, but what they're armed with is more state of the art than anything we should find in Peru."

"I do," Bridget broke in, drawing everyone's attention. He knew *why* she knew guns, and he wasn't surprised she was still embarrassed about it. "Your average infantry are typically armed with an M4. It's good for both close quarters and medium range, and the rounds are common all over the world. Did anyone see *Black Hawk Down*? That's the gun they were using. These guys? The rifles are about the same size as an M4, but I'm unfamiliar with the body or that scope they've got mounted on top."

Bridget's father was a colonel, and she'd grown up living and breathing that stuff. She'd dragged Blair to the opening night of everything from *Saving Private Ryan* to the aforementioned *Black Hawk Down*. She'd spent countless evenings playing *Call of Duty* and waiting in line every time a new game came out.

"So, what?" Alejandro finally spoke up, glancing up from the heater. "Is this not a good thing? There are very many men protecting us, and they have lots of fancy guns. Not only do we not pay for this, but they pay us a fortune to become pivotal figures in the legends that will spring from this place. We are the few who will see the world's understanding of the past change forever. We will *shape* that change. Are you not honored to be here?"

"You have to be alive to enjoy that, Alejandro," Dr. Roberts said quietly. His gaze softened. "We've all seen Steve. The man is suffering. I'm no medical doctor, but he has severe burns all over his skin. The kind found after Hiroshima or Chernobyl. That's saying nothing about his behavior. How many of you has he attacked now? Sheila, I know he came after you with a trowel last week. We've all seen the bruises Bridget tries to cover up. The man is melting down in there, maybe literally. What in the hell could cause that?"

"We already know that place eats signals. If you bring your cell phone in, the battery is drained in minutes. That can't be a coincidence," Blair said. "Dr. Roberts believes this place thrust itself from the earth. That takes power. Enormous power, I'd wager. It has to have been dormant for a dozen millennia, given your dating, yet it has a reservoir of power that somehow survived that long."

"There's only one type of power that could last that long, at least any power source we've discovered," Bridget said, eyes widening as the group put the pieces together. "Steve has radiation poisoning."

"Maybe, but we don't have a medical doctor, so there's no way to be sure," Sheila said, seizing the conversation once more. "What we are sure about is that the people who brought us here know a lot more about this place than they're letting on. Either they were expecting this place, or they move faster than any company I've ever seen. They had base camp set up within twenty-four hours of this place appearing. They know the central chamber is dangerous, but they've forced Steve inside, and now they're forcing Blair. How long until he starts exhibiting the same symptoms?"

"I haven't felt any adverse effects yet," Blair said. The idea of the madness being somehow infectious had already crept into his mind, and Blair had spent the last several days practically having minor heart attacks every time he imagined a symptom.

"Are we willing to risk it without more data?" she asked. "I mean, come on, it's our lives at stake here. I'm happy to explore this place, but if there are dangers, we need to be aware of them."

"I agree," Dr. Roberts said. "We've signed their NDAs and contracts. It's not like we can tell anyone anything, but if our lives are at risk we deserve to at least have all the facts."

"What do you propose we do?" Alejandro asked. His sharp tone made it clear he didn't share their fear. "Should we run to them and *demand* answers? They owe us nothing. We signed forms agreeing to this. We are paid very handsomely not just for our expertise but also for our discretion. If knowing what they know would help us unravel the mystery of this place, I have no doubt they would share. Is there some risk? Perhaps. Is this not always the case when exploring a new frontier?"

"Typically, that risk doesn't result in your skin melting," Sheila retorted. She glanced back up the rise, and Blair followed her gaze. It had settled on Commander Jordan's tent, perched like a hawk on the ridge overlooking camp. "I'm not expecting you to do anything. I just need to know where everyone stands. If we present a united front, we're far more likely to get some answers. They might be able to replace one of us, but replacing the entire team would take weeks or even months. I'm betting they don't want to spend that time."

"I am deeply sorry, but I will not be a party to this. Do as you will," Alejandro said, shaking his head. He wore the expression reserved for a child that has done something extremely disappointing. The normally jovial man picked up his coffee and left the pavilion, moving off toward the ridge.

There was a long silence as the group eyed each other uncomfortably. Dr. Roberts finally leaned in and drew their attention.

"He's free to make his own decisions. Do the rest of us have a consensus that something should be done?" Dr. Roberts asked. Sheila nodded immediately of course, and then Bridget followed suit a moment later.

"We have to do something," Blair said, crossing his arms. "I don't want to think anything ill of our benefactors, but all we're asking is a little more information. I do think we need to approach the matter delicately, though."

"That, we can do," Sheila said, darting a glance over her shoulder. "I'll give it some thought, and we'll come up with a way to approach Commander Jordan tomorrow."

10

ANSWERS

Jordan checked the slide on his .457, inspecting the heavy pistol for debris of any kind. Basic weapon maintenance was the first thing every soldier learned. If your equipment failed in combat, you died. It was that simple.

Satisfied with the weapon's condition, he slammed the slide home and slid the weapon into the holster strapped to his thigh. The matte-black gun was larger than any he'd ever used, and he was still getting used to it. Even after Jordan spent countless hours at the gym, it kicked like a mule. He much preferred a .45, which could be fired one handed in a pinch and was incredibly accurate at close range. But then he'd never had to fight a werewolf before. If that thing returned he'd damned well be ready, and that meant his sidearm needed all the stopping power he could get. That thing had gotten up after having over a hundred rounds emptied into it. He didn't have room to play around.

Footsteps approached outside the tent. There was a muffled exchange of voices, Yuri's thickly accented Russian and a softer male voice. It was most likely one of the scientists. Jordan snapped the nylon holster strap over the pistol's grip and exited the tent into the late-morning glare. Jordan found it so odd that the high desert was both so bright and so cold at the same time. He slid on his sunglasses, giving his eyes a moment to adjust.

Alejandro's diminutive form stared up at the Russian, expression guiltier than a kid caught red-handed at the cookie jar. Jordan liked the little Latino, maybe because he wore his emotions so openly. There was no subterfuge to the man.

"What can I do for you, Alejandro?" he asked, stepping up to join them. He gave a smile as warm as he could muster, given the constant vigil. That thing could return at any time. He prayed it would come during the day, if it did.

"Oh, Commander. There you are. I am so sorry to disturb you, but I come with troubling news," Alejandro said, shifting his attention from Yuri.

"Was going to wake you," Yuri rumbled with a shrug, raising an eyebrow.

"I wasn't sleeping. It's six thirty. I've been up for two hours," Jordan replied. Sleep had been elusive since his encounter with that thing. "Why is it you want me to see, Alejandro?"

"The others are gathered below. They are angry and feel you are withholding information from us."

Jordan considered the situation carefully. It was hardly surprising. The scientists were all intelligent, particularly Smith, though he was both the last to arrive and the only one among them without an advanced degree. It made sense that they were piecing things together, even with the limited information they'd been provided.

What was surprising was Alejandro coming forward about this meeting. The smaller man was loyal to a fault, and breaking ranks seemed out of character. He was always trying to keep the peace, not make waves.

"I appreciate you coming forward, Alejandro. You're risking the enmity of your peers by doing so," he finally replied. Jordan glanced away from the man and at the cluster of figures in the pavilion below. They were near enough that he could make out faces but not expressions.

"I know. I regret having to do so, but I wish to contain this situation before it gets out of hand. It is my hope that you will accompany me back to the group to address their concerns. I realize you can tell us very little, but if you give them something, it would calm the others, and work would proceed uninterrupted."

"And if I don't, I'll have a mutiny on my hands; is that it?" Jordan asked, turning his gaze back to Alejandro. The man's dark face paled.

"I don't know that it would go that far, but people will not do their best work if they are afraid," he replied, shifting from foot to foot like a child needing to pee.

What the hell should he do? Jordan couldn't reveal the entire situation; the Director would flay him alive. But if he let the situation fester, the scientists would drag their heels. Some might even try to leave. If that thing were still out there, they'd be easy prey.

"You did the right thing, Alejandro. Let's see what we can do to allay their fears," he said, squeezing the man's shoulder in what he hoped was a comfortable manner. Alejandro flinched.

"Escort?" Yuri asked, raising an eyebrow over his sunglasses.

"No, I don't want them to feel more threatened than they already do," Jordan replied, shaking his head. "I'll go down with Alejandro and get this sorted out. Keep the men away from the camp for now."

Yuri nodded. Jordan turned for the camp, setting a brisk pace that Alejandro had trouble matching. The shorter man scurried along, slightly out of breath from the elevation as they closed the gap to the pavilion where the scientists had gathered. It didn't take them long to spot his approach, and the assembled group closed ranks like a herd of elephants protecting a calf from a lion.

They said nothing as he strode into their midst.

"Alejandro tells me that you're unhappy with the lack of information provided," he said, letting his gaze roam the assembled group. Bridget and Roberts dropped their eyes immediately. Sheila held his stare for a moment, but then she, too, looked away. Only Smith met Jordan's gaze without difficulty.

"I can't say I agree with him approaching you like this, but Alejandro is right. We want to know just what the hell is happening down in the central chamber. You know a lot more than you're telling us," Smith said. Jordan still had a hard time thinking of him as Blair.

"Yes, we do," Jordan admitted, matter-of-factly and without a hint of either reproach or guilt. "I don't want to trot out tired clichés, but all information about this dig is need-to-know. We've ensured that each of you has the data needed to do your job."

"What about our health, Jordan? We're no good to you dead. You know that place is killing Steve," Dr. Roberts said, taking a step toward the giant soldier.

The scene was comical to Jordan, really. Roberts was a Chihuahua yipping at his heels.

"That is a definite concern," Jordan said, sighing softly. "My men are spending time down there too, albeit in more limited quantities than Dr. Galk. Be that as it may, we all have a job to do, and you accepted the risks when you signed your contracts. You're free to leave at any time, and you will keep your retainer, provided you adhere to the NDA you signed. We're not holding anyone against their will."

Blair looked shocked, and Jordan understood why. The scientists undoubtedly expected him to be cagey and antagonistic, to imprison them for questioning the situation. Wasn't that how the plot of every sci-fi movie went, with the evil military arrogantly withholding information?

"So are you going to tell us what you know about the central chamber? Why it's dangerous?" he asked cautiously. The others perked up as they awaited his answer.

"No, Professor Smith, I am not," Jordan replied. Smith wasn't a professor, but Jordan had seen the way the other scientists respected him, so he granted the honorific anyway. "We all answer to someone, and my boss has restricted that information. You have my deepest sympathy, but I cannot tell you anything beyond what you already know," Jordan said, giving an uncomfortable shrug. "I will say this, though. The faster you complete your work in the central chamber, the less exposure we'll all have to the dangers that place poses."

"What about Steve?" Bridget asked. She picked up her coffee, hand trembling. She didn't meet his gaze. That wasn't surprising, given the body language she displayed around Smith. There was a lot going on under the surface there.

"It's my sincere hope that Dr. Galk recovers from his ordeal, but if not, his sacrifice is not just for science but for all of humanity. You've been inside. You know this place changes everything," Jordan said, removing his sunglasses. He exhaled heavily. "I know you want more answers. I wish I could give them, but I can't. Accept that and stay, or pick up your marbles and go home. Decide. Right now. Am I ordering a transport to take some of you home?"

His gaze raked the lot of them, blue eyes icy. One by one, they dropped their gazes. It seemed the crew weren't willing to miss this, even though it might cost their lives.

"Excellent, I'm glad we understand each other. Now, I'll get out of your hair so you can get back to work," he said, keeping his tone mild. It wouldn't do to gloat. He needed them to feel like they mattered, not like they were being bullied.

"About that..." Smith broke the silence. "I may have found a way into the rest of the structure."

Jordan smiled. This man was *definitely* smarter than the rest of the uppity scientists the Director had assembled. Well, most of them were uppity. Bridget wasn't half bad. At least she talked to him like a human being.

"Excellent. Let's get down there. I'll have an escort prepared."

"Not just yet," Smith said, a predatory smile growing. "If you want inside, then I want a little information first."

"You're on dangerous ground, Smith. You've been paid quite handsomely, and I expect you to obey the terms of your contract," he replied. "If you know how to get inside, then you're obligated to share it. Otherwise you're wasting my time."

"I'm pretty sure I can get us inside. It's taken a lot of study, but the civilization that built this place left clues, if you know where to look. With Steve's deteriorating health, I'm the only person within four thousand miles that can solve this," Smith said, glancing at Bridget. Perhaps for support? Interesting.

"Professor Smith, we're both professionals. Let's grant each other professional courtesy. Yes, you're the only man who can get me inside. Yes, I need to get in as soon as humanly possible and don't have time to hunt for a replacement to solve this mystery of yours. You clearly want something over and above the enormous compensation we've offered. What are you after?"

"We want to know what the hell is going on down in that central chamber. Tell us what's happening to Steve and whatever else you know about this place, and I'll open the door," Smith said.

Jordan paused, reaching for a pot of coffee and filling a blue plastic mug. "Okay."

"That's it? Okay?" Smith asked. The archeologists, once again, looked shocked. Jordan suppressed a smile. He wasn't doing a very good job as the evil military commander keeping the noble scientists in the dark.

"Yeah, that's it. I'm here because I'm very good at sizing up tactical situations, Professor Smith. You have something I need. You will not give it to me unless I give you something in return. You want answers. Ask."

"Why didn't you tell us everything you knew about this place?" Smith asked, without hesitation.

"I know it sounds trite, but we've kept you in the dark because the information is on a need-to-know basis. The Director, the man I report to, felt knowing the full extent of the truth might disrupt your focus."

"Knowing everything about this place is the whole point, isn't it?" Sheila hurled her words like spears.

"Your *employer* knowing everything is the point, yes," Jordan countered. Sheila was tall and straight-backed, with a fire most crusading teachers had long since abandoned. He respected her, though he was almost positive the feeling wasn't mutual. "You were not the first team on site. We swept this place within twelve hours of it appearing. Our first team found several very curious anomalies. First, this place eats signals, as I'm sure you're aware by now. There is one spectrum it seems to allow, one that it also seems to be broadcasting. Something we call ELF—"

"Extremely low frequency waves," Dr. Roberts interrupted, wiping powdered eggs from his beard. "There have been some very interesting experiments involving ELF on human DNA. Apparently, if you have two test tubes within several inches of each other, one with DNA and the other with the correct proteins to synthesize it, the first test tube will use ELF to assemble DNA in the second, despite the fact that they have no direct contact."

Jordan would have to mention that to the Director. That might be worth following up on. Maybe they could bring in the person who'd conducted that study.

"Very succinctly put, Dr. Roberts. We have no idea what the ELF are used for, but we know two things: First, that they emanate from the central chamber. Second, it would require a very unique power source to continue broadcasting for as long as we believe it has."

"We already figured that part out. It couldn't have tunneled out of the earth without some sort of power. That room is full of radiation, isn't it?" Blair asked, setting his coffee down on the folding table.

"Yes," Jordan replied. There was no point in denying it, not when they'd clearly puzzled out the truth. "We believe that to be the cause of Dr. Galk's deteriorating health."

"Yet you're sending us in there anyway?" Bridget asked. "Steve could die. We could die."

"That's a risk all of you were aware of when you signed your contracts, as was I."

"Don't pull that legal bullshit with us," Sheila snarled, poking him in the chest with an outstretched finger. "You owe us more than that. If that place is dangerous, you should get us hazmat suits, or—"

"They wouldn't help," Jordan said, cutting her off with a wave. "This radiation isn't the most friendly variety. It pierces cloth. It pierces metal. If you're down there, you're going to be exposed; it's that simple. That means some, or maybe even all of us, might die exploring this place. That sacrifice is necessary."

"Why?" Blair asked.

"Because of who built this place. We know nothing about them, but their technology could exceed our own. This place returned on a very specific date, and if my employer has any idea why it's above my pay grade. For all we know, it could be a giant bomb. Until we know otherwise, this thing is a threat, and you've been hired to help us neutralize that threat," Jordan explained. The Director would be furious that he was revealing so much of their mandate, but what choice did he have? These people were going to mutiny if he didn't give them something. Even if they didn't, Smith could withhold the information he desperately needed.

"He's right," Smith said, drawing surprised looks from his colleagues. Only Bridget seemed of like mind, reaching up to squeeze his shoulder. He flinched, just slightly, but enough for Jordan to catch the pain in his eyes. "We have to get inside, have to learn how or why this place was built. That's worth the risk. Besides, I think I can get us in. We only have to be down there for a few hours more. Hopefully that much exposure will be safe."

"Excellent, Professor Smith. I'm glad you understand. How do we proceed?"

"How the hell could you possibly know how to get inside? We're nowhere near understanding their language," Sheila said, rounding on Smith.

"We don't need to understand their language. Many of their glyphs are highly detailed pictographs that tell a story. I've spent a great deal of time studying the passages in the south corridor, the one Bridget showed me when we first went inside," Smith explained. His eyes were alight, and the others seemed to pick up on his enthusiasm. "We assume it's some sort of rite of passage. This wolf-headed goddess raises up champions to help battle whatever the red figures depicted are. In every case, the ritual begins with her grasping their hand. This symbol is repeated over and over."

"Oh my God," Sheila said, her oatmeal tumbling to the floor. "The statue in the central chamber. It represents the wolf goddess."

"Right. So if we grasp the hand, I'm betting we'll initiate whatever rite of passage we see depicted in the glyphs," Smith said, grinning now. He was clearly proud of his discovery, and he had a right to be. Jordan was impressed.

He fished his radio from a vest pocket. "Yuri, assemble Alpha. Have them set up all four turrets in the central chamber. Also, send a priority message to HQ and let the Director know that Professor Smith may have found a way into the inner structure."

11

THE MOTHER'S HAND

"I have never been so terrified in my life," Sheila murmured so faintly Blair could barely make it out. She was crouched behind him in the shelter of the doorway. He couldn't blame her. The longer he spent in the central chamber, the less he trusted it. That was *before* Jordan had revealed the truth about the radiation. The wondrous had become the sinister.

The ramp descended into deep shadow, completely swallowed around halfway down. The room was more brightly lit than he'd ever seen it. Fuel for the generator was sparse, and not because of money. Their employers had no lack of that. No, the logistics of carting hundreds of gallons of gasoline made supply an issue.

The stand lamps in each corner fought a losing war with the darkness, but they gave shape to the room. Blair had seen the obelisks with his headlamp, but this was the first time they had any real context. They sat at perfect cardinal directions, the one in the center nearly twice as tall as the others.

Below each obelisk sat a boxy turret that would have been at home in the movie *Aliens*, each about waist height with a broad body atop a tripod. They clicked and hummed as they scanned the darkness, a bright red beam shining from each.

"Steve?" he called into the darkness. In spite of the better illumination, there was no sign of the man. Somehow, that made sense.

As he took a step down the ramp, a wave of dizziness overcame him, a flash of something bright robbing him of sight. It was an image, a stern but beautiful woman with silver hair and commanding eyes. She held a golden staff clutched in one hand and wore regalia that wouldn't have been out of place in Egypt.

"Smith, are you all right?" Blair heard in the distance. He blinked, turning slowly to face Jordan. The man looked...Was that concern?

Blair turned to face Jordan, the soldier filling the space beside him like some movable wall. "Do you feel that? It's almost like a humming in the air."

"Is right. Yuri feel it too," the Russian rumbled, emerging from the shadow of one of the smaller obelisks. He held aloft a small tablet that displayed a fluorescent green graph. "Readings increase forty percent in last hour. If continues, all dead in four hours."

"Readings?" Blair asked. The dizziness was passing.

"Radiation. This place is getting more dangerous by the minute. Let's get this done," the commander said, striding boldly down the ramp without waiting for a reply, not that Blair had one ready. How could one respond to that?

"Blair?" came a raspy voice from the shadows near the southern obelisk. A figure moved in the darkness. Jordan had a pistol out and aimed before Blair even registered the fact that he'd moved. Another gun cocked behind him, probably Yuri's.

"Blair, did you solve it? We have to open the..." Steve mumbled, lurching into a pool of light. His dark hair was matted to the side of his face, greasy with sweat. The clothing draping his skeletal form was crusted from weeks of wear, and the pungent odor of the long homeless wafted through the room.

Steve's gaze focused as he noticed Jordan, Bridget, and Sheila. His face twisted, spittle flying as he roared, "Why did you bring them? They're not of the blood. They don't belong here. Their very presence taints this holy place. The whelps will be punished for this insolence."

He lunged for Blair, hissing like a snake. There was nothing left of the man he'd known, only a shell of rage and madness. Blair stumbled backward, shielding himself with his arms. Then Jordan glided forward, jerking the butt of his pistol down on the back of Steve's skull. He collapsed like a puppet whose strings had been cut, falling limply at Blair's feet.

"Steve," Bridget shrieked, her headlamp bobbing as she hurried down the ramp. She knelt next to Steve, raising two fingers to his throat. She turned a glare at Jordan. "He'll live, but I'm betting he's got a concussion. We should carry him up. He'll need medical attention."

"He's dying of radiation poisoning. A concussion is the least of his worries. Yuri, restrain the man in case he's still agitated when he wakes," Jordan ordered, dismissing Bridget with a wave as he holstered his pistol. Sheila gave a squawk of protest as she finally entered the room, but Jordan silenced her with a look. "I'm not in the habit of explaining myself, but as I still need your cooperation, I will make a final exception. We've entered a combat situation. Dr. Galk was a threat to Professor Smith. Professor Smith is our best chance of finding this secret chamber, so I eliminated the threat. I will do the same to any other threat without hesitation. Now, let's get in and out as quickly as possible. Unless you all want to end up just like the poor doctor."

Yuri knelt next to Steve, rolling him onto his stomach. The Russian gave a snort of disgust, removing a white zip tie from his pocket and binding Steve's wrists together. He repeated the process with the ankles leaving Steve trussed and bleeding on the marble. Part of Blair was horrified, but he mostly felt relieved. Whatever Steve had become terrified him.

Blair moved to the floodlights that had been carted in, flipping the heavy red lever to crank the generator from medium to high. It read *Aziz* in bright green letters, shiny enough that the thing could have been made yesterday. Light flooded the chamber as the generator roared to life. The stench of gasoline and carbon monoxide belched from the motor, but the chamber was large enough that airflow wasn't a problem.

The light didn't quite banish the shadows, but it did reveal the reason they'd come. A nine-foot statue stood at the far side of the room near the south wall, its right hand extended in a gesture that might have been friendly had it not been for the statue's bestial countenance. The nobility, the exquisite detail with which the obviously feminine features had been crafted, once again struck Blair. It made the Egyptians' finest work look like the macaroni pictures hung on your fridge. The statue also confirmed his earlier observation. Except for the gender, this *was* Wepwawet. An indisputable connection to ancient Egypt, on a continent thousands of miles away.

Blair strode through the lingering darkness, standing beneath the magnificent statue. He glanced behind himself as booted steps echoed dully. Jordan stepped up next to him, with Bridget and Sheila just a few paces behind. Yuri scanned the darkness, rifle in a death grip.

"So how do we activate it?" Jordan asked. He stood coiled, like a snake ready to strike. Blair was strangely comforted by his presence, though he doubted anything he did here would require armed intervention from the soldiers.

"I don't know," Blair said. He placed his palm against the statue's. "There might be a lever or a way t—"

The statue's hand tightened around his, locking it in an implacable grip. The hand didn't grind or move like stone. The way it twisted had been just like a living person's.

"Smith?" Jordan asked, raising an eyebrow as he inspected the statue.

"The grip isn't painful, but my hand is stuck. Hold on a sec; the stone is getting warm," he explained. An odd blend of curiosity and unease settled over him.

"Yuri, do you have the bolt cutters?" Jordan called over his shoulder.

"Hold on; let's not be hasty," Blair said, waving his free hand. "We want to get inside, don't we? This might be part of the process."

"Or it could be a trap," Bridget countered, moving from Steve's side to inspect the statue. She shot him a worried glance. "I don't see a way to loosen it. We'll have to break the hand off. Jordan is right about the bolt cutters."

"You might be right. It's getting hot now. Really hot," Blair grunted, tugging as hard as he could. The statue held him fast. He gave Bridget an earnest look. "Just be careful. I write with this hand." Sweat flowed freely down his face. The generator's acrid exhaust stung his eyes. His nerves were jagged glass, like the early stages of a migraine.

"Have bolt cutters, but stone too thick," Yuri explained, gesturing with a two-and-a-half-foot tool. "Explosives, maybe. Or bullets if desperate."

Jordan moved behind the statue, examining the wrist. "I can shatter this with a few well-placed shots. Marble is tough, but it can't handle this kind of ordnance."

"Are we that stupid now?" Sheila said, muscling her way past Jordan to the statue. "If you fire at that arm, the bullet will ricochet through the room. Even if it didn't, it's going to send chips of high-velocity stone right at Blair. Not to mention damaging the most price-less archeological find in history. No, what we need to do is—"

The statue grew hot, as if it had been left in the afternoon sun for the weight of the day. Blair twitched and flopped, fire flowing up his arm and into his chest. It surged through his body like flame over gasoline, obliterating all except the pain, a deep, white agony. Even his eyes were thick with it.

In the first instant, he longed for death. What felt like an eternity later, he knew death had betrayed him, unwilling to free him from the pain. So he endured. The inferno rampaged through him as though he were a dry forest. When its fury was finally spent, he found himself huddled at the base of the statue.

"Commander, south wall. Ten o'clock," Yuri barked, ducking behind an obelisk.

"Handle it," Jordan called back, looming over Blair with outstretched hands. The Commander's eyes had widened. So odd, that tiny gesture. The man had a level of control Blair had never witnessed, yet something he'd just seen had rattled him. The soldier was shocked. Shock. Blair was in shock, wasn't he?

"Blair?" Bridget called. She seemed a hundred miles away. She knelt next to him, her clean fragrance a welcome balm to the echoes of pain haunting his limbs. "Look at me. I think you've just been electrocuted. Can you tell me your name?"

She seized his chin, forcing him to look her in the eye. Such pretty eyes. Pools of brown. Some of his happiest memories dwelt there.

"Gash. Abnat," Blair said, shaking his head to clear it. A distant part of his mind recognized the aphasia, but he was powerless to articulate that.

"Jordan, how quickly can you get a doctor out here?" Bridget asked, looking up at Jordan.

Something rumbled behind him, but Blair was too weak to find out what. The best he could manage was to loll his head to the side. Instantly alert, Jordan and Yuri snapped their rifles up. Sheila had stumbled backward, both hands clasped over her mouth. Clean white light burst all around Blair, overpowering the sad stand lamps.

Bridget squatted next to him, squeezing his shoulder. "You're going to be all right. We'll get you out of here."

"No," Blair croaked, pausing as he gathered another breath. "I want to...to see. Show me."

"Jordan?" Bridget called. Her voice was further away now. "Jordan, can you carry him inside?"

Inside? Inside where? Jordan's daunting arms were suddenly around him, hoisting him effortlessly into the air. Blair's vision spun, finally coming to rest on a wide chamber where the wall had been moments before. It was the single greatest discovery in history, more momentous than the cave paintings the Cro-Magnon left in France thirty millennia earlier. It changed everything.

The clean white light emanated from the room's ceiling, clearly illuminating the brilliant hieroglyphs lining every wall. Unlike the others, these were quicksilver, each symbol flowing and alive. Seven sarcophagi radiated around the room from a central point, each a pure block of glass inset with rubies and emeralds and diamonds. Pulses of light flowed between the gems in precise lines.

Only one sarcophagus was occupied, yet Blair couldn't make out much about the occupant. Darkness ate at the edges of his vision. His heartbeat had slowed, awarding a grudging beat every few moments. Every breath was a battle, a ragged gasp for whatever oxygen he could find.

"My God," Sheila said, staggering toward the sarcophagus. She planted her palms against the glass, ignoring the pulses of light that flowed around her. "It's not possible. She's breathing. This woman is alive."

Blair fought for another breath, but this time his lungs refused to obey. He waited for another thud, but his heart was stubbornly silent. He wasn't a medical doctor, but he didn't need to be to understand the darkening of his vision. Blair was dying, poisoned by whatever the statue had done.

"Blair? Blaaair!" Bridget screamed.

12

BLAIR'S DEAD

Jordan compartmentalized the situation, allowing his training to take over in the face of the incomprehensible. He knelt swiftly, laying Smith on the ground just outside the chamber they'd discovered. Blair's eyes were closed, his chest unmoving. Jordan feared the worst. He applied two fingers to the man's throat, giving a long count to ten. Nothing.

"Yuri, get the scientists topside. Radio HQ and tell the director we're initiating containment protocol. We need a team here ASAP," he barked, shrugging out of his windbreaker and laying it gently over Smith's limp body.

"What are you doing?" Bridget shrieked, dropping beside him and yanking the jacket away. "Blair? Blair, can you hear me?" She shook the man, but there was no response.

"Yuri," Jordan barked, shooting the man a glare.

The beefy Russian gathered Bridget in a tight grip, hauling the woman to her feet and away from the body. She resisted violently, fists beating against Yuri's chest as she raged. "Let me go. You can't do this!"

"He might still be alive," Sheila pleaded, eyes shining with unshed tears. "There might be something we can do."

"You know there isn't," Jordan countered, replacing the windbreaker. Smith deserved some peace. "We have no idea what killed him, but make no mistake. This man is dead. I understand he was a friend and colleague, but that doesn't change my job. I have to protect the rest of the team. Whatever killed him could be contagious."

"Then we're all exposed," Sheila roared, balling her fists. "We should all be quarantined, which means there's no reason not to stay down here and see if we can do anything for Blair."

"You can't just give up on him," Bridget said, finally calming. Yuri still held her, but his grip had relaxed.

"We don't have a choice," Jordan replied, shaking his head. "The radiation was bad down here before. Opening that chamber dramatically increased it. Right now we're facing an unknown threat, and that calls for a tactical retreat. We'll have a containment team here in twelve hours, and then we can find some answers."

"Blair will be dead by then," Bridget said, eyes flashing. It was the first time Jordan had seen her truly angry. She hadn't shown nearly so much emotion for Dr. Galk.

"He's dead now. I understand you don't agree with my decision. I don't care. You can grieve topside," he said, seizing Sheila by the arm. He shoved her toward the ramp leading to the surface. "Move. Now. I'd rather leave you your dignity, but I'll throw you over my shoulder if I have to."

"What about Steve?" Bridget asked.

Jordan considered his answer carefully. Dr. Galk was dying, his mind deteriorated past use. There was no point in wasting resources trying to save him. "He's already received a lethal dose. We don't have to be doctors to see it. Even if he hadn't, I can't risk spreading a potential contagion. It could be radiation, but if whatever's killing him is communicable, we're all in danger. He stays down here."

Sheila and Bridget looked at each other, apparently coming to a silent understanding. Neither resisted as they were herded up the ramp, Yuri in front and Jordan bringing up the rear.

Jordan paused at the edge of the central chamber, giving the new room a final look. If that woman really was alive, she'd survived for ten millennia or more. These people possessed technology that vastly eclipsed their own. What the hell had they unleashed on the world when they'd opened this place? More importantly, what had happened to the creature they'd found within?

13

THE WORST THIEF OF ALL

A higa leapt skyward, seizing a granite outcrop jutting into the naked sky. He dangled there, sucking in deep breaths as he gazed down at the lush jungle a dizzying distance below his mountain perch. The darker green vein of the River of Life wound through the lighter trees, snaking off into the distance. He'd spent many precious days locating villages along its banks, performing the grisly work that might shield the world from the coming darkness.

A sudden gust of wind dried the sheen of sweat coating his brow, drawing a cool sigh. Climbing was harder than it should have been. Partly that was due to the weak moon, bereft of the life-giving energy he'd known in his day. Yet the greater part had been stolen by the most cunning thief of all, time.

He leapt again, powerful arms propelling him to another outcrop near the mountain's peak. Mother willing, the going would be easier when he reached the leeward side. He'd forgotten just how massive this continent was, how long it took to travel between jungle and mountains.

Picking up a strange metal canister corroded by rain, Ahiga knelt. What had its purpose been? The memories he'd pilfered allowed him to decipher the odd writing. *Coke.* That was the word formed by the glyphs used by these moderns. The word meant nothing. He dropped the can with a clink, shaking his head. Mankind had spread like a cancer, leaving refuse in their wake. That would come to an end soon, for good or ill.

Ahiga shielded his eyes from the sun's harsh rays. Wispy clouds danced below him, wreathing the mountain as if paying homage. He stared past neighboring peaks, toward the distant valley where the Ark lay. He'd managed to brew such a troubling predicament. He must return and wake the Mother. Yet, getting inside would mean battling the soldiers. His strength had waned during his long hibernation. Did enough remain?

A sudden tremor brought him to his knees, spilling his limp body on the ground mere inches from a fall that would kill even him. Ahiga struggled to pull himself away from the abyss, but his body refused to obey. Energy raged through him, a bolt of lightning in reverse. Instead of striking, it departed. A beam of silver poured from his mouth, streaking through the sky, toward the distant Ark. It moved so swiftly that in a single heartbeat it had passed beyond his enhanced vision.

Ka-Dun, it cannot be. The voice of the beast inside him carried more alarm than Ahiga'd ever heard, despite being bonded for centuries. He shared the panic, for the impossible had occurred.

"It cannot, yet it is. Someone has taken the access key," he said, hot shame pushing back the chill wind. His failure was complete.

Only one of the blood could have wrested the key, and then only if they knew the ritual.

"It is so," Ahiga agreed, finally rising to his knees. His body felt like a wrung-out wraf. "Someone was found worthy. I am no longer guardian."

There was only one course now. He must return and find this new guardian, or the Mother would never awaken. This strange new world would burn.

14

BLAIR'S FUNERAL

"We shouldn't have just left him there," Sheila said. Her hot tears rained on the dry soil. She knew she was hysterical, but didn't she have a right to be? Blair was *dead*.

"I understand that," Jordan replied, his tone thick with uncharacteristic patience. Damn, she hated the man. He rested a comforting hand on her shoulder. "We didn't have a choice. We don't know what killed him. What if it turns out to be an airborne pathogen? Pulling back was the right thing to do. I've already arranged for a team to investigate, and quarantined us from the rest of the soldiers until we know we're safe to be around. We'll have you back in the inner chamber inside of forty-eight hours."

"Is *that* what you think we care about?" Bridget hissed, rising from her blue canvas camp chair and glaring at the big man. "Blair is *dead*. We don't know how or why. He was more than a friend...to all of us."

"You have my sincere condolences. Professor Smith was a brilliant man, and we all feel his loss. Keenly. I'm not trying to trivialize that. At the same time, I still have a job to do. That job is protecting the living," Jordan replied, removing his hand from Sheila's slumped shoulder. Its weight had actually been reassuring. Jordan shook his head, turning from the group and striding off into the night.

Bridget rested in a neighboring chair. Her legs were pulled tight against her chest, and her head was down so her hair screened her face. Alejandro and Dr. Roberts sat at the far side of the pavilion. They conversed in low tones and significant glances. Were they worried that she or Bridget might do something crazy? Good. Let them know a shadow of the pain she labored under. It *wasn't* okay.

"I'm going for a walk," Sheila announced, rising suddenly to her feet. She just couldn't be around these people and their lingering looks.

"Can I go with you?" Bridget asked hesitantly, glancing up with swollen eyes.

That took Sheila aback. The two hadn't been friends for almost three years. They weren't active enemies, but their decade-old friendship had died the moment Bridget betrayed Blair. The man had never been the same. Right up until the end, she'd seen the pain in his gaze whenever it landed on her former friend. Horrible bitch.

"Why not?" Sheila agreed, surprising herself. Maybe she just didn't want to be alone. Or maybe she wanted to be with someone who knew Blair as well as she did. Or, maybe, she just wanted to get Bridget alone so she could choke the smugness out of her.

The pair left the pavilion in silence, neither speaking of a destination. It wasn't long before they found themselves on the western side of the pyramid. The ancient structure was bathed in moonlight and would have been beautiful under other circumstances. Almost luminescent, the stone drank in the light. The workmanship was incredible, as were the pictographs, all fantastic colors and bold symbols. Yet it no longer held any joy for her.

"I want to go back inside," Sheila said, not sure if that would help but desperate for anything that might salve the wound. She started forward without waiting for Bridget's reply.

"Sheila, wait." Bridget grabbed her shoulder. She pointed at the mouth of the tunnel leading into the pyramid's cavernous depths.

"Jordan left Yuri to guard the entrance. He isn't just going to let us inside. You know that."

"Sure, he is," Sheila growled, plunging forward with quick, deliberate strides. No ignorant soldier was going to stop her.

The shorter woman fell wordlessly into step beside her as they stepped beneath the oppressive stone tunnel. Yuri lurked in the darkness near the doors, arms clasped behind his back. His submachine gun dangled from a strap over his shoulder, and he still wore his sunglasses. Who wore sunglasses at night? Especially when they were on guard duty.

"Should not be here," he rumbled, taking a step toward them as they approached. A slight red glow came from behind his glasses. Apparently they were more than they appeared. "Return to the camp site. Pyramid off limits."

"No it isn't," Sheila said, moving around him, toward the doorway. He stepped into her path, raising a hand to stop her. Sheila batted his hand aside, taking a step backward. "Don't touch me. I'm going inside. So is Bridget. You might be able to stop one of us, but not both. Not unless you're willing to shoot us. Are you?"

Yuri looked decidedly uncomfortable, raising a hand to adjust his glasses as he considered the answer. "Is dangerous inside. Why go?"

"Because our friends' bodies are down there, discarded like garbage. Steve and Blair deserve better than that. They deserve a funeral," Bridget interrupted, stepping up to join Sheila. She thrust a finger up at Yuri. "If you want to run back and tell Jordan, go right ahead. We'll be inside, but unless you're going to physically restrain us, you can't stop us. We know this is a signal dead zone, so it's not like you can use a radio." Bridget plunged past him into the darkness, leaving the bemused soldier in her wake. Sheila smiled grimly and followed.

"Wait," Yuri called. Sheila paused, turning to face the man. "Ten minutes. Get down, find bodies, come back. Smith was good man. You're right. Deserved better." Maybe he was human after all.

The air was slightly warmer inside, making the hair stand up on Sheila's arms for some reason. Something was different. The air was charged, like the night sky just before a bolt of lightning, or just after. What did it mean? She considered asking Bridget, but anger kept the words firmly lodged in her throat.

"You hate me, don't you?" Bridget asked, bracing as if she were expecting a blow as they advanced up the corridor. Their footsteps echoed dully around them, the only sounds as Sheila considered her reply.

"Yes. I hated you before, and I hate you more now that he's dead," she admitted, eyeing the shorter woman's silhouette in the shadows cast by the headlamp. Bridget winced. Good. "Does that surprise you? Do you even know why?"

"I can guess."

"Then guess. I want to hear it from you," Sheila demanded, burying her grief in anger.

"You always liked Blair. I mean romantically," Bridget whispered, hair screening her face. It was an image the men *loved*.

"God, no. You couldn't have it more backward. I had a thing for Steve, especially in the beginning. You remember how confident he was, how he kept court in the lecture hall during lunch," Sheila said slowly, to keep the anger in check. "When you chose Blair, I figured I had a shot. We actually started to get close for a while there, spent a lot of time together."

"Then I ruined that, just like I do everything else."

"Yeah, you did. Good thing for me, though. I guess I dodged a bullet. I had no idea what Steve was really like," Sheila said. She wasn't going to sugar coat this. "I still remember when you had the affair. You two did it right under his nose. He was the *very last* to know. Why, Bridget? Blair wasn't enough for you?"

"You have no idea what it was like," Bridget said, meeting Sheila's gaze with a sudden ferocity. She paused, headlamp casting odd shadows in the corridor. "He was completely wrapped up in his work. He didn't come to bed. I barely saw him for months. Steve was there. Whatever I needed, he dropped his work to make it happen. One day...well, it just sort of happened."

"Happened to destroy Blair," Sheila barked, starting down the corridor again. Bridget could come or not; she didn't care. "He was never the same. You know you're the reason he quit fieldwork, right? And that he hasn't been in a long-term relationship since?"

"I didn't," Bridget answered, sudden fire apparently sapped by guilt.

"You broke his heart and took away his best friend in a single day. What did you think was going to happen? Then you show up here and start fawning over him, acting like Steve is dead. Did you really think you could have them both? God, what the hell is wrong with you?" Sheila said, finally having an outlet for the anger that had been building for three years. "What did you think your flirting with Blair would do? Did you even stop to think how it might affect him? Or Steve?"

"You're right. I'm a horrible person," Bridget said so softly the soft wind whistling through the tunnel nearly stole the words. "I never meant for any of it to happen like it did. I loved them both, you know. I feel like I've lost them."

"You didn't deserve either of them, you miserable bitch," Sheila hissed. She was lashing out, but damn if the woman didn't deserve it.

"Don't you think I know that? Blair only came on the dig because I asked him to. He's dead because of *me,* Sheila. I killed him as much as anything in that pyramid," Bridget said, voice cracking as tears blazed a trail down her dust-caked cheeks. She sagged to her knees in the middle of the corridor, sobs wracking the tiny woman.

Sheila couldn't explain why she did what she did next, but she sank to her knees and gathered Bridget into her arms. She let Bridget sob into her shoulder, and before she knew it, she was crying too. They poured out their grief in a cathartic release, trembling and crying as they clung to each other. Somehow it bridged the gap between them, beginning the healing that might mend their friendship.

It made Sheila vulnerable, and she almost confessed her secret to Bridget, that a disease was eating away at her. Every day the HIV made it harder to get out of bed.

The moment was broken as a feral and panicked shriek echoed

up from the bowels of the pyramid. The sound rolled down her spine with icy fingers, reaching into the primitive animal that ruled all mankind. Run, it said. Run fast and far, and do not look back.

"What was that?" Bridget asked. They pulled away from each other, touching gazes under the thin illumination of the headlamps.

"It must have been Steve. We should go see if he's okay..." Sheila trailed off as a bestial howl rolled up from the depths. It was raw and visceral, like that of a wolf circling its prey, only much, much deeper. As if it were coming from the throat of a considerably larger creature.

"Run," Bridget screeched, lurching back the way they'd come. She stumbled, head careening into the wall. Bridget's headlamp clattered to the stone, casting crazy shadows as she scrambled back up the corridor.

Sheila froze. She wanted to follow, but she couldn't move. Some corner of her mind cataloged and labeled the emotional response. Her brain's limbic system was cutting off the flow of blood to her prefrontal cortex. Her animal instinct had taken control and was tending to her survival. It knew that if she moved, she might advertise her presence. But Sheila knew it was wrong. She had to move.

Her breath came in shallow gasps, and she began to tremble. Something was moving down in the darkness, in the central chamber. She'd been in enough tombs to sense such things, to feel the flow of the air. The thing was moving quickly. Sheila scanned her immediate surroundings with her headlamp. The walls were lined with large statues, anthropomorphic gods from a bygone age. It was her only chance.

She dove at the wall, huddling beneath the protective arms of a statue. Her trembling hand rose of its own accord, switching off the headlamp and plunging the corridor into near darkness. All that remained was Bridget's discarded headlamp some twenty feet closer to the exit. The lamp cast a steady beam of light against the wall next to it, creating a puddle of illumination.

Something clicked against stone with a steady cadence, tapping its way closer. Movement. A massive shadow flitted by her hiding place. Sheila wanted to squeeze her eyes shut, but even that small freedom was denied her by the terror. She couldn't even breathe. The noise might be the end of her, slight as it would be. With the grace of a predator the shadow landed near the headlamp.

It had to be eight feet tall. Its frame was heavily muscled and thick with dark fur. An alarming mix of wolf and man shaped its head, adorned with an elongated snout but clearly human eyes. A word existed to describe such a creature, but her mind refused to allow it. This wasn't a movie.

The creature picked up the headlamp, examining it with terrible purpose. It seemed puzzled by the light, shining it up and down the hallway. The beam splashed within a few inches of Sheila's right foot. She shrank in on herself, becoming a part of the wall. Lack of oxygen was making her lightheaded, but she didn't dare breathe.

The beast stared in her direction, scanning the darkness, searching. Its grey fur made it eerily similar to the Egyptian god Wepwawet Blair had mentioned, the wolf-headed warrior son of Anubis. But this was far, far more terrifying than any hieroglyph or statue. The blood and gore slicking its neck and chest gave voice to that fact.

The audible click of the headlamp's switch being flipped ushered the hallway into sudden darkness. Heavy breathing broke the silence, broken by a few huffs as the creature sought a scent—her scent. How much longer could she hold her breath?

15

THE BEAST

The beast stirred from the sleep of ages, reborn into a time far removed from its own. It rose gracefully on powerful legs, uncurling fur-covered limbs corded with muscle. Clawed fingers flexed experimentally as it tested its new body. This vessel was suffused with power, far more than it should have contained this early in the cycle. That could only mean that its host had lingered near a source.

The beast was aware of the host's consciousness, fluttering like a trapped bird. It would grow stronger with time, but for now the beast's control was total. It had the freedom to accomplish the tasks for which it had been created, uninterrupted by whatever morals or confusion its host might be afflicted with.

A careful survey of its surroundings revealed the Mother's rejuvenation chamber. It was in many ways the very heart of the Ark. Her slumbering form was still shielded by the rejuvenator, which emitted wave after wave of energy from the array of gems scattered across its surface. The beast basked in their glow for several minutes, filling its reserves until its fur nearly glowed. It had no idea how abundant such energy would be outside the Ark, so every scrap could be vital.

The beast raised its muzzle, drinking in a dozen interwoven scents through wet, black nostrils. Unblooded had been here recently, perhaps a half dozen in total. One scent overpowered the others, thick and pungent. It was masculine but sickly. That would make sense if the fool had been in the antechamber for any length of time. The energy here was many times more intense than the trickle provided by the moon. An unblooded would die in a matter of weeks from prolonged exposure.

The beast stalked through the doorway into the much larger antechamber, padding silently past the dormant obelisks despite its incredible size. Such grace came naturally, a gift from its creator. The room was cloaked in shadow, but the beast's keen vision spotted a huddled form in the far corner. This wretch was the source of the stench. The fool's hands and feet were bound. Had it been left as a sacrifice? That seemed unlikely. The beast flexed both hands. It unlimbered claws that itched to rend.

"Blair?" a scratchy voice called. The beast plucked the word from the sheaf of memories fluttering through its host's imprisoned consciousness. The word was significant. It was the host's name. Perhaps the limp form was a friend or colleague of the host. Not that it mattered. The pathetic mortal was in the final throws of energy sickness, mere hours from an agonizing death. "Is t-that you? Have you seen the inner chamber? It's wonderful. The Mother, she's beautiful...so beautiful. We must wake her..."

The beast rose to its full height, looming over the pitiful wretch. The man's gaze cleared like the sky after a storm as he twisted in his bonds to stare up at the instrument of his execution. In a moment of lucidity, he seemed to realize exactly what he was looking at. The light of understanding filled his gaze.

"Champion," he whispered, wiggling into a prostrated position. He pressed his forehead to the cool marble floor. "I am ready for the sacrifice. Judge me."

Interesting. The beast had not expected any supplicants. How was such a thing possible? It considered for long moments, squatting next to the sacrifice. If this poor fool had lingered near the Mother for any length of time, her mind could have imparted memories. She was that strong. That must be it.

It was a pity there weren't more like him, but the beast hadn't expected there to be. That would have been far too easy. No, he would have to hunt them. He would find their villages even if they were buried in the heart of the jungles choking much of this continent. Then he would blaze through them in a raging inferno. They would resist, of course, but that would merely hone long-dormant skills in preparation for the true battle.

The beast seized the man by the neck, claws sinking into his soft flesh. Hot, coppery blood rained to the floor as he hefted the supplicant. The beast's mouth filled with saliva. It hungered. The man let out an ear-piercing shriek that echoed through the chamber. Apparently, his faith was a flimsy thing in the face of pain.

The beast lunged for the man's throat, ending the tortured shriek. It bathed in the sweet, tangy blood as it tore loose head and spine. The limp form slumped to the ground, blessedly silent. The beast let out a low howl of victory, reveling in the coming slaughter. Then it fed for the first time.

16

IT'S BACK

"Commander," Yuri panted, skidding up to the pavilion in a shower of dust. His chest heaved under his bulky black Kevlar vest, but he didn't let that delay his report. "Yuri disobeyed orders. Allowed Sheila and Bridget to enter pyramid."

"You let them in?" Jordan growled, rising from his perch on the edge of a large black crate. He set his tablet down, forgetting a half-written message to the Director. "You had strict orders. No one inside without my direct authorization."

"Is true, but Yuri ordered not to use force against noncoms. Women go inside unless Yuri stop. Besides, they wish to retrieve Smith. What they do is right. Smith deserves burial," Yuri said, snapping to attention. He wasn't offering excuses, just reporting the facts. He knew he'd be punished, but he reported his own crime anyway. The man had such an odd sense of honor.

Jordan would probably be forced to mete out something unpleasant since a direct order had been disobeyed. That would come later. For now he had to recover those women. "How long ago?"

"Four minutes, twenty-four seconds," Yuri answered. His breathing had eased, but his pale face was slick with sweat.

Jordan considered the best tactical response. They had no idea how Smith had died or what potential risks had been unleashed. He didn't believe in curses, but he did worry about a virus or disease that modern humans had no resistance to. It was unlikely, but if he was wrong, the cost could be more lives than he'd be able to overcome losing and still sleep at night.

Going back in presented the significant risk of spreading a contagion. Should he write the women off? He stowed the human drive to protect, forcing himself to consider only logic. They were experts in their field, and that made them the best chance of learning more about this place. Losing such skilled assets would be painful, but replacements could be found.

"Commander, what's going on?" Alejandro asked from his tense perch in one of the folding chairs at the neighboring pavilion.

"Sheila and Bridget went back inside the structure," he admitted. No sense hiding the facts. "We're going to quarantine them there. No one else will be allowed to enter or exit until Mohn's science team arrives."

"And how long will that be?" Dr. Roberts demanded. He rose from the chair next to Alejandro's, crossing to Jordan's pavilion like he was spoiling for a fight.

"I'm going to guess tomorrow afternoon sometime. They'll arrive by chopper. It will be a team with hazmat suits to scan every inch of that chamber. A field lab will be constructed on-site, and they'll begin processing data within hours," Jordan replied, rising and taking a single step toward Roberts. He loomed over the stubborn geologist, but the man didn't seem deterred.

"How many of us will be dead by then? We don't even know what killed Blair...or what's going on with Bridget and Sheila. We should be sending your men and their guns down to find them, not sitting here waiting for them to die." He met Jordan's gaze.

The commander had seen this sort of defiance before. It wasn't going to be quieted short of violence, but he had to try.

"Heeeeelp!" A woman's shriek echoed through the ravine. Bridget. Jordan spun to face the pyramid. There was only one thing he knew of that could evoke that kind of terror. That *thing* had come back, or there was another one in the pyramid.

"Yuri, get the men set up with the heavy ordnance. I want the western side of the pyramid under lockdown. If it isn't our girls, and it moves, I want it dead," he ordered. Yuri snapped a salute, sprinting off toward the soldiers' camp.

Jordan crossed the pavilion to a long black case he'd hoped that he wouldn't have to open. He knelt, using his thumb on the scanner set into the front of the black plastic. It snapped open, rising of its own accord. He reached for the pieces within, assembling the rifle he'd acquired in Panama with practiced ease. Assembly took only moments, but for Jordan an eternity had passed before he slipped the strap over his shoulder and slammed the clip home.

The sniper rifle had been modeled after an old-school Barrette, but it was newer, sleeker, and—most importantly—it was automatic. It was far larger than the modified M4s the rest of the squad would be using. That made it worthless at close range, but it might let him get the drop on this thing.

"What about us, Commander?" Roberts asked. Some of the fire had gone out of him, but his stance was defiant.

"You and Alejandro head east. Get at least a hundred yards from camp and hide in the boulders," he ordered, pulling his sidearm from its holster. He offered it grip first to Alejandro. "Take this. It's a .457 so you'll need to hold it with both hands when you fire it. All you have to do is flip the safety, point, and pull the trigger. Can you do that?"

"I can do that." Alejandro nodded, taking the pistol gingerly in both hands. "It's heavy."

"Dr. Roberts..." Jordan said, reaching for the 9mm he kept tucked into his boot.

"I've never fired a gun in my life, and I'm not about to start now. She could simply have encountered a spider for all we know. You're overreacting," he replied, crossing his arms and leaning against a crate.

A low, deep howl echoed from the depths of the pyramid and up the ravine. It was otherworldly. Terrifying. Jordan had heard something similar in Alaska, but this was deeper and more primal.

"Run. Now!" he barked, giving Roberts a little shove. The man rounded on him, about to protest. Jordan cut him off. "Didn't you fucking hear me? Move. Fucking MOVE."

Alejandro was already in motion, eating up ground like a rabbit fleeing a fox. Dr. Roberts watched him go, and then turned and lumbered into a run as well. That was the best Jordan could do for them right now. His priority was downing that werewolf. More than just their lives could depend on it.

Jordan cradled the heavy rifle, sprinting into the dusk. The moon hadn't risen yet, but he could already make out the faint glow on the horizon. He hoped it wouldn't make the thing stronger. He circled wide around the structure's southern face. Going this way would take longer, but he didn't want to risk getting close. He'd seen how quickly that thing could move, and if it got the drop on him, he was done. That meant more than his life. If his team couldn't bring the beast down, the thing could kill with impunity. The village of Villa Milagros was just a few miles north.

"Deploying now, Commander," Yuri's voice crackled over the com. "In position, forty seconds."

Bridget's petite form burst from the darkness just as Jordan rounded the southwest corner. She staggered forward a few paces, and then her ankle folded and she spilled into a dirt mound. She tried to struggle to her feet but wasn't making any real progress. Exhausted from her flight out of the pyramid, she was helpless.

Jordan's training took over. He dropped to one knee and set the rifle's stock against his shoulder. He sighted down the scope, hoping Mohn's toy had a way to track the werewolf. Night vision revealed nothing. The shot was going to be hard at this range. He wished he had another hundred yards between him and the target, but he'd just have to trust his reflexes.

"Come on, you bastard," he muttered, conscious of Bridget's flailing as she sought to regain her feet. He considered the options for a split second, weighing her usefulness as bait against the risk to an entire village. He didn't have a choice. She was expendable.

Something large blurred into the scope's field of view and then out again before he could squeeze the trigger. The creature was just too fast. His scope didn't catch up to the beast until it paused, looming over Bridget's cowering form like some avenging god. He didn't waste time wondering what it was. The creature had a discernible anatomy. That was a head. He bet it needed that.

Jordan's finger slid over the trigger, already depressing it when his brain registered what he was seeing. The beast lunged so swiftly that his finger couldn't complete its arc in time. Blood fountained as Bridget's shrieks were finally silenced. *BaDOOOM*. A foot-long streak of white tore a line through the side of the beast's silver head, lifting the entire creature and launching it into the darkness in a spray of gore. The beast didn't rise.

Was it dead? He didn't know. He could try approaching and helping Bridget. He didn't like leaving her out there, but even at this distance, he knew she was beyond saving. The lowlight vision revealed a slowly spreading pool underneath her, and her neck was bent at an unnatural angle. He swung the scope back into alignment with the patch of shadow where the beast had fallen.

"You can't be fucking serious," Jordan said, refusing to accept what he was seeing.

The beast was back on its feet, form half revealed by the moon-light. Its head was completely whole. There was no sign of a wound other than a smattering of blood on the creature's fur. Even more alarming were the thing's eyes. They were human, glittering with intelligence as the beast searched the darkness for threats. It was looking for him. Methodically, like a trained soldier.

Jordan centered his sights on the creature's thick torso. He had no idea if the beast could even be killed, but killing it was his only hope of saving his team and the villagers. He needed to do massive damage to this thing. Jordan stroked the trigger, sending a gout of flame from the muzzle and a boom through the ravine. The bullet punched through the creature's torso, inflicting damage no living creature should survive. Most of its internal organs *should* have become pulp. But it didn't fall.

The beast's gaze locked on him. He'd given away his position with the muzzle flare, and the creature had instantly capitalized on that. Jordan stroked the trigger again, but the beast flashed upwards and the shot splintered marble instead. The animal bounded out of sight, disappearing up the same trail they'd taken down into the ravine.

"Yuri, fall back to the jeeps. That thing is getting away," he said into the com. His voice was calm in spite of his pounding heart.

"Acknowledge," Yuri said. Jordan watched the four men who'd been skulking through the shadows to his west pivot and head back to base camp.

"Also, set up the sat link. The Director needs to know just how screwed we are."

17

DR. LIZ

"It hurts, Dr. Liz," Emilie whispered, a single tear sliding down the child's cheek. She used the back of her free hand to hurriedly wipe it away, as if embarrassed by the sign of weakness. It was a sobering action for a six-year-old. They grew up so fast here.

"I know," Liz said, deftly severing the stitch's loose end, though she'd never done anything like this as recently as a few months ago. She reached for a cotton swab and dabbed it with alcohol before returning to the child's wound. Emilie would have a scar, but that was a small price to pay. She could have lost the finger. "We're almost done. Just a little bit more, and you can go home. You've been so brave. I'm very proud of you."

Liz dabbed the wound, drawing a wince from the child. Emilie's lips were tightly drawn, but she didn't complain as Liz finished cleaning the wound. Liz wrapped the hand in clean gauze, hoping the child wouldn't go digging in the fields for a few days. She'd have to speak with Emilie's mother, though she doubted it would do any good. Harvest was coming, and the family needed every hand, even the wounded ones.

"There we go. All finished." She tousled the child's hair. "Tell your mother I'd like to speak to her, all right? She can—"

"Dr. Liz?" a male voice called from the street outside. The bell above the door chimed as Rafael entered the clinic. "Jefe says he needs you right away. Very important. He says come now."

"Did he say why?" she asked, removing her latex gloves and dropping them into the waste bin. She hated the residue they left behind. The white powder made her feel like some nerdy doctor, which, regardless of the title they gave her, couldn't be further from the truth. She slipped on her prescription sunglasses. Her regular ones had broken almost three months ago, but being in a remote Peruvian village made replacing them nearly impossible. At least she could see outside. During the day at least.

"No, but he asked Rufi to gas up the jeep," Rafael said, holding open the door for Emilie as the child darted through. "Esperanzo came down from Villa Milagros. He was white, like he seen something bad. Don't know what. Jefe ain't told nobody."

Liz followed him out to the town's one road, muddy furrows from the rare car still drying from the storm that had passed through sometime the previous night. The black clouds blanketing the southern horizon threatened to do the same tonight. She and Rafael hurried up the side of the road. A battered Ford truck bulging with chicken cages rumbled by so close they had to press themselves flat against the adobe walls of the clinic.

"Slow down, chupa," Rafael yelled at the vehicle's retreating form. He gave up with a half-hearted shake of his head. "Old fool's going to kill someone one of these days. Michela needs to take his keys away."

They picked their way down the muddy road, past a dozen familiar buildings. The street was hardly crowded, but there were perhaps twenty other villagers, from old Tia to a few children chasing a soccer ball. The pace was so much slower than it was in the states, neighbors chatting and people enjoying the afternoon from battered wicker rocking chairs on porches.

"Dr. Liz, when you gonna stop by?" Sanchez called from the back of his mule on the far side of the street. His grey hair fluttered in the wind like an overgrown hedge as he delivered a gap-toothed smile. "You can try my tequila. Best in Peru."

"She's not interested in your tequila, or anything else you've got," Rafael said, interposing himself between Liz and the skinny old man. "Jefe needs her right away. We got business, you old letch."

"What kind of business?" Sanchez asked, jerking the reins of his mule to get it to slow. The mule had other ideas. It kept plodding down the road, unconcerned with its master's insistence on turning it around.

Liz couldn't help but chuckle as they quickened their pace and left the old man behind. He was one of the reasons she loved Villa Consuelo. Everyone here had such personality, and they all knew each other. This place painted life back in the states with an impersonal brush. In the states, you could feel like you were alone even when surrounded by people. *This* was community.

They passed Luca's Café, the town's only restaurant and the last structure before the north road. Jefe was waiting in the jeep. He wore his signature uniform, a pair of faded blue jeans and a black leather jacket. His salt-and-pepper hair was slicked back, reminding Liz of *The Fonz*, from that old show Happy Days.

"Liz. Get in, please. We have much to discuss. Rafael, go down to the station and tell them I want a patrol sent north. Turn back anyone heading up to Villa Milagros. No access. Tell them it's quarantined," Jefe commanded. She'd never met someone with such a confident air. His demeanor was something the entire village relied on. He was part mayor, part police chief.

"Yes, Jefe," Rafael replied with a quick bob of his head. He hurried back into town at a fast walk while Liz slid into the passenger side of the battered jeep. The door gave a groan of protest as it slammed shut, spattering her white shirt with mud.

"Great." Liz flicked off what dirt she could.

"You've heard I served in Desert Storm, right?" he asked as the jeep lurched up the dirt track. The locals called it a road, but Liz disagreed. Roads were paved. This was more like a goat trail, and calling it that was being generous. It jounced them about like a horse trying to shake its rider.

"Yes, I'd heard that," she called back, over the roar of the engine. Jefe hadn't ever discussed his past with her. Something big must be going on for him to let his guard down even this much. "Is that why your English is so good?"

"It is," he admitted, resting a commanding gaze on her before shifting back to the road. "I saw a lot of really bad things there, things I won't ever talk about. This is worse. I must ask your forgiveness for showing you this horror, but I don't have any idea what killed these people. I need you to tell me what did this."

"Killed?" Liz repeated, numb from the weight of the words. Her hair whipped in the wind as the jeep reached an alarming pace. "People are dead? How many? How did they die?"

"All of them. Except one," Jefe replied flatly. The man was stone, as unconcerned by the hazardous drive as he was by the murders. "He's still alive, and we don't know why. We haven't been able to wake him. I'm hoping you can, because if you can't I'm not sure we'll ever know what happened. I think he's an American, maybe European. Blond hair."

"What can you tell me? Is it sickness?" she asked, unaware of any disease that could wipe out an entire village in so short a time, unless some sort of chemical warfare was involved.

"No, not sickness."

"But you told Rafael that Milagros is quarantined," she said. The jeep ground over a steep rise, nearly toppling backward. Jefe just kept driving.

"Because I don't want anyone seeing what really happened. These people were murdered, Liz. Violently," he explained. His tone was as dispassionate as if he were counting bushels of corn.

"By who?" she asked so softly she wasn't sure if he heard. The jeep jounced another fifty paces before he finally answered.

"No by who. By what," he said, gunning the engine. The muffler belched a cloud of acrid exhaust as it labored up the trail, burning her eyes. "It looks like some sort of animal, like a bear or a lion."

"But we don't have either here. There isn't anything capable of killing a man, let alone an entire village. There isn't even a zoo for a couple hundred miles," she replied, her mind working furiously to conjure something that could have killed so many.

"You begin to see why I brought you. Nothing I've ever heard of could do something like this," Jefe said, shifting into a low gear as the jeep angled up a slope no sane man would attempt to drive over. She clenched her eyes shut, gripping the seat for all she was worth. This was the spot Liz hated the most on the road to Milagros. "If it is an animal, then we must find and kill it. If it is a man, then we must find him, though I do not see how such a thing could be possible. No man could do this, no matter how evil."

They fell into silence as the jeep lumbered up the hill, dense foliage pressing the trail from both sides. A cloud of green macaws burst from one of the trees, winging their way north in a riot of noise and color. The birds were beautiful in a way she knew she'd never find back home in California. She wished she could share the sight with Trevor. He was so serious most of the time, but she knew the flock would have brought out one of her brother's boyish grins.

"We're nearly there," Jefe said, rather unnecessarily. She could clearly see the ramshackle houses in the distance. Villa Milagros was even more poverty stricken than Villa Consuelo, and she always had a difficult time coming up here.

Normally both parents and children would be in the cornfields by now, weeding and pruning to ensure the best harvest possible. The rows of corn on three sides of the little town stood empty, untroubled save for the slight summer breeze. There was no sign of anyone moving between the homes, in and out of the town's shops, or even around the bar. Marta's little Honda Civic was parked outside her house, and Sandoval's tractor stood idle next to his field. Until she got closer, Liz thought the place looked deserted. Then she saw the shattered doors hanging in frames, the spatters of blood on dirty windows. There were furrows in the mud where something heavy had been dragged.

Jefe parked the jeep just outside town, close enough to see where the carnage had apparently taken place but far enough away to not smell the blood. It was still closer than Liz would like, and she was thankful that the breeze was coming from the south, blocking whatever unwelcome odors filled the town. No longer caring about the mud spattering her t-shirt, she exited the vehicle. Mud seemed so trivial in light of the tragedy that had befallen these people.

"Gonzalez has been gathering the bodies into a grave," Jefe said, his voice subdued for once. He started up the road, pausing long enough for her to catch up. "I'd like you to examine them before they are buried. Just to see if you can identify the wounds. Then we will take you to the survivor and see if you can wake him."

The pair walked in silence as they navigated the dirt road through the town. Like Villa Consuelo, the town only had one road, so they passed every house and business as they walked. All had been damaged. Doors kicked in or a window shattered. A few had bullet holes, though those were rare. Who had been shooting? And at what?

"Over here," Jefe said, leaving the road to pass through rows of corn.

Liz followed, growing increasingly nervous about what horror might lie waiting. She'd seen a dead body once, but the woman had died in her sleep. It wasn't at all the same thing. She steeled herself as they finally left the corn, emerging near the clearing the village used as a graveyard. Gonzalez stood shirtless in a hole that came to his waist, shoulders flexing as he heaved another shovelful of dirt from the mass grave he was digging.

Next to him lay neatly stacked bodies, dozens of them. Men, women, and children. All were covered in blood. Some were missing a limb, others a head. A few had been torn entirely in half. Most had been partially eaten. The gore was more than Liz could take, and she dropped to her knees, retching the remains of her breakfast onto the damp soil.

"Take your time, Liz," Jefe said, resting a calloused hand on her shoulder. "I am sorry you have to see this, but we must know what caused these wounds."

Liz wiped her mouth with the back of a hand and wobbled to her feet. She approached the stack of bodies, which had already attracted a thick carpet of flies. The corpses stank, cloying and acrid at the same time. She knelt next to one of the bodies, a partially eaten man.

"Jesus, I need a cigarette. You know I'm not a real doctor, right? Everything I know about forensics comes from TV shows," she admitted, when she could finally speak.

"I know. You're all we have, Liz."

"I'll do what I can. I'm guessing the jaw is canine, from this bite," she said, voice quavering but as steady as she could make it. "I don't see any obvious claw marks, not the sort you'd expect from a great cat. It might be a bear, but the wounds are the wrong shape for that. This is like a dog attack. Or a wolf, maybe. Something with a muzzle."

"If it was, then it must have been a really big dog," Gonzalez said, pausing to wipe sweat from his forehead. He didn't meet Liz's gaze.

"So, a dog then. Perhaps a mastiff or a large pit bull?" Jefe asked.

"Maybe, but I doubt it. Look at this. The arm has been crushed, like in a vice. This thing must have had one hell of a grip," Liz said, strangely fascinated by the carnage. What had attacked these people?

"Is there anything else you can tell us?" Jefe asked, placid calm back in place.

"No, not without a real autopsy. That's not something I'm qualified to perform, anyway."

"Very well," Jefe said, moving to the far side of the grave. He squatted near the base of an enormous sycamore tree, its wide canopy providing the only shelter from the sweltering sun. "Come and take a look at this. I have never seen the like."

Liz followed Jefe, picking a trail through the thick mud. She knelt next to the area he'd indicated, understanding immediately why he wanted her opinion. The track was far too large to be that of a wolf or a dog. It might even be too large to have been a bear, but she suspected the markings might be around the right size for a grizzly. The shape was all wrong, though.

"What do you think?" Jefe asked after allowing her to study the track.

"From the size, I want to say it's a bear, but the track is too long.

It's more what I'd expect to see of a primate, like a gorilla," she mused, picking up a stick that had fallen from the sycamore. She used it to illustrate as she spoke. "But see the front end of the foot? It has four pads just like a dog. I have no idea what it is. Maybe we can take a picture and send it on to the university at Cajamarca?"

"I'll get my camera from the jeep, but first we have business to attend to," Jefe said, rising to his feet. "It's time to wake the survivor and see what he knows."

18

NOT DEAD

Blair returned to consciousness by degrees. His own deep, sure breaths were the first things he latched onto. They felt so different from the ragged gasps he last remembered. Then came his heartbeat, strong and steady. He shivered, eyes opening as he remembered his heart stopping. It was the last thing he remembered. Should have been the *final* thing he remembered. Dying.

He raised his head and examined his surroundings. That was something else he shouldn't be able to do. Where were his glasses? He was all but blind without them, or at least he should have been. Yet he *wasn't* blind. He could see with a clarity not even his glasses had afforded him. Details leapt out at him: the rust spots on the metal counter, the worn plastic of the four chairs arrayed near the door, the faded lettering on the stoppered bottles in the wooden cabinet across the room. *Penicillin.* This place must be a clinic.

A detached part of his mind guessed that the team had flown him to a hospital, but the rest was latching onto the obvious. Not only was he alive, but he'd also been changed. Changed by whatever had happened with the statue. The incident paralleled a number of bad movies, really. The mousy scholar inherits super powers from a long-dead alien race, or in this case, a vanished culture.

Blair looked down and realized that he was naked save for a thin white sheet. Well, not quite naked. There was a handcuff around his right wrist, and it was chained to the bed's ancient metal frame. What the hell? That wasn't all he noticed. His carefully cultivated wine gut was gone, replaced by abs Hugh Jackman would envy. *Prehistoric Aliens*—even better than the gym.

It is part of the change, Ka-Dun.

He froze, unable to process the voice that had just echoed in his own head. It was deep. Powerful. And it could hear his thoughts. Before he could answer, his neck whipped around, toward a new sound.

"He is inside. Doesn't seem hurt, but he won't wake up," a gruff voice said from outside the warped wooden door in the front of the small clinic. Footsteps were approaching, thundering in his ears. Three distinct sets—two heavier and one, either a woman or a child, lighter.

"It could be a concussion. Head wounds sometimes cause trauma, and if there's swelling in the brain, it could prevent him from waking up," came a muffled female voice. Was that a Californian accent?

The door groaned open, the top hinge very nearly pulling free from the wall as it did so. The breeze that accompanied it made Blair aware of just how stifling the room was. He was drenched in sweat. He relaxed, feigning sleep while watching the door's warped reflection on the metal cabinets beneath the counter.

Two blurry figures entered the room while a third cast a shadow across the doorway from somewhere outside. The first wore a leather jacket and was definitely tall. His companion was a shorter woman with long copper hair. He couldn't make out much from the reflection, but tan shorts exposed long, creamy legs.

"We think the killing happened last night. Gonzalez found the bodies this morning, and this man was unconscious, covered in blood. Gonzalez cuffed him to the bed in case he goes crazy when he wakes up," the man explained. Who the hell were these people? And why were they worried he might go crazy?

"He's already awake," the woman said, circling the bed. She kept carefully out of his reach. "His back is too tense, and I can see him watching our reflection in that metal cabinet."

Blair rolled over slowly. No sense in hiding anymore. He pulled his knees to the kind of chest he'd always envied, stifling questions as he took a better look at the pair. The woman's hair fell just past her shoulders, and she wore the sort of large sunglasses Audrey Hepburn had made famous. She had a mud-spattered t-shirt and khakis that revealed shapely legs. Very shapely.

Her companion had slicked-back hair and eyes like flint. His gaze seized Blair, weighing him on some invisible scale as he took slow steps toward the bed. Blair could glean nothing from the man's expression, but the way his hand rested on the gun belted to his side spoke volumes.

"Who are you?" the man asked, looming over the bed. His breath stank of tobacco.

"Who are *you*?" Blair growled back, taken aback by a surge of anger. His shoulders squared almost of their own accord, and he held the man's gaze without flinching. "Where am I? Why am I cuffed to a bed? And why the hell am I naked?"

Silence grew. The man reached into his jacket and withdrew a pack of cigarettes. He offered one to the woman, who seemed on the verge of taking one before finally shaking her head. The man turned back to Blair.

"Most interesting. You are angry and confused by your predicament. And why not? You awake naked and chained to a bed. Not a position to envy," the man drawled, tapping the pack against his palm. "We, too, have a predicament. We are distraught over the slaughter of this entire village. Let us put emotions aside and try to reason this out. Why don't we begin with names? I am called Jefe. This is Dr. Liz. The man you can't see outside is Gonzalez. And now it is your turn."

"All right, I can be reasonable. My name is Blair Smith. *Professor* Blair Smith," he said. He emphasized the title Jordan had given him, thinking it might make him sound more legitimate than a teacher at a junior college. And right now, he needed any credibility he could muster. He was acutely aware of his nakedness. It was unsettling. It made him feel trapped. Anxious.

"Very well, Professor Blair Smith," Jefe continued, dragging a plastic chair toward the bed and turning it to face Blair. He slouched down into it, slipping out of his leather jacket and allowing it to wrap over the back of the chair. The pack of cigarettes was still clutched in one hand. "Why don't you tell me what you remember last?"

The woman he'd identified as Liz pulled up a chair of her own, though she kept it much further from the bed. He didn't blame her for being cautious. Naked American teachers were probably a pretty rare sight.

"I was at a dig site up in the mountains, someplace called Cajamarca. There's a pyramid there. A very old pyramid," he said, fumbling through the fog in search of memories. "We found a way into the inner chamber, but the door was trapped. I was poisoned, I think. I thought I was dead."

"You had companions with you? People that can verify this dig site?" Jefe asked, posture straightening as his gaze intensified. Blair got the sense that his next words were very important.

"I had a team with me, but I don't know where they are. I guess it's possible they could have brought me here for treatment," Blair reasoned, glancing at the doctor. He couldn't read her with those sunglasses on. "You know, you probably know more than I do. Why am I cuffed? And what was the point of taking my clothes?"

"You were naked when we found you," Jefe said, finally tapping a cigarette out of the pack. He cupped the end with one hand and lit it with a lighter fished from another pocket. He took a long drag before continuing. "We cuffed you because everyone in this village is dead. Everyone except you."

Blair collapsed against the bed, strength deserting him even faster than Steve and Bridget had. Everyone was dead? What about Bridget? Or Sheila? Were they dead too? If they were, how had he gotten here? And what had happened to these people?

"Look at his reaction," Liz broke in, rising from her chair and taking a step closer to the bed. "You can see from his expression he's as shocked as we are. He doesn't know anything."

"Maybe," Jefe said, blowing a lungful of smoke in Blair's direction. "Maybe not. He could be a good liar. Or he could be crazy. What if he doesn't remember what he did?"

"Let's give him a chance," Liz demanded, staring hard at Jefe over the rim of her sunglasses. It was Blair's first glimpse of her eyes, shockingly blue, like a patch of sky just after a storm. "Blair, we're in the Cajamarca region of Peru. Can you describe this dig site? Where was it?"

"It was in a ravine between these two large mountains. One of them looked like an old man with big eyebrows," he said, doing his best to recall any other significant features. "I know the closest town was supposed to be Villa Milagros."

"See?" Liz said, tone challenging as she focused on Jefe. "His story checks out. He's talking about Yanacocha. That's just a few miles further up the mountain. There was that caravan of jeeps a few weeks back. Maybe he was with them."

"He could be making it up," Jefe growled, leaning forward in his chair and skewering Blair with his gaze. "Are you lying? If you are, the truth's going to come out. We can verify your story about the dig. If that valley's empty, we'll know you killed these people. If that's the case, I won't hesitate to execute you."

Sudden rage crashed over Blair. *He* was the one naked and chained for no reason he could see. What gave this bastard the right to sit in judgment over him?

"I didn't kill anyone," Blair roared, a wave of heat surging through him. Jefe's eyes widened, and his hand fell to the pistol holstered at his side. "You've got me chained to a bed against my will even though I haven't done anything. So let me make this very clear. You *will* release me and let me have my clothes back." That last part came out as a growl.

"I will do nothing of the kind," Jefe retorted. He'd recovered his composure, staring dispassionately at Blair. "First we will investigate your story, and then we will see what to do. Gonzalez will take the jeep up to Yanacocha. He can be back in just a few hours. That will give us plenty of time to discuss your story."

"Can't we at least get him some clothing?" Liz asked, drawing Jefe's gaze. Blair could tell the man had a soft spot for her, and it wasn't hard to understand why.

"I will find him something," Jefe agreed, taking a step toward the door. "Do not get too close to him. Do not let your guard down. I know he seems innocent, but appearances can be deceiving. This man could be a killer."

"I'll be careful," Liz agreed as Jefe left the clinic. She turned to face Blair, sinking into a plastic chair and pulling it a bit closer to the bed. She was still out of reach.

"Well, this is awkward," Blair said after several moments of tense silence. "I'm sorry you have to be involved in this. Though, honestly, I'm not sure what 'this' is. I can't even imagine how I ended up here."

"You don't remember anything? About coming here?" she asked, moving to one of the chrome drawers. She opened it and removed a wad of bandages. She moved to the bed, eyeing him warily as she began to roll it around his chest. He glanced down, noticing a six-inch slash that had already scabbed over. The edges were an angry red, though it didn't hurt like any infection he'd ever had. Where had that come from?

"I..." Blair began, realizing that perhaps he did know something. Fragmented images danced just out of reach. Scenes from a nightmare. Screaming, people dying. "No, I don't. You said those people are dead. How many? I mean I know that's morbid, but I just...I need to know."

"Almost thirty," Liz answered, still wearing those dark sunglasses. Her voice was soft, subdued. "What were you digging for? There aren't any ruins around here."

"There are, actually. Ruins like you've never seen," Blair said, repositioning himself on the bed in an attempt to get comfortable. The cuffs made that difficult. "The pyramid we found predates any culture on this continent by at least six thousand years. What's more, the structure was built by an advanced civilization, one we've never encountered before."

"Next you're going to tell me about aliens," Liz replied. He could sense the eye roll even if he couldn't see it. She finished winding the gauze, applying a pair of butterfly clips to cinch it in place. "I hope, for your sake, you're telling the truth. If you killed those people, the penalty here is death. Jefe won't be shy about meting out justice. I doubt he'll even wait to get you to Cajamarca. He'll do it himself."

"If I'm the killer, he'd be right to do it," Blair said, unable to suppress a sigh. "I know you don't believe me, but I honestly have no idea how I got here. I'm just a teacher trying to make ends meet."

"I guess we'll find out soon enough." Her tone was skeptical enough to alarm him. He had to do something.

"Think about it," Blair said, hoping she'd see reason. He needed an ally, however flimsy that alliance might be. "If I killed these people, why would I have stuck around? Why lay here apparently naked and covered in blood?"

"Maybe Jefe's right. You could be crazy."

"Maybe, but he said you're a doctor, right? Use Occam's razor. What's the simplest explanation? Let's examine the facts. How were these people killed?"

"By some sort of animal," Liz admitted, dropping back into her plastic chair now that her work was done. "I've never seen wounds quite like these."

"That alone should clear me," Blair continued, though somewhere in the recesses of his mind fangs flashed. He remembered the taste of raw flesh, hot and wonderful. "If it was me, I must have needed some sort of weapon, right? Where is that weapon? I bet you didn't find one. So what's the simplest explanation?"

"That the people here were killed by an animal. For some reason, it didn't kill you."

"Good, you can see reason. Listen, I don't know what killed these people. I don't even know how I got here. But that's not the real question you should be asking."

"What should I be asking?" Liz said, sarcasm not lost on him.

"Where is that animal now?"

19

NUMB

Sheila was too numb to be terrified, emotions wrung out of her like so much dirty dishwater. She sat atop a rock, watching the flurry of activity engulf the camp around her. None of the soldiers scurrying about paid her any mind, though they had to be aware of her. There were over two dozen now, most erecting new tents around the large jeeps that had come in just before dawn.

A few more clustered around one of four new helicopters. Three were the larger types that had disgorged a seemingly endless supply of crates and men. The last was sleeker, smaller. It had a pair of deadly looking guns slung under short, stubby wings, and a cockpit designed to seat two.

Yuri sat in one, wearing a headset that covered his ears alongside his ever-present sunglasses. Commander Jordan stood a few feet away, a similar headset clutched in one hand. The other held a tablet, which had been handed to him by one of the black-clad techs moving between the soldiers.

"Commander," one of the techs called, trotting over from a hastily erected tent. "We have the results. The DNA is a match, sir."

Jordan looked up slowly from the tablet. Large bags under eyes seemed to bear the weight of the world. "So, let me see if I understand this. Professor Smith rose from the dead, then killed most of the scientists?"

"So far as we can tell, sir," the man said, adjusting owlish glasses. He winced as the rotors on the helicopter began to spin. Slowly at first, but gradually picking up speed. "The DNA from the wounds on the bodies is a perfect match. That thing, whatever it is, used to be Smith. There's more, sir. There's an irregular pathogen in the saliva. We haven't been able to identify it."

"Is it communicable?" Jordan asked, tensing.

"We don't know, sir," the tech shrugged.

"For the time being, we have to assume it is. Requisition whatever you need to study it and have a report on my desk in two hours. Have you gotten the satellite photos I asked for?" Jordan asked, tucking the tablet under his arm and putting on the headset.

"Yes, sir. You'll find them on the tablet. It's linked to the copter's Wi-Fi, but you may not be able to access it until you're away from the pyramid," the man replied, glancing uneasily at the structure.

"Sum it up for me then," Jordan said drily. He turned to the copter and tossed the tablet onto the rear seat. Yuri shifted slightly as it sailed by but kept his focus on the dashboard. How the Russian remained so calm, Sheila didn't know. She envied him.

"The citizens of Villa Milagros are all dead, sir. The bodies have been gathered into a mass grave. As of two hours ago, there was one civilian digging a grave outside and a heat signature in one of the buildings."

"Acknowledged," Jordan said. He waved dismissively, and the tech trotted away.

Jordan turned in Sheila's direction, stalking over to her rock like a panther. He stood there for a long moment, heavy eyes studying her. "Sheila, are you all right?"

"No," Sheila replied, shaking her head slowly. "No, I'm not. Have you found any sign of Alejandro or Dr. Roberts?"

"The creature caught up with them last night," Jordan said, a brief expression of pain flitting across his features. "I'm sorry, Sheila."

Just like that, she became the sole survivor of the science team.

Blair, dead. Steve, Bridget, dead. Now Alejandro and Roberts. Shouldn't she feel something? Grief? Anger? She must be in shock.

"We're going after it," Jordan said, reaching out to squeeze her shoulder. The gesture was oddly human coming from the man she'd thought of as a corporate robot. "It's slaughtered a village not far from here, and it could do the same to others if we don't stop it. We'll be back in a few hours. Why don't you get some sleep in the meantime?"

"That's a good idea," she mumbled, dropping her gaze to hide the lie. She wasn't sure she could ever sleep again. If she did, she knew what she'd find lurking there—those terrible eyes.

Sheila was vaguely aware of the crunching gravel as Jordan turned and headed for the helicopter. The whirring of the rotors grew more high-pitched. She hoped he'd give that thing some payback.

20

HUNTED

Liz wobbled to her feet, plastic chair clattering to the floor behind her. Fear sank deep roots, cunning and insidious. The man on the bed eyed her, something unreadable in his gaze. His muscles tensed, chest and shoulders rippling as he straightened.

She knew he was probably trying to manipulate her, but he'd spoken sense. She wasn't a vet and didn't know a lot about forensics, but the wounds did appear to have been inflicted by an animal. If that was the case, then it was still out there. It might even be watching them. Waiting. Stalking.

"I have to talk to Jefe," she said, shouldering open the stuck door and half stumbling from the stifling room. Blair said nothing as she exited.

Jefe was ambling back toward the clinic in that nonchalant way of his, placid as a still pond despite the horrific situation. He carried a pair of jeans and a ragged white t-shirt under one arm, waving as Gonzalez's jeep roared up the road behind him. It made for the pass above, a narrow track leading to Yanacocha, where Blair's story could be verified.

"He tell you anything?" Jefe called as he approached, a thin streamer of pungent smoke rising from the cigarette clutched in his right hand. Liz closed the distance before answering.

"What if he isn't the killer?" she asked, words jumbled together just like her thoughts. She must sound hysterical. "If an animal attacked these people, then it's still out there. What if it comes back? You have a gun, right?"

"Yes." Jefe nodded, placing a calloused hand on her shoulder. "If there is a beast and it comes back, we will deal with it. But I do not believe there is one. A man killed these people, and I believe he is in that room, cuffed to the bed."

"What makes you think it was that guy we've got chained in there? Those wounds look like they were inflicted by a large predator, not a man," she said, convinced Jefe was wrong. Blair lacked the means to do this, much less the motive. "Besides, those bodies were partially eaten. No human could have done that, especially not so quickly. These bodies are fresh. Probably from last night, or maybe yesterday."

"Those are interesting facts, but I have cause to believe it was the work of this man. Walk with me and I will show you," he said, guiding her up the road and toward a cluster of ramshackle houses. Each stood atop short stilts to avoid the thick mud that came with the rains. The late afternoon sun made them appear forlorn, especially in the absence of their owners. "Do you see that house over there? The one with the red door?"

"I see it," she replied, studying the structure. It looked the same as the other houses, at least as far as she could see.

"Look at the door," Jefe said, eyeing her as if waiting for her to realize something obvious.

The paint was faded and cracked, but there was nothing out of place with the door. It stood closed, looking none the worse for wear after the previous night's attack. What was she supposed to be seeing?

"Oh my God," she said, looking at three other nearby doors. All had been shattered. "This door wasn't broken. Why not? What's different about this house?"

"It's the first one in the row," Jefe explained, turning to face her. He used his forearm to wipe sweat from his forehead. "If you were to enter town from the north, this is the first house you'd encounter. If you were looking to kill everyone, you'd sneak into the first house..."

"...But after that there would be no need to be quiet," Liz reasoned, suddenly understanding. She approached the house with Jefe, voicing her suspicions. "If the people in the first house screamed, the rest of the village would know they were being attacked. So shattering the doors would make sense, because you'd no longer have the element of surprise."

"Exactly. Bravo, Dr. Liz. You would make a fine soldier," Jefe said, giving her an affectionate smile. He approached the door and turned the handle, pushing it open slowly.

The door creaked as it exposed the interior of the house's single room. Blood had soaked the packed-earth floor, but the bodies had been removed. Shelves dotted the walls around an iron stove that had to be fifty years old. Most held cooking implements, though she spotted a dog-eared Bible on one of the shelves. It hadn't saved the occupants.

"See over here?" Jefe asked, holding open a curtain that led into the small sleeping chamber in the corner. "The attacker waited for the first person to come through the curtain. He killed them right here, then moved in to kill the others. It was too methodical to be an animal. An animal would have torn the curtain down. This was done by a man."

"I think you're right," Liz admitted, feeling nauseated. She needed to get outside.

She pushed the door open, barely able to contain whatever was left of breakfast as she left the acrid smell of blood. She leaned forward, resting her hands on her khakis as she took slow breaths. Calm down, Liz, she admonished herself. Panicking and getting sick weren't going to help anything. Besides, if Jefe was right, they'd already caught the killer. So what was there to worry about? They'd know soon enough, when Gonzalez returned.

Liz glanced up the road to see if she could still spy the jeep.

There. It was picking its way up a ridge most goats would avoid, nearing the top of the pass. It would be out of sight soon.

"It is a lot to take in, I know," Jefe said, emerging from the horrible house. "I am sorry that I had to show this to you, any of it. But you can see why I asked. Why I need your help."

"Yes, I can see. Bringing me was the right thing to do," she said, still focused on the retreating jeep.

She was completely unprepared for what happened next. As Gonzalez crept up the hill, she spotted movement on the other side of the peak. A helicopter came into view, the *whup-whup-whup* echoing down the mountainside. It hovered like an angry wasp, spinning to face the jeep. Then one of the massive black guns under the wings began to spin. A moment later a deafening roar filled the valley, projectiles streaking from the horrible weapon. Crack after crack thundered down at her, impossibly loud despite the distance.

Bullets punched through the jeep, spinning it like a block kicked by a child. Gonzalez hunkered down in the driver's seat, using the vehicle for cover. It didn't help. More and more bullets rained down on the jeep, which careened off the trail and plummeted into the valley. Liz watched in horror as it fell, impacting on the valley floor in a ball of flame and debris. She'd known Gonzalez since the first day she'd arrived in Villa Consuelo. He had a baby goat he fed with a bottle.

"Jefe!" she shrieked, spinning to face him. Her heart thudded heavily in her chest as she tried to get her mind around what had just happened. "Who are they? What the hell is going on?"

"Run," he hissed, grabbing her roughly by the shoulder and shoving her in the direction of the clinic. "I don't know who they are, but they are here to silence us. I begin to believe there may be something up at Yanacocha. Something these people would kill to protect."

They ran fast and low, darting between fence posts and through front yards. Jefe reached the door to the clinic first, holding it open long enough for her to slip through before slamming it shut. Blair sat upright on the bed, whole body more tense than any spring she'd ever seen. He craned his neck, struggling to look out the window in the direction of the gunfire.

"What's going on?" he demanded, shifting his gaze between the two of them. "I heard gunshots. A lot of gunshots."

"Be quiet," Jefe hissed, slamming the door and jumping into a crouch next to one of the windows.

Liz crept to the window, staring out as much as the dirty glass would allow. She couldn't see the helicopter, but its angry buzzing was growing closer.

"What if they start shooting at us?" she asked Jefe, careful to keep her voice low.

"Then we die," Jefe answered, rubbing dirt from the cloudy glass. He peered outside, pulling a pistol from inside his jacket. "Those miniguns fire fifty-caliber bullets. Our only chance is that they did not see us. If they have, they will descend on this village and wipe us out. I do not know why, but they wish to silence anyone who saw whatever they found."

"They're coming for me," Blair said so softly Liz barely heard. She wasn't sure if he was speaking to them, or just out loud. His gaze was far away. "Something happened in the inner chamber. They want to know what. And how. They're coming for me."

"Who is 'they'?" Jefe asked, voice like a whip. He left the window and dropped the full weight of his gaze on Blair.

"Mohn Corporation," Blair growled, eyes wild.

"The private army? That Mohn?" Jefe asked, looking back out the window. "Then we are truly dead."

The *whup-whup* of the helicopter was directly above now. The walls shook from the wind it kicked up as the dark shape descended into their view through the dirty glass. It spun to face them, like some predator discovering cornered prey. A high-pitched hum began as the guns that had killed Gonzalez began to spin again.

21

NOWHERE TO RUN

Time slowed to a near stop, advancing frame by frame as Blair watched the helicopter's black profile descend into view through the grimy windows. A high-pitched whirring kept terrible counterpoint with the deeper *whup-whup* of the rotors as the gigantic barrels set under the wings began to spin.

He lingered in eternity. The worst part wouldn't be *his* death. As far as he was concerned, he was already dead. He'd died back in the pyramid, and that made every moment after borrowed time. The same wasn't true of Liz, or her angry companion. Neither had asked to be here, yet both were about to die because of him. Guilt, anger and shame warred within him.

The power is there if you but take it, Ka-Dun, the strange voice said, echoing through his mind for a second time. *Prepare yourself. There will be pain.*

Blair's body went rigid. Fire flooded his limbs, liquid agony much like what he'd experienced when he'd touched the statue. What the hell was happening? His back arched, throat constricting to strangle a scream. Muscles spasmed, rippling and tugging under his skin. They writhed like snakes, growing larger and more defined under his horrified gaze. Beneath the agony, part of him realized that what he was seeing wasn't possible. Yet his eyes bore witness to the terrible miracle.

Pain ceased. His legs were thicker than any athlete's, his arms and chest like something out of a superhero movie. There was no time to ask how or why. Answers could come later, assuming he lived through this. Blair wrenched the wrist bound to the bed, and the cuffs' links exploded, steel fragments burning thin lines in his chest. But he was free.

The high-pitched whirring grew more urgent as time returned to its normal flow. Blair moved. He glided across the room with bestial grace, soaring into Liz and bearing her roughly to the dirt floor. She landed on her side, his body between her and the wooden wall that offered nothing against the horrible roar behind him.

The room exploded. Splinters of wood, flecks of plaster, and broken bottles burst around them. Jefe was caught in the crossfire, arms covering his head as if that might offer some protection from the maelstrom of debris. For a moment it seemed like that scant defense might be enough, but then a streak of fire from the weapon outside caught him in the chest. He was lifted like a rag doll, flung against the back wall with such violent force that he punched through and out of sight.

Blair pulled himself further atop Liz, who thrashed like a wild thing in an attempt to dislodge him. Fire blossomed in his back, ripping him from her and sending him careening through the room. He slammed into the bed's metal frame, right arm snapping with a violent crack. Behind him Liz screamed and crawled toward the hole left by Jefe's form. She didn't make it.

A round punched through her back, driving her into the ground with such force that she slid all the way to the wall. She didn't rise. Blood covered her back, and the wound was horrible to look upon.

She may yet be saved, the voice thrummed in his head. *But you must relinquish control to me. Are you willing, Ka-Dun?*

"I'll do whatever it takes. Save her," he grunted through clenched teeth. The corona of pain from his wounds ate at the edges of his vision.

First we must heal the injuries you have suffered. Will it so.

Blair had no choice but to trust the voice. It was impossible, of course, but so were a great many things that had happened in the last few days. Something flowed through him, liquid and vibrant like life itself. Touching it was like touching the face of the universe. His shattered forearm began to vibrate. Then an audible crack split the silence left in the wake of the massive gun. His arm twisted into place of its own volition, bone knitting together with incredible speed. His skin rippled around the wound, rapidly covering the bloody carnage. Within moments, it was whole. Even his hair had grown back. He flexed his arm in wonder, awed by what had just happened.

Hurry. That was merely their opening volley. Your foes will come in earnest now. Their weapons cannot kill you, but healing will tax you. You can spare neither time nor strength.

"How can I save her?" he asked, rising to a crouch behind the bed's twisted metal frame. It wouldn't protect him if the gun started firing again, but at least it hid him from anyone who might be looking in from outside.

Surrender to me. Give in to your rage. I will slay the interlopers and, Mother willing, I will save your she.

"I don't know what that means," he barked. There was movement outside the window. The helicopter was beginning to rise out of sight. Were they leaving? Perhaps they had assumed everyone was dead.

They have raised arms against you. Your she lies dying. I will redress these wrongs, if you give me leave.

It was right. Mohn was killing innocent people. His gaze settled on Liz's limp form, awash in blood and shrapnel. She was already dead. She had to be. They were responsible. They would pay. Pay in blood.

"Whatever it takes. Kill them. Kill them all," he growled, adrenaline surging through his system. Rage enveloped him in a furious inferno, burning away all other emotion.

It shall be so, Ka-Dun.

The agony returned, but this time Blair welcomed it. His entire body spasmed, back arching as lightning seared every nerve. The change that had begun in his limbs continued, more violently and far more terrifying. His fingers elongated, thickening as they grew. He cried out as sharp claws emerged from his fingertips, rending his flesh as easily as they would their victims'.

Every pore burst open, silver fur forcing its way from his skin. It grew and writhed like a sea of tiny snakes, enshrouding his body. His jaw broke, unhinging as it sprouted thick rows of fangs. His nose popped and cracked as it grew into a muzzle more at home on wolf than man. His chest grew still thicker, muscles undulating as they had before. Bones snapped from sockets as his body rearranged itself. He was taller. Stronger. Faster.

He could hear the men above, chattering into their radios. He could hear their heartbeats, slow and confident. They smelled of sweat but not fear.

They do not yet know that they are prey.

Black nylon ropes dropped into view through the shattered windows. With rifles slung over shoulders, soldiers in midnight body armor descended into view two at a time. They moved with military precision, each with a patch on his or her right shoulder. The patch depicted a large green triangle with a smaller silver one set inside it. Mohn Corp.

Sleep, Ka-Dun. I will bear your will to the interlopers. They will know your terrible vengeance.

Blair relinquished control, falling into darkness.

22

NOT JUST AN ANIMAL

The helicopter didn't so much as buck as both squads rappelled out the sides. Jordan had only worked with Yuri a short time, and the man's piloting skills continued to impress him. The Russian was tight-lipped about his past but seemed awfully comfortable in Vietnam-era American hardware.

Jordan waited for both squads to reach the ground before he stabbed a blue button on the console. The winches set into the cargo bay spun, retracting the nylon ropes the men had used to descend. "Yuri, pull us up to fifty meters."

The Russian expertly guided the craft skyward, rotor elevating in pitch to match their altitude. As they rose, the canopy tilted to afford a view of the ramshackle building below. Jordan couldn't see anything through the now shattered windows, thanks to the cloud of dust from the fifty-caliber rounds they'd filled the building with.

They'd seen two figures enter when they'd first crested the ridge. Neither looked anything like the beast, but Jordan couldn't take any chances. There could be a contagion at work here, and even if there wasn't he knew exactly what the Director's orders would be. Silence anyone who might leak word about the pyramid. Jordan wasn't sure the man would be wrong to give those orders, given what they'd found. The very idea of werewolves being real had taken a potshot at his reality, but the fact that a woman might have survived for over ten thousand years was even more terrifying.

"Alpha, take up defensive positions in the street. Use the cars for cover. Bravo, get to the rear of the building and watch that cornfield. If it gets in there, we'll lose it," he ordered, shifting his attention to the large tablet hastily installed in the center console.

The touch screen lived amidst the dials and buttons in the antiquated aircraft, the old mingling not so seamlessly with new. The weld housing the tablet definitely wasn't pretty. Not that it mattered. The burnished console around the screen was unfinished, built for function rather than aesthetics. All the old hardware was like that. It came cheap though, or at least cheaper than anything made in the last two decades. The helicopter was one of the few pieces of equipment Mohn had employed that wasn't state of the art. It seemed oddly out of place for a company that spared no expense. For anything.

The tablet displayed all eight helmet-cams, Alpha on top and Bravo on bottom. The men's points of view added up to a fairly detailed picture of the situation below. It supplied him with tactical data while keeping him relatively safe. That was paramount, and not just because it meant he got to live. Getting footage to base camp was vital. The troops had to know what they were dealing with.

"Alpha in position," Williams barked, his men sprinting into cover behind the battered vehicles the villagers in Peru favored. They set up a crossfire on the building's front, ready to cut down anything that emerged. The new XN8 rifles they used were compact but close enough to M4s that the troops had acclimated quickly. If they'd be enough remained to be seen.

The troops moved with an efficiency any modern military would have envied, because every soldier there had served in one army or another. There were eight men and women from as many countries, each with a different background but a similar set of skills. They were the best he'd ever worked with.

"Bravo in position. I don't like this, sir. We're too exposed out here. There's no hard cover."

"Noted, Corporal," Jordan said over the mic jutting from his helmet. He studied the building below. If the creature was inside, it could be biding its time, waiting for them to make a mistake.

"Orders, Commander?" Williams asked after a precise sixty seconds. His troops were wound tightly. They couldn't hold that focus long.

"Put a gas canister in the building and see what that flushes out. Be ready. This thing moves faster than anything I've ever encountered," Jordan replied, flicking off the mic. How high could that thing jump? "Yuri, take us up another thirty meters."

The Russian tilted the stick, obligingly carrying them higher.

"Alpha, weapons hot. Make sure the target goes down before it reaches cover," Williams ordered, his camera bobbing as he sprinted to another car.

"Roger that," his squad chorused.

"Fire in the hole," Williams shouted.

Jordan watched Williams's feed as he lunged from cover long enough to lob a silver canister through the hole where the window used to be. Chalky smoke billowed from all sides of the building, obscuring any view of the interior. It was a calculated risk. They wouldn't see anything until the creature emerged, but the grenade should, quite literally, smoke it out.

The ceiling exploded outward in a shower of plaster and wood. A terrifyingly familiar figure landed on the southeastern corner of the roof, its silver form shrouded by the smoke pouring from the hole the thing had created. Jordan studied it as the beast took in its surroundings. Its head swiveled from man to man, pausing on each long enough to assess it. This sort of eloquent body language was exactly what he'd expect from a highly trained soldier. It wasn't at all what one would see from a Hollywood monster.

"It's on the roof," Jordan barked into his mic. They weren't moving fast enough.

"It's too fast to track," Williams shot back, voice on the ragged edge of panic.

He was right. The beast had already vacated its perch. It dropped silently to the ground, bounding toward Bravo. Jewel was its first target. She fought to align the barrel of her rifle, but the beast was too swift. It raked her chest with wicked claws that sent the tiny blond woman spinning away in a fountain of her own blood. Her body was still airborne when the beast leapt, twisting over the rest of the squad and landing in the thick rows of corn. They rustled briefly, and then it was gone.

"Oh my God. Oh my God, Jewel is down. It's in the corn. Watch the corn," Tarkus called, backing away from his companion's body as he slowly walked his rifle over the wall of corn.

Jordan knew with cold certainly that the man was about to break, training or no. This was going south. Bigger guns didn't mean shit, just like he'd told the Director.

Yuri angled the helicopter without needing to be told, drifting over the corn as they scanned for the beast. It was in there somewhere.

"Sit tight," Williams's voice crackled. "Alpha, circle north. Let's see if we can flank this thing."

Williams's group broke cover and sprinted through the wide alley between the clinic and the neighboring house. They emerged near the cornfield, breaking left in a staggered formation. The maneuver was executed with textbook precision and gave them command of the entire western edge. It was exactly the right call.

The creature burst from the corn, closing the distance to Tarkus in three massive bounds. It planted its shoulder against his midsection, tackling the hapless soldier through the building's rear wall. The corporal's weapon clattered to the ground as the pair disappeared from view. The smoke had dissipated, but enough haze remained that Jordan couldn't make out the interior. He reached for the touch screen, tapping Tarkus's display. It filled the screen, revealing nothing but odd shapes in the darkness. Then a face appeared. It was all wolf, that face, all but the eyes. They glowed with amber malevolence, examining the camera with all-too-human intelligence.

The screen went black as the feed died. Jordan tapped the screen, returning to the entire squad. Not focusing on the black spot where Tarkus's feed had been was difficult. Jewel's camera was tilted at a crazy angle, by some chance having landed on her mangled form. He compartmentalized it, focusing on the larger situation. No distractions.

The creature was already moving. It punched a new hole through the clinic, emerging in the alley behind Noelo, the last member of Alpha. The former marine spun and unloaded a burst from his XN8 into the creature's head. It roared in pain, face a mask of blood. Then it seized the beefy man in both clawed hands, sinking a maw full of fangs into his throat. It ripped loose a huge chunk of meat, wolfing it down before discarding Noelo. The last member of Alpha tumbled to the ground like a cigarette butt, limp and lifeless. The beast blurred back to the corn, vanishing like sleep after the crack of thunder.

"Bravo, be advised Alpha has been eliminated. You're on your own," Jordan announced, nodding to Yuri. The Russian eased back on the stick, gaining elevation. No sense in taking chances. "The creature has reentered the cornfield. Get some distance and watch your six. It can cover fifty meters in about two seconds."

"Roger that. You heard the man. Let's move, people," Williams ordered, impressively calm despite the carnage. Ever the professional, that one.

His team fell back, putting seventy-five meters between them and the field where the creature lay waiting. The move would buy them reaction time at the cost of accuracy. They formed a rough triangle, setting up an overlapping field of fire. It was textbook perfect, as always.

Ninety seconds passed. One twenty. Nothing stirred in that corn except the wind.

"Command, is this Bravo. Any sign of movement?" Williams's voice crackled over the com. He was starting to fray, and his men were probably in even worse shape.

"Negative," Jordan replied, scanning as the helicopter slowly circled the field. The corn was still as the dead.

The men stood frozen, each at the edge of action. Ready in the truest sense of the word.

"Request instructions. Commander, should we withdraw?"

"Negative. Hold your position," Jordan answered, a bead of sweat trickling down his cheek. Where the hell had the creature gone?

The beast came at them sideways, bursting from cover exactly where it had entered. It blurred in a zig-zag pattern, scooping up Tarkus's XN8 and flipping atop the clinic's smoky roof. It crouched to minimize its profile and then looked straight at Jordan. The beast brought up the muzzle of its newly acquired weapon, smoothly aiming with one outstretched arm.

The rifle barked a hail of rounds in Jordan's direction. They punched through the canopy, stitching a line toward his face. Horrible pings echoed through the canopy as the rounds came closer. He held his breath, wincing in preparation for the bullet. It never came. He darted a glance over the now shattered canopy. *Holy shit.* The beast had withdrawn the clip and appeared to be looking around for more. Jordan wasn't sticking around long enough for it to find one.

"Get us out of here," he ordered Yuri, tuning out screams as the helicopter limped toward base camp.

23

WRATH

The beast sifted through the Ka-Dun's memories, plucking relevant details. The strange weapons the warriors wielded were known as guns. The Ka-Dun understood them in a conceptual sense but had never had need of them. He was a scholar, not a warrior. This denied the beast the skill to use them effectively, but they were not complicated. The gun proved remarkably easy to control, as he'd learned when attacking the angry black bird in the sky. The helicopter, his Ka-Dun knew it as.

He'd driven the machine from the field of battle, which left four warriors to deal with. That and the cleansing of the Ka-Dun's she. That she would join the great pack was unlikely, but nothing was lost in the attempt. It must be done quickly, yet doing so would leave him vulnerable. These warriors were skilled, and while he didn't fear their weapons, he was aware of the cost of the wounds they might inflict. Conservation of energy was critical with the sun so early in the cycle.

He sank into a crouch, testing the cool air in the alley with powerful nostrils. The troops were approaching slowly. They smelled wary. He cocked an ear, waiting for them to betray their presence. There. A boot crunched on a piece of adobe blown loose during the battle. He glanced at the building next to him, a crude structure long exposed to the elements.

A pair of wooden shutters stood open, revealing the shadowed interior. It was nearly devoid of furniture, save for a single rickety table and a set of plastic chairs around it. Interesting. He probed memories until he understood plastic. A superb material.

"Does anyone have a visual?" a voice crackled from around the corner, next to the inner wall of the house. It came through the communication device used by the warriors. Radios. Useful, but such a dangerous folly to play so ignorantly with signals.

"Negative," another voice crackled back. All but one had been male so far. Strange, but fortunate. She's were the fiercest, cunning and deadly.

The beast gathered on its haunches, leaping over the lip of the window and rolling to its feet on the dirt floor inside. Its eyes adjusted instantly to the dim light, and it cocked its ears as it prowled toward the wall. *Crunch.* A boot fell just on the other side of the wall. The warrior's body was pressed against it. A fatal mistake.

It lunged forward with all its considerable strength, punching a hole that belched a cloud of plaster into the hapless warrior's face. Before the man could recover, the beast's hand closed around his helmet, wrenching him back through the hole the creature had created. The violent motion widened the hole, ripping away much of the wall as the warrior thrashed in the beast's grip. The effort was futile.

The beast clenched its fist, crushing both the black helmet and the skull beneath. The twitching stopped. It seized the corpse with both hands, ripping loose a hunk of flesh from the neck and shoulder. It lacked the time to feed properly, but even small morsels would fuel its strength.

The beast was already moving before the corpse tumbled to the floor, gliding soundlessly through the front door onto the muddy track outside. Even the Ka-Dun didn't consider this a proper road, though his memories showed many places in the world where such a primitive way of life held sway. The world had changed much. Lost much.

The beast darted across the mouth of the alley, making it to the ruined face of the clinic without incident. The other three warriors would be cautious, and that would give it the time to cleanse the Ka-Dun's she. It ducked through the gaping hole in the front of the clinic, rolling over debris and landing near the she's limp form.

She was covered in blood and plaster, the life having already fled from her. Time was fast vanishing. The beast knelt next to her body, gently exposing her shattered neck. Bone jutted from ruined skin. The wounds were hideous. No matter.

The beast fed. Even if the she did not rise, her flesh would provide sustenance.

"Target acquired," a voice crackled at the edge of its hearing. The beast rose, but it was too late.

Bullets punched through the walls, tearing into its thigh and shoulder. The wounds throbbed, but the pain sharpened its senses. It rolled backward, dropping prone amidst the dirt and debris. Energy flowed to the wounded area. Within moments both bullets were expelled from its flesh, falling to the ground with tiny clinks. The wounds sealed, and the beast was whole.

"Is there movement?" another voice crackled, closer than the one before. They were approaching. It would show them movement.

The beast leapt straight up, through the hole it had created earlier. It landed lightly atop the corner of the structure, wooden beam groaning under its considerable weight. The three warriors were in a triangular formation, already bringing their weapons to bear.

It leapt toward the closest, clawed feet punching through the man's chest. The beast bore the warrior to the ground, crushing the fool before he could cry out. The other two warriors spun to face it, one quickly enough to align his weapon. The black rifle expelled a hail of slugs, ripping into the beast's midsection and sending it staggering backward.

The beast roared its pain and anger, leaping nearly a dozen feet into the air. It landed behind the warrior who'd attacked, raking him across the throat with razor-sharp claws as the man spun to face it. The warrior was flung violently backward in a fountain of his own blood, limp body rolling across the ground to land at the feet of his companion.

The final warrior stared, trembling. His will was broken. He turned and ran. It would not save him.

24

NEED A DRINK

Blair heaved another body into the pit, already brimming with butchered villagers. He leaned against a stunted poplar tree, but not because he was winded. It was the weight of all those deaths. Neither the frigid wind nor the rapidly sinking sun accounted for the deep chill that coursed through him.

Those people had been slaughtered by the strange consciousness imparted by the statue; he was convinced of it. He stared down at them, the ragged remains of the living, the once vibrant natives. Dozens of them. The pile now included eight soldiers, all with the grey and green triangle emblazoned on the shoulder of their rumpled black uniforms. The same uniform Jordan had worn. Mohn Corp. It gave Blair something to hate. A target. The resulting rage was the only thing keeping him moving. It smoldered within him, warm and vigilant.

He dropped the last of the soldiers into the pit, surprised at how little exertion it took, especially because he'd been at this for hours. That seemed a solid estimate based on sun's position just over the western peaks. He was stronger now. Tougher. Both were tied to the thing inside him, though he couldn't begin to understand how or why. It shouldn't be scientifically possible, not based on his admittedly limited understanding of genetics.

He needed room to think, to study this and get his mind around it. Unfortunately, he still had work to do. One body remained, one that he hadn't been able to force himself to move. Liz. Despite giving its word to save the pretty young doctor, the beast had savagely murdered her and then fed upon her corpse. Just like it had every other person it encountered. He'd been a fool to trust it, but there had been no other option. What could he have done against trained soldiers armed with state-of-the-art weaponry?

You accuse me unjustly, Ka-Dun.

Blair froze. He'd heard the same voice just before the chaos of combat. He'd been too busy to really think about it then, but now he had nothing but time.

"What are you?" he asked, studying the pile he'd assembled next to the pit. There were eight matte-black rifles with thick stocks and short muzzles. He had no idea what they were called or what sort of bullet they fired, though he was confident he could learn to use one if he had to. Next to them was a smaller pile of pistols, also matte black. They were metal, as he'd imagined, but lighter than expected.

I am a part of you, Ka-Dun. Imparted by the Mother's blessing when you accepted the Mantle of Champion.

Blair's lip curled up at the irony. "Champion? You murdered an entire village, and you used my body to do it."

Necessary work, Ka-Dun. We must prepare for what is to come.

"You said you were going to save her," Blair hissed, a single tear sliding down his cheek. It was the first he'd shed since the day he'd found out about Bridget and Steve.

I have honored our accord, Ka-Dun.

"Get out of my head," Blair snarled. "If you can't do that, then at least be silent."

As you wish, Ka-Dun.

Blair wasn't sure how he knew, but something told him the beast had retreated. He was left in awful solitude, alone to contemplate the horror before him. He needed to add Liz's body to the pile, but how could he face those lifeless eyes? Knowing he was responsible for her death made that unbearable. He knew almost nothing about her, save that she was American and had come here to investigate the grisly murders he was inadvertently responsible for. Where had she come from? Would her people send someone to look for her and the men she'd been with? What would they do when they arrived? He shouldn't be here when that happened. Otherwise, those people would probably die too.

Blair turned from the pit, already under assault by an endless army of buzzing black flies. There was probably more he could or should be doing, like planning his escape from the area. Maybe gathering supplies or looking at a map. Right now he just needed a drink. Surely there must be a bar in this little town, assuming it had survived the chaos and blood of the past day.

He picked a path through the debris, back to the dirt track masquerading as a street. His hands were tucked in the pockets of the tattered grey overalls he'd found after he'd awoken. They were too large, as was the bright red shirt. He felt like a scarecrow in them, especially with the length of cord he'd used as a makeshift belt. The clothing was far baggier than it would have been the day before, except in the arms and chest, where it was tighter than it had a right to be. That shouldn't be possible, but then neither was being turned into a werewolf after opening a pyramid from the Mesolithic. Mummy curse, eat your heart out.

The sun sank behind the jagged western peaks, painting the sky with reds and golds. He wondered if Liz would have thought it beautiful. A particularly morbid thought.

"God, but I need a drink," he muttered, casting the woman from his mind as diligently as he'd done with Bridget. It was becoming a habit.

Blair stood in the middle of the road, studying the cluster of buildings around him. The trouble with Peruvian villages was that they didn't label buildings properly. He was used to homes and shops being clearly defined, but these people didn't seem to differentiate. They were just as likely to sell corn cakes out a side window as they were to have dinner in the same building. They didn't distill alcohol that he knew of, but where there were people, there was booze. He'd just need to find it.

He scanned the row of ramshackle houses, looking for anything that stood out. A squat building was wider than most of the others. Its shutters had been repaired recently. Some of the slats were lighter in color, as if they had just been added. Maybe the owners had a bit more money than their neighbors, and if that was the case, there might be something to drink inside. If not, maybe he could scrounge some food. That was probably important too, though he felt strangely satiated despite not having eaten since the previous morning. He refused to consider the reason why.

Blair picked his way up the path to the doorway, a simple set-up covered by a grey blanket with embroidered red edges. It, too, was new, probably a recent and treasured addition. He pushed it aside and ducked into a single large room. Nearly a dozen chairs were arrayed in a horseshoe around a ring of stones used as a fire pit. A metal spit charred black by repeated use straddled the stones.

Long shelves lined opposite walls. They were made from older wood, bowed in the middle from crockery, bottles, and a wide assortment of kitchen tools. One of the shelves had a half-dozen dark bottles. The unlabeled glass wasn't familiar, but the wax-sealed corks certainly were. Someone had a taste for wine, quite surprising in this part of the world. He'd expected beer or perhaps stronger liquor, but certainly not wine. It had probably travelled a long way to end up here. That didn't matter. Whatever it was would do nicely.

Blair shuffled across the dirt floor to the shelf, hefting one of the bottles. Dark liquid sloshed inside. Red of some form. He preferred that to white at the best of times, and given the circumstances, its resemblance to blood seemed fitting.

"Now to open you," he muttered, scanning the gloom for a corkscrew. It stood to reason there would be one. How else would they open their wine?

His search revealed a pitted iron corkscrew on the bottom shelf, just under the wine. It was stamped with a *JR*, probably a long-dead maker's mark from when the thing had been cast decades ago. The tip was stained, a battle scar from opening hundreds of bottles.

Blair sagged into one of the chairs, strength flowing from him as the weight of events pressed down on his shoulders. How the hell had he ended up here? Where was here, exactly? And where was he supposed to go now? How could he even begin to quantify what had happened to him?

He set the bottle between his legs and began twisting the corkscrew. It bit eagerly into the cork, which pulled free with almost no effort. That was going to take some getting used to. He'd never been strong, but now that he was, he rather liked it.

Blair lifted the bottle and savored a mouthful of the dark liquid. It was harsh. Not quite ready to be consumed, probably a Cab or some similar cousin. It didn't matter, though. He gulped it down like it was water after a trek through the Sahara. It washed down his chin and neck, staining his newly acquired clothing. Again, he didn't care. All that mattered now was obliterating his consciousness, even if only for a few hours.

"Arrrrrroooooooooo!" The otherworldly howl tore through the twilight. The bottle tumbled to the earthen floor, forgotten.

The cry was close. Terrifyingly close. He recognized it instantly, though it had been years since he'd gone to Canada. He and Bridget had gone to hear the wolves, and their song had been amazing. This was a deeper, more primal version of that same song, as if it had been born in the throat of a much larger animal. There was only one thing he could think of that might make such a sound. It was a werewolf. But if he'd just heard the howl, then that meant *he* couldn't be the werewolf, didn't it? Maybe he wasn't responsible for all these murders.

Sudden relief washed over him, lessening the guilt he'd been wrestling with. If he wasn't the werewolf, someone or something else was. Then it hit him. That something would be hunting for the closest prey it could find. Him. The wine was already fogging his mind, making him sluggish.

Should he hide? Would it even matter? Wolves could track by

scent. That meant the beast could find him if he remained here. But was running a better option? If he fled, the beast would hear him. It would be on him within moments if he left the safety of the house. No, remaining was his only option. The beast *might* find him if he remained. It would definitely find him if he fled.

Blair crept to the shutters facing the street. He held his breath as he gently pushed a slat, moving it just enough to peer into the gloom. Night had not truly fallen, but the mountains denied the village the last of the sun. Anything could be moving out there, and he'd never know it. Was the beast listening to his heartbeat even now? After experiencing the things he'd experienced, he knew that was possible.

Wait. Maybe he could tap into that now. Part of him resisted, for acknowledging the changes meant accepting what he'd become, accepting that he was the monster that had brought these people to their end. But if there was another werewolf, didn't that mean it might be responsible? That triggered more questions. Where had it come from? Had it been unleashed in the pyramid somehow?

Thump, thump. Thump, thump. He could hear the beast's heartbeat now, low and heavy. Slower than he'd have expected but also terrifyingly powerful. It was approaching.

25

YOUR SHE

Blair froze. The creature was out there in the gathering darkness, hunting him. He could *feel* it, somehow. There was more than just the heartbeat. There was a scent. Powerful. Earthy. Feminine in some bizarre way, though why that would matter he couldn't possibly imagine. Just the ramblings of a mind desperately seeking escape from a situation over which it had no control. What the hell was he going to do?

He peered through the slats in the door, out at the road, the squat houses now nothing more than looming shapes. The sun had fully surrendered, leaving fading scarlet in its wake to the west. The moon wouldn't rise for hours. That too, he could feel. It was an itch between his shoulder blades. He could point to the exact spot the moon would rise over the jagged peaks to the northeast, though such knowledge didn't help his immediate situation.

Something moved in the street, not more than a dozen paces away. It was large. Taller than a man and far, far broader. Blair silently cursed the darkness. This creature might mean the end of him, but if that were the case he wanted to at least see the architect of that end. He wanted to know what he could about it before it tore him apart and feasted on his corpse.

Blair stared through the wooden slats, unable to look away from the figure. Something glittered in the darkness. Eyes, pale and yellow, like tiny reflections of the moon. There was no source of light to reflect, no illumination of any kind, yet they glowed with their own amber malevolence. Another mystery he wouldn't live to solve.

"Arrrrroooooooooo," the beast howled a second time, raising its head skyward and unleashing an eerie song that was at once beautiful and terrible. It called to him in a way he didn't understand, and for an eternal instant he longed to join it, adding his voice in a terrible choir.

Somewhere in the distance another howl answered. Then another. Then a third. They mingled and flowed, a melodic choir that froze his blood and quickened his heart. It was powerful. Mesmerizing. Yet it didn't quiet the sudden terror. How many of these things were there? Where had they come from? Had they been trapped in the pyramid, freed when he touched the statue? No, some part of him sensed that wasn't the answer. So where did they come from?

The howl ended, and the amber eyes turned on his hiding place once more. The beast whiffed the night air with powerful nostrils, surely tracking his scent in the same way he picked up hers. That awful gaze locked on him, and he knew with terrible certainly he was about to die.

It bounded forward on powerful legs, clearing twenty feet in a single jump. Two more hops brought it to the rubble-strewn yard outside the building, a mere handful of feet from the door he cowered behind. The beast tentatively sniffed again, as if it were seeking something. But what? She—he was sure it was a she now—seemed confused by his scent.

Then her eyes narrowed. Midnight lips rose as she bared ivory fangs. The beast lunged, arm punching through the shutter with blinding speed. It shattered into splinters, peppering his face and neck with tiny wounds as he tumbled backward. Only his newly acquired reflexes saved him. Claws rent the air mere inches from his face as he scrambled back, desperate to avoid the horrible monster. The werewolf, a part of his mind admitted.

It leapt through the window, landing heavily on the dirt floor next to him. Blair rolled, barely avoiding another swipe as the creature advanced. It blurred toward him, a terrible and ancient god that moved faster than any mortal could possibly react. Yet react he did. He narrowly avoided another swipe, flipping to his feet and leaping over a tree-trunk arm covered in scarlet fur. The beast lunged again, powerful jaws snapping shut on the space his neck had just vacated.

Blair dropped to his knees, rolling forward between the beast's legs. It pivoted, faster than he could scramble away. Lines of fire tore into his back as a swipe finally landed. He could feel the hot blood fountain from the wound, smell its metallic tang as droplets hung frozen about him in the air. The moment stretched, just as it had when the helicopter appeared. Everything but him slowed a crawl, including the werewolf.

It lasted only an instant, then time sped up and the blood hanging in the air splattered to the dirt. A detached part of him knew the wound wasn't fatal, but it was enough to slow him. That meant death, especially given that he wasn't fast enough even before he'd been wounded. But it didn't mean he was going to go quietly. There had to be something he could do.

He shot a quick glance around the room, taking in every detail. The shelves lining the walls provided nothing of use. The plastic chairs were no better. Four wooden pillars, each about eight inches thick, supported the roof. He didn't recognize the dark wood, but that hardly mattered. Even if they'd been cut from oak, the beast would shred them like paper. He could use that to his advantage.

Time returned to its normal flow. Blair stumbled to his feet, charging the nearest load-bearing pillar with the beast in pursuit. Claws raked the air behind him, the force of the blow fanning his back with a slight breeze as it sailed by. He dove for the pillar, grabbing it with a well-muscled arm. His new strength still surprised him as he swung around the pillar, positioning it between him and the werewolf. The creature barreled into it, snapping it like kindling.

The roof groaned above them; then plaster and timber rained down from above. A beam slammed into the beast's back, knocking it atop Blair and pinning them both to the ground. A cacophony of splintering wood and tumbling shingles drowned out his agonized scream as the beast's full weight pressed down on his wounded back. Fire surged through him, just barely preventing him from passing out from pain.

Then there was silence. Was the beast dead? Could it have been that easy?

No, Ka-Dun. She lives and will be upon you in moments. It is wise to flee from an enraged female, but she lacks the energy for sustained combat. If you are canny, you will best her.

The werewolf stirred, knocking aside the beam that pinned it as easily as a parent could heft a sleepy toddler. Rubble shifted, partially burying Blair as the beast rose to its feet. There was no fleeing, no escape. She was faster and much larger than him.

He could feel her tensing above him and sensed the blow an instant before it landed. That foreknowledge didn't save him. The beast's clawed fingers punched into his back, ripping past his spine and emerging from his chest in a spray of gore and pain. She hefted him into the air as life bled from him. All he could do was stare at the bloody clawed hand protruding from his chest, fur slicked with his blood. It was a bad way to die. Fuck that. He wasn't going out, not like this.

Yes. Channel your rage, Ka-Dun.

Something rippled within him. Something bright and potent and heady lay within his grasp. Blair seized it, channeling the rage until heat suffused his entire body. His muscles were suddenly aflame, swelling as they had just before the helicopter had cut down Liz. The memory of her being flung against the wall like a discarded doll compounded the rage, drawing it into a single point—the fist protruding from his chest.

No. He was not impotent. If he was going to die, he would sell his life dearly. The beast had destroyed his life, his career. Murdered an entire village. Possibly killed his oldest friends and colleagues. It was going to feel a tiny fragment of the pain it had inflicted.

The energy rolled through his body. Muscles swelled. Silvery fur burst from his skin, writhing like a million tiny snakes. His face throbbed as bones cracked and popped. Fangs burst from his jaw as a muzzle forced itself free of his face. He knew what was happening. The change was the same as before, but this time it came much, much faster.

Even as the process continued, Blair attacked. He gathered his legs under him, planting his feet against the beast's belly. He kicked off with all the force his new muscles could muster, legs tensing like powerful springs. The beast's clawed hand ripped free of his chest with a squishy pop, and Blair tumbled into the rubble near its feet.

The area around the wound burned, and a quick glance revealed muscle and skin knitting back together with shocking speed. He didn't have time to revel in the miracle.

Blair seized the end of a thick beam with both hands, heaving it skyward with the incredible strength imparted by the strange metamorphosis. The oak connected with the beast's shocked face, its expression comically human as it watched Blair struggle to his feet. The force of the blow lifted the female off its feet, despite its massive size. It flung the beast in a long arc, knocking it free of the rubble and into the street some thirty or forty feet away.

He wasn't done. Blair bounded forward in the same manner the beast had used. The fury inside him was a living thing, fed by all the pain, shock, and stress of the last few days. This thing was the reason for all of it, and if he could eradicate it, then perhaps the pain and rage would vanish.

Well done, Ka-Dun. Few master the change so quickly. You are strong. It bodes well for your species.

Blair ignored the voice. It was responsible for Liz's death, or at least it hadn't prevented it as promised. A distant part of him knew that was irrational, but he brutally repressed it. There was only rage right now. This beast would die at his hands. Maybe he couldn't kill the voice in his head or change what he'd become, but he could ensure that the thing in front of him didn't kill anyone else.

You do not understand, Ka-dun. This IS your she. I have done as you asked.

26

HELD ACCOUNTABLE

J ordan steeled himself as he ducked inside the lofty command
tent, raising the zipper on his jacket until it covered his neck.
His stomach roiled, and his forehead was beaded with sweat
despite the frigid Peruvian morning. The sun hadn't cleared
the eastern peaks around the pyramid's ravine, but scarlet streaks
foretold its coming.

He'd rarely experienced this type of trepidation, the fear of
confronting one's superiors. But then he'd never failed quite so spec-
tacularly as he had with this operation, particularly in Villa Milagros,
where he'd allowed the creature to not only slaughter his men but
also drive him from the field of battle. Jordan straightened, squaring
his shoulders. He had to take responsibility for what was ultimately
his screw up. He could make excuses, but he'd been commander of a
failed operation.

He strode boldly between banks of laptops on tables manned by
white-clad technicians. He made for the cluster of people at the far
side of the tent. The outer ring consisted of white-coated scientists
flanked by black-clad soldiers. All were focused on the pair of men
standing before a gigantic flat-panel monitor that currently displayed
a map of the Cajamarca region sprinkled with alarmingly red dots.

"What are you telling me?" the taller man rumbled, each word clipped for efficiency. The Director stared down at a quailing scientist, his silvered widow's peak transforming him into the bird of prey. "Are you seriously going to stand there and say that you have *nothing*?"

"That's exactly what I'm saying," the smaller man shot back, defiantly adjusting his glasses. "I know you want to get into that sarcophagus. We all do. But wishes aren't going to change anything. We don't even know what it's made of, much less how to open it. Or even what the power source is. We've tried everything from explosives to laser torches. Nothing has even scratched it. All we do know is—"

"Shit!" the Director roared, silencing the man with a swipe of his hand. "What you know is shit. You're supposed to be the top minds in your field. You have every resource money can buy. I need answers. I need them now. If we can't get inside that thing, hundreds of thousands of people could die. Millions. Isn't that what you told me? If you need more equipment, we'll get it. If you need more people, we'll find them. Now find me a way to get inside that sarcophagus, or get me someone who can."

Slipping past the last few tables to the empty area surrounding the large screen, Jordan moved closer as the tongue-lashing continued. Nervous technicians hunched over glowing screens as they analyzed data, doing their best to ignore the Director's tirade. Thick black cables snaked from the tent and toward the pyramid, which explained how so many of the screens displayed feeds of its hallways and chambers. Hard lines were the only way around the signal dead zone.

It really underscored how little they knew about this place. The room was littered with Ivy League scientists, men and women from across the world. Scholars with resumes that boasted dozens of languages and degrees he didn't pretend to understand. Yet the pyramid and its contents baffled them. What did that say about their society? Just how much more advanced had the builders been?

"Get out of my sight until you have something useful to report," the Director growled. The knot of figures surrounding him wilted under his gaze, all clearly wishing they had anywhere else to be. Jordan cursed his height as the Director's gaze settled on him. "Commander Jordan. I have to admit I'm surprised you came back. Most men have enough instinct for self-preservation to flee after they have fucked up as monumentally as you have. Get your ass up here."

Jordan didn't flinch under the weight of that gaze, though he certainly wanted to. Instead he cut a path through the crowd, their relieved faces slipping eagerly out of his path as they realized he was the Director's next target. Only one showed sympathy, one he was surprised to see. Sheila had donned a white coat like the rest of the scientists. She gave him a tentative smile and a squeeze on the shoulder as he passed. It helped more than she knew.

"The report I received an hour ago can't possibly be correct, can it?" the Director barked, eyes so hot they threatened to ignite the very air. "They claim you not only let Subject Alpha escape, but that you lost two of our best squads doing it. Can you even begin to comprehend the magnitude of that fuck up, Jordan? Answer me. It's not a rhetorical question."

"No, sir," Jordan gave back evenly, stopping next to the Director.

The man lapsed into his famed silence, like the eye of some implacable storm. He gazed fixedly at the monitor with hands clasped behind his back. Anyone who didn't know him might have called the stance languid, yet Jordan recognized it as the deceptive pose of a lion about to pounce. The Director's midnight suit was pressed and crisp despite the heat and humidity. His tie was perfectly centered at the nape of his starched white shirt, shoes glowing under the halogen lamps on tall titanium tripods.

"This could be the end of everything. They'll say that your failure today marked the beginning of the end, the moment when humanity lost the battle for its own survival," the Director began, voice low and calm despite the gravity of his words. He gestured at the map. "There are seven instances, all within twenty miles of Villa Milagros. Seven, Jordan. Do you see them?"

"Yes, sir," he answered, studying the map. The points formed a clear dispersal pattern with the village at the center. They were spreading. Fast. "Do we have eyes on the ground?"

"No, we don't fucking have eyes on the ground. You *were* the eyes on the ground, before you tucked tail and ran. What we do have is a panicked populace who have no idea what you and your team have unleashed on them. Specialist Gage, put up some media feeds for Commander Jordan," the Director growled over his shoulder, gaze flicking back to the screen as he waited to be obeyed.

The map flickered and disappeared, replaced by four panels. Each displayed a local news feed, and although Jordan didn't speak Spanish, interpreting wasn't hard. They were all variations of the same grisly scene. In one, a blond reporter spoke outside of what appeared to be a local bar. The door had been shattered in its frame, and a bloody handprint streaked the wall. The woman's face was pale under her tanned skin. Her eyes held a haunted look, and her tone was somber.

Each of the other three were similar. Ghastly murder scenes spattered with blood. Numbers flashed across two of the screens. Seventeen. Twenty-four. If they were accurate, over a hundred people had died, and this was only the beginning. How many more would be slaughtered in the days to come?

"I can see you're beginning to grasp the situation," the Director said, voice pitched low. He turned from the screen and caught Jordan's gaze. "At least three more of these creatures originated in Villa Milagros. Whatever plague we've unleashed spreads as these things kill. It's too early for accurate projections, but ops guesses roughly one in twenty killed will come back as one. Five percent of the victims rise as another monster, spreading this thing."

"My God," Jordan gasped, sudden realization crashing down on him as he did the math. "Sir, if they reach a sizable population center, we could be facing hundreds. Thousands. Two of our best squads couldn't even kill one."

"You're thinking too small," the Director said, loosening his tie. His shoulders sagged, a tangible sign of exhaustion. Not in all the years they'd worked together had Jordan seen him unbend even that much. "If we can't contain this, we're looking at the extinction of the human race. Gage, put the projections up, please."

"Yes, sir," the white-coated tech said. The news feeds disappeared, this time replaced by a global map. Red dots bloomed across South America, beginning in Peru. They surged through Central America and into the United States. Dots appeared in Europe and then on every continent. By the end of the sixty-second simulation cancerous red covered the world.

"We stop these things here, or we don't stop them at all. The next few days are critical. We need to learn everything we can about them: their weaknesses, how they can be killed, how they hunt. Most importantly, we need to understand how the disease is transmitted," the Director explained, a little of his fire returning.

"Understood, sir. What's our next step?"

"I want you to meet with the science team for a debriefing. They'll explain what we already know. Then we need to locate Subject Alpha. He's the source of the contagion, so studying him might be our only hope of understanding what we're dealing with. We've got ops working around the clock and have feelers out to the Peruvian government, offering them help in containing the spread."

"Sir, do we have any way of knowing which of these attacks could be him?" Jordan asked, already considering options for finding Smith. He studied the map on the screen, keenly aware of the gravity of his failure.

The Director was silent for a long moment. He squared his shoulders, turning to face the room full of busy technicians. They worked diligently under the halogen glow, processing data and no doubt looking for the shred of evidence that would deliver their quarry. They were the best, but what they were searching for was tantamount to a black grain of sand on a white beach.

"No. We have to hope he makes a mistake. Uses a credit card. Ends up on camera somewhere. We've already arranged taps for his families and associates, and I'll alert you if anything comes of it. In the meantime you're going to have to think like him. We assume he's probably trying to find a way back to the States," the Director replied. He turned his gaze back to Jordan. "I understand I'm asking a lot, but you need to find him, Jordan. Quickly. Don't fuck up this time. We won't get another chance."

27

NAKED

Liz had to pee. Urgently. Her teeth chattered as a breeze caressed her bare back. She blinked away sleep, pushing herself into a sitting position. There were mountains to the east. A surf pounded somewhere in the distance. Where was she? And why was she naked? Her heart nearly stopped when she realized there was a well-muscled arm draped over her legs. What the hell was going on? She scrambled away from the strange man, pain spiking through her left foot as it came down on a jagged rock. She careened off a tree that had somehow snuck up on her, barely catching herself on the sycamore's lowest limb. She was trembling violently, and not just from the chill.

Her heart thundered, and she could only manage shallow breaths. What was the scarlet mess all over her neck and chest? The dried ichor flaked when she brushed it with her index finger. It was blood. She raised her hands to her cheeks. They were covered with the stuff. Where had it come from? What had she done? She remembered dimly lit dreams, horrible and dark. She remembered rending. Ripping. Rutting like an animal.

Her head whipped toward the stranger as she caught a flash of movement. He scooted sleepily into the spot she'd just occupied, scratching a mop of dirty-blond hair. He had an angular face that might border on handsome had it not been covered in gore. A chest wide enough for the cover of a trashy novel bore tendrils of tattered medical gauze—familiar gauze. She dimly recalled the clinic in Villa Milagros. Yes, he was the unconscious stranger. What had his name been? She'd lost it in the chaos. Apparently she'd lost a lot more than just that.

She scanned the beach to the west. A two-lane road dotted with gas stations paralleled it. To the north lay a smattering of buildings maybe twice as large as Villa Milagros. There would be a phone there. Maybe even police. The hike was a good ten miles, most if it through thickly tangled bushes or over rocks that would soon grow intolerably hot. Wonderful.

Hot, coppery anger flooded her. She didn't even have shoes. It was time to get some answers.

"Hey," she said, steeling her courage and hobbling toward the man. She prodded him roughly with a foot and then hopped to a safe distance. "Wake up. I said *wake up*."

"Wuzzat?" the man asked, drowsily sitting up. He patted the ground next to him as if he were searching for something. Glasses, probably. Liz knew what that was like. Speaking of which, where were hers? And how could she see so clearly without them?

"Wake up," she demanded with all the authority she could muster. It wasn't easy when naked, lost, and covered with blood. "Where the hell are we? How did I get here? There's plenty of rocks, and I'm going to start aiming for your head if I don't get some answers."

His deep brown eyes blinked into focus as he drank in her legs and ever so slowly lifted his gaze to her chest. He was blushing by the time he reached her face. In other circumstances she might have welcomed the attention, but right now the behavior only stoked her anger.

"I, uh, I don't know. Look, I know this has got to be confusing," he said, averting his gaze as he rose gracefully. At least he had manners. "Your name is Liz, right? You're a doctor too? A medical one?"

"No," she snapped, hackles relaxing slightly. There had been such strange nightmares, but they grew more distant as the sun picked skyward through the clouds.

"No? I could have sworn that Jefe guy introduced you as Dr. Liz. Anyway, my name is Blair Smith. I'm an anthropologist—well, a teacher with an anthropology degree, anyway. How much do you remember from the clinic?" He spoke gently without looking at her, as if placating a wild animal. Did she really look that hysterical? Maybe she was.

"I..." she trailed off, tugging at the thread of memory. "Jefe drove me up to Villa Milagros. The villagers were dead. Killed by..." Killed by what? Fangs flashed in the jumbled corners of her mind.

"Killed by me," the man interjected, heavy eyes finally returning to her. His face was stone. "Or by something inside me. A monster. The same one inside of you. I realize how crazy that sounds, but it's true. We're dealing with something I can't even begin to comprehend, much less explain."

"Yeah, great. Monsters. Got it. How did we get here? Why did you kidnap me, and for the love of God, where are my clothes?" she growled, anger surging as the tirade gained momentum. She didn't know what was happening, but this man was at the heart of it. She fished a rock from the ground and hurled it at his face. Much to her surprise, it hit, snapping his head back as his mouth filled with blood.

"Oh my God," she said, horrified by her own actions. It didn't matter what he'd done. This wasn't like her. She looked around the brush-covered hill for anything to staunch the flow.

Blair's face twisted, and he took a threatening step toward her.

"Don't. Do. That. Again," he said, taking another step forward. He was taller than her and obviously stronger, but she didn't budge. There was a curious lack of fear. "Whatever happened to me also happened to you. Where do you think all that blood came from? Look at yourself. Take a long look, Liz. You might not be a doctor, but you've been to college, right? Examine the fucking situation."

She did. She was naked, but so was he. He was covered in blood, but so was she. Whatever was going on had affected him just as it had her. If he'd wanted to kidnap her, he'd be clothed and would probably have a gun. He'd also have bound her. The anger ebbed, leaving exhaustion in its wake.

"Tell me what you mean by monsters. Explain everything. Talk slow, like I'm stupid," she said as calmly as she could manage.

"It's complicated."

"So *un*complicate it. How about something simple? Where are we?" she asked, anger returning in a sudden surge. She actually took a step toward *him*. They were inches apart now, each refusing to back down.

"I don't know," he growled, glaring down at her. "I was just woken up, remember? How the hell do I know where we are? And what is it you think I did, exactly? Carried you naked down a mountainside and rolled you around in some blood?"

Liz didn't have an immediate answer, and that just made the anger worse. She wanted answers and he didn't have them. Yet he was the only target for her rage. She seethed silently.

"Listen, I know this is all a lot to take in, but we don't have time for you to get hysterical. Think you've got it bad?" he blared, voice thundering over the waves. "I'm in a foreign country. I don't speak the language. I'm naked. I have no money. My friends are dead. Oh, and I'm a fucking werewolf."

She just stared, counterargument dying unspoken. His lip was knitting itself back together, the flesh literally closing before her eyes. Blair started to cough, raising a hand to his mouth. When the hacking ceased, he showed it to her, palm up. There were two broken teeth, clearly expelled from his mouth. In their place were two brand new replacements, clear and white in stark contrast to their neighbors.

"Wha-what just happened?" she asked in a tiny voice, though she was positive she didn't want to hear the answer.

"You can probably answer that better than I can. That isn't the only thing. Look," he tugged at the remains of the bandage around his midsection, exposing smooth, pale skin. "If that isn't proof enough for you, think back to that clinic. Do you remember the helicopter? Your friend dying, the guy in the leather jacket?"

"Jefe," she muttered, mind tangled in what she'd just witnessed. Spontaneous regeneration happened in starfish, not people. Even then, reforming a limb took days. The amount of energy required to do it instantly was nearly incalculable. It was impossible, but she'd just seen it.

"Yeah, Jefe," Blair continued, seemingly oblivious to her stupor. He started pacing the rocky terrain, studying the area below them. "You know what they sent after us. Soldiers. Why do you think that is? Why do you have no memory of coming here? I'll bet you had nightmares. Violent ones. Deny it, if I'm wrong."

The fire inside her sputtered out, smothered by the weight of his words.

"I can't," she admitted, hating him for the truth. She sank into a crouch, hugging her chest to her knees. "What I just saw is impossible. And I did have nightmares."

"That's something, I guess," Blair said, hopping atop a small boulder. She tried not to watch him, but even given the circumstances they were in, it was hard not to notice the way the muscles bunched in his legs. Such an odd thing to feel at a time like this. He turned a steely gaze on her. "I was called in to a dig site a few weeks back. Up in the mountains, near a mine."

"Yanacocha," she said, staring him in the face. It made ignoring... other things easier. He seemed to be doing the same, eyes focused on her face. "It's the largest goldmine in South America."

"Okay, Yanacocha. We were studying an enormous pyramid, bigger than anything ever discovered on this continent or any other." He shaded his eyes against the sun. He watched the town to the north. "We have no idea who built it, and the structure demonstrates command of a technology we can't begin to understand. It changes our whole understanding of the ancient world."

"So let me see if I have this straight," Liz broke in, fanning an ember of her earlier anger. She gently stoked it into indignation. "You want me to believe that you were studying some pyramid built by *aliens*? If this thing is so gigantic, why wasn't it discovered before? Some random kid in Georgia would have found it with Google Earth."

"Why do people always assume it's aliens?" Blair rolled his eyes. "We don't know what culture built it, but it was humans, not little green men. I don't know much about them yet, or why they disappeared. What I can tell you is that they designed a pyramid that can cause earthquakes."

"And werewolves," she added, answering his eye roll with one of her own. "So our mysterious lost people of Atlantis made werewolves? Seriously? What next, sparkly vampires? I believe in some things people think are pretty out there, but come on."

"Listen, lady. You do whatever the hell you want. I'm done trying to convince you," he said, sliding off the rock and moving toward the town in the distance.

"Where are you going?" she called, rising and trotting after him. She didn't trust him, but she also didn't want to be alone. Especially alone and naked.

"To that village. I need clothes. And a phone." He paused, turning to face her. "I don't know what's happened to us, but I intend to find out."

"Exactly how are you going to do that?" she asked, planting her hands on hips, like weapons. "Are you a doctor? Can you sequence DNA? Because if you can't, you're going to fail."

"I'm guessing you can? I thought you weren't a doctor," he countered, turning a glare on her.

"Grad student. I've had a lot of training, and I understand how DNA works. If we can get to a lab, I might be able to get us some answers."

"Great. First we'll get some clothes. Then we'll find a lab," he said, turning back toward the village and setting a ground-eating pace down the rocky hill.

She hobbled after him, favoring her right foot and abruptly realizing she didn't need to. The pain was gone.

"My foot," she said, lifting a leg to inspect the sole of her foot. "The wound. It's gone." She ran a hand over smooth, unbroken skin.

"I told you. Whatever this is, we're in it together," Blair said, neither turning to face her nor slowing. "The faster we reach that town, the better. We can be there by nightfall, but we're both going to look like lobsters. Wish I had some sunscreen."

28

SUNBURNED

Blair dropped into a low crouch in the deep shadows next to the salt-weathered fence. He rested a hand on one of the rough slats, peering at the ramshackle house and the deserted highway behind it. A wan glow came through what he took for a kitchen window, thick with the kind of filmy grime that built up near the ocean. The rest of the place was dark, and the only sound was the pounding of surf in the distance. Even the wind was barely audible, though he felt its salty caress. They were cloaked in darkness, save for the fat sliver of moon just above the horizon. He stared up at it, fixed on its surface, iridescent like he'd never seen before.

"Yeah, I feel it too. Makes me itch for some reason," Liz said, settling in next to him as she peered up at the moon. They were still naked, though the darkness mercifully obscured certain details.

The hike had been difficult, and not solely because of the blistering sun. She was beautiful. Long copper hair and...And he needed to focus.

"Wish I understood what the hell is going on. Nothing makes sense anymore," he said, unsure if he meant the attraction or the moon. Perhaps both.

"If my brother were here, he'd have some sort of theory, but I haven't the faintest idea why I can close my eyes and point straight at the moon. I mean, I get that we're werewolves so it sort of makes sense. I just don't get *why*. Anyway, I don't see any cars coming. Do you think we should knock?" Liz asked, rocking back and forth on her heels in the soft sand. It had the appearance of a nervous habit.

"You know more about local customs than I do. If this was California, the owners would either call the police or come out with a shotgun. How will they react to a pair of naked strangers on their doorstep? How do we explain what happened?" he asked, voice pitched low even though there was little risk of being heard over the waves.

"I'll tell them we camped at the beach and were robbed while swimming," she replied, evidently having given the matter thought during their mostly silent hike. Liz rose to her feet and started for the front door. "Come on. I doubt they'll answer with a shotgun, and even if they do, what choice do we have? It's getting chilly this close to the water, and I don't like the idea of another night outdoors."

"All right," he agreed, loping after her through the thick sand. At least it was better than the rocks. "I'll let you handle the talking. Just be ready to run."

They rounded the fence, crossing the cracked cement walkway. It led past an old pickup truck to a shadowed porch. He wished he knew what time it was. Eight? Nine?

"Maybe we shouldn't do this," Liz hissed, turning as if to go.

"We have no choice," he hissed back, threading a way up the driveway and past the truck. "Come. On. I can't do this alone. I need you to translate."

She froze for several agonizing heartbeats and then followed Blair up the driveway. He stepped aside just before the porch so she'd be the first to reach the door. She gave him a tentative glance, somehow visible despite the near darkness. Then she seemed to find her courage, and she gave the plywood door three sharp raps. A tense breath later, light flared within. A muffled Spanish voice called out and was answered by a woman. Footsteps approached, two sets.

The floor creaked on the other side of the door. Then a bolt clicked. The door creaked open, revealing a bleary-eyed man topped by a greying rat's nest that hadn't seen a brush in years. He flicked a switch next to the door, and the porch light flared to life. Blair blinked away spots as the old man studied Liz's naked form. He gave a little frown and then called something in Spanish over his shoulder.

A portly woman in a floral dress advanced up the hall, calling something back to the man Blair assumed to be her husband. She stared suspiciously at Liz, gaze darting to the man as if to confirm he wasn't enjoying the sight. The man opened the door a bit wider and turned his attention to Blair, face hardening as he did so. Not surprising. Finding a lone naked woman on your doorstep is more curious than disturbing. Add a man into the mix, and that whole impression changes.

There was a rapid exchange in Spanish between the old man and Liz, and then he stepped aside and gestured for them to enter. Whatever she'd said had worked. The woman's expression went from hostile to sympathetic. Liz bobbed her head gratefully as she ducked inside. He moved to follow, but he found the man's arm blocking his path. The old man's face was harder than granite, and he raised a finger first to his eye and then to Blair. *I'm watching you.* Great.

To make matters worse, the itching between Blair's shoulder blades had gotten worse. He didn't need to turn around to know that was the part of his body being caressed by the moonlight. Well, why not? If he was a werewolf, then it made sense. The scientist in him demanded answers, though. He wanted not just to know how a werewolf could exist, but also how or why the moon would matter.

The old man finally moved his arm and waited patiently as Blair ducked under the door. The floorboards creaked as he made his way up the hallway and into a tiny kitchen. Liz was already seated at a table just large enough for two, with a frayed grey blanket wrapped around her shoulders. That hadn't taken long. An old thirteen-inch television droned quietly on the counter behind them, featuring an attractive Latina reporter in front of some store.

The husband thumped down the hall, passing Blair and

heading into the house's one, small bedroom. He emerged a moment later with a thin green robe that Blair gratefully accepted. It only hung to his thighs, and it itched, but at least he wasn't naked any more. The old woman scurried across the linoleum, grabbing him by the arm and hustling him to the chair across from Liz.

"Gracias," he said, exhausting his supply of Spanish.

"De nada," the matronly woman replied with a smile, turning to rattle off another flurry at Liz.

"She says we can stay the night. Tomorrow she'll bring us to the police station so we can tell them we were robbed," Liz replied. Blair heard her heart speed at the word "police," and he couldn't help but shiver when he realized what he was doing—hearing heartbeats.

"Mira. Mira," The old woman said, face going pale as she gestured at the television. Blair didn't need to understand Spanish to get the gist of what the reporter was saying. She was gesturing at a storefront. The metal bars outside the door had been bent and the door itself ripped off its hinges. Something massive had broken its way inside the shop.

"Oh my God, Blair. You don't think?" Liz whispered, eyes finding his.

"Maybe. Ask them where that is," he replied grimly, still watching as the reporter solemnly relayed a story he feared he would understand all too well.

Liz obligingly spoke to the woman in Spanish, but it was the man who answered. His voice was hostile, and he gestured accusingly at the pair of them. His wife reacted, blinking rapidly as though seeing them for the first time.

"Blair," Liz began, heart racing as she prepared to bolt. She pulled the blanket tighter as if that might offer some protection. "They want to know why we're not sunburned if we spent all day walking. He says we're lying, and I don't think I can convince them otherwise."

Now that she'd called attention to it, Blair realized he wasn't burned. Neither was Liz, and her skin was fair enough that there was no way to explain it. Their mysterious new ailment was the only answer. Werewolves healed their own wounds; perhaps they could heal sunburns too.

The man darted across the kitchen, reaching into the nook next to the ancient white refrigerator. He emerged with a shotgun, which was promptly leveled at Blair's chest. Blair tensed but was careful to make no threatening gesture.

Slay him, Ka-Dun. He is less than nothing. His weapon cannot harm you.

The voice shocked Blair, and he jerked erect without thinking. It was a mistake. The old man stroked the trigger, and the gun roared. Acrid smoke burned his eyes as a cloud of pellets took him in the chest. The force of the blow hurled him backward, knocking the table into Liz and sending him sprawling. He couldn't draw in a breath, but he managed to roll onto his stomach. He was still struggling to his feet when he heard the growl.

Liz had been knocked from her chair, but she flipped to her feet so rapidly that only his new senses allowed him to see more than a blur. The blanket was pooled at her feet, and her entire body began to tremble. Her eyes were malevolent pools of amber, bestial and enraged. She tilted her head backward, canines elongating even as a deep howl burst from her like the vengeance of the damned.

It shook the room, sending the old man staggering back into the refrigerator. His hands shook as he snapped the shotgun open and tapped out the shells. He fumbled at a drawer that probably contained more rounds as his wife ran shrieking from the room.

Liz continued her transformation, auburn fur bursting from every part of her body. It raced to cover her nakedness as her body swelled. She grew taller, more muscular. Claws burst from each finger. Bones broke as a wolf's muzzle replaced her face. It all happened so fast, no more than a few heartbeats. Then a nine-foot monstrosity stood where the beautiful woman had been.

The beast lunged, wicked claws punching through the man's abdomen with a sickening crunch of bone. The shotgun clattered to the floor as one of her furry arms hefted him effortlessly. Hot blood rained to the linoleum, and the man's heart raced like a rabbit. Blair staggered to his feet, wanting to stop her but knowing it was impossible.

Not so, Ka-Dun. You are a shaper. Impose your will and she will obey.

"How?" Blair cried, staring in horror.

It was too late. The beast sank her fangs into the old man's neck, nearly severing his spine as she tore violently at his flesh. Blood painted the room, fountaining across her auburn fur until she resembled an avenging demon Hollywood would envy. The old woman bolted down the hall, barreling out the front door with a shriek that wouldn't end. The beast took a step as if to follow.

Blair wasn't sure what he did, but something surged within him. It was the same fire he'd felt when he first changed, a crackling energy that threatened to burst from him. He grabbed at it, using it to fuel *something*.

"Stop," he roared. Power suffused his words, lending a palpable authority. The beast paused and then turned to face him. Blood dripped down a chest recognizably human, even under all that fur. Every muscle strained to reach him, claws flexed in anticipation. She wanted to destroy him. He could feel the malevolence, feel her struggling against his will. How long before she broke free and killed him?

29

CLASH OF WILLS

Liz was terrified. She stared down at Blair through alien eyes, powerless to control the actions of the monstrous body she now inhabited. She was not alone. A palpable presence lurked within her, exposed now that she'd somehow unleashed it. The thing was all rage, wrapped in a fury so potent that it frightened her even more than her helplessness. Below her Blair glared upwards, blood-speckled shoulders squared and face locked in grim determination. Something lurked in the recesses of those deep brown eyes, a power and authority he'd lacked before.

"Stop...fighting me," Blair said, taking a step closer. His face hardened, determination and anger etched there. "I know the beast wants you to kill. I know that better than anyone possibly could. But I also know you can fight it. You can control it. Fight the beast, Liz. Take back your power."

He is a shaper, Ka-Ken. His witchery is all that keeps us from rending his frail little body. Join your will to mine, and we will slay this impudent male.

No! she railed, screaming within the confines of her head. Frustration and anger formed an alloy of resolve. She wasn't helpless. *I will not help you murder him. Give me my body back.*

We are one, Ka-Ken. If this form displeases you, then change it. But first let us deal with the shaper. Let us smash his witchery and feast on his flesh.

I said no. He's the only one who knows what's happened to me, she shot back, girded in a grim armor of determination. *Why don't you flee back into whatever corner of my mind you were hiding in? Go. Away.*

This one will stop us from killing the unblooded who fled. She will alert warriors that we lack the energy to fight. She must die.

No. I won't let you kill her. Now give me back my body, she roared, voice echoing in her mind. She had to regain control before anyone else died. Her will strained against the beast's, wrestling for dominance. The beast was strong, implacable. Yet so was she. She marshaled all the fury, all the humiliation, all the pain and confusion. *No more.*

Your will is strong, Ka-Ken. I relinquish control, but be wary. His kind are treacherous. They lack honor.

Just like that, the struggle ended. The voice, whatever it was, receded into the shadowed recesses of her mind. She became aware of her body, suddenly in control of the hulking form. It was unfamiliar but dizzyingly powerful. She possessed a strength she'd never imagined. Her senses were alive. She could taste the blood on the walls, smell the family of mice under the floor boards. Blair's heartbeat thundered around her. Yet none of that power would enable her to move so much as a muscle. Whatever Blair was doing had stopped everything but her breathing and heartbeat.

Liquid fire roiled within her. She hurled it against her captor, unsure of what she was doing or why. A burning desire for freedom blazed within. Panic mixed with indignation. It was far worse than claustrophobia, something she'd wrestled with her entire life.

"Fine. You want me to let you go? I will," Blair said, heartbeat slowing. He still glared up defiantly. "Just remember that her death will be on your hands. Can you deal with that, Liz?"

Blair took a large step back, tensed muscles finally relaxing. The force holding her vanished. It didn't fade. It was just gone. Sudden fatigue washed over her as the fury dissipated. She just wanted to sleep. To hide from what happened to her, even if it was only for a few hours. She sagged to her knees, muzzle resting against a chest covered in gore-slicked auburn fur.

Her muscles spasmed violently as something receded within her. Every part of her skin itched as fur slithered back within her body. Bones cracked and popped as her body reorganized itself. The pain was immense, but it was fleeting. Within moments she lay naked on the linoleum, ragged sobs bursting out. Several moments later, a blanket settled over her, covering her from the neck down. It was a small kindness, but an important one. She wasn't alone.

"I just killed a man. Ripped him apart in front of his wife. I murdered him." She tasted the words, looking for the emotion they lacked. Why didn't she feel anything? That was going to catch up with her.

"Do you drink?" Blair asked.

The question bewildered her. It was too normal.

"Let me see what I can find," he continued as if she'd answered. His form moved behind her, and a moment later the refrigerator door creaked open. "Aha. Beer." Bottles clinked; then she heard the familiar hiss as he popped the tops. She rose into a sitting position, clutching the blanket to hide both her nakedness and the remnants of the murder she'd committed. Blair turned from the counter and offered her a Corona. She took it numbly.

"I'm struggling to get my mind around this too, but we have to focus on what we can do now. We have to get out of here. Someone must have heard that shotgun blast and probably the screams. Liz, we can't stay."

"Let me think for a minute. I just need a sec," Liz replied, taking a long swallow. The cool liquid slid down her throat, tangy and familiar. She stumbled to her feet, careful to drop neither the beer nor the blanket. The TV still droned in the background. The scenario was shockingly normal. "The wife will run to her closest neighbor, and they'll call the police. It will probably take some time for them to respond, but you're right. They're coming. We have to get out of here. But where do we go?"

"Should we see if they have any money? Maybe some clothes?"

Blair suggested, gaze filled with something unreadable. Did she look that horrible? She probably wouldn't have been able to look at him either if their roles had been reversed.

"You're right," she agreed with a tight nod. Gulping down the rest of the beer fueled her resolve. It was liquid courage. "I'll search the bedroom for clothes. See if you can find some money in the kitchen. Most people don't trust the bank here, so they usually keep something stashed. It could also be in the bedroom."

She didn't wait for a response, setting the empty bottle on the counter and heading for the hall. Exhaustion pulsed through every muscle, leaving her a trembling wreck. She threaded the wreckage in the kitchen, ignoring the sweet smell of blood and choosing to focus on the familiar tang of the beer. The hallway was dark, but she had no problem making out the picture frames on the wall, and the dark carpet that muffled her steps. It led to a small room at the back of the house, cluttered with dark, bulky shapes and the musty scent of mildew. Liz fumbled a hand along the wall near the doorway, probing until she located the light switch. She gave it a flick, revealing too much about the couple who'd called this place home until her arrival.

The room was dominated by a queen-sized bed draped with a floral-print comforter and enough pillows to supply a Boy Scout troop. The bed was flanked by mismatched nightstands, one holding the brass lamp that had sprung to life when she'd flicked the light switch. The other held a tattered bible and an old green rotary phone. It also held two drawers that were as good a place to start as any. Liz sat heavily on the bed. She slid open the top drawer, revealing a pile of old pictures. Near the back of the drawer was a small black wallet, the sort her grandfather might have used.

Hating herself, she plucked it from the pictures and checked the contents. A small wad of multicolored bills stared back at her. It wasn't a fortune, but it would get them away from here and maybe hire a boat to take them to Mexico. Hot tears rained down on the bills. This had to be a nightmare. She wasn't a killer. Werewolves didn't exist. She was going insane.

A floorboard creaked behind her.

"I couldn't find any money, but there are some clothes in the hall closet," Blair said, appearing in the doorway. He seemed reluctant to enter. "Hey, we should get moving. Did you find anything?"

"Money," she said, sudden rage surging. She held the wallet up, hot tears still streaming. It was too much. "That's enough to hire a boat. To get us to Mexico at least."

"I get it, Liz. This all sucks. Monumentally," he said, buttoning an awful Hawaiian shirt. "We have no idea what we've become, or how. Mohn wants us. The police will be after us now too. The best thing we can do is get out. That will save lives. You saw what happens when we're threatened. If we want to protect people, we have to keep moving. Then maybe we can piece together what's happened to us. Maybe even find a cure."

"I just need a minute," she whispered, refusing to look at him.

"All right, I'm going to pack some food and get dressed. Make it quick," he said, disappearing back up the hallway. She envied his composure in the face of mythological monsters.

On a whim, Liz picked up the phone. She held the hideously green plastic to her ear. The dial tone brought her a small piece of sanity in an ocean of impossibility. Trevor would know what to do. She dialed the number methodically, waiting as the dial reset after each digit. There was a series of clicks as it routed her to the United States, and then it finally began ringing. What time was it? That probably didn't matter. Her brother was a night owl. He always had been.

"This is Trevor," he answered, his voice a rock she clung to.

"Thank God. I was so worried I'd get your voice mail. Trevor, I'm scared," she said. Suppressing a sob of relief took everything she had. She stood from the bed, clinging the phone's base to her chest as she faced a cracked full-length mirror. She needed clothes. "I'm in trouble. People are dead. There's blood everywhere. I don't know what to do."

30

LA MULTA

Blair closed the bedroom door, affording Liz the privacy he'd have wanted were the roles reversed. Unfortunately, his new hearing made that impossible. Her ragged pulse beat a staccato against his temples. The voice on the other end of the phone cracked like thunder.

"Liz? Hey, it's gonna be okay," he said with empathy. "Calm down. Start at the beginning. Whatever it is, we'll get through it. Where are you?"

"I don't know. Somewhere in north Peru, near Cajamarca," she explained, sucking in shallow little breaths as she fought for control. Her heartbeat slowed. "I'm traveling with a...man. I don't really know him. There are men chasing us. Men with guns."

"Guns? Liz what the hell happened?" Trevor fired back, voice exploding through the receiver. "Is he holding you against your will? Can you go to the police?"

Blair strode up the hallway, toward the kitchen, wishing he could turn off his hearing.

"I don't think they can help. These men, they've got rifles and military gear. There was a helicopter. They work for a company called Mohn Corp." Liz's voice softened despite the gravity of her words. "This man I'm traveling with, Blair, he's an anthropologist. He found something, and these soldiers want it. They've tried to kill us both. They did kill my friend. Listen, Trev. How I got involved isn't important. I'm scared, and I need to find a way home. Can you help me?"

"Of course, Liz. Just tell me what you need me to do."

Blair entered the kitchen and cracked open the fridge door. It stopped after just a few inches, blocked by the still-warm corpse Liz's alter ego had just slain. After all that had happened, he was simply too exhausted to react in any sort of rational way. He reached in and grabbed another beer, popping the top with his thumb. It was a fear he couldn't have managed just a few days ago. One of many changes he couldn't explain. He needed to find answers and find them quickly. What had he become? What kind of psychopath would have left such a plague?

You insult the Mother, Ka-Dun. The Ark is the vessel of your salvation. The champions are the slim shield staving off your species' annihilation.

He jerked violently around, spilling his beer as he searched the kitchen for the speaker. There was no one, of course. The voice was in his head, but it still rattled him. He couldn't shake the feeling that it was coming from behind him, even though there was no direction in his mind.

"What are you?" he asked aloud, partly to muffle the conversation in the bedroom. "What do you want with me?"

I am your guide. It is my duty to shape you into the weapon that will defend your people.

"Thus far all you've done is slaughter everyone around me. Who are my people? And what am I defending them from?" he asked. This was the most forthcoming the voice had been. Blair leaned against the counter, sipping his beer in deliberate protest of the carnage.

I have killed because you do not yet have the will to do so. It is your purpose, your reason for existence. You must cull the unblooded before it is too late. The enemy's return is imminent. The sun will soon enter the next phase of the cycle.

"The enemy? No more riddles. No games. I want answers," he

growled, wishing the beast had a physical form he could attack. He recognized the feeling as something that would have been out of character just a few days ago. The realization chilled him. "Why are you talking to me, anyway? You've been silent for days."

The moon provides sacred sustenance when she is large in the sky. Her energy gives us strength. Without this I must sleep. This leaves you vulnerable. This is why you must husband your strength, why you must learn.

"Who are you talking to?" Liz asked from the doorway. Her sudden appearance startled him. How had she snuck up on him like that?

"You know who. The voice," he riposted, setting the half-empty Corona on the counter. "You've got one too, don't you? Like a whisper in the back of your mind. Something that takes control when we sleep, that turns us into that *thing*."

"Yes," Liz answered, pausing for an eternity before taking a tentative step into the kitchen. "It's there, lurking. I can feel it slithering through my mind. Watching even when I'm in control. It's especially bad tonight. Stronger. Do you think that has something to do with the moon?" Her words were an eerie echo to the beast's.

"It must be. Every myth about werewolves ties them to the moon, especially the full moon. Maybe it's some sort of radiation, or...well, shit. I don't know a lot about physics or astronomy, but there must be some scientific explanation," he rambled, letting the ideas flow as he considered the ramifications. He met Liz's gaze. "I need to get back to the pyramid. If I can get access to my notes and some of the photos, I can figure out who left this and why they did it. The answers to whatever we are now are up there. I know it."

"We both know what we are now," Liz shot back unflinchingly. She righted one of the chairs and sank heavily into it. The ankle-length skirt and the baggy white blouse she now wore must have come from the bedroom. "Let's face facts. We're werewolves. No more 'what we've become.' Just call us what we are."

"Fine, we're werewolves. I'll stick to that. So, are you willing to help me get back to the pyramid?" he asked, immensely relieved to have someone to discuss the situation with. He moved to the second chair, sitting just a few feet away.

"Are you crazy?" She gaped at him like he'd gone insane. Maybe he had. "If we try to get back there, Mohn will kill us. I bet they have a whole army by now. There's no way we'd even get close. Blair, we have to run. To get somewhere that we can investigate what's happened to us. Maybe if we understand that, we can reverse it."

"You're right," he agreed, wishing she weren't. He rose to his feet. "You said something about testing our DNA. What do you need to perform those tests?"

"We need a real lab, something back in the States. Somewhere with both the resources to do the tests and people that can help us interpret the results. My brother can probably get us access to a lab at SDSU," she replied. Apparently he'd missed that part of her phone conversation.

"All right, so how do we get to San Diego?" he asked, relieved that they had something close to a plan. He turned on the faucet and used the sponge to dab the blood away from his neck and face. "There's no way we can board a plane or even a boat without a passport, right?"

"This isn't the United States. Customs is corrupt. When I got here, they charged something called 'La Multa,' the fine. It's an open bribe. Any captain will take it. We just need to find a boat that will take us to Acapulco. My brother has a copy of my passport just in case I ever lost mine. He can ship it there, and pick it up when we arrive," Liz explained, rising. She made for the hallway.

Blair turned off the faucet and followed.

"That will help you, but what about me? I don't have a backup, and I doubt Mohn is going to let me pick it up from the pyramid," Blair said as he trailed after her. She made for the door but glanced over her shoulder to indicate she was listening. "Do you have a plan to get me on a plane in Acapulco?"

"Yes, and we'll talk about it on the way. Come on, we have to get out of here," she replied, cracking the door and peering outside. "I don't see any lights on out there. The neighbors are probably too afraid to get involved, but I'm sure they've already called the police."

"Let's get moving, then. We can run along the beach. There shouldn't be anyone there, and the waves will wash away our trail," he said. Liz darted down the porch and into the night. If not for his new senses, he would have lost her. Even as it was, he could barely track her form as she sprinted across the road, toward the pounding waves.

He trailed after, low and quiet. Here and there he detected a heartbeat, low and steady as if its owner were asleep. That surprised him. He'd expected the quiet little town to erupt like a kicked anthill after the shotgun blast and the wife's screaming. Still, he wasn't one to question good fortune. He sprinted after Liz, closing the gap shortly after his newly acquired sandals began to crunch the sand.

"You asked if I had a plan," Liz said, half of her face illuminated by the heavy moon above. "We won't be able to get you on an international flight, but we can probably convince them you lost your passport and to let us fly to Tijuana or Ensenada. From there it's easy to get you across the border into San Diego."

"Guess we don't have much choice. Let's hope that it..." He instinctively turned toward the foothills they'd traversed the day before. He wasn't sure how, but energy pulsed through him. His eyes grew warm. Thin moonlight now lit the land like dusk. Shrubs and boulders leapt at him with impossible clarity, as if he were gazing through a powerful set of binoculars.

In the distance a four-legged figure stood atop a rise. It was a wolf. A very large wolf.

"What is it?" Liz asked, scanning the horizon in the direction he was facing.

"There's something out there, and it's watching us," Blair said, a chill working it's way down his spine. "Liz, it's a werewolf. I'm sure of it."

31

ONE WHO FIGHTS

A higa seethed with indignation, pacing back and forth across the rocky outcrop as he gazed at the tiny village next to the ocean. His heavy lupine body tingled with power from the moon above. The trickle of energy was thin, but he drank it in eagerly.

Impudent and powerful as only the Mother's direct progeny could be, the interloper who'd usurped his link with the Mother glared defiantly back at him from the distant shore. In time the whelp might eclipse even him, *must* eclipse him if he were to fulfill the duty he had unknowingly usurped. It was a mantle that must be borne *now*, though there was no way the whelp could be prepared in time, or at all, if Ahiga couldn't even reach him.

What moments remained were vital. The unblooded must be culled. The tainted must be eradicated before they began spreading their vile plague. Yet he could not do these things. He must train the whelp and awaken the Mother. It was a slender thread of hope that bore the weight of an entire world.

"Where do you run to, little cub?" he mused, studying the strange buildings clustered along the shore. A road stretched into the distance, made from some strange black substance. Alien, like much of this place.

The whelp moved along the shore instead of using the road. Why? Perhaps he fled the soldiers who'd conquered the Ark, or maybe he sought passage to another land. Perhaps both. There was a way to know, but Ahiga's soul cried out at the crime of it. He could force his way into the whelp's mind and pilfer his destination. Yet such an act against the blooded was the worst sort of violation. The Mother would be ashamed. But what cost if he did not? What if this fool fled to the far corners of the world, leaving the Mother to slumber through the coming apocalypse? Ahiga waged an internal war, each side marshaling its forces. What should he do?

The whelp trotted up the shore. He would be out of sight soon, breaking the visual link Ahiga needed to invade his mind. He must act quickly if he were to act at all. Would this betrayal haunt him later? Could the whelp accept him as a teacher after such a violation? It didn't matter. He *must* learn where the whelp was going. He reached deep into the well of power within himself, pulling forth a thick surge that resonated through him.

Ahiga channeled his will into a spike, focusing upon the whelp to the exclusion of all else. Then he struck, piercing the whelp's pitiful defenses and slipping into his mind. The world disappeared, replaced by a flowing sea of memory. Experiences flitted by like birds, fluttering about in a multicolored storm. He ignored most, sifting through the mass to reach the most recent.

Something flashed by and he snagged it between two fingers, pausing to examine the memory. It showed a female shifting. The whelp wasn't alone. Why hadn't he spotted the female? Had she already mastered the shadows? Ahiga sifted more memories. Liz, that was her name. Blair, that of the whelp. They were running, hard and fast like prey before the hunt. Just like prey, running would mean their destruction unless he somehow intervened.

Where were they going? Ahiga sifted again, this time latching onto a snippet of conversation. Acapulco, a city to the north. They planned to travel by ship. Very well, he could do the same. He would catch them in Acapulco. The whelp would return to the Mother no matter the cost.

Who are you? a voice thundered. The memories scattered, leaving Ahiga standing on an obsidian slab stretching to the horizon. Above him loomed the host he'd invaded. The whelp's eyes glittered with righteous rage, and he stood ready despite his ignorance. Even the whelp's instincts might be dangerous in the confines of his own mind. He held all the advantages here.

I am Ahiga. It means one who fights, he explained, sketching a bow. Respect was the only thing that might salvage things. *Please accept my sincere apologies for touching your mind without permission. The need is dire enough that I have broken one of our greatest taboos. You must come to me, Blair. You have set great events in motion and time grows short. The Mother must be awakened.*

You're talking about the woman in the pyramid, aren't you? he asked, stance softening just a little.

Yes, and she can only be awakened by one who shares a link with the Ark. A link you forged when you touched the Mother's hand, Ahiga explained, reaching for words Blair might grasp. He sank into a cross-legged position and gestured for Blair to do the same. *Please, there is much you need to know. I cannot maintain this link long. Sit. Join me.*

Even if I wanted to wake her, I can't, Blair explained, ignoring the proffered spot. *She's surrounded by soldiers. Going back would get me killed.*

It will be dangerous, but you do not grasp the severity of the situation, Ahiga replied, anger bubbling up. He struggled to keep it from his voice, with limited success. *If we do not wake the Mother, the world is doomed. Countless unblooded will fall to the enemy, each victim increasing their strength. If you continue to flee, this fate is inevitable. Can you live with that, whelp? It will be your fault.*

My fault? Blair thundered. His beast must have sunk deep roots for him to be able to summon so much rage this soon after his bonding. *You've turned me into a monster. I've slaughtered women. Children. Not an hour ago, Liz killed a man whose only crime was helping a couple of strangers. I don't know what you did, but I'm going to find a way to undo it. Tell me, if I help you wake this Mother, can she cure me?*

Cure? Are you mad? Of course not, Ahiga replied. He rose gracefully to his feet. There was no reaching the whelp.

Then I want nothing to do with you, the whelp thundered. A sudden gale sprang up, whipping at Ahiga with incredibly fury. It picked him up, hurling him from the whelp's mind.

32

SURPRISE GUESTS

J ordan shook his head, marveling at the three-story structure squatting at the base of the pyramid's exterior. It hadn't existed the previous morning. An army of black-uniformed Mohn employees had used a gigantic 3D printer to construct pieces. Like toddlers with Legos, they then assembled their field headquarters. They'd even found time to erect a small array of satellite dishes atop the roof. The dishes were aimed at the angry black clouds blanketing the sky. A storm was coming. How appropriate.

"Sir," one of two gate guards said. Both snapped to attention as Jordan ducked under the doorway and into Ops. It was far more organized than the pavilion had been, with techs hurrying between machines. They were analyzing all the data gathered thus far. They'd learned nothing significant from what he could tell.

Jordan wove through rows of tables, angling for the one furthest from the door. Sheila hunched over a desk, open manila folders scattered everywhere. He picked up a photo from the one closest to him. It was some of the vivid hieroglyphs discovered in the main chamber. "This is Professor Smith's work. Have you had any luck with his notes?"

"Some," Sheila drawled in her peculiar yet endearing way. "I don't have a true translation since we lack their alphabet, but the fact that they used pictograms is helpful. Blair laid the groundwork for a few dozen symbols, and I've expanded on that. I've focused mostly on the inner chamber, and I don't like what I'm learning. I'm starting to suspect why this place was built, but I'm not confident enough to share the research with the team. I need more data."

"What does your gut tell you?" he asked. Science was great, but it was intuition that had kept him alive.

"That we've stumbled into something we don't understand," she said, spinning her chair around to face him. She straightened her glasses. "This place is massive. It's clear from the sarcophagus chamber that this place is much bigger than we initially guessed. We have no idea how deep underground it goes. Building something like this would take the concerted effort of nations to duplicate today, assuming we could even do it." Her face paled. "I've also realized something, and it scares me. We dated the pyramid by the sediment it was buried in, but the truth is we have no idea how long it was buried. This thing's true age could be much older than the thirteen-thousand-year-old sediment layer."

"How much older?" he asked, unsure why she was alarmed. To him old was old. What did a few millennia matter, give or take?

"I don't know. What I do know is that they clearly intended for it to awaken at a specific date and time. The question is why. What was significant about that date?" she asked, though he sensed the question was rhetorical. Obviously she had a theory. Sheila plowed on. "You have to have heard all that garbage about 2012 being the end of the world. What a lot of people don't know is why that year matters so much. It marks the end of the long count in the Mayan calendar. According to their mythology, it marked the end of the old world and the beginning of the new, and they weren't the only ones to leap to that conclusion."

Pieces clicked together in Jordan's head. It wasn't accidental that Mohn had sent them to an empty ravine just moments before the pyramid had appeared. Somehow his employers had known to expect it. That suggested they knew something about Sheila's mysterious date.

"Have you ever heard that old song, 'The Age of Aquarius'?" she asked, humming the name of the song to a very familiar melody. Jordan's mother had loved the musical *Hair*, so he'd heard the song often, growing up.

"Yeah, I know it," he said, stroking the stubble he hadn't had time to deal with. "What does a bad song from the '60s have to do with this ancient culture?"

"The Age of Aquarius is supposed to begin soon, or to have already begun. Scholars hotly debate when we'll enter it. It's part of something called the Galactic Procession, divided into thirteen parts. Each corresponds to a Zodiac sign," she explained, bouncing in her chair excitedly. "Each sign lasts about two thousand years, which means we complete a galactic rotation once every twenty-six thousand years. The Mayans knew that. So did the Greeks. So did a lot of ancient cultures. What if that knowledge trickled down from this ancient culture? What if the pyramid came back at this time for a reason? It could have been programmed, for lack of a better term, to return when the new age began."

"It clearly had a trigger of some sort, but why come back now? What exactly happens when we enter a new age? And why leave a trap that turns people into werewolves?" Jordan asked, leaning against her desk and crossing his arms over his chest. "There are dozens of sightings already. From Mexico to Argentina. There was even an attack in Texas at a clinic. The media had a field day with that one."

Sheila paled at his last words, avoiding his gaze. She seemed to collect herself after a moment.

"I have a theory about why the werewolves were created," Sheila said softly. She looked shaken. "Blair's notes mention some sort of ancient enemy. What if the werewolves were engineered to fight something?"

"Like what?" he replied, chilled at the possibility of an enemy that required such a ferocious creation.

"I don't know. Blair was still working with that part, and I haven't had a lot of luck. But the answer is in there somewhere," she said, brow furrowing. That simple gesture said more about her level of frustration than cursing would. "I wish I had some help. There's just too much ground to cover. I wish Blair was here. Or even Steve."

"What if I could get you that help?" he asked. It was a gamble the Director might not like, but if it gave them answers, it would be worth it.

"Then I'd say get it. I don't know that you're going to find someone as good as Blair though," she replied, turning back to the files on her desk.

"Sheila, come with me," he said, resting a hand on her shoulder to get her attention. She was already engrossed in her work again.

"Hmm? Where are we going?" she asked, finally looking up.

"I have something to show you. I could get in a lot of trouble for this, but I think it might provide the answers you need," he said, voice low so none of the surrounding techs could hear. "Come on. Follow me."

He offered a hand and helped her to her feet. The pair threaded back through the desks, unnoticed by the small army of drone-like techs. They had been assigned unrealistic workloads that would consume their attention entirely. Jordan and Sheila reached the exit without being noticed. The guards snapped to attention but said nothing as they passed.

"Where are we going?" Sheila hissed, darting a nervous glance back at the guards. "I'm not supposed to leave without authorization."

"Are you willing to take a risk?" he asked, slowing his pace to give her time to think.

"Yes. I'm not getting anywhere, so if you have anything that might help, I want it. I'll take the risk." She delivered the words with a tight nod.

"Good. We're heading into the stockade," he said, steering her toward the squat black building. It lacked windows and had one shiny metallic door. "They'll let me in, and I doubt they'll ask about you. If they do, you're here to examine the prisoners, all right?"

"Prisoners?" she asked, brow furrowing again as she considered his words. The mannerism made her resemble an owl. She snapped her fingers in sudden understanding. "You caught one of them. We have a live specimen, don't we?"

"You'll see soon enough," he replied, striding boldly up to the pair of guards at attention outside the stockade. These were more alert, assessing his threat level even though they recognized him, as their training demanded. He stopped before the pair. "I'm accessing the prisoners in cell six. I expect to be inside for no more than twenty minutes."

"Yes, sir," one guard barked, words clipped as tightly as the man's shaved head. "Per regulations, all visitors must be logged. Please sign this." He offered a clipboard, which Jordan signed after a cursory examination. He handed it to Sheila, who added her signature. That would be damning evidence later.

"You're clear, sir," the soldier said, taking a step back and opening the door with a sharp hiss. He gestured inside.

Jordan plunged forward, shoulders squared with every bit of the authority he could muster. Sheila followed behind, clearly nervous. He hoped they'd chalk that up to the idea of examining werewolves. The door snapped shut behind them, sealing itself with a series of clicks. Inside lay a single long corridor that stretched the length of the building. It was lined with doors at ten-foot intervals, each set with a two-way mirror to allow the captors to observe their prisoners without their knowledge.

He strode boldly down the hall, noting Sheila's gaze as it swept between the cells they passed. All were empty, save for the last one at the end of the hall. That's where Jordan finally stopped, gesturing at the mirror to allow his companion to study the occupants. Sheila adjusted her glasses as she peered into the featureless cell. Two figures sat on the padded floor. They were at opposite ends of the room, clearly trying to stay as far from one another as possible.

"Is that? Jordan, it can't be. What am I seeing?" Sheila asked, her weight sagging against him as shock overcame her.

"Exactly what you think you see. That's Bridget. And Steve," he explained, supporting her. Both the occupants wore plain white hospital gowns, but their faces were unmistakable. She had to recognize them. "They rose the morning after the initial attack. Steve was easy enough to take down, but Bridget took out three of my men before she could be contained. Our initial findings suggest females are larger and a great deal more violent than males, though we have no idea why."

"I...Why are you showing me this?" Sheila asked, finally supporting her own weight. She was still watching the prisoners.

"You said you needed help. This is it. They can help you solve the language problem, to find out what we're dealing with," he said, leaning over to push the red button next to the door before she could protest. "Steve, I'm here with Sheila. She has a request she'd like to make."

At the sound of Jordan's voice, Steve leapt to his feet so swiftly Sheila stumbled back from the door. He was a different man than he had been at the initial dig site. More confident, calm, and self-possessed. He emanated strength. Bridget didn't react at all, just huddled in the corner with her head pressed against her knees.

"Hello, Jordan," he said, tone that of a dinner party host welcoming his guests. He took a step closer to the window. "Hello, Sheila. Are you trying to open the Mother's sarcophagus? If so, you're out of luck. It's genetically locked to the person who bonded the Ark. No Blair, no Mother."

"Why would we want to wake up whoever's in there?" Jordan countered. "Thus far, the people who built this place have managed to unleash a plague that could wipe out our civilization unless we find a way to stop it. Do you really think waking up the woman who might have caused it is a good idea?"

"More importantly," Sheila said, breaking in before Steve could reply, "who is the Mother, and how do you know anything about her? Or that Blair is the one who can open her sarcophagus? What the hell is a genetic lock?"

"She told me," he said, predatory grin spreading. It took a lot to rattle Jordan, but this guy did it. "She touched my mind. She's still asleep, but even now her will is so powerful that it bleeds out and touches everyone around her. Have you had dreams lately, Sheila? I know you have..."

"Commander Jordan, this is Ops. We have a situation. Are you on the line?" the radio at Jordan's side blared, breaking off all conversation. He snatched it from his belt and thumbed the receiver.

"This is Jordan. Go ahead," he replied, thumbing the red button to kill the feed into the cell.

"We just intercepted a local police call in a small town near the Peruvian coast. A woman claims two foreigners turned up on her doorstep in the middle of the night. One turned into a monster and killed her husband," the voice explained. It was a balding tech named Sandoval.

"How is this attack any different than the dozens of others?" Jordan asked, irritation leaking into his voice. He eyed Steve through the mirror. He was certain the man, even in a sealed cell, knew he and Sheila were still there.

"Sir, they described the two people. One of them is Subject Alpha."

33

THE BOAT

Blair stared down at the white-tipped waves, hands braced on the ship's chrome railing. Thick spray washed over him, smelling of salt and brine. It felt wonderful. It tasted of freedom. He inhaled deeply, smiling up at the moon's thickening crescent. There was movement behind him.

"I'm sorry." Liz's voice was soft enough that he might have missed it if not for his augmented hearing. "About the other day, when we woke up. I mean, how I reacted."

Blair turned to face her, reply lost. He couldn't help but stare. The moonlight polished her eyes to brilliant sapphires and painted her river of bronze hair into platinum. She was a wholly different person than he'd met what felt a lifetime ago but was, in reality, a handful of days. The change was not just physical, though she'd changed dramatically in that way too. Soft curves had transformed into the toned muscles of a lifelong athlete, just as his own body had transformed.

The changes went deeper though. The determination and borderline hostility in her gaze had softened, hinting at a vulnerability he doubted she'd ever willingly show him, or anyone for that matter. Though he'd only known her briefly, he had the sense that she prided herself on being self-sufficient. She'd have to be to travel South America as a lone foreign woman. That took a mix of courage and savvy.

"For pelting me in the face with a rock?" Blair said, flashing a grin. He leaned back against the railing, exalting in the spray as another wave crashed against the bow of the freighter. "Can't really blame you for that, given that you woke up naked next to a man you didn't really know."

The moonlight hid her blush, if there was one. She momentarily averted her gaze before replying. "Still, I shouldn't have taken it out on you. You're just as much a victim of this whole thing as I am."

"Don't I know it," Blair said, snorting as she moved to the railing next to him.

Silence stretched as she stared out over the waves, wind playing with her hair in a way that made his hands twitch. He wondered what it felt like. Blair glanced up to the higher deck, but other than the bearded captain steering the boat they were completely alone. He was out of earshot, giving them as much privacy as they could really expect.

"I've been doing a lot of thinking," she said, glancing at him as she spoke. She brushed away a lock of hair that had blown into her face, "about what we've become and how it happened. About this pyramid and why it might have come back now. Have you ever wondered about all the myths about werewolves and elves and vampires? I think there's more truth in them than we ever could have guessed. What if our legends are half-remembered stories?"

"I think that's a bit of a stretch," Blair said, caught a bit off guard by the question. During all the running, he hadn't thought much about the origins of the werewolves. "Not the werewolves, obviously, but vampires or elves. I haven't seen anything to suggest either exist."

"You have to wonder at least. This pyramid turns everything we know on its head. If werewolves exist, why not other mythological creatures?" she said, delivering a slight smile. "There's a lot more to the universe than most people are willing to admit. Do you know why I was in Peru to begin with?"

"I've been wondering," Blair admitted. He turned around, resting his forearms on the railing as he turned his gaze to the ocean. It glittered under the caress of the moon, like a field of carelessly discarded diamonds.

"I came to meet with a shaman, a spirit guide who helps the locals," she admitted, eyeing him sidelong as if waiting for a reaction. He said nothing. "I took ayahuasca. I went on a spirit quest."

"So you believe in all that supernatural stuff then?" he said, before he could catch the words. Her face hardened, mask back in place immediately.

"Yeah, I believe in that woo-woo stuff," she shot back, tone heated. "You can make fun of it if you want, but there's a lot more to it than just superstition and mumbo jumbo."

"Next you're going to tell me you think the pyramids were built by aliens," Blair said, rolling his eyes. He didn't want to slight her beliefs, but he'd dealt with this uninformed crap for too many years.

"Who's to say they weren't? Or if not aliens, then something modern people would consider to be magic," Liz said, brushing her hair from her face again.

"History," Blair countered, moderating her tone. If he wanted her to listen, he couldn't be an ass about this. "We know when and how the pyramids were built. We've even found a complex built by Pharaoh Khufu to house the workers who did it. We've been able to piece together their lives, from the beer they drank to the games they played. The Egyptians were very meticulous in their record keeping."

"What about Abu Gorash?" she asked, eyes alight with triumph.

Blair was taken aback. Very few people knew about Abu Gorash, the pyramid atop a mountain, so remote that almost no tourists visited it. The stonework was so fine that it appeared to have been machined.

"I watched a documentary on the pyramids, on Netflix. It said that the pyramids were used as a power source and that you can still feel the electrical charge at their tips. Even if that wasn't true, how did the Egyptians get all those stone blocks to the top of a mountain?" she said, clearly enjoying herself now. "Magic, or something we'd consider to be magic. We haven't had any proof that it exists, at least until now. You said the pyramid you discovered is larger than the Egyptian ones and that it caused an earthquake, right? How much more proof do you need?"

"That's true," he admitted, considering the notion. Could she be right? It just wasn't possible. There was too much proof showing that the Egyptians had used conventional labor to build their monuments. "It's possible the Egyptians were aping an earlier culture, but their work is elementary compared to what we found in those mountains. Clearly this culture had technology so advanced we might call it magic, but if the Egyptians did, why was their work so primitive in comparison? Why did future cultures not use this 'magic'?"

"Maybe some of them did," Liz said, giving a pleased smile. "The Mayans built pyramids. The Celts built Stonehenge. What about the moai statues on Easter Island? There's evidence all around us."

"Okay, let's say you're right. You're not—we have too much evidence to the contrary—but let's say, for the sake of argument, that all these places were built with magic," Blair allowed, crossing his arms and giving a smile of his own. He had her now. "What happened to the magic, Liz? Why did these cultures stop using it? Why don't we use it today? People all over the world call themselves magicians or shamans, but not a single one anywhere can demonstrate anything concrete. They're not throwing fireballs or conjuring demons. They're not healing the sick or levitating twenty-ton stone blocks through the air. Why not, Liz?"

She was quiet for a long moment, staring up at the moon while she bit her lower lip. Then she straightened suddenly, eyes alight as she turned back to him. "This pyramid came *now*, of all the times it could have appeared. You remember all those 2012 prophecies, that the world was going to end? It was based on the Mayans; their calendar ended in 2012."

"I'm familiar with it. They called it the long count," Blair said, quirking an eyebrow. "I don't see where you're going with this."

"The Mayans believed time was circular, that it flowed in a great cycle. So what if magic is a part of this cycle, that it comes and goes," she said, as excited as Blair had ever seen her. Liz's energy reminded him a little of Bridget. "Maybe magic has been gone for a really long time, thousands of years. We have legends about it, but people today can't duplicate it because it's been gone for some reason."

"And you think it's back now?" Blair asked. He wasn't sure what to think. On the one hand, it sounded crazy. It was just the sort of ratio-nalized pseudo-science that he'd contended with his entire career. On the other hand, he'd turned into a *werewolf*, and a pyramid from the Mesolithic had appeared all on its own. Like magic.

"Exactly. Maybe it's been building up slowly and we've hit some sort of tipping point," she said. It was obviously a topic she was passionate about, and that passion made her even more beautiful. "If it's cyclic, maybe the magic got weaker, and that's why by the time the Egyptians built the pyramids, they had to do a lot of it with conven-tional labor. That explains the evidence you said we've found. It could also explain why they built them to conduct energy. Magic."

"If you're right, if there is some sort of energy we'd think of as magic, then that makes a kind of sense," Blair said. He didn't like where this was going, but he couldn't fault her logic. "If it was fading away, then the Pyramids could have focused what remained. Maybe it was a last gambit to keep their magic alive. The Pyramids were built during the fourth dynasty, what we call the Old Kingdom. Maybe they worked for a little while, but by the time the Middle Kingdom rolled around, they were just lumps of stone. That could also explain why they don't have any adornment inside. The Egyptians love to decorate their monuments, but the insides of the Pyramids are completely bare. If they were functional, not decorative, that would make sense."

"We'd have to rethink history," Liz said, with a genuine smile. "Every ancient civilization has their myths about magic. Atlantis. King Arthur. Ancestor worship. Gaining strength through human sacrifice. What if all those legends are based on something real? They were real in the beginning, but as magic faded, all the miracles stopped. That's why no one believes in it today."

"This is an interesting theory, but I'm not comfortable calling it magic," Blair said, shaking his head. The boat creaked as it crested a wave. He squinted. There were city lights on the horizon.

"Then what do you want to call it?" Liz asked. She leaned against his shoulder. It wasn't a cold night, but her warmth was welcome for other reasons.

"Something the beast in my head said. Shaping," he said, wondering exactly what the word meant.

34

A SPIRAL

Ahiga laboriously placed the last stone, as large as a man's head. He added it to the growling spiral, hot sand kissing his bare feet as he completed the spiral's third revolution. It was far larger than the ones he'd created in ages past, but power was thin, and he needed all the focus the stones could provide. It was the only way to accomplish what he must.

He shaded his eyes against the harsh sun, large in the sky over the western horizon. It nearly touched the water, its yellow brilliance already fading to orange. Soon it would become red; then it would vanish into the ocean, like some slowly cooling ember. Already, the moon hung in the sky, the fat crescent pale and weak. Drowned out by the sun's lingering majesty.

Ahiga took slow, deliberate steps across the sand. He followed the spiral inward, his breathing shallow as he approached the center. When he reached it he squatted, knees out-thrust slightly with his forearms resting against his thighs. He closed his eyes, crouched at the exact center of the spiral. The apex of the power it could provide.

"What are you doing?" a voice said, the high shrill of a young child.

Ahiga's eyes snapped open, and he turned his gaze on the unexpected interruption. The beach was empty save for a small girl of perhaps six or seven. She wore a bright-blue bathing suit, and her long, dark hair sent runnels of water down her bare shoulders. Too young to fear a stranger and armed with all the curiosity such a young child could muster, she watched him with large, dark eyes.

He scanned the beach and spied two figures in the distance. A bare-chested man sat on a bright-red blanket while his mate emerged from the deep-green waves. She wore tiny white garments that barely covered her chest and crotch, highlighting bronzed curves rather than hiding them. The child bore a strong resemblance, the same hair and heart-shaped face.

"I am gathering power," Ahiga told the child, turning his attention back to her. She was too young to accept the gift.

The child's parents are of the age, his beast rumbled, voice echoing through his mind. *They could be slain quickly.*

He considered that option; then discarded it. Imparting the gift would cost both power and time, and he had precious little of either. He would need all that he possessed for the ritual he must enact. He had to know how quickly the champions were spreading. More importantly, he had to locate the whelp, or all would be lost.

"No, you aren't," the child said, planting her hands on hips. "You're just playing with rocks."

He blinked, taken aback. Few among the blooded questioned his word. None among the unblooded would dare. Yet here was this simple child doing just that. Ahiga leaned his head back and laughed.

"I am, child. These stones help to focus my power. They will enable me to perform a ritual of great power, one that will send my consciousness winging across the sky. Higher than any bird can soar," he said, though he knew she couldn't possibly understand what he was doing.

"The rocks are going to help you fly?" the child asked, her tone dubious. "People can't fly. Not like birds. We have to take an airplane."

Ahiga didn't need to pluck the concept from her mind to understand. The strange silver birds in the sky were conveyances, carrying people from land to land with shocking speed. He'd already puzzled that much out.

"I will show you," he said, closing his eyes. Establishing a link to the child's mind took a bare trickle of energy compared to the vast expenditure required by the ritual.

He focused on the first stone, feeling the weight and substance of it with his mind. Then the second. Then the third. Faster and faster, he touched them, working his way outward across the spire. The world faded away, the crashing of the waves and the hot sand gone as he rose from his body and into the sky. He could see pinpricks of light dotting the world beneath him, dozens of them.

They radiated out from the Ark, like the arms of an octopus. One arm curled down into the River of Life and the vast jungle that surrounded it. The rest snaked through the mountains, toward the ocean, growing wider as they reached the strangely sprawling cities. Excellent. Many had reached large population centers, and that meant the champions could spread swiftly.

The lights closer to the Ark pulsed strongly, while many of those in the cities were weaker. Each indicated the relative strength of a champion. None were potent enough to be the whelp he sought, but then he hadn't expected them to be. Ahiga cast his will north, across the waves. He followed them until he found a pair of lights in the vast ocean of darkness. They blazed like the full moon, both potent. The whelp and his direct progeny.

He studied the ocean around them, casting his will still further north until he located the land they would arrive in. It had housed a great empire in his day, but the climate had shifted dramatically over the millennia. Arid plains were now choked with jungle, and only a few cities dotted the land. That was good, in a way. It limited the destinations the whelp could be seeking. The tall structures dotting the beaches must be this *Acapulco* he had plucked from the whelp's mind. Their vessel crawled sluggishly toward it, perhaps a day or two away from the crowded port.

It would cost him, but Ahiga could move far more swiftly than they. Wolves were strong swimmers, especially when fueled by the power of the moon. He would reach this city on the heels of his quarry. Ahiga released the vision, returning to his body with a dizzying sense of vertigo.

He opened his eyes, unsurprised to find the child slack-jawed and gaping at him. Her chin quivered, eyes even larger. She backed a step away, turned abruptly, and started sprinting across the sand to her parents. She began to wail, terrified by the vision he'd shared with her.

Ahiga smiled and then rose from the spiral and strode toward the water. He hated swimming, especially across such a vast distance. Would that he possessed a slipsail. He chided himself for the thought. There was no sense lamenting what he did not have.

Ahiga dove into the water, energy flowing through his body as he began the change.

35

ACAPULCO

Blair peered through the filmy cab window as it rumbled to a halt outside the Crowne Plaza, a towering structure with sloped sides, a little too reminiscent of a pyramid. Palm trees decorated with streams of hanging lights blazed away on the walk outside the building, which perched in opulence on the boardwalk along Av Costera Miguel Aléman, the main artery running through Acapulco. A 747 dipped across the sky, disappearing somewhere to the north.

"This is it," Liz said, squeezing Blair's arm. She leaned forward to speak to the driver. "Cuánto te debo?" The two had a rapid exchange. The driver seemed angry, and Liz had gone tense. Blair wished again that he'd paid a little more attention in his high school Spanish classes.

"He says it's thirteen pesos for each of us, and he won't take the money we brought from Peru. He will take American currency though," she explained, opening the cab door and slipping out. She leaned her head back into the car. "I'm going to run inside and grab the package my brother sent. Then we can pay the cab and get our room. I told him you'd stay here." She slammed the door, hurrying up the walk and disappearing through the glass doors into the hotel.

Slay this wretch, Ka-Dun. He should be honored to render service for the blooded. If he will not serve in life, let him serve in death.

"I'm not going to kill the man to save a few pesos," Blair whispered under his breath. The driver had sharp ears, his gaze shooting up to the rearview mirror when Blair spoke. The man probably thought he was crazy. He might not be wrong.

They waited in silence for an eternity, just Blair and the driver. The cab had been considerably more crowded, but apparently theirs was the man's last stop. The system was an odd one. The cabs just kept picking up passengers until they were full, more like a bus than an American taxi. Of course, they were also really cheap, which was a very good thing for people with limited means. What little cash they had wasn't going to get them far, unless Liz's brother had sent them enough to afford airfare to northern Mexico. Staying at the Crowne Plaza seemed an unnecessary waste, but because Liz's brother was paying for it, Blair supposed he shouldn't complain.

He lost himself in the drone of car horns and the steady stream of drunken tourists winding their way down the boulevard. This city had a reputation for never sleeping, and from what he saw of the clubs they'd passed, he found the reputation to be well earned. Hundreds of bikini-clad women and bare-chested men clogged the streets as far as the eye could see, most cradling brightly colored plastic glasses. It reminded him a great deal of the Vegas Strip, though most of the people were darker skinned and probably didn't speak much English.

Within minutes a familiar heartbeat approached. Blair looked up to see Liz, her bulky white blouse and matronly skirt decidedly out of place amidst the frolicking tourists. She clutched a rubber-band-wrapped bundle in one hand, pausing to withdraw a twenty-dollar bill as she stopped next to the cab's now open window. Blair popped open the door and joined her on the curb as she settled their fare with the driver. He handed back a wad of brightly colored Mexican bills and then sped off before Liz had a chance to count them. The battered cab left a cloud of acrid exhaust in its wake, disappearing into the cacophony of the busy thoroughfare.

"How much did your brother send us?" Blair asked as the two headed up the walkway, toward the lobby.

"A thousand dollars," Liz answered, pausing to thread around a cluster of drunken teenagers. "That should be enough to get us some new clothes and tickets to Tijuana. Trevor will meet us at the border into San Diego. From there we should be able to find a lab and hopefully get some answers."

"You think it will be that easy?" Blair asked, dropping his voice as the sliding glass doors closed behind them. The lobby was like a library compared to the oppressive noise outside. "I'm still not sure they're going to let me on a plane without some sort of identification."

"You'll find that Mexico is quite a bit different than the states," Liz said, beaming a grin at him. It was the first time he could remember her smiling. "The corruption here is more or less the same, but they're a lot more blatant about it. If we slip the clerk some cash, they'll overlook your lack of ID, at least as long as we're only flying within the county. I *do* think it will be that easy. Mohn has no idea where we are. We've got money, and we've got a plan. Things are going to work out."

Blair returned the smile, though privately he still had his doubts. He trailed after Liz as she strode boldly to the concierge. He was a short, wiry man with slicked-back hair and a neatly trimmed goatee. His clothing was in sharp contrast to the tourists', a white dress shirt with the first two buttons undone and a pair of tight-fitting black slacks. He leaned forward on the marble countertop, ready to serve as they approached.

"Good evening, Ms. Gregg," he said with the grace of one well trained to serve. He gestured toward the elevators on the far side of the lobby. "I've taken the liberty of preparing your room. Take those elevators to the seventeenth floor and turn right. You're in 1706. Is there anything else I might provide to make your stay more enjoyable?"

"Is there a place we can pick up some clothes? I know it's late," Liz asked, gesturing at her travel-stained blouse.

"Of course, Ms. Gregg. The hotel gift shop is open until eleven p.m. You'll find suitable attire there. Toiletries are available in the room, and if you need anything further, please don't hesitate to call the front desk. We're happy to provide you with whatever you require," he said, clearly admiring Liz's figure. Not that Blair could blame the man.

They walked to the center of the marble floor, traffic flowing around them as they got their bearings.

"There it is. I'd kill to get out of these clothes. Let's see what we can find," Liz said, heading in the direction of a large shop with wide windows. Through the glass, he could see an array of t-shirts, stuffed bears, and all the other crap one would expect of a tourist trap.

Fifteen minutes later they boarded the elevator with an armload of bags. Blair had selected a black shirt with palm trees and the word *Acapulco* emblazoned across the chest. A pair of sandals and comfortable swim trunks completed his purchases. All the other bags belonged to Liz, who'd bought two full changes of clothing and a green bikini that he hoped she would have a chance to wear. The elevator dinged, and the doors slid closed. It rose smoothly, numbers ticking by until it stopped on the seventeenth floor. They exited onto a plush green carpet that could have been installed the day before.

Blair picked out a sign that indicated their block of rooms lay to the right. They wound up the hallway, too exhausted to speak as they passed the last fifty feet to relative safety. He could scarcely believe it when they reached the matte-black door with a bronze placard that read *1706*. Liz slid in the white keycard, and a green light above the lock flared. She pushed the door open, revealing a spacious room with two queen-sized beds. Blair tossed his packages on the floor near the closest bed, flopping onto the floral comforter and relaxing against the pillows. Liz sat heavily on her bed, massaging her neck as the door clicked shut behind them.

"I can't believe we made it," Blair said, rising restlessly to his feet. They were here; why couldn't he enjoy it? He crossed the room and pulled open a white curtain to reveal a narrow balcony with two patio chairs and a small glass-topped table. The city blazed beneath them, thousands of tourists completely unaware that a pair of werewolves had just arrived in their midst. "So, your brother is going to meet us in Tijuana, right? Have you told him about our...situation?"

"Sure, I told him we're werewolves," Liz said, rolling her eyes. She removed her hand from her neck and rose to join him at the balcony. He slid the door open, and they stepped into the balmy night. The city flowed below them, and they took in the noise of car horns and laughter. Neon lights and people flirting. "How would you react if someone told you that? Trevor is the consummate scientist. He's even more of a skeptic than you are. He'll believe it if I can show him proof, but if I told him now, he'd just assume it was the ayahuasca."

"He knew why you went to Peru?" Blair asked. The way she'd described her brother, Blair expected him to be straight laced and anti-drug. Most of the academics Blair knew were like that, at least the ones involved in the hard sciences and higher math. A few were okay with marijuana, but they wouldn't be caught dead near anything more exotic.

"Yeah, and he isn't much surprised. Trevor is no saint either. Besides, in this case he knows it wasn't for recreational use. I came down to get my head on straight," she said, trailing off. Her eyes narrowed, back straightening as she turned to face the door to the hallway.

Blair cocked his head, listening. What had she heard? There it was, footsteps approaching. It was possible the passerby was just some hotel guest finding the right room, but they'd both seen too much to assume that to be the case. Besides, whomever it was moved with near silence, breathing and heartbeat measured. Controlled. The footsteps stopped outside their door. Liz and Blair both jumped when three sharp raps sounded.

"Should we run?" Liz mouthed. She pointed over the balcony, clearly contemplating the impossible. Seventeen stories. Their healing was miraculous, but could they recover from something like that?

"No one knows we're here except your brother, right?" he whispered. She nodded her agreement.

Another series of raps. Blair steeled himself and crossed the room to the door. He stared through the peephole, intrigued by the figure on the other side of the door. It was a tall man in his late fifties with long silver hair and weathered features. His eyes were a sharp, clear grey and held the weight of ages. He'd seen those eyes before, but he couldn't recall where.

"Please open the door. I know you're standing there," the man said, words precisely clipped as if they weren't in his native tongue. Blair couldn't place the accent.

He rested his hand on the knob, hesitating before turning it. The door clicked open, and he stepped back to get a better view of the man. There was something infuriatingly familiar about him, but Blair just couldn't place it.

"May I enter?" he asked, sketching an odd little bow.

"Who are you?" Blair demanded, tensing and readying to shift if need be. He doubted the man worked for Mohn, but trust was a precious commodity. He was aware of Liz behind him. Her heart beat swiftly as she moved closer to the door.

"My name is Ahiga," he said, delivering another shallow bow. "I am a champion, like you. What you know as a werewolf."

36

MORE QUESTIONS

B lair shifted his gaze to Liz, arching an eyebrow. She gave a tight nod, standing on the balls of her feet as if prepared for a fight. He turned back to Ahiga, opening the door wide and gesturing for the old man to enter. The old man moved with the grace of a predator, stalking a path to the plush chair in the corner.

Atop the chair, the old man drew his legs underneath him as Blair and Liz each sat on their respective beds. He took several moments to compose himself, avoiding eye contact until he'd finished. Then those piercing grey eyes flashed up, hard as ice.

"How did you find us?" Blair asked, seizing the initiative. The old man's gaze tightened as he discarded whatever he'd been about to say.

"With great difficulty," he admitted, a frown creasing his weathered face. "I have spent nearly an entire lunar cycle chasing you. This is a delay we can ill afford. Events spiral out of control. We *must* wake the Mother so preparations can begin."

"Yeah, you said pretty much exactly the same thing back in Peru. When you got inside my head," Blair shot back, spearing the old man with his gaze. He crossed his arms, leaning back into the pillows.

"We'll get to that. First, answer my question. How did you know how to find us here?"

"I plucked the destination from your mind," the old man explained. His expression softened, just for an instant. "What I have done brings me great shame, yet I had no other choice. I had to find you, Blair Smith. Through happenstance, or perhaps fate, you have become the locus of events. The arbiter of the future, to either usher in an age of darkness or be the last guttering candle sheltering mankind from its black embrace. Melodramatic, I realize, but true nevertheless."

"You've been here about two minutes, and I've already had enough of this Yoda crap," Liz interrupted, snatching her purse from the bed as she stalked to the balcony. She withdrew a pack of cigarettes she'd bought in the gift shop, tapping one into her hand. It was the first time Blair had seen her smoke. A nervous habit? "I'll accept that you're from the past, some immortal werewolf or something. What I don't buy is that you have some benevolent purpose. You've turned us into *killing machines*. We slaughter relentlessly. Without mercy. Why? What could they possibly have done to make you want to kill them so indiscriminately?"

"I understand that it is difficult to understand. Your culture clearly places a high value on life, something that I would normally say is laudable," the man said, crossing his arms as he stared dispassionately at Liz. Blair got the sense that he was annoyed, though he seemed like he was struggling to contain it. "You cannot possibly understand what is coming, why our kind were created, or what we shield the world from. I will answer all your questions, but all you need understand right now is that every moment is precious. We must return to the land you call Peru. We must go now."

Blair leaned forward, catching the old man's gaze. "If waking this *Mother* is so important, then convincing me to help you is critical, right? You want my help? Then you'd better become a whole lot more talkative. Answer our questions; help us understand what we've become. How to control the thing inside us. Then maybe, just maybe, talk about helping you. Right now we don't know you, and we *certainly* don't trust you. You could be lying to get us to wake this woman so she can end the world. Hell, it seems like we're already off to a good start, and we haven't even woken her up yet."

"You are right," the old man replied, heaving a sigh. He wore the weariness of a man assigned an impossible task with an unrealistic deadline. "I have gone about this badly, but I was woefully unprepared for such a turn of events. When the Ark opened, I was to wake the Mother from her slumber. It was my purpose, the reason I was left as guardian. I spent countless centuries meditating, drawing upon the Ark's latent energy to fuel my body. Even still, time has ravaged me. My survival was a near thing.

"When the Ark finally initiated itself, I made the gravest of errors," he said, expression portraying self-inflicted agony now. "I crept to the surface to have a look at this new world. I wanted to see what remained. I told myself I'd wake the Mother upon my return. Yet when I reached the surface, the soldiers of Mohn were already there, waiting. Somehow they knew of the Ark's return before it happened. I wished to stay and fight, to drive them from the Ark, but my body bears the terrible weight of years. I fled, ceding control to them."

"So you were locked in the pyramid from the very beginning? That must have been thousands of years," Blair asked once the man paused. He leaned back into the bed, relaxing slightly. He didn't trust the old man. The story sounded plausible, but it did nothing to explain why they'd been transformed into werewolves or why they were compelled to slaughter everyone around them.

"Yes, thirteen thousand by your calendar. Half of the longest count," he said, running bony fingers through his hair. "It was a terrible price to pay, but someone had to be there to wake the Mother. The Ark was damaged, you see. It no longer possessed the capacity to steward the Mother. It needed a living caretaker, one who could activate her rejuvenator at the proper moment."

"Great, so you don't need us," Liz said, leaning back against the balcony. She took a long drag from her cigarette, blowing the smoke over her shoulder. "Just head back and do your job. Wake this Mother and let her do whatever it is that you feel is so important."

"I cannot," he growled, eyes smoldering as a glimmer of life returned. "When this whelp grasped the Mother's Hand he bonded with the Ark. That link overrode my own, and I am too weak to forge another. Only he can deactivate her rejuvenator."

"Okay, so that explains how you found us and what you want from us," Blair said, back stiffening at the bite of the man's words. What right did he have to be angry? He wasn't the one who'd been turned into a killing machine against his will. "Now let's talk about what we want from you. We need to understand what we've become. What happened to me when I touched the statue? Obviously it changed me, but how? Into what?"

"We lack the time for me to relieve you of your ignorance. Suffice it to say that you were given a great gift which allows you to draw on the light of the moon," Ahiga explained. "This energy fuels your shaping, to suffuse your body with the strength of the wolf. In the case of males, it also allows us to shape our surroundings. You have probably already experienced this at least once. If you haven't, you soon will."

"What you're describing sounds like a virus," Liz interjected, tamping her cigarette out on the railing. "It infects the host and modifies our DNA somehow."

"I do not understand this word, 'virus,'" Ahiga said with a shrug, clearly irritated by the idea of not knowing something. "The Mother created the gift. She understands much that I do not. You speak as she does. She, too, is a healer, a learned one."

"What about the voice in our heads?" Blair asked. "It's taken control of me at least once. Will that keep happening?"

"We call it the beast," the old man explained. He rose smoothly to join Liz at the balcony. "It is imparted by the gift. The Mother imbued it with what she called racial memory, though I do not fully understand what she meant by that. The beast is a part of you, both servant and protector. It may seize control in the beginning, but as your will grows, it will yield. Its knowledge can help protect you, if you are wise enough to listen."

"Wise enough to listen?" Blair snapped, surging to his feet and taking a step toward the old man. "It used me to slaughter an entire village. Dozens of people. *That's* what you think we should listen to?"

"Their deaths are insignificant if they birth the champions we need to protect us." The old man rose smoothly to his feet, now just a step away from Blair. His acrid breath stank of decay. Of age.

"So that's what this is about," Blair said, finally understanding. His eyes narrowed. "You want us to make more werewolves. A certain percentage of people killed come back. But most don't, right? What is it, one in ten that survives? The rest just die. That's it, right?"

"More like one in twenty. Less for those killed by weaker bloodlines," Ahiga confirmed. Something unnatural smoldered in his eyes, something Blair could *feel*. "It is a price we pay gladly, for the alternative is unthinkable. If we do not cull them, the enemy will subvert them, increasing their own strength. Of course, you cannot know these things. You have no understanding of the horrors to come. You speak from rationality, wrapped in ignorance of the world's true nature. Make no mistake, whelp. The ancient enemy is coming, and its will is terrifying.

"Already, you can feel its touch on your world," he continued, shifting his attention to Liz. "You are a healer. Tell me, do you know of a disease that attacks the body's ability to defend itself? It would have appeared within the last two or three generations, probably on the continent across the eastern ocean—the birthplace of the ancestors."

"HIV," she answered without hesitation, straightening from the balcony. "You're talking about HIV. The first case was discovered in the late nineteen-sixties. It came from South Africa, and the vast majority of the world's outbreaks are on that continent."

"This disease, this HIV. Let me tell you about it," he growled, taking a step away from Blair to face Liz. "Before I do, I raise a question. How could I possibly know so much about this disease having so recently wakened? Ask yourselves that as I tell you of this disease.

It is transmitted through blood or semen or saliva. It weakens the victim so that they are more susceptible to other sickness. Then, after months or even years, the victim finally dies. Does this sound like your HIV?"

Liz gave Blair a worried look; then she turned back to the old man. "It does. It sounds *exactly* like HIV, right down to the place of origin. So how do you know so much about it if you've been asleep?"

"Because the disease is older than your entire civilization," he answered, raising his arms for emphasis. "It is older even than I. The Mother knows of its creation, though she seldom speaks of it. Ask yourselves, if this disease is so ancient, why did it only just now appear? What is now different about the world?"

"There are a lot of differences," Blair countered angrily. "Whatever you're getting at, just tell us. We don't need this cryptic bullshit. Why has the virus suddenly come back?"

"Plants require the sun for nourishment. Your science tells you this, does it not?" the old man asked, infuriatingly calm as he settled back into the chair.

"You're talking about photosynthesis," Liz interjected from the balcony as she tamped her cigarette out on the railing. "Yes, we're familiar with it."

"This disease is much the same. It requires the sun to survive. It absorbs energy, using it to fuel the destruction of the host. The stronger the energy, the faster the death," Ahiga explained. The old man glanced out the window, in the direction Blair knew to be the moon. "Imagine if the energy from the sun, the lifeblood of this virus, were to suddenly and dramatically increase. What might happen if the disease accelerated? What if it could kill every last host in a single day?"

"That's horrible," Liz said, her concerned glance sweeping the pair of them. "If that's the case, every HIV patient in the world could die. We're talking millions of people."

"You do not yet grasp the full horror, girl. What if the afflicted became a tool of the ancient enemy? They are called deathless for a reason, for after the death of their host they will continue on. A vast army of undead corpses intent on wiping out all life. I can tell you with certainty this will happen, though I know not when," the old man said with a deeply troubled sigh. "The day must be near, or the Ark would not have initiated itself. We will see a gradual shift for a lunar cycle. Perhaps two. Then there will be a sudden explosion of light from the sun. The disease will flourish. This is why we must awaken the Mother. The champions must be there to oppose the enemy, and she must be here to lead us."

"So let me see if I understand this correctly," Blair said, voice heavy with sarcasm. "The sun is going to go into overdrive, and that will kill every HIV patient in the world. Their bodies rise as zombies, becoming some sort of evil army. You want to make a bunch of werewolves to fight them, slaughtering your way though the populace to do it?"

"That's the heart of it, yes."

"Get the fuck out of our hotel room," he growled, close enough to violence that he knew Liz could feel it. He shot her a glance.

"Get out, before we throw you out," Liz hissed, taking a threatening step toward the old man. "Or you're going to regret making more werewolves. We might not know as much as you do, but we can still use our claws."

"You fools!" Ahiga roared, shooting to his feet. He bared his teeth in a snarl and raised a single hand.

A dazzling wave of silvery blue light burst from his palm. It washed over Blair, sinking into his muscles like acid. He screamed, long and loud, until no more breath would come. Then he collapsed bonelessly to the carpet, paralyzed. A moment later, Liz thudded to the floor next to him. Ahiga squatted next to Blair's head, grabbing his chin roughly in one hand. "You know *nothing*, whelp. Now we are going to have a talk about manners and about priorities. Yes?"

37

OLD

"**Y**ou do not have the *luxury* of obstinance, whelp," Ahiga hissed, hauling Blair's limp form up until their noses nearly touched. "You lack the time to adjust to your circumstances. I am the teacher, you the student. You *will* learn, whether you wish it or no. You *will* stifle your impertinence, and you will listen. I have much to teach and precious little time remaining to teach it. So while you lie there, consider the wealth of powers I command, the myriad of things you cannot possibly understand. In my age, we respected our elders, even if we despised them." He released the pup, allowing Blair's body to crash to the floor.

Ahiga rose and strode purposefully to the door, pausing to turn with his hand resting on the handle. "I give you this simple gift, whelp. Investigate the disease. Study the sun. Learn the truth of my words. If you are honest with yourself, you will have no choice but to accept that the ancient enemy is coming. That everyone and everything you know is on the brink of destruction. When at last you accept these things, your beast will help you seek me out.

"Do not meander in this quest," Ahiga continued, shaking from the strain of keeping them both paralyzed. If it weren't for several recent nights under the moon, he'd have been forced to release them.

"If you tarry too long you will force my hand. If needed, I will find and kill every last thing that you love. Your family. Your friends. Whatever it takes, whelp. That goes for you as well, female. Help this whelp find wisdom, or I will see that your worlds burn before everyone else's."

The door clicked open, and he exited the room. A heartbeat after the door clicked shut behind him, Ahiga collapsed against the wall, spent from the energy required to overpower the impudent whelps. It underscored just how frail he was now, how much he had lost during his long slumber. He was weaker than he should have been, even given his low reserves. There was only one possible cause. Age. When he'd taken up stewardship all those millennia ago, he'd been a young man in the prime season of power and life. Yet the centuries had leeched that vitality from him, had pushed him to the very end of a life span all others would call eternal. The sacrifice had been necessary. Someone had to remain behind, to awaken the Mother when the time came.

Ahiga staggered to his feet, weaving like a drunkard down the plush carpet. He already knew where the pup would go next. A city called San Diego. There was much to prepare before meeting him there, where he would stand ready for Blair to accept his duty. If he did not, the fool would learn that Ahiga made no idle boasts.

38

TWO WORDS

"Sit down, Jordan," the Director ordered, tone lacking its usual steel. He gestured to a nylon camp chair across from his plastic desk. The room was a hastily erected caricature of the man's San Francisco office. It was flanked by identical white file cabinets, all of which were sheltered by an unadorned dark canvas pavilion. It was exactly his style, out in the open where everyone could reach him quickly.

Jordan did as ordered, waiting patiently as the older man shuffled through a ream of file folders. Most probably detailed recent attacks, but he studiously avoided looking. The Director scrubbed fingers through manicured hair that had more salt than pepper. Jordan remembered when it had been the other way around, just a handful of years ago.

"You know why I called you here," the Director said, eyes watery as they met Jordan's. He looked so weary. "Allowing Sheila access to Subjects Beta and Gamma was an inexcusable lapse in judgment. They are both considered compromised, so sharing our limited intel with them could have catastrophic consequences. What if they can communicate with others of their kind, spreading word of our ignorance and weakness? What if Beta had gotten loose and killed the both of you? We'd have lost a command officer and our best remaining scientist. For what? It was a bad call, Jordan." Then he fell silent, waiting.

"It was the right call," Jordan replied unapologetically. He leaned forward, placing his hands on the desk's cool plastic. "We've learned more about their language in the last week than we did the four prior. Steve has been invaluable, and Bridget's been pulling her weight. That knowledge could be vital to stopping this thing."

"What happens when Bridget goes berserk and tears Sheila apart?" the Director barked, slapping the desk and shooting to his feet. He was silent for a moment, eyes promising a venomous death if Jordan uttered a word. Then the Director quietly placed his palms on the desk in a rough parody of Jordan. His voice made the high altitude chill even frostier. "We know nothing about them. What they are. What they can do. That's why they're in isolation. Can you imagine what might happen if they got access to the pyramid? There could be weapons of mass destruction in there. It might even be that we've already found it. Or rather her.

"These visits with Sheila stop, now. I know you disagree. I don't care. You're putting the welfare of the human race in the hands of unknown variables," the Director said, gaze steady. His voice was still calm, despite the gravity of his words. "I'm going to tend to that situation personally. To cover up for your lapse. I want two words, Commander."

"Yes, sir," Jordan agreed placidly, fuming inside. Arguing would change nothing.

"Good, because we have work to do. Are you up to speed on the spread?" he asked, nodding at the global map. A new pin had been added to London. Another in Dubai. The steady march of red covered far too much of South and Central America. It had begun to bleed into North America as well.

"Yes, sir. I'm up to speed. We're not going to get a handle on this, not without a whole lot more firepower," he said, hating how much it resembled an excuse. He straightened in his chair, holding the Director's gaze. "These things can devour a squad, taking shot after shot and not going down. We're just outclassed. Even if we weren't, if we could take them down without losing a fistful of men, they're just spreading too quickly."

"I know."

The simple admission was deafening. It staggered him.

"We're losing, Jordan. There are too many of them and not enough of us. We only have one chance. Find Subject Alpha. So that's what you're going to do. I've pulled in every resource I can. R&D has created some pretty amazing toys. There aren't many, but what we have is going with you," he explained, stepping out from behind the desk and leaving the pavilion's temporary shelter from the heat. "Follow me. I'd like your assessment of the new hardware."

Jordan followed mechanically, still shelled from what he'd just seen. He knew things were bad, but this...

The Director set a brisk pace across the packed dirt path. His tie fluttered in the wind, and his form was nearly obscured by the dust kicked up from a passing jeep. He strode past Ops, ignoring the steady stream of black-clad soldiers filing in and out. They left the smoother path for the rougher terrain that had been set aside for troop maneuvers. The Director's goal seemed to be a blue canvas pavilion that had to have been erected in the last twenty-four hours.

Several men in black tank tops and matching fatigues were unboxing unfamiliar ordnance. It looked like something straight out of a sci-fi movie. Yuri was the center of the activity. He'd stripped down to his fatigues and was seated atop a pile of small crates. His legs were already covered in sculpted matte-black body armor, and two men were lifting a chest piece into place.

"What are they working on?" Jordan asked as they closed the distance to the pavilion. He ran a hand across his brow, removing a sheen of sweat that the brisk breeze had neglected to remove.

"Something you'll be very interested in, I think. It's the center-piece of our new arsenal," the Director answered, keeping his measured pace. He was unaffected by the chill. "It's the X-12 personal body armor created by R&D. I brought in the two prototypes we've created. They quadruple a man's strength, allowing you to bend steel. Top speed of forty miles per hour. They have induction coils that slowly recharge through skin contact. If you don't tax them too heavily, they're powered almost indefinitely."

"What kind of ordnance do they pack?" Jordan asked, assessing the armor as they neared the pavilion. It was bulky enough to throw off a man's center of gravity. That could probably be compensated for with practice, but the armor would require an experienced pilot to be of real combat use. Did something this new even have pilots?

"Each one has a shoulder-mounted Raptor missile launcher with four rounds," the Director explained, pointing to the unit mounted to the armor's right shoulder as they stepped under the pavilion. A small space heater mitigated a bit of the cold. "Each wrist is equipped with a pair of twelve-inch titanium spurs for close combat. Beyond that, the armor is designed to carry handheld weaponry. The rifle of choice is a .50 caliber, and the armor can fire it while running."

Jordan gave a low whistle. A .50 caliber rifle could core a tank, but they usually needed to be anchored in place to be fired. Snipers normally stuck to stationary vantages, making them vulnerable. If the armor could fire accurately at a run it would be a formidable weapon, maybe even one that might have a chance against the werewolves shredding his forces.

By the time they reached the pavilion, the pair of soldiers had encased Yuri in armor. The arms were less bulky than the chest and seemed to provide a full range of movement, while the helmet was a featureless black faceplate. The corporal rose from the pile of crates, taking an experimental first step. He wobbled but kept his footing. An armored arm snapped into a salute when its owner noticed Jordan and the Director. His two companions rapidly joined him; their boyish grins faded into surprise when they realized the base commander had snuck up on them.

"At ease," the Director said, waving dismissively. He crossed to an open case, hefting the large rifle cradled in black foam. It was similar to the one Jordan had used when Subject Alpha first escaped the pyramid, but it was heavier and had a longer barrel. Too heavy for a man to fire without breaking his collarbone. The Director offered it to the corporal, who seized it awkwardly in one armored hand, something Jordan wasn't sure even he could manage. "Yuri, why don't you show the commander what the armor can do? See that hawk circling the ridge? Take it out."

The Russian flashed through the dust, leaping into the air and landing with a crunch on a boulder nearly thirty feet away. He cradled the rifle effortlessly in his right hand until he snapped the stock up to his shoulder and sighted down the scope. He tracked his target for roughly two seconds; then the rifle boomed. A two-foot gout of flame erupted from the muzzle, but Yuri's shoulder barely moved as the projectile turned its target into a cloud of greasy black feathers nearly two hundred yards above them.

"Impressive," Jordan admitted, stepping back under the pavilion's welcome shade. "I'm curious to see how it performs against a real enemy, though. The werewolves are fast, strong, and nearly un-killable."

"Let's find out," the Director replied, turning to the black-clad soldiers who'd helped Yuri don the armor. "Get the commander set up in the second suit. Give him the rundown on its use." He reached for the radio at his belt, depressing the talk button. "Ops, this is Director Phillips. Send a squad to escort Subject Gamma to the firing range."

"Sir?" Jordan asked, shocked by the move. The Director had to know how dangerous letting Steve loose would be. Slaughtering a squad would be effortless if he shifted.

"Just get the armor on, soldier," the Director ordered, steely gaze settling on Jordan with the weight of determination. "You wanted a test. You're going to get it."

"But sir, we should—" Jordan began.

"We don't have time," the Director snarled, turning a heated glare in Jordan's direction. "The reports on Gamma are clear. He knows more than he should. He's admitted to being in some sort of telepathic contact with the sleeping woman. We have no idea if our security measures are adequate to hold him. We also need to know how that armor performs in a live-fire exercise against a real target. I want two words, Jordan."

"Yes. Sir," Jordan said, through gritted teeth.

39

FIELD TEST

"See this symbol here, the one that looks like a pyramid with two lines coming out the top? It repeats at odd intervals throughout the first, second, and seventh stanzas," Sheila said, tapping a symbol near the center of the sheet of paper. She slid it across the padded floor toward Bridget, who picked it up in both hands. The petite woman had little choice because the silver cuffs wouldn't allow her hands more than three inches apart. A similar pair was clamped around her ankles, though its chain was eight inches long to allow a shuffling walk.

The manacles weren't just silver in color. They *were* silver. Mohn had run some very early tests on their prisoners and had found the substance to be effective. Sheila didn't know why that was, something about silver being toxic if mixed into their blood. If Bridget attempted to shift, her wrists and ankles would swell in size, and the restraints would slice off her feet and hands.

Steve wore an identical set, but his hands were in his lap. He pointedly ignored the two women. He lounged against the white padding lining the cell, eyes closed, though Sheila knew he was listening. He'd stopped helping days ago when Sheila had refused to listen to his arguments about waking the strange woman he called the Mother. She got the sense that he knew more than he was willing to share with her or Bridget, that he could read the strange language just as easily as she could read English.

"Yeah, I know it's significant, but I haven't the faintest clue what it means," Bridget responded, eyes on the paper Sheila had handed her. "At first I thought it must represent the structure itself, but I think it's more than a reference to this place. It shows up too often and in too many different contexts. It's maddening."

"I have a theory," Sheila replied, unable to suppress a grin. She knew she was on to something, and it thrilled her, because she knew Bridget would be just as excited. Just like she had been in the old days. "What if the symbol is a type of building? What if this pyramid is just one of many, if that symbol isn't saying this place, but rather this *type* of place? What if there are other pyramids, either here or in different parts of the world? Why, it could mean that..."

She trailed off, glancing behind her at the sharp hiss that heralded the door opening. Was it already time for the guards to collect her? She should have another two hours, unless something had gone wrong. Had they found Blair? The door swung outward, revealing two black-clad soldiers armed with lethal rifles and matching expressions. One leveled his weapon at Steve, the other at Bridget.

"There's no need for those," Sheila said, rising slowly to her feet. The men ignored her, keeping their weapons trained on her friends. "Where's Commander Jordan? And why are you interrupting? Our work is important, and I was told th—"

"Dr. Steven Galk," the lead soldier barked, ignoring Sheila. He was a freckled youth not much more than twenty, yet his gaze was steady. Confident. "Rise slowly and keep your hands down. Proceed down the hallway with your eyes down. Any deviation from these instructions will be met with terminal force."

Steve sat silently for a long moment and then raised his head languidly. His eyes opened, piercing blue shards landing on the man who'd spoken. Steve watched the soldier coldly as he rose to his feet, smooth and graceful, like the predator he was. The guards tensed, fingers tightening on triggers as they prepared to sell their lives.

Death would be quick for them if Steve somehow broke free of those restraints. Sheila had seen what a werewolf could do and just how little they feared bullets. So why had the powers that be sent only two guards? It seemed reckless. Jordan would undoubtedly have an answer, probably pointing out that there was nowhere for Steve to go. If he killed these guards, he'd face dozens of others outside the building who would mobilize the instant a shot was fired.

"As you wish, soldier," Steve said. His words were soft but distinctly audible over the uncomfortable silence. He shuffled toward the door, hands obligingly low in front of him.

"Where are you taking him?" Sheila asked, surging to her feet. Whatever they intended couldn't be good.

"Respectfully, that's none of your business, ma'am," the freckled soldier shot back, eyes never leaving Steve. He and his companion backed out of the room, allowing Steve to exit behind them.

"I'm not a prisoner." She bristled, stepping into the hallway next to Steve. "You don't have a right to keep me in there."

Bridget finally rose to her feet. Her stance was timid, but her expression showed a hint of steel. The timing was incredibly bad, but Sheila was glad the woman was recovering. Recent events had hit her hard.

"Where are you taking him?" Bridget demanded, taking a short step toward the door. The taller soldier snapped the butt of his rifle to his shoulder, muzzle aimed straight at her face.

"It's all right, Bridget," Steve called into the room. His voice was calm, as if this were all perfectly ordinary. "Don't make a scene. I'm sure they just have a few more tests they want to run. I'll be back shortly." Bridget's expression showed how unlikely she thought that prospect was, but she said nothing as the soldier quickly closed the door, leaving her in the featureless white room.

"Walk slowly, and don't make any sudden moves," the freckled soldier ordered. Steve started up the hallway, trudging toward the exit as if he were striding through a park. Sheila wondered what he knew that she didn't. He seemed so...resigned.

The motley little group exited the hastily constructed building, passing another pair of guards as they stepped into the chilly afternoon. A few clouds stubbornly dotted the sky, a patch of shade drawing a shiver from her as it passed over them.

Sheila fished her oversized sunglasses from a side pocket of her khaki shorts, donning them to keep the glare at bay. The soldiers gestured for Steve to leave the trail and head across the rougher terrain. They threaded past boulders and around scrubby little bushes, toward a stand-alone black pavilion.

None of the soldiers at any of the newly erected buildings paid them any mind. If the prospect of having a werewolf loose among them was disconcerting, they certainly didn't show it. Either they knew something she didn't, or they were prepared for anything Steve might try.

As they approached the pavilion, she made out a knot of men enjoying its shade. Two wore the uniforms she was familiar with, but two others wore bulky black armor complete with faceplates. The equipment was new and definitely strange, but she'd never cared much for such things. She was far more interested in the last figure, a man she knew by reputation but had never spoken with—the Director, whose title was so powerful that a name wasn't even needed. He wore a light-grey Armani suit set off by a deep-blue tie of the finest silk. Somehow, even standing amidst armored soldiers, he made it look perfectly natural.

He stood talking to one of the armored figures, nodding in the group's direction as he became aware of their approach. The Director stepped from the shade, raising a hand to shield his eyes despite wearing a pair of dark sunglasses. The man studied them like a flat-eyed reptile, no hint of his thoughts touching his expression.

"Sir," the freckled soldier called. Now that they were close enough to be heard, he trotted ahead of their group, leaving them in the care of his silent companion. He paused next to the Director, offering a tight salute and saying something low enough that Sheila couldn't hear it.

One of the armored figures stepped forward, looming over the Director. He said something, voice carried away by the wind. Whatever it was caused the Director's face to tighten.

"Reckless? Is that what you think? Commander, we are out of time. If we can't beat one of them now, on our own ground, what choice do we have in the field? Private, give me your sidearm," the Director barked, turning toward the freckled soldier. He studied Steve through those dark black lenses. The soldier drew the weapon without hesitation, offering it grip first to the Director, who took it in his right hand.

He flicked the safety off; then in one smooth motion, he raised the gun and aimed at Steve. The weapon coughed, ejecting a shiny brass cartridge that flashed in the sun as it spun over the Director. The acrid smell of hot gunpowder stung Sheila's eyes even as the round punched into Steve's chest. It picked him up, flinging him backward in a tangle of limbs.

Sheila could do nothing but stare in shock, unable to process the event. The Director had just shot Steve. Why? It didn't make any sense. If the Director wanted Steve dead, why not have the soldiers take care of it back in the cell? Why drag him all the way up here?

"All right. Commander, it's time to see what that suit can do," the Director said, turning to face the armored figure who'd questioned him a moment before. The Director lowered his weapon. "My guess is you've got about ten seconds before he shifts. Once he does, I want you to take him down. Hard. Yuri, back him up, but don't intervene unless the commander fails to contain the situation."

Commander? The man in the closest suit must be Jordan. That he was a part of this travesty, the killing of a man as some sort of test, galled her. Yet he was a soldier, and although she doubted he'd agree with the Director's method, he was unlikely to disobey orders.

She shifted her horrified glance to Steve's writhing form. The man twisted and groaned on the ground, cuffed hands clutching at the scarlet stain spreading across the belly of his white hospital gown.

His back arched and his eyes became unfocused. He mewed pitifully, fighting to draw in a breath.

Then the change began. The process was shockingly rapid, fur bursting from every pore even as Steve's bones popped and broke. They rearranged themselves, allowing for the sudden swell of muscle as he increased dramatically in size. Two sharp pings sounded as the cuffs exploded from his wrists and then from his ankles. So much for the silver. Within moments Steve the man was gone, replaced by a black-furred werewolf. The amber eyes glittering over that canine muzzle held alarming intelligence. How much of that was still Steve?

"Sheila, get back," Jordan ordered, stepping between her and Steve. His form was obscured by the armor, but his voice was unmistakable. "All of you, get clear now!"

Everyone but the Director took several hasty steps backward, fleeing for the illusory safety of the pavilion. That left the two combatants eyeing each other like strange cats, circling slowly as if seeking an advantage in their as yet silent struggle.

40

CLASH OF THE TITANS

Jordan's breath thundered in his ears, echoing in the tight confines of the armored suit. He instinctively dropped into a combat stance, feet sliding apart for better balance. The suit reacted instantly, the faceplate overlaying a head-up display over his vision. The HUD provided a variety of useful information, from his elevation to the current count of his Raptor missiles.

Bright-red crosshairs appeared over the creature that had been Dr. Galk just moments before. Jordan wondered idly how the suit identified enemies, but the thought skittered away like butter on a hot pan as the creature began its first attack. It blurred forward, moving so quickly even the suit had difficulty tracking it.

The only thing that saved Jordan was the foreknowledge of just how fast these things were. Jordan leapt backward, the suit exaggerating the motion and carrying him forty feet. He landed heavily, thrown off balance by the unexpected power of the movement. Jordan rolled over backward, tucking his limbs and coming back to his feet.

The werewolf was already after him, but this time it was merely inhumanly fast instead of impossible to track. Jordan readied himself, popping a set of matte-black claws from one wrist. He lunged forward with all the power he could muster, aiming for the werewolf's throat. The wickedly sharp weapons hummed through the air as they whooshed through the spot the werewolf's neck had just occupied. The beast danced backward, incredibly nimble despite its size.

Steve, if he could still be called that, responded with a vicious downward slash. Ebony claws every bit as sharp as their metal counterparts descended toward Jordan's face. He dropped into a crouch, shifting slightly to the right as the claws sailed harmlessly by. The shift left him open to a sudden kick from the werewolf, the force of the blow hurling him back across the rocky ground in a cloud of dust and debris.

The armor protected him from the worst of the hit, but it still hurt like hell. Jordan rolled to his feet, knowing he had only moments before his opponent was on him again. The werewolf possessed the advantages of speed and size. Jordan would have to outthink it if he was going to have a prayer of winning. That was problematic enough. Dr. Galk was incredibly intelligent, and Jordan had a feeling that whatever he'd become could draw on that intellect. Worse, the thing seemed to draw on the kind of battle-honed instincts that could only be earned through a lifetime of combat.

Jordan looked up to find the werewolf in the air above him, furry arms spread wide as it brought down two sets of claws in one incredibly vicious strike. He managed to block the first with a raised forearm, but the second sent up a shower of sparks as claws skittered across his chest plate. The metal held, but the claws carved furrows in their wake. The force of the blow knocked him back a step, metal servos whirring as the armor fought to keep him in place.

Metal was pitted against flesh, and Jordan knew there could only be one outcome in a contest of strength. He had to use finesse. Jordan went limp, allowing himself to fall flat on his back. The sudden move caught the werewolf off guard, and the beast stumbled forward, toppling in his direction. Jordan was ready. He planted his feet against the creature's gut, kicking with all the incredible force the power armor could muster.

The move launched the beast into a high arc, almost thirty feet into the air. Since its feet were no longer touching the ground, all that muscle meant nothing. It flew in a predictable pattern, powerless to change the direction of its flight. Jordan led the target, making a gesture with his left thumb to activate a Raptor missile. There was a deep clunk from the launcher on his left shoulder and then a sudden burst of recoil that even the armor had a difficult time suppressing.

A white contrail snaked from his shoulder as a thumb-thick missile streaked toward its target. It had to be moving several hundred miles per hour, yet despite that, the werewolf somehow had time to tuck into a fetal position. It turned in midair, presenting its right shoulder to the blow. Jordan's jaw dropped as he grasped his opponent's logic. If the missile struck a leg, the beast wouldn't be able to move and the fight would be over. Take a missile to the back or torso, and it would lose vital organs, with the same outcome.

Instead, the creature took the missile in the side. A concussion of light and sound erupted, momentarily turning the suit's HUD white. When it cleared a moment later, it showed a huge cloud of dust and smoke. There was no sign of the creature. Jordan scanned the area, but apart from soldiers and scientists scurrying away, there was no sign of movement.

The beast emerged from the thickest bellow of smoke, its fangs bared in a snarl of rage. One arm was simply gone, shoulder ending in a ruined mass of flesh charred black. It raised its remaining hand, fingers spread wide as they pointed in his direction. Jordan tensed. What the hell was that thing doing?

He tried to reach for the rifle slung across the armor's back but found himself unable to move. His entire body had gone rigid, as if he'd stuck his finger in a light socket and the flow of electricity had paralyzed his muscles. Jordan strained against his own body, yet his limbs refused to obey

"Director, I can't move," Jordan's panicked voice boomed, amplified by the suit's speakers. "Everyone, get clear. Get clear *now*."

The werewolf blurred. One moment it stood thirty feet away, the next it loomed over him. The beast wrapped its remaining clawed hand around Jordan's neck, squeezing until the metal began to buckle with a hideous metallic scream. It hoisted him into the air, Jordan's limbs dangling like a broken doll's. The creature brought the armor's faceplate close to its own, showing its fangs as it stared directly at him with the terrible gaze of an avenging god.

If he was going out, then by God, he was taking this thing with him. Jordan concentrated, willing his thumb to move. He waged a silent battle, fighting with everything he had to get that one digit to disobey the paralysis this thing had somehow inflicted. The metal groaned again, tightening around his throat. Breathing became difficult.

Jordan's thumb finally broke free. He jerked it three times, each motion causing another clunk from the missile launcher. Three separate streaks leapt from the boxy launcher into the beast's chest just a few feet away. The rapid explosions hurled him into the air, and the last thing he saw was the ground rushing crazily up at him.

41

THE HUNGER

"This is never going to work. Not with our luck," Blair said, sweat trickling uncomfortably down the back of the purple Hawaiian shirt he'd picked back at the Tijuana airport. The heat was bad, but the stench of sweat and urine filling the tunnel around him was worse. There were too many people too close together, a hundred heartbeats he couldn't tune out.

Liz gave a long look over the rim of her newly acquired sunglasses. "It'll work. We're obviously Americans, and I have a passport with a photo ID."

"That gets *you* out of trouble, but what about me? You know we can't let them take us. Mohn will know about it in hours," Blair replied, scanning the line of bored tourists packing the narrow bridge. It was enclosed in steel and concrete, straddling the four-lane artery connecting Mexico to the United States.

"They'll let us through. Listen, we're obviously American, and I'll just tell them you lost your wallet. They'll buy it. It happens all the time," she said, nudging him with an elbow. She smiled gloriously up at him in a way that would have thrilled him in any other circumstances. "Fifty more feet and we're home free, Blair. We've made it. My brother will get us to a lab, and we'll finally get some answers."

"I hope so," he grunted, lowering a hand to his side. Something hot flared in his belly, the second time since this morning. He suppressed a groan, inching forward against the knives in his side as the line moved. It was suddenly so cold. Blair raised a trembling hand, staring fixedly at the disobedient fingers that swam across his vision. What in the hell was happening?

"Are you all right?" Liz asked from somewhere miles away. She leaned in close, blue cotton shirt pressed against his bare arm. Suddenly her arm was around him, supporting his weight. "You just turned white. Like too white. You look like you're going to keel over. Lean on me. I've got you."

"I..." he croaked, staggering forward as the line moved again. "I'll be fine."

You must feed, Ka-Dun. The voice rang through his mind, familiar and unwelcome.

"Just give me a straight answer for once. What's wrong with me?" he muttered, hoping no one heard him. Talking to yourself made people think you were crazy, and crazy people drew attention.

Your body brims with power. The flesh cannot contain so much fury. You must feed to sustain yourself. There is prey before you. Consume them. You will gain strength, and others will rise to aid our cause.

"Why do I even bother?" he said, leaning against Liz as she helped him forward. A few neighbors darted curious glances, but only an elderly Asian woman seemed genuinely interested. Their eyes touched, and she glanced hurriedly away, blanching at whatever she'd seen.

"You're talking to it, aren't you?" Liz whispered. She was supporting almost all of his weight, and it seemed effortless.

"Yes," he replied, suddenly warm again. The pain faded to a dull smoldering. "It wants me to feed. Something about being full of power. You know how cryptic they are."

"I do," she replied, inching forward again. There were still at least a dozen people ahead of them, but they were close enough to see a pair of tables. People handed across their identification and were waved forward. "It makes sense that we'd need to feed. The things we do have to consume an enormous amount of calories. Can you suppress it for now?"

"Yes," he replied, forcing himself to straighten. A sheen of new sweat soaked through his shirt, but fortunately that was hardly out of place among the press of bodies. He wouldn't give in, not here and not now. If he did, all these people would die. "I will. I have to. I'm not going to murder these people, no matter what the voice says."

Ka-Dun, your control is admirable, but you must feed. Soon. Your body demands it, and if you do not heed its wishes, I will be forced to assume control.

"I won't give in to you," he hissed, voice pitched low so only Liz could hear. She darted an alarmed gaze at him, her grip tightening around his waist.

"Blair, what's it saying?" she asked, scanning the crowd around them. He could feel the tension in her body. She knew he was losing control. If that happened, the slaughter would be horrific.

"More of the same," he grunted, forcing a step forward. He probably looked drunk, but with the number of returning college students in the crowd, that wasn't anything out of place either. "Listen, beast. That's what the old man called you. You say you're here to advise me, right?"

Of course, Ka-Dun. I am a part of you, created to aid you in battle.

"Then fucking aid me. Give me an alternative. I'm not killing these people," he barked, catching a wide-eyed look from a chubby ten-year-old with a chocolate stain on his shirt. Blair glared at the boy, who spun back to face a mother with enough arm hair to be mistaken for a werewolf herself.

There is another path, a foolhardy path. If you refuse to feed, then you must deplete your reserves of energy. Burn it away and so, too, will the hunger burn away. I must counsel against this course. It will leave you vulnerable, weak before the coming storm. You will need your strength.

"I'm not killing them. How do I burn it away?" he asked, forcing another step. Deceptively small and just inches away, Liz stood ready to catch him.

Use your higher abilities. Touch the minds around you. Or shift into a beast. Your instincts will guide you. Trust them.

Blair turned to Liz, meeting her gaze with a steadiness he'd lacked just moments ago. Touch others' minds. It sounded so sci-fi, but wasn't that exactly what the old man had done to him back on the beach in Peru? He'd seen a wolf miles away, a wolf he'd known was a man. That man had reached into his mind across an incredible distance. So why couldn't he?

Liz, can you hear me? Blair thought, somehow *pushing* toward her. Something electric crackled between them as her eyes widened.

"Did you just?" she asked, releasing him as she clutched both hands at her chest. It was a defensive gesture, and he couldn't blame her. He'd told her about his experience with Ahiga, and she'd felt the old man's power back in Acapulco. She was putting the pieces together with dizzying speed. "Can you do it at will? What am I thinking now?"

Blair concentrated, staring deep into her eyes. What had it felt like when Ahiga entered his mind? How could he duplicate such a bizarre feat? At first he felt foolish, so close that Liz's heady scent was almost overpowering. It was awkward and intimate, but he forced himself not to break eye contact. This release of energy was vital. If he failed, if the voice could be believed, he might fly into a rage and kill everyone around them. Blair pushed, straining against *something*. It was like trying to move a car up a hill by himself, and he began to pant despite the fact that he hadn't moved or physically exerted himself in any way.

Females possess an implacable will. They cannot utilize shaping, but piercing their minds is extremely difficult. Your will must be honed, a slender dagger to pierce her psyche.

He suppressed the questions that bubbled up. Exactly what was shaping? Why couldn't females do it? That didn't matter right now. All that mattered was finding a way inside Liz's mind. It wasn't a *should* or a *maybe*. It was a *must*. So he pushed. And pushed. He gathered his will, trying to focus it into a slender dagger as the voice had suggested. It felt like molding putty, especially since he was so unsure of what he was doing. He pictured a steak knife, pouring all his will, his need into it. Then he thrust, shoving with all his might. Liz gasped, eyes widening. The world vanished.

Blair was lost in a sea of darkness, unsure of where or why. Then he became aware of something twinkling in the distance, a tiny pinprick of golden light. Others joined it, a sea of stars all around him. It was if he lay at the center of a hollow globe, looking out into space. Was this the inside of Liz's mind? One cluster of lights was much closer than the rest, so Blair moved toward it. The sensation felt like swimming, or perhaps this was what flying was like. As he neared the golden cluster, each dot resolved into a separate globe with images dancing within. He saw people and places he was unfamiliar with, and he sifted through them until he finally found one he recognized. It was him, wearing the same clothing he'd purchased at the airport. Standing in the same crowded walkway. He was seeing himself through Liz's eyes.

A shadow loomed behind him, and Blair spun to face it. There, in the distance, stood an impossibly tall monster. The auburn werewolf he was coming to know so well. Its hackles were raised, teeth bared. Its gaze had settled on him. She was coming for him. Blair panicked, unsure of what might happen if he stayed. So he fled, far and fast, away from the lights. There was a sudden shock, and he staggered backward, suddenly in his own body again. Liz darted forward, catching him before he collapsed into the chipped stone wall to his right.

"It's all right. I've got you," she said, easing him back to his feet. Her hands were cool despite the heat. "What happened? Did you see something?"

"I saw inside your mind," he replied, raising a trembling hand to his temple. His head throbbed, but the hunger had abated at least a little. "There were a million stars. Memories, I think. I was able to sift through them. To see things you've seen."

"You went through my memories?" Liz asked, eyes turning dangerous. "Did you see anything I need to know about?"

"No. I saw...me. Me through your eyes," he admitted, still feeling dizzy as they inched up the corridor with the rest of the cattle. "Then there was this giant werewolf. Your beast, maybe? It came after me, so I ran. The next thing I knew I was standing here."

"I guess that's what I get for asking you to read my mind," Liz replied, gaze softening. She took another step forward. They were only a few people away from the uniformed immigration guards waving people past. "Remember, just let me do the talking and we'll be fine."

Blair wasn't so sure. He was coated in sweat, weaving like a drunk.

42

BRUCE

Liz sucked in a deep breath as she stepped into the space vacated by a leathery-skinned man in a 49ers t-shirt, gagging from the stench of grease and beer he'd left in his wake. The overpowering sense of smell was one of the downsides of her newly acquired senses.

A bored-looking woman squatted in an uncomfortable metal chair at the head of the line, the sweat-stained fabric of her blue uniform straining to contain her bulk. It was a battle the garment threatened to lose at any moment. Pinned to the top of the uniform was a lopsided brass tag that read *Brenda*. Brenda's gaze roamed up and down Liz, apparently classifying her as nothing worthy of attention. She accepted the passport Liz offered, flipping open the blue leather cover and inspecting the image inside.

"Welcome to the United States," she said in the plodding way reserved for those doomed to repeat the same phrase thousands of times a week. She shifted her gaze to Blair. "Passport or driver's license, please."

"My boyfriend lost his wallet," she interjected as Blair shot her a nervous glance. He was drenched in sweat, his Hawaiian shirt so sodden he looked to have been dunked in a pool. Perspiration plastered the garment to his chest, showing off the wall of muscle underneath. The blond stubble and mussed hair gave him a rumpled look, but that wasn't out of the ordinary in the steady flow of hung-over tourists.

"No ID?" the woman asked, mouth tightening as she adjusted her bulk. The chair creaked alarmingly. "I'll have to call over a supervisor. Step off to the right." She gestured at a painted red square a little ways apart from the flow of tourists.

Blair shot her a look, every muscle tensing. He reeked of impending violence. She put a hand on his shoulder and shook her head. *Not right now,* she thought. Hopefully he could hear that. If so, he didn't respond, though he did relax ever so slightly. They hurried over to the area the woman had indicated, standing alone as people threaded by.

Several moments later a tall black man with a shockingly pink scar on his chin approached. He wore the same uniform as the other bored workers, but his complemented broad shoulders and thick arms. Like those of a bird of prey, his clear brown eyes studied them as he approached. He was clearly used to every flavor of bullshit border crossing. His name tag read *Bruce*.

"I'm given to understand that one of you doesn't have any form of identification. Is that correct?" he rumbled, voice like a landslide. He raised an eyebrow. "I'm also given to understand that one of you looks like death warmed over, but now I'm thinking that was an understatement."

"That's right," Liz broke in before Blair could speak. She hoped he'd keep his mouth shut and over-zealous Bruce would just assume he was whipped. "My boyfriend lost his wallet on the beach, and to top it all off, he has food poisoning. Bad shrimp down in Ensenada. We just came down for a weekend vacation. That's not a problem, is it?" She kept her tone light and shot the man her best smile. He wasn't impressed.

"What's your name, sir?" he asked, gaze fastening on Blair. The silence stretched uncomfortably.

"Blair Smith," he finally said, scowl deepening. "Listen, I'm sicker than a dog. More than a little hung over. I'm tired, and I really want to lay down. You can tell I'm an American. People must lose their wallets all the time. Just let me by."

It was a great mix of confrontation and entitlement, just the sort of thing an upper-middle-class tourist might say when returning to the states. Liz breathed a silent sigh of relief. He was playing along instead of giving in to the beast.

"I understand your discomfort, sir, but it's my job to make sure we don't allow terrorists into the country. Do you have any way to substantiate your identity?" he asked, unmoved by Blair's apparent ire.

"I guess we could call the university I work at. You could talk to one of my coworkers," he offered with a shrug. Liz could kick him. If the man obliged, Mohn would know about it within minutes.

"Is that really necessary? I can substantiate his identity. I'm his girlfriend," she asked, leaning a bit closer and resting her hand on the officer's forearm. "Listen, Bruce, I know you're just doing your job, but we're in kind of a hurry. We have to meet my brother for dinner, and we're already two hours late. I don't suppose you could just let us through? I know your time must be valuable."

He gave her an appraising look, which darkened when he turned to Blair. "You're lucky your girlfriend has some manners. I'm within my rights to detain you until your identity is ascertained. Now get out of my sight before I change my mind."

"Thank you," Blair said, visibly relaxing. Liz seized his hand and dragged him past the man before anything else could happen.

They entered the second half of the bridge straddling the traffic-clogged freeway, picking their way past slower families as they made for the red spiral staircase leading down to the parking level. It was ringed by thick metal bars and made Liz uneasy, despite having made the crossing before. It reminded her too much of a cage.

"Looks like you were right," Blair admitted once they were out of earshot. "Thank God that's over. Now what? We meet your brother?"

"Yeah, we meet Trevor and head back to his place. I'll tell him we need to do a blood test and we'll see what he can arrange. Either we'll have him bring a kit home, or maybe he'll take us to SDSU where his office is," she answered, squinting at the sudden brightness as she entered the stairwell.

"I'm hoping you come up with something," Blair answered, following her down the concrete steps. They were black with grime, discarded gum, and other things she couldn't identify. "I want to know how we're able to change. And how I'm able to read minds. I don't believe in magic. There's got to be an explanation."

"I *do* believe in magic, but even that has to be based on sound principles. I have a theory. We're surrounded by signals everywhere these days, right?" she asked, pausing to slide around a mom leading her two-year-old down the wide stairs.

"Yeah, cell phones and Wi-Fi are everywhere now," Blair said, following just a step behind.

"So one of the websites I spend some time on claims that these waves could be altering our behavior. I know, I know...It makes me sound like a conspiracy nut. But if you'd said the same thing about werewolves and ancient super-powered civilizations a few weeks ago, how would people have reacted?" Liz asked, pausing to catch Blair's gaze. People tended to react badly if she brought up some of the sites she frequented, especially people in academia. She'd never so much as mentioned them to her brother.

"So you think that I'm using a signal to establish some sort of link with someone's brain? That could explain what Ahiga did to us. He sent out some sort of pulse that paralyzed us both," Blair theorized, brow furrowed in thought. He was quick. "Wouldn't that take some sort of power source?"

"The brain is just a complex electrical system. I don't see any reason it couldn't act like a receiver, picking up signals that you broadcast. Waves bounce, so the same waves would return back to you. I bet that's what establishes the link," she answered, growing more excited. The theory made sense. "That doesn't explain the gender difference, though. How is it you can do this *shaping* thing the beast talked about, but I can't?"

"That part is easier to get my head around," Blair replied, dodging a puddle of something viscous as they neared the ground level. "We're a sexually dimorphic species. Men are generally taller and stronger. Women are more resistant to pain, and in my opinion much better looking. We have different chromosomes and different hormones, like testosterone. It makes sense that whatever this virus is could affect us differently. What I'm wondering is if there's a way to test our hypothetical signals? That might grant some insight about our abilities."

"Not that I can think of. There's a lot we don't understand about signals in general, even though most of our technology is based on them. Maybe your ancient civilization did, but if they left us any clues, they'd be in that pyramid," Liz said, stepping out of the stair-well and onto the asphalt. She shielded her eyes as she scanned the parking lot for Trevor's Land Rover.

"If only we could get back inside. Given time, I could learn their language and get us some answers," he replied, joining her on the curb. "I'm still not sure how to explain how we change forms, and I'm betting they left some sort of user's manual. If nothing else, the woman inside must know."

"You've mentioned her a couple times. Keeping her alive that long should be impossible," Liz said, biting her lip as she scanned the incoming traffic for Trevor.

"So should being a werewolf or reading minds. We'd be smart not to underestimate what these people might have been capable of. The woman was breathing," Blair said, more than a bit defensively.

"I believe you. It's just the scope of that...Well, it's hard to accept, even for someone like me. Just give me a bit of time, all right?"

"Are you going to tell your brother the truth?" Blair asked. It was a question she was still struggling to answer. Would doing so put her brother in danger? What if Mohn came after them? He was a bit of a gun nut, but these people way outclassed any concerned citizen, even one as militant as her brother.

"I don't know," she replied, a bit surprised at her honesty. Showing vulnerability was difficult at the best of times, and Blair was a relative stranger. Maybe the shared experience was what made her more comfortable, or maybe it was some inexplicable twist of genetic manipulation now that they'd both been infected with the same virus. "Let's keep quiet about it for now. We'll go with the story we discussed on the plane. You were at a dig in Peru, and Mohn wanted whatever you found there. We'll just leave out the whole werewolf part."

"All right," Blair agreed with a shrug. His shirt was finally starting to dry, but it all but pulsed with his scent. "It's your brother. I'll do my best to play this off, but how are you going to explain the tests you're running?"

"I'm going to tell him the truth eventually, I just need to figure out how," she replied, rising to her tiptoes. There it was. A forest-green Land Rover slid into a spot a couple rows over. She couldn't help but hop up and down when a familiar shock of red hair appeared outside the driver's side door. Trevor was the stereotypical ginger, just like her. "There he is. I'm going to go meet him. Give us a sec before you head over."

She trotted through the parking lot, pausing to let a blue Camry pass before entering the row where she'd seen Trevor's SUV. Trevor caught sight of her, lighting up with a big grin as he strode toward her. His goatee had a couple grey hairs, and there were a few more lines around the eyes, but other than that he looked just like he always had.

Liz couldn't help herself, bursting into tears as she sprinted into a rib-crushing hug.

"God, I've missed you," she sobbed, all the pent-up emotion finally finding release. "Thank you so much for coming, Trev."

"Of course, Wizzer. You know I'm always here for you," he said, tousling her hair just like he had when they'd been children. There was something so comforting about her older brother, even in the face of all that had happened.

"Don't call me that," she said, unable to suppress a grin.

"I won't say it in front of this Blair guy, but you've got to give it to me straight. I don't need to know what trouble you're in, at least not yet. But do you trust him? Your phone call sounded frantic, and if he's got some sort of hold over you, I can deal with it."

She disengaged reluctantly, turning as Blair approached. "He's a friend, Trev. He's saved my life more than once over the last few weeks. I trust him. Whatever we've fallen into, we're in it together."

"Later we're going to have a talk about what that is," Trev said, his smile melting. He'd gone into business mode.

"You'll get the whole story, I promise," she mouthed, gesturing at Blair as he darted around a battered pickup with a tentative wave. "Trevor, this is my friend Blair. Blair, this is my brother, Trevor."

Trevor renewed his smile as he offered a hand to Blair. "Welcome to San Diego. Sounds like it's been a hell of a trip."

43

WATCHED

Ahiga stopped next to an odd metal conveyance the locals called a car. They were larger and much more ornate than those found on the southern continent. The sapphire hue on this one was strange to him, its unnatural sheen something that would have been near impossible to fabricate in his own time. He pretended to be opening the door, fumbling with the keys he'd taken from his last victim. The whelp and his female seemed unaware of his presence as they met with a fiery-haired man near a larger vehicle of the deepest green.

He'd known a moment of worry when he'd stood so near the whelp in the press of bodies seeking entrance to this nation. Fortunately, the stench of the clothing's previous owner had masked his scent, particularly the red shirt emblazoned with the word *49ers*. It had indicated the owner's loyalty to a particular tribe of warriors, if he understood the garment's purpose. He'd shaped his face into an exact replica of the man who'd worn it, and that subterfuge appeared to have worked. His presence was still secret.

Where was Blair going? Frustration boiled in him as he considered the bare handful of days remaining. He understood that the whelp must find his own acceptance of the powerful new body he'd suddenly been thrust into, but time was a luxury they could ill afford. Yet he could do nothing to sway the whelp. His own energy was all but spent, and the female would tear him apart if he attempted another direct confrontation.

Ahiga reached for the fiery-haired man's mind, slipping past his rudimentary defenses like wind through a forest. He plucked the man's destination with a deftness earned through centuries of practice. It was a town known as Bonita, nestled near the edge of this strange, sprawling sea of concrete and pollution. He would follow them and make one final plea to the whelp.

He must convince him, must show him the rudiments of shaping. If the whelp could not be prepared, all of them would pay the price.

44

HELIO-SEISMOLOGY

Trevor slid into the driver's seat, yanking the heavy door shut with its comforting metallic groan. The tan leather was cracked and faded, but the Land Rover was as reliable as the sunrise. He buckled the frayed seat belt, adjusting his wire-frame glasses as Liz slid into the passenger side. Her companion hopped in the rear passenger side, buckling his belt over a wide chest that spoke loudly of time in the gym. Trevor used the opportunity to study this Blair through the rearview mirror, taking in the sweat-stained shirt and stubbly face. Strangely haunted eyes darted around the parking lot, probably scanning for some sort of pursuit.

What could possibly be worth chasing them all the way from Peru? He glanced again at Blair. Putting that kind of fear into someone took a special kind of people, the sort who didn't balk at leaving bodies.

"So, uh, Trevor, what do you do for a living?" the man asked, shifting uncomfortably under Trevor's gaze. He eased the Rover out of its spot and into the line waiting for the on-ramp to 5 North.

"I'm a helio-seismologist." Trevor said, waiting for the inevitable confusion. He was used to it.

"Helio-seismologist. Sun vibrations?" Blair asked, straightening in sudden interest. That was certainly a surprise. "How does that work, exactly? I'd think it's too hot to get any sort of accurate measurements."

"That was the prevailing belief for a long time. It's part of why helio-seismology is such a young science. We only recently discovered that the sun has many different layers. By analyzing the P-modes and G-modes, we learn about the composition and density of those layers," Trevor explained. Most people couldn't care less about what he did.

He eased onto the on-ramp, flicking his turn signal as he maneuvered into the flow of traffic.

"So why helio-seismology? That's an oddly specific field," Blair said. Trevor was aware that Blair was steering the conversation away from himself, but that was fine for now. There'd be time to find out the circumstances surrounding their flight from Peru after they were safely back at his place.

"When we were kids, my sister Jessie and I called Trevor *Spaceboy*. We still do. He's always been an astronomer," Liz interjected. Leather squeaked as she craned her neck to give Blair a smile. Something significant passed between them, a look that said *don't talk about it*. That Liz would keep secrets bothered him, regardless of the circumstances. He'd always assumed she'd trust him with anything.

"I've always loved the night sky, but I found helio-seismology in junior high. I was in seventh grade waaay back in 1989—you know, before rocks were invented? Anyway, I saw a news story about how six million people in Canada were without power after a solar event called a coronal mass ejection," Trevor explained, weaving into the fast lane as the Rover roared to a triumphant eighty miles per hour. "I was a big sci-fi buff, and it seemed so post-apocalyptic to me, the idea that we could all suddenly be without power. I wanted to know what had caused it, so I spent most of that summer in the library. Are you familiar with coronal mass ejections?"

"No, but I can take a stab at what they are from the name," Blair mused. "Some sort of mass ejected from the sun's corona?"

"That's it exactly," Trevor replied, unable to suppress a grin.

Except for his sister and a few professors, he didn't often get to have conversations like this. "The sun sends out two bursts, the first traveling at the speed of light. It hits our magnetosphere, warning us that the mass of charged particles will be arriving a few days later. Those particles wash through the magnetosphere too, and if they're strong enough, they surge through our atmosphere like they did back in 1989. There was an even worse event back in 1859, one many times stronger. We didn't have the kind of instrumentation to track it like we can today, but from what we understand, something like the Carrington Event could be catastrophic if it happened today.

"These events wreak havoc on electronics, and if a wave were strong enough, it could probably knock power out to most of the world. Since replacement transformers only come from a couple different places, it could take the world months to recover. I did my thesis on that possibility, and it got the attention of not just the federal government but a private corporation called HELIOS. They recruited me to a research team that monitors solar flares and other activity; we're tracking a big one right now, actually. If we see a large enough wave, we're hoping we can warn the world to turn off the lights before power grids get fried. It's pretty scary stuff. So how about you, Blair? You seem pretty sharp. What do you do?"

"I'm an anthropologist. I study Meso and South American cultures. You know, pyramids and that sort of—"

"Trevor, I'm starving," Liz cut in, glaring over her sunglasses at Blair. It was uncharacteristically blunt of her, an obvious attempt to steer the conversation.

"We're only ten minutes out. I've got some venison steaks ready for the grill," he said, wondering what it was she didn't want him to know. "So, Blair, you study pyramids and ruins? Is that why you were down in South America?"

"Trev, don't grill him. We just got here, and it's been a really stressful couple of weeks. Can we maybe talk about this after dinner?" Liz asked, slumping in her seat. She looked like she'd been through hell.

"It's all right, Liz," Blair said, leaning forward until his face was even with her headrest. "Yes, Trevor. I study pyramids. That's what I was doing in Peru. I don't want to give you the whole story right now, but we found something that some unfriendly people want very badly."

"Does it have anything to do with the attacks down in Peru?" Trevor asked, praying the answer was no.

The question seemed to catch the pair totally off guard. Neither answered. Nor would they look at him. If he didn't know better, he'd say Blair was eyeing the door as if he were considering the risks of ejecting himself into traffic. The silence was damning.

"Well, does it?" Trevor asked again, tone firming. He switched on his blinker and glided into the slow lane.

"Listen, Trev, now really isn't—" Liz began. He hit his hazards, jamming on the breaks and pulling onto the shoulder in a spray of gravel.

"Think very carefully about your next words, Liz," Trevor said, his voice as soft as death. "I sent you a big chunk of my savings along with that passport and picked you up at the border, knowing you've likely committed some sort of crime. I will *not* be toyed with or kept in the dark. It's me, Liz. Let me in on this and I'll help." He locked eyes with her, reaching over to give her hand a squeeze.

She was silent for a long moment, face betraying signs of her inner battle. The fact that she even had to think about it suggested whatever she was involved in was worse than he could possibly imagine.

"Blair, we have to tell him. Everything," she said, not breaking eye contact.

"Liz, there's no way he'll believe us. He's going to think—" Blair began, raising a hand to his door lock.

"He'll believe us," she said, quietly but with the determination Trevor had always loved about her. "I trust him more than anyone. He's my brother. Look what he's already done for us."

"All right," Blair said, lowering his hand. "Trevor, I don't know your sister well yet, but I've come to trust her. If she thinks you'll listen, then I'll tell you the truth, but you're not going to believe it."

"Try me," Trevor said, shifting to face Blair as best he could from the driver's seat. "We're not going anywhere until I at least know how you're connected to those killings."

"You want to do this, or should I?" Blair asked, turning to Liz. Then the oddest thing happened. Their gazes locked over the rim of their respective sunglasses. Something crackled between them, static electricity, maybe? He had no idea what to make of it.

"It's your story," Liz answered, electricity dissipating. She turned to face him. "Trevor, everything he's about to say is true. You know I wouldn't lie to you. Hear us out." She turned back to Blair. "Go ahead."

"I was called in to study a pyramid in Peru, the oldest ever found anywhere. It appeared all by itself about two months ago," Blair began, slouching back into his seat. The tension bled from him, as if telling his tale set him free somehow. "The people who built it are far more advanced than anything we've ever seen. And before you go there, no, there was no evidence of aliens. No gate with a wormhole to another world. But these people accomplished things we can only guess at."

Trevor quietly turned back to the road, flicking off his hazards and turning his blinker on. He waited for an opening and then gunned the engine. The Rover roared back into traffic as Blair continued.

"I was called in to find a hidden central chamber the Peruvian government suspected was there. They were backed by the Mohn Corporation," he said, pausing for a reaction.

"I've heard of them. Private mercenaries. Contractors, they call themselves."

"Mercenaries with an agenda," Blair gave back. "They were the ones running the show, not the Peruvian government. They knew about the pyramid before anyone else and had already checked the place out before they brought my team in. They held back a lot of important information, like the radiation coming from the central chamber. I watched a good friend wither into a madman."

Trevor stayed in the slow lane, angling toward the 805 exit. The man seemed earnest thus far, but Trevor had a feeling there was still a bomb to be dropped.

"When I finally solved the puzzle, I sprung a trap. I was injected with something. Something lethal," he continued, pace slowing as he neared a topic he clearly didn't want to discuss. "Trevor, I died. My heart stopped. When I woke up, I was in a clinic with your sister. We were attacked by Mohn, but we got away—"

"Bullshit," Trevor said, drifting past a black Mazda and back into the fast lane. "You don't just 'get away' from Mohn, particularly in a backwater like Peru. If they wanted you dead, they'd have killed you. So how did you 'get away'?"

"You asked how we were linked to the attacks. Whatever I was injected with turned me into something. It altered my DNA, if your sister's theories are right. Mohn didn't let us get away. I tore them apart and they ran," he finished, turning to stare out the window as if waiting for condemnation.

Silenced reigned for a long time as Trevor considered the story. It was implausible for a lot of reasons, but it didn't sound like a lie. It *couldn't* be a lie, because Liz wouldn't lie to him, not once he'd confronted her like this. She was scared in a way he'd never seen.

Then there were the attacks, grisly murders that reporters couldn't explain. Like animal attacks but on a scale that made no sense. As outlandish as Blair's tale was thus far, it *could* explain them. Still, something bothered him.

"So you turn into some sort of creature," Trevor allowed, glancing over his shoulder. "Did you kill all those people, then?"

"No," Blair said, a little too quickly. "A percentage of those killed come back as the same kind of creature. That's how the attacks are spreading, at least that's our best guess."

"So what kind of creature is this, exactly?"

"Trevor," Liz interrupted, squeezing his hand in exactly the same way he'd done. "This is the part you aren't going to believe."

45

RECONCILIATION

Bridget rose to her feet and began to pace again. It was a precise twelve steps from one corner of the unrelieved white wall to the other, twelve shuffling steps forced by her manacles. The room wasn't tiny, but it was completely barren. No decorations. No furniture. Nothing to entertain a mind that had grown desperate from boredom.

The only thing she had to stare at was the black serial number etched into the thick manacles binding her wrists. 2746891. The silver sat atop some sort of rubber compression bands, noticeably stronger than the originals. If she stretched or flexed, they moved with her, ostensibly to prevent her from tearing them off if she shifted.

Mohn Corp. had performed extensive tests of her abilities after Steve had disappeared, and she'd been warned that the manacles were tough enough to withstand her incredible strength. She didn't care to test the theory. Where would she go even if she could somehow break free? The place was, no doubt, ringed with soldiers, and even if she got past them, there was nowhere left for her.

Blair might live if he'd risen in the same way she had, but she had no way to find him. What would he say if she did? Steve hadn't returned after the horrible day where they'd removed him, though in a way that had been a relief. He'd ignored her, refusing to speak no matter how many times she approached him.

Could she blame him? Not really. She'd grown attached to Blair again after his arrival. All the old attraction had come flooding back, and even in Steve's deranged state, he must have been aware of it. Steve had been dead to her. He'd wasted away, a shell of his former self. A man who'd fawned over her for years was suddenly cold, angry, and even violent. Yet that changed nothing. She'd been horrible, both to him and to Blair.

It was funny, really. Here she was, in the midst of the worst personal crisis of her life. She'd become a mythological monster and was locked away from the world, probably never to be released. Yet what really haunted her was her treatment of the only two men she'd ever really loved. If she had to do it over again, what would she do differently? Nothing. That was the truly agonizing part. She was trapped in a web of emotions, one of her own making. She loved them both.

Bridget froze, head cocked toward the door. Footsteps echoed in the hall outside. Two pairs were approaching, a soldier to escort and one real visitor. But who were they allowing to see her? Or was it time for her execution? More tests, maybe? The possibilities danced before her as she squatted down into the least threatening position possible.

The seal around the door hissed as it popped open to reveal one of the black-clad soldiers, a bearded man with dark skin. His eyes were glued to her chest through the embarrassingly flimsy gown they'd given her. She'd grown used to that reaction, but that they couldn't be more professional still irritated her. Were there really that few women in camp?

The soldier held the door open, eyes still fixed on her breasts as Sheila stepped into the room. She looked so odd in her black fatigues and white tank top. Were they mandating uniforms even for the research team now? And why had she come?

"Make this fast," the soldier said, finally prying his gaze from Bridget's chest as he stared disapprovingly at Sheila. "I'll be right outside. If you're not out in three minutes, I'm dragging you out."

"I understand," Sheila answered, patting his arm. "Thank you so much for this. I'll be quick."

The soldier slipped from the room, shooting Bridget one more leer before the door snapped shut with another hiss. Sheila met her gaze, nodding to the camera. Then she stepped forward, gathering Bridget's much smaller frame into a hug.

"They can't know you have this," her former friend whispered, pressing a small bundle into her hands. Bridget slipped it inside her gown, dropping into a crouch to further hide it. It was small but thick. A book, maybe?

"So you're probably wondering why I came to see you," Sheila said, much louder for the camera's benefit. She leaned against the wall next to the door. She ran the back of her hand across her forehead, cheeks still flushed from the cold. Bridget had almost forgotten how wintery it was outside.

"I'll admit I'm surprised," Bridget replied, pressing her back against the wall and cradling the book under her gown. "I know we worked together for a while when you came to see Steve and I, but all that stopped. I thought you were done with me. You said you hated me."

"I did. For a long time, I did," Sheila said, her back sliding down the wall as she settled opposite Bridget. "You know why. Not just what you did to Blair, but also what you did to Steve."

"So why come, then? Nothing's changed there. I can't erase the sins of the past."

"Perspective, that's what changed," she said, scrubbing a hand through dark-brown hair that had recently reached her shoulders. It looked much better long. "I started thinking. What would I have done in your shoes? If Steve had wanted me, I'd have taken him. But what if Blair had wanted me too? What if I'd been the pretty one? The one all the men fawn over.

"I can't honestly say I'd have done anything differently than you. Maybe I'd have been you if our roles were reversed," she continued, seemingly unable to make eye contact. "When you died, I really questioned my actions. Should I have cut you off, or tried to understand you? Then you came back. I had a second chance. I watched you closely while we were working together, the way you were around Steve now. You genuinely feel guilty, don't you? I can see it weighing on you."

"Yes," Bridget replied without hesitation. "It eats at me. I was weak. I'll admit it. I liked the attention, from both of them. And I love both of them. How fucked up is that? I can't pick. I want them both. Now I have neither."

"I'm sorry for that," Sheila said, finally meeting her gaze.

"You mean that, don't you?" Bridget asked, utterly shocked by the statement.

"You made a real mess of things, but we were friends for over a decade. You're not a horrible person, Bridget. Maybe a little self-centered, but no one deserves what you've been through."

"I—Sheila, I don't know what to say. What changed your mind?"

"My health is deteriorating," Sheila said, as if talking about the weather. "This was probably going to be my last dig, no matter what."

"Cancer?"

"No, HIV. I've had it almost three years," she admitted, using the wall to help her back to her feet. "I'm not going to die or anything, but the disease has really made me question my own mortality. My symptoms were mild until about six months ago, but since then they've been getting steadily worse. I can barely get out of bed a lot of days."

"Sheila, HIV is treatable. You can get help," Bridget said, eyes tearing up. She'd just regained her friend and felt like she was already losing her. "Can't you talk to Mohn? There must be something they can do."

"I've been to all sorts of doctors, tried all the latest medications. It does provide a lot of relief, but I'm tired all the time," Sheila said, pausing. She cocked her head and gave a warm smile. "I'm not going to be able to do field work forever. I want to spend what time I have left doing the things I love. Learning and discovering, just like we always have. So that's what I'm going to do. I just needed someone to know, and despite everything that's happened, you're still my best friend."

"That means more to me than you'll ever know," Bridget said, overcome with emotion.

The door hissed a third time, popping open to reveal the soldier again. "Come on. I could get in serious trouble for this. You're done here."

Sheila turned to the man with a nod, one teardrop sliding down her cheek as she exited. She didn't look back as the door closed, leaving Bridget in silence.

Bridget glanced up at the ever-present camera, shifting against the wall until she faced away from it. She carefully removed the bundle from under her gown, making very sure to interpose her body between it and the camera.

It was a pocket-sized leather-bound book, the sort of journal Sheila loved to use. A small letter was tucked inside. Bridget carefully removed the yellow paper, quickly scanning the contents.

Bridget,

I came to make peace today and hope I was able to do that. I wasn't sure I'd be able to find the words, so hopefully I did. That wasn't the only reason I came to see you. I've learned some truly frightening things since we last spoke.

Using Blair's notes and our work with Steve I have a pretty good understanding of the inner chamber now. I believe I've puzzled out why this exists. Something horrible is coming. I believe it's tied to the Galactic Procession. Every 13,000 years something strange happens with our sun. I don't know what or how, but this ancient culture warned that it could end all life on the planet.

They believe that werewolves were our only chance of survival. They refer to them as champions and that they're our only defense against whatever catastrophe is coming. That's why I had to see you. You're one of them now, and if the ancients are right we're going to need your help.

I'm doing my best to get you out. I've grown close with Jordan and am hoping to persuade him to aid in your escape. Until then sit tight, but be ready to move. In the meantime I've included all my research notes in case they're useful. If nothing else, hopefully it will alleviate the boredom you must be feeling.

I'm sorry for everything that's happened between us. I hope we get a chance to start over after all of this is done.

Your Friend,
Sheila

Hot tears rained on the page. Knowing that Sheila had forgiven her felt wonderful. Maybe she would have a chance to start over, assuming she survived whatever impending apocalypse was coming.

46

MOONLIGHT

"You still take sugar, right? It's in the cupboard above the coffee maker," Trevor asked her, leaning against the island in the center of the kitchen. Liz nodded absently in Trevor's direction, admiring the dark wood as she opened the cabinet.

"These are new," she said, fishing out the small bag of white sugar and dumping a liberal portion into the heavenly black liquid filling her mug. "Did you install them yourself?"

"Yeah, I got tired of looking at the old ones. Pour me a cup too?" he asked, withdrawing his wallet and keys and dropping them on the counter. "I'll fire up the grill. Coffee and venison isn't exactly conventional, but given what you've told me, I'm guessing we've got a long night ahead of us."

Blair entered the kitchen from the broad hallway leading to the front door. Liz could smell the soap from the bathroom on his hands, mingled with the pungent scent of sweat.

"Trevor, do you have a computer I can use?" he asked, oblivious to the conversation he'd interrupted. "I'd like to do some research on the glyphs in the pyramid."

"Sure, my office is through that door on the right. Computer's on the desk," Trevor replied, accepting the mug that Liz handed him. He paused long enough for Blair to enter the office before turning back to her. "So, give it to me straight. What exactly do you think happened to you guys? Virus? Disease of some form?"

"We'll have to get some blood work done to know for certain, but my gut says virus," Liz said, leaning heavily on the counter behind her. Her vision swam, just for a moment. The feeling faded, sending a shiver down her spine as her skin itched the way it had in Peru, under the moon. She ignored it.

Trevor considered her words for several moments, sipping at his coffee. The soft hiss of an air conditioner came on behind him, quietly battling the warmth that had accumulated in the home over the last few hours. "Whatever it is seems to have altered your DNA at a fundamental level; it would have to in order to make the things you describe even possible. I'm guessing if we sequenced your genome, we'd find that it's rewritten entire segments. But I have no idea how it inserted a wholly separate consciousness into your heads. That's way beyond anything modern science has achieved. Into that woo-woo stuff you and Mom love."

"Yeah okay, Agent Scully. You used to love it too," Liz chided, sipping her own coffee. "Besides, doesn't look so much like woo woo anymore, does it? Blair can read minds. If that isn't woo woo, I don't know what it is."

"Okay, okay, you have a point," Trevor said, delivering one of those boyish grins. "You and Mom owe me a big 'I told you so.' Listen, I have a friend that runs a small startup in San Francisco. They make microscopes that attach to your smartphone, and Erik owes me a favor. I can probably get him to send me one so we can do a blood test without the risk of bringing you guys out into public."

"Thank you," she replied. "That would be a huge help."

"I'm hungry. How about you?" Trevor asked, setting down his coffee and replacing it with the platter of steaks. "Shall we take this outside while I grill?"

Liz had a moment of worry when she looked at the generous slabs of meat. Every horror movie she'd ever seen said that she should crave raw meat. She rose to follow him, leaving her coffee on the counter. The instant she stepped outside, something hot and angry flared in her belly, like cramps, only far, far worse.

The porch light came on, illuminating the back deck. The wooden planks had been stained the same color as the cabinets, and was now ringed by a newly installed fence. It stood nearly seven feet tall, enough to screen them from neighboring houses, had there been any. They were surrounded by shrub-covered hillside extending beyond the house. Her brother had the most precious commodity in Southern California—privacy.

Trevor opened a chrome grill large enough for an entire cow, setting the plate with the steaks on the platform built into the grill's right side. He grabbed a tightly bristled brush and began scraping it along the grill.

"So you think it's some sort of virus that was engineered by a prehistoric culture somehow advanced enough to understand genetics," he said, glancing at her as he used a pair of tongs to move steaks onto the grill. "If that's true, their choice of animals seems odd. Why wolves? Why not bears or tigers or something? Wolves are predators, but they're hardly the most successful hunters in the animal kingdom."

Liz's freshman biology class supplied the answer. "At a guess? Canines have the most malleable DNA of any mammal. Almost every breed of dog was created in the last two centuries. You can radically alter a dog in just a couple generations," she explained, pulling one of Trevor's folding chairs toward the grill. She collapsed heavily into it. A tingling itch spread across the back of her neck. It wasn't hard to figure out why. The moon's fat crescent hung low over the eastern horizon, nearly touching a mountain in the distance.

"That's plausible," Trevor said, clicking the igniter. The grill lit with a soft whoosh. He was studying her the way one might an animal at the zoo. "So you mentioned that you could feel something in the moonlight. Do you feel it now?"

"Yes. It's almost painful, like standing in the sun long enough to burn," she said, glancing up at the offending ivory crescent. Was she experiencing the same sort of overload Blair had faced back at the border crossing? It would make sense.

Yes, Ka-Ken. You must feed, and soon. The voice startled and chilled her in equal measure.

"Now that's definitely interesting," Trevor said, pulling a Star Wars apron their sister Jessie had given him for Christmas around his neck and tying it behind his back. "All light is just a certain bandwidth of radiation. Plants use it for photosynthesis. We use it for solar power. There's no reason whatever this virus is couldn't use it as a power source. I suspect Erik might find chlorophyll or something very similar when we do your blood work. That still leaves the question of why moonlight instead of sunlight. Have you felt anything odd during the day?"

"Not so far. Neither has Blair. It always happens with the moon," she replied, fidgeting in her chair. She just couldn't get comfortable, and she was starting to feel nauseated. The symptoms were alarmingly close to what Blair had described. "That seems odd. Sunlight is a lot more plentiful than moonlight. If I were going to design a virus, sunlight would make more sense."

"Every ray of light has a certain wavelength. Light reflected off the moon would have a different signature than that of the sun," Trevor mused, deftly flipping the steaks. "You're right that sunlight is a lot more constant than moonlight, but I think I might understand why moonlight would work better. If you absorbed sunlight, it would risk overload if you stood in the sun all day. Have you ever seen what happens to a battery you let charge too long?"

"Yeah, it melts," Liz said, almost certain she was about to share the same fate as the hypothetical battery. She wobbled to her feet, right hand using the lawn chair for support. "I think I'm going to wait inside, out of the moonlight. I'm not feeling too well."

"All right," Trevor said, giving her a worried look as she stepped inside. She felt immediate relief, though she was still sick to her stomach. Her brother followed her to the doorway, tongs still clutched in one hand. "Here's the thing. The light we see reflected from the moon is only one bandwidth. There are others we can't see.

Those can still reach you even indoors. So that will help, but it isn't going to protect you entirely. If we need to, we can get you into the panic room. That should shield you from the bandwidths we can't see."

"I think that might be a good idea," she said, doubling over in sudden agony as fire spread through her gut.

You MUST feed, Ka-Ken. Slay this one. If he is strong, he will rise to join you. If not, you spare him a fate worse than death.

I won't, she thought back, leaning heavily against the wall just inside the sliding glass door.

You must. The male can bleed his energy with shaping. You cannot. If you do not feed, you will relinquish control to me whether I will it or no. You brim with power, and it must find release.

"Trevor," she began, voice quavering. She was shaking uncontrollably now. Sweat poured from every pore, drenching her shirt in seconds. "Trevor, you need to get into your gun safe and lock the door, now."

"Gun safe?" Trevor asked, stepping closer to the door. "Liz, you look like you need a hospital. You're white as a sheet. Are you okay?"

"I think I'm going to shift. The last time that happened, I killed a man," she said, sagging to her knees and cradling her gut. This couldn't be happening. Not again. "Trevor, I can't control myself when I shift. Please, get away. Quickly. Before it's too late."

Trevor flicked the knob on the grill, killing the heat. Then he darted inside, undoing his apron as he moved. He knelt next to her, placing a hand against her forehead. She could see in his eyes that he still didn't quite believe that she was going to turn into a werewolf. Who could blame him? It was still an implausible story as far as he was concerned.

"Trevor, please," she begged, back arching as the transformation began. Fire flooded her body as the beast seized control.

His eyes widened as he finally realized what he was seeing. Trevor rose unsteadily to his feet, pausing to watch her as the change took hold. Didn't he understand how dangerous this was?

"Trevor, *run!*" she shrieked.

47

GUN SAFE

Trevor was transfixed by the sight before him. Liz's back arched, bones cracking and snapping as a low, horrifying wail burst from her throat. It warbled and changed, deepening into a howl. Her blouse and skirt split at the seams as her body expanded and changed, fur bursting from her skin like bad special effects in some B movie. It didn't even look real. But it was.

He'd seen enough horror movies to know what came next. She would become a rampaging monster that would tear everyone and everything around her apart. If Trevor was still here when she'd finished her transformation, he was going to die. It was time to run, despite the fact that none of this should have been possible. He discarded logic, giving in to the primitive limbic system that had kept mankind's ancestors alive for over three million years.

Trevor bolted up the hallway, past the office where Blair was working. He didn't bother warning the anthropologist, because he figured Blair was safe. After all, Blair could just turn into a werewolf and fight back. Trevor didn't have that luxury.

He skidded to a halt in front of the reinforced door leading to the garage, cursing himself for keeping the deadbolt locked. His keys were in the kitchen. He reversed course back up the hallway, skidding across the linoleum. He'd have fallen if he hadn't caught himself against the wall with one arm. There, on the island. The slender ring with five keys, two for the house, one for the walk-in safe, and one for each vehicle. He seized them triumphantly, already turning when something large rose from the spot Liz had just occupied.

Covered in thick auburn fur, it stood on tree-trunk legs. The creature slouched, but its back and shoulders still knocked a shower of plaster from the high ceiling. Beady eyes of alarming amber landed on him, and he was shocked to see how human they appeared. The creature bared its fangs at him exactly the same way a dog would; then it flexed massive hands tipped with ebony claws. He was going to die if he didn't move.

Trevor bolted back down the hallway, skidding around the corner past the refrigerator as the thing bounded after him. Each footfall tore furrows in the hard wood, but its enormous weight prevented it from finding solid footing. It careened into his refrigerator with a tremendous bang before he lost sight of it.

Several precious seconds later Trevor reached the door to the garage. Trembling fingers fumbled at the lock, and he breathed a sigh of relief when the key slid home. He jerked the handle, pushing the door open and slipping inside the garage. A quick glance up the hall confirmed every nightmare he'd ever had.

The werewolf charged forward, ripping free another shower of plaster as its head smashed into the ceiling. It bounded toward him, and he barely had time to slam the heavy door before something massive crashed into it.

He inserted the key into the deadbolt, twisting it with a satisfying click. Would that even slow the thing down? He couldn't assume that it would, though he certainly hoped so. The frame was reinforced steel, just like the front and back doors. A lot of his friends thought he was paranoid, but when you lived in such a remote place being targeted for home invasion was common. Even a SWAT team with a battering ram would take time to get through that door.

Now what? He surveyed the garage for options. The white '65 Mustang he'd spent the last two years restoring dominated one side.

Several workbenches occupied the other. There were tools over there, from heavier hammers to a machete he'd brought with him on a hunting trip. None of that would slow down a rampaging werewolf.

Gun safe, maybe? It ran the entire length of the garage and was walled off with steel-reinforced concrete, a narrow steel door standing open at one end. His ex had demanded he build it because she'd been uncomfortable with the idea of guns in the house.

He'd designed it to keep things in, not out. It was a combination door, so even if the werewolf was smart, it wouldn't have easy access. Once inside he'd be trapped, though. Would there be enough oxygen? He didn't know. Trevor hesitated for an agonizing moment as something heavy thudded into the door behind him. The door shivered in its frame but held. He was running out of time.

Trevor darted into the gun safe, flicking the light switch just inside the door. Fluorescent light illuminated a gun collection he'd accumulated over his adult life, each weapon complete with the memory of both acquiring it and learning to fire it. He scanned the wall, considering which option might save him in the face of a life-threatening werewolf. Another hollow boom came from behind him, this one accompanied by the tortured shriek of metal. Shit.

He considered the H&K USP .45 caliber, but the pistol would take too long to load. Most of the rifles needed more room than the garage would afford. That left either the Remington pump-action shotgun or the Browning A5 his dad had given him for his sixteenth birthday. He settled on that one, its wooden stock familiar as he removed it from the wall and grabbed a box of shells.

Trevor poked his head through the gun safe's door. His jaw dropped when he saw the ruined door leading into the house. The frame had held, but the werewolf had battered the center portion until both metal and wood were giving way. A large hole gaped in the middle, not large enough for a person but certainly getting there.

He slid a trio of shells into the side of the shotgun, cocking the bolt after each one. The motion was automatic, learned over thousands of hours of shooting. It was the gun he was most familiar with, and it packed one hell of a punch at short range. Trevor tipped the box's remaining shells into his jacket pocket, advancing slowly toward the door as he prepared to defend himself.

Maybe falling back into the gun safe right now would be the smartest thing, but this was his home, damn it. He wasn't going to give up without a fight. Besides, his sister was still inside that thing somewhere. Maybe she could fight it for control. If not, he just prayed he'd be fast enough to retreat into the safe. The idea of being trapped in an airtight box wasn't appealing, but if he needed to retreat that would be better than dying.

The beast's monstrous head and shoulders plowed into the door, ripping steel as it forced its way through. Trevor didn't think. He brought the stock smoothly up to his shoulder and sighted down the barrel, aligning it with the beast's face. The gun coughed, kicking into his shoulder as the acrid smell of gunpowder filled the garage.

The beast jerked backward, one eye exploding into ruined gore. The furious howl it gave was deafening as it went berserk, tearing apart more of the door in an attempt to reach him. Trevor fired again. The beast's other eye disappeared, the howl going from furious to agonized. Tough to fight when you're blind.

Then his jaw sagged. Flesh and bone vibrated as the thing's face began to knit back together. Both eyes scrunched shut, and when they opened a moment later, the beast glared furiously at him through both eyes. The only trace of the damage was the blood-matted fur covering its face.

The beast roared, bursting through the remains of the door in a shower of metal fragments. Trevor recoiled, shielding his face as the shrapnel whirled past him. Something bit into his arm, but he ignored it. He was already moving toward the gun safe, conscious of the enormous form so close behind him that he felt hot breath waft over his neck.

Trevor went low in a baseball slide, flipping onto his back and aiming the shotgun at the thing's knee. He fired, a momentary surge of triumph filling him as the beast's knee exploded. It stumbled, catching itself with ungainly arms. That only bought him seconds, but he hoped it would be enough.

He scrambled inside, staggering to his feet and yanking the door. The heavy metal closed slowly, inching inward as he strained against it. The gap closed to just a few inches. He pulled harder, willing it shut. Furry claws appeared, grabbing the door the very instant before it would have slammed shut. They arrested the door's momentum, and it began to swing open.

Trevor darted a glance at the wall full of weapons, but they may as well have been miles away. He'd never have time to load them. He was going to die.

48

BLUR

lair sat down in the leather-backed computer chair, swiveling it to face the twenty-seven-inch iMac dominating the cherrywood desk. He'd always preferred PCs, but Macs were more common in the academic world, so he had no problem firing up the machine and launching Safari. He typed, "Mayan glyphs" into the search bar and then browsed the top several results.

The first link showed the glyphs at Tayasal, a small island in Guatemala that had once served as the capital of the Mayan empire. He studied the style of the glyphs with an eye for the patterns he'd seen on the pyramid in Cajamarca, noting distinct similarities. The language was certainly less complex, but there were similar markers in the same way that Latin words had crept into English. The similarities were hardly definitive but suggested that the Mayan language might have its roots in the language of the ancients.

He leaned back in the chair, absently running his fingers through his hair as he studied the images. What was the connection? The pyramid had been buried, and the two were separated by a dozen millennia. How was it even remotely possible that the Mayans knew anything about the ancients? The question was maddening because to even approach an answer would take a team of scientists months of research. Months he didn't have.

Be wary, Ka-Dun. The Ka-Ken stirs.

His concentration shattered as an all-too-familiar howl sounded from the kitchen. Blair shot to his feet, spilling the chair onto its side. Trevor's form flashed by the doorway as he pounded toward the garage. Blair was still deciding what to do when Trevor barreled the other direction, back into the kitchen where the howl had originated. There was a clatter of keys; then Trevor sprinted past again.

A moment later a hulking auburn form pounded past with murderous intent. Blair was sure she was going to kill her brother unless he did something.

She is suffused with power, Ka-Dun. You will not find it easy to invade her mind this time. Shaping will be of little use. You must best her in combat if you seek to save this unblooded, and that is nearly impossible against a raging Ka-Ken.

"She's larger, stronger, and faster. I can't win that fight," Blair said, hurrying to the door and peering down the hall. The floor was littered with plaster, and the linoleum had been scored in many places by sharp claws. The werewolf beat at the heavy door Trevor had managed to close behind him, but it didn't look like getting through would take her long.

Larger and stronger, yes. You can be faster than any female if you will it so.

"Faster, how?" Blair asked, wincing as Liz-wolf's fist punched through the door leading into the garage. At least she hadn't noticed him yet.

You must blur. The ability enables you to move faster than the eye can see. It is taxing, but when facing a female in combat, it is our only hope of victory. You have already tasted the power, though you still lack conscious control.

"Worth a try, I guess," Blair replied. He was tempted to ask the beast how to activate the ability, but he knew all he'd get back was some cryptic Yoda crap. He stepped into the hallway and took a deep breath. The werewolf didn't even glance at him, instead shattering the door into kindling as she burst into the garage.

Blair shifted. It came easily now, his body tearing through his clothing with shocking speed as it rearranged itself into a now-familiar lupine form. Damn it, he should have taken his clothes off first. Oh well.

He had to admit that he enjoyed the rush of strength, the sharpened senses. He felt invincible. Could he be killed? He'd never seen a werewolf die, but he reasoned that if one took enough damage, it could be killed.

We can die, Ka-Dun, if we lack the energy to heal or if we suffer grievous-enough injury.

"Great," Blair said, imagining what the much larger Liz-wolf could do to him. He peered around the corner again in time to see Liz-wolf's head and shoulders disappear through the remains of the door. A shotgun roared in the garage. The noise was deafening to his augmented hearing, and he stumbled backward with a wince.

Liz-wolf's head rocked backward, but that was the only visible effect. A second shot came a moment later, resulting in a similar jerk. Then Liz-wolf went berserk, tearing through the doorway and into the garage. Her nails skittered across the concrete as she chased Trevor out of sight.

Blair followed, pausing in the ruined doorway to survey the garage. A pristine white Mustang from the '60s was flanked by a number of workbenches. On one of them, a black car-sized tarp sat neatly folded next to a can of wax and a white rag. A third shotgun blast roared, drawing his eyes to the far side of the garage. Liz-wolf tumbled to the ground in a spray of blood and a crack of bone as Trevor scrambled through a narrow doorway with a steel frame set into the concrete wall.

He reached out and yanked on a thick metal door, frantically struggling to pull it shut as Liz-wolf regained her feet. She bounded forward, seizing the edge of the door just before it could slam shut.

If she got it open, Trevor was a dead man. Not only would they lose their only ally, but Liz would never forgive herself for the attack.

Blair *had* to stop it, for both their sakes. He sprinted forward, willing himself to move faster. He had no idea what he was doing, no idea how to harness the strange abilities he'd been cursed with.

Perhaps it was his need, or conviction or just damned luck. Regardless, his limbs filled with liquid warmth. It was like the fire of the change, but instead of pain, he felt something akin to massive adrenaline. It was heady. Powerful. And with it, he moved like the wind. Or rather the world slowed to a crawl.

He had an eternity to study the situation, to decide what to do. Blair was moving normally, but the rest of the world was bathed in molasses. Liz-wolf's muscles tensed, and the door inched open with agonizing finality. Blair sized up the room again, forming a plan.

He blurred forward, the world slowing still further as he seized the tarp and leapt into the air. He unfolded it, roughly forming a bag. Then he slammed it down over Liz-wolf's upper body. It came down to her waist, obscuring both her arms and murderous fangs.

He landed nimbly and then delivered a vicious kick to the same knee Trevor had shot just a few moments before. Liz-wolf toppled to the ground, tangled up in the tarp. Blair leapt into the air as she began to rise, coming down on her back with his considerable weight. She was off balance from her wounded leg and what he hoped was unexpected blindness, and the move knocked her into the wall so hard that cinder blocks shattered under the blow.

Blair clung to her back, arms encircling her over the tarp. A sharp tearing sounded, and Liz-wolf's head tore free from the tarp. Murderous amber eyes gazed back at him over her shoulder as her lips came up in a snarl.

"Uh oh," Blair said, panting now. He felt like he'd run a marathon, limbs trembling from the exertion of the blur.

Liz-wolf gave a furious roar, leaping to her feet with Blair still on her back. Her arms strained against his, flexing with incredible strength. Then she gave a sudden burst, ripping from his grasp and tearing away the remains of the tarp. He tumbled to the garage floor, his elbow coming down painfully. Before he could rise, Liz spun, raking at his chest with wickedly sharp claws.

What fear for one's life could do was amazing. The blur returned, sending Blair straight up. He seized her suddenly sluggish wrist with both hands. He twisted in mid-flight, maneuvering behind her and raking into her back with his own claws. The wound sent forth a stream of blood and knocked Liz forward a step. She recovered quickly, turning to face him as he danced backward to gain room to breathe. He was more agile than her, but he'd delivered his best attacks and she didn't seem even slightly phased.

She launched a flurry of swipes, claws touching nothing but air as he flowed desperately around each attack. Frustration lit Liz-wolf's features as she fell back a pace, dropping into a low crouch. She studied him, slowly circling. Every few seconds, her gaze would dart to their surroundings, scanning the garage as if seeking a weakness she could exploit. Was she trying to flee?

Then she vanished, body melting into the deep shadows cast by lonely halogen lights Trevor must have turned on when he'd entered the garage. Blair froze, straining to catch a hint of her heartbeat. It should thunder in his ears, but instead he heard nothing. There was the cry of a bat somewhere high above. A neighbor's dog barked in the distance. There was nothing else.

The massive metal door swung silently open, drawing Blair's gaze. Trevor emerged with a rifle slung over his back, a black pistol belted to his waist, and a pump-action shotgun cradled between his arms. He snapped the shotgun to his shoulder. Just a few feet from Blair's face, the mouth of the barrel was huge.

Trevor's finger began to tighten on the trigger. Blair blurred. He rolled forward, coming to his feet behind Trevor as the shotgun roared. The blast rang Blair's ears like a gong as the stench of gunpowder renewed.

"Trevor," he roared, voice deep and bestial. It was the first time he'd spoken as a werewolf. "It's Blair. I won't hurt you. I can help you stop Liz."

Trevor spun, already bringing the shotgun to bear. Blair was faster. He seized the barrel in one furry fist, aiming it at the ground.

Trevor began to reach for the pistol holstered at his side but hesitated. His gaze held fear, but it was steady. Every part of his body was loose. Relaxed. It was the same way Jordan had moved, back in Cajamarca. He sounded calm despite the fact that his sister and her houseguest had just turned into monsters. Definitely not your average astronomer.

"How do I know you won't tear me apart the second I let my guard down?" Trevor asked.

"Because we're talking right now. If I wanted to kill you, then you'd be dead," Blair replied, releasing the shotgun and taking a step backward. He raised his hands in what he hoped was a placating gesture, palms out. "Liz is out of control. Her body is full of too much energy. Radiation, I think. I experienced something similar, but I'm in control now. She will be too if we give her time to burn off that excess."

She does not burn her reserves nearly so quickly as you do. Be wary, Ka-Dun. Such feats of speed are costly. Your strength wanes. You must conserve it for the trials ahead.

The beast's logic made sense. How much juice did he have left in whatever metaphysical battery powered his abilities? How quickly could the moonlight recharge him? The answers were essential to his survival.

"All right," Trevor said, lowering the shotgun. "What do we do?"

"We survive," Blair said in a low growl, stalking to the doorway of the house. He scanned the garage, but nothing stirred. It was far too quiet, the stillness just before a predator strikes. "Liz disappeared somehow. I have a number of abilities I don't fully understand, so it stands to reason that she does too. There's a division between the sexes. We can cover the specifics later, but the bottom line is I don't know what she's capable of. I do know she's larger, stronger, and just about impossible to kill."

"I almost took her face off with a shotgun, and she was fine just a few seconds later. We need to incapacitate her, but I have no idea what that's going to take. She can grow back an eye. Can she regrow limbs?" Trevor asked, putting his back to the wall near the door leading into the house. It gave him a vantage of both doors, probably a smart move.

Any wound can be healed, no matter how grievous, so long as you expend enough energy.

"As long as she has energy, she can knit herself back together. I'm not sure we *can* kill her," Blair rumbled, shifting his attention to the shattered door leading into the house. It gaped ominously. Everything was still, other than their heartbeats. No cicadas. No bats. Nothing. The whole yard outside was holding its breath, fervently attempting to avoid the notice of the predator lurking in its midst.

"Regenerating takes time though, right? At least a little. If we can disable her long enough to restrain her, we can give her time to regain control," Trevor said. It made sense.

"Now we just have to find her," Blair growled.

"We won't have to. She'll find us," the wiry man replied, feeding shells into the shotgun.

49

FEED

Liz railed within the confines of her own mind, helpless to stop the beast from slaughtering those she cared about. She'd hurled her will at the thing when it first pursued Trevor, to no avail. It had batted aside her attempts to wrest control, like a parent controlling a child's tantrum. Later, when the beast had been about to enter the gun room, she'd tried again. This time she'd reached into reserves she hadn't known she possessed and had managed to force the beast to pause. It had bought a few precious seconds, seconds during which she could have killed her brother.

Then Blair had attacked and the beast had regained control. She'd watched helplessly while it attempted to kill him, cheering every time he melted away from an attack with inhuman speed.

The beast was patient, though. It had somehow melded into the shadows, wearing them like a cloak. It slinked back into the house. Watching. Waiting. Studying. It now lurked in the hallway just beyond the shattered door leading to the garage, massive body invisible in the gathered darkness. Even Blair's heightened senses seemed unable to detect it. If only she could do something to betray the beast's presence.

It cannot be, Ka-Ken. We must feed, and soon. The male will give us the greatest strength, but the unblooded will suffice. He could prove a valuable ally if his blood is pure. He is near kin to you. The danger is less.

She considered reasoning with the beast but discarded the notion as foolish. It respected strength. The only way she was going to regain control was to take it by force. If it could be cunning, so could she. Liz offered no protest, merely watching. The beast would be distracted when it attacked. She could make her move then and, hopefully, wrest control.

The beast whiffed the air, inhaling deeply as it sorted the myriad of scents. Sweat. Fear. Gunpowder. It flowed to the doorway, wrapping the shadows more tightly about it. They clung to its fur, blotting out all light. It was an incredible ability, and even amidst the horror of her situation, she couldn't help but marvel at it. How was it done? Her brother would probably talk about refracting light or some other equally scientific explanation. He might even be right.

The beast studied the room's two occupants. Blair's furred form slouched against a waist-high red toolbox, the wheeled kind that held more tools than a person could ever possibly hope to use.

Do not be deceived by his posture. Every part of him strains to detect us. He is powerful. And dangerous. He must be dealt with first.

Her brother stood with a shotgun in hand, a rifle slung across his back, and a pistol holstered at his side. He scanned the very space they occupied, but his gaze roamed past them without any hint of recognition.

"We won't have to. She'll find us," he said, adding more shells to the Remington. She remembered when Dad had bought it for him.

The male is vulnerable. He dies.

Blair had turned to face Trevor, leaving his back to the doorway where the beast lurked. She felt it gather its weight on powerful legs and then leap into the air. Their form rose silently, descending toward Blair's unprotected back with incredible speed.

Somehow he saw it coming, already spinning toward them. It was too late. The beast tackled Blair's smaller form, pinning his arms as its jaw latched onto his throat. It bit down in a spray of blood, hot and coppery and wonderful.

The beast seized Blair's wrists, yanking his arms in opposite directions until they popped free of their sockets. Blair gave a gurgling scream, marred by his ruined throat. The wounds were mortal, at least on a human. The assault was a savage one, designed to cripple a foe before it could react. It worked perfectly. Blair sagged weakly, eyes rolling back into his head. He was dead unless she could do something.

Liz poured everything into seizing control of her arms, just that one part of her. She would *not* allow this to continue. The beast would be stopped. She was in control here.

No, Ka-Ken. You know not what you do. He is vulnerable. We can claim his strength. He is the Mother's direct progeny. We will become much greater, gain strength to combat the evil to come.

She was horrified. The beast wanted her to *devour* Blair. She could feel its thoughts, and they made her furious. She was tired of being the victim, of letting this thing commit atrocity after atrocity while wearing her skin. Never again would she allow this. It was time to put a collar on this fucking thing. Her body grew rigid, no longer pulling Blair's arms. She could *feel*. Those were her hands. *Her* toes.

Then a shape loomed to her side, something metallic flashing in the garage's wan light. Pain struck like an adder. She watched in shock as her right wrist was severed in a spray of blood. She released Blair, seizing the severed stump with her other hand. Liz could only gape at the sight of her brother already raising the machete for a second strike.

The beast charged from the back of her mind, seizing control once more. It shot out the whole arm, grabbing Trevor around the neck and hoisting him into the air. Then it began to squeeze. Her brother's eyes bulged in agony. He was a hairbreadth from having his larynx crushed. He seized the machete in both hands, bringing it up in a tight arc. The weapon bit into the beast's wrist, severing a tendon.

Trevor dropped to the floor, dropping the machete with a clatter as he rolled backward and came to his feet. He drew a huge black pistol from the thigh holster, both hands wrapped tightly around the grip as he brought the muzzle into alignment with her belly. She tried twisting away but was too late. The gun bucked once, twice, and then a third time. All three rounds caught her in the gut, searing into her vital organs and forcing her to take staggering steps backward.

The beast went wild, battling her with an intensity she'd never imagined. Liz clung to control, maintaining the tiniest grip in the face of the assault. She had to buy them time to kill her, because the alternative was unthinkable. Trevor was her brother, and while she'd only known Blair a short time, he was the only one who understood what she was going through.

Hairy arms wrapped around her neck, yanking her from her feet. Blair tightened the crook of his arm around her throat, every muscle straining as he cut off her air supply. The beast sought to dislodge him, bucking wildly and nearly tossing the smaller werewolf away. Blair clung like a spider, refusing to let go.

"Kill me, Blair," Liz roared, forcing her arms to drop to her sides. "Do it. Quickly. I won't fight you."

His grip tightened. Blackness ate at her vision.

50

BONITA

Ahiga studied the house below. A structure suitable for a large family, set by itself atop a squat hill. The place was a welcome relief from the mad clusters of buildings he'd passed to get here. People living on top of each other, filling every available space. Dwellings so tightly clustered had been unheard of in his time but seemed common in this new world of pollution and appallingly crowded cities. Yet the structure was larger than many he'd seen. Did it mark the home's owner as a man of prestige or power? If so, this man could make a potent ally for the whelp's fledgling pack. One they would sorely need in the days ahead.

The house was bathed in the light of the gibbous moon. A steady light burned in what Ahiga took to be the kitchen. He'd learned that term from one of the hosts he'd consumed. During his own time food had been both prepared and eaten in the same area. The idea that one needed separate rooms for each task was wholly alien, but then so were the size and opulence of these dwellings. The homes he'd known were both smaller and less ostentatious than those possessed by even the lowest of the unblooded he'd seen.

Several shapes loped through the darkness, ranging the rocky ground as they sought field mice or rabbits. Ahiga had called the coyotes to his service, and they recognized him as their alpha. They would serve as additional eyes and ears, and could even aid in combat if needed. He'd have preferred the ferocity of wolves, but one made due with the tools at hand.

Ahiga glanced at the moon, mood souring. It was the second cycle since he'd awoken, and he'd still neither revived the Mother nor convinced the whelp to do so. What would the Mother say when she finally woke? She wasn't known for her temperament and had occasionally destroyed those who failed her. What would she do to someone who'd failed as monumentally as he?

It spurred him to action. Ahiga concentrated, using a surge of energy to make his body malleable. He shifted, but not into the powerful werewolf his kind had become known for. No, this required more finesse. Ahiga became a small brown wolf, one that an observer might mistake for a very large coyote. In many ways the form was more familiar to him than that of a man.

He trotted through the darkness, winding past scrubby bushes and boulders of various sizes. His path brought him closer and closer to the house, allowing him to hear the trio of heartbeats within. All beat slow and steady. They were confident. Or at least not immediately afraid, not like they had been mere hours ago when the female had gone berserk in an energy rage. Both Blair and their new human companion had been lucky to survive that encounter. An enraged female was nothing to trifle with.

Ahiga found a boulder not far from the window where the strange boxes they called computers were kept. The whelp's newest ally sat in front of the box, holding a small black communication device to his ear. Trevor, that was the man's name.

"Thanks, David. I appreciate you covering for me. Has anyone asked why I wasn't there today?" his host asked. He paused for a moment as he listened to the response. "Hey, are you following the data we've been tracking on that sun spot?"

There was another pause. Ahiga could hear a voice on the other end of the speaking device, but couldn't make out the words.

"I've been a little busy," Trevor replied. The lack of context was maddening. Another pause.

"Yeah, well, they're going to want to make time for this. If this thing keeps growing, it could release a CME bigger than the Carrington Event. That could do catastrophic damage to the world's power grid," Trevor said, tone somber. Ahiga was pleased that the unblooded seemed to understand the magnitude of what was to come. A part of it at least. "Have you notified the Director?"

"Are you kidding?" The voice on the other end said, finally loud enough for Ahiga to make out words. "The Director doesn't take calls from me. I'm just your sidekick. You want to notify the guy? You're going to have to call him yourself."

Ahiga left his perch, circling the house until he was near one of the other heartbeats. It was low and strong, familiar. There. Blair stood in the backyard, eyes closed, presumably so he could focus on his hearing. He was studying his surroundings but had not yet found Ahiga. The whelp was learning in spite of himself. Ahiga could not help but revel in the sight. It was a tiny ember of hope, but it was more than he'd had just moments ago.

He retreated back up the hillside, loping on four legs at a ground-eating pace he could maintain for hours. Soon it would be time to present himself, but first Blair and his pack must have the time to discover the truth. Only then could Ahiga hope to sway them to his cause.

51

SORRY

Blair inhaled deeply, eyes closing as he savored the nectar of the gods—coffee. He opened them, sipping at the scalding liquid as footsteps padded into the kitchen behind him. The first hint of sunrise touched the eastern horizon, almost banishing the horrors of the night before.

"So, uh, sorry for ripping out your throat," Liz said, rubbing at sleep-tousled hair as she entered the kitchen from the hallway that led back to the bedrooms. She didn't meet Blair's gaze.

She wore a thick white bathrobe that fell to her ankles. Trevor had supplied one for Blair as well, and the warm fluffy fleece was heavenly. He took another sip of his coffee as he considered a response. The rational world had died back in Peru. How screwed up was it when getting your arms pulled out of your sockets was perhaps the third most notable thing that had happened to you on a given evening?

"Now, that's not something you hear every day. I'm sorry I put a bag over your head and tackled you into a wall," Blair replied, lowering his mug and shooting her a grin.

"I'm *not* sorry for shooting you in the face," Trevor said, expression deadpan. Until Liz smiled, Blair didn't understand he was joking.

Trevor stood at the stove, frying up some scrambled eggs in a huge cast-iron skillet. "I mean, you did tear apart my garage, and it's going to take the next few weeks to fix the holes you put in my ceiling."

"Trevor, I don't even know what to say..." Liz said, trailing off as she stared up at the wide furrow in the dining room ceiling. Bits of plaster still dusted the carpet, the trail leading into the kitchen where they stood.

"I'm totally telling Mom," he said, but his lips quivered at the edge of a smile. He removed his glasses to clean them on the SDSU t-shirt he'd emerged with just after Blair had awoken. "You're going to be grounded for weeks, and don't think that 'but I'm a werewolf' thing is going to hold any weight with Mom."

"I take it back. I'm not sorry for tearing your house apart," Liz said, grabbing a blue mug from the cabinet and pouring some coffee. She took a moment to slug Trevor in the shoulder before adding sugar. "All joking aside, I have got to find a way to control this."

"You will. Blair has, if what I saw last night is any indication," Trevor said, turning the gas off and ladling the eggs into a large bowl. He had already set out orange juice and toast. "It's just going to take some study. All three of us are scientists—well, two of us, anyway. I think your belief in woo woo disqualifies you, Liz. You're one of those hippie liberal arts scientists." Trevor grinned, setting the bowl of eggs on the table and sliding into one of the blocky chairs.

"Environmental conservation is a real degree," Liz growled, though with no real heat. She took the chair to Trevor's right, folding her legs underneath her as she ladled some eggs onto her plate. "Listen, I know this is a lot to take on. We didn't have anywhere else to go."

"Liz, you're family. Even if you weren't, this is bigger than you," Trevor said, setting a piece of toast on the edge of his plate. "These attacks are spreading fast. Faster than anything we've ever seen. They're all over South and Central America, and there've been a few incidents in Los Angeles too. If we can't get a handle on this, the human race is in real trouble. Do you remember when we were kids and we talked about the *Aliens* movie? What would happen if one of those things got loose down here? Liz, this is the same thing. It's already out of control, and given what I saw last night, there's no way even the military is going to be able to contain this."

"I think it's even worse that that," Blair said. He set his fork down meticulously and then folded his hands in his lap. "We were stalked by a werewolf that came out of the pyramid. He claimed to be inside the whole time that thing was buried, and from what I've seen I believe it's true. He claims some sort of ancient enemy is coming. That we're all in terrible danger. He says werewolves were created to serve as champions. So even if we do manage to contain this, there's something worse coming."

"Something worse?" Trevor asked. He took a liberal swallow of his juice. Blair didn't know the guy well, but considering the subject, he seemed far too calm.

"Yes," Liz interjected. She rested her elbows on the table, gesturing at Trevor with her fork. "We don't know what, exactly. This werewolf claimed that the HIV virus was the key. He says it's not new. He says it existed thousands of years ago. Many thousands, apparently."

"If HIV is so ancient, why did we just discover it a few decades ago? Wouldn't it have been there all along?" Trevor asked. He dabbed at his goatee with a napkin, a bit of egg spoiling his serious demeanor.

"That's something you might be qualified to answer, actually," Blair said, wolfing down a mouthful of eggs. They were hot but incredibly good. "Ahiga—that's the old man—claimed that the virus thrives on sunlight. He compared it to plants. He says that we've entered a new age and that the sun is changing. He also said that a more massive change is coming soon. That we're running out of time."

"Shit," Trevor said, setting his fork down. The blood had drained from his face.

"What is it?" Liz asked, laying a concerned hand on his forearm. Blair went cold. He wasn't sure he wanted to hear what came next.

"Well, he's definitely right about the sun changing. We've seen more activity in the last six months than in the previous two years. And the previous two years were more active than the previous ten. About six weeks ago a sunspot began developing. Normally they blow after a few days, maybe a week. This one is still growing," Trevor explained, leaning back in his chair. "If this Ahiga is right, he could be talking about a coronal mass ejection far, far worse than the one back in 1989. If that's the case, our power grid will be in shambles. It would be the perfect time for this ancient enemy to make an appearance. Or for an ever-growing army of werewolves to spread across the globe."

"So if that's the case, what can we do about it?" Blair asked, setting his fork down. He'd lost his appetite. "Is there a government agency we can warn or some emergency backup plan we can get them to activate?"

"Sort of. I can try contacting the agency I report to, warning them about what's coming," Trevor said, finishing his juice. He set down the empty glass, and he shuffled eggs across his plate. "The government definitely won't listen. The group I'm a part of monitors CMEs, but we don't have a plan in place for a massive event. Even if I did, we don't have hard data to show them. Getting it is a serious problem just due to the nature of CMEs. They come in two parts. The first wave will hit earth about eight minutes after it leaves the sun. The second wave, the dangerous part, will arrive two to three days later. No one in the government will take a warning seriously until we see the first part. The best I can do is monitor for that."

"The whole HIV thing will sound even more far-fetched," Liz said, leaning back in her chair as she brushed a lock of hair from her face. "Those poor people have been persecuted for decades. Even if Ahiga is right, we have no proof. It will just sound like another unjustified rant from the religious right."

Everyone was silent as they considered the implications. They knew what was going to happen but couldn't convince anyone of the truth.

"So what *can* we do?" Blair finally asked.

"Hmm," Trevor said. His face lit up a moment later. "Technically, I work for the government, but most of our budget comes from a grant from a private corporation. The government won't listen, but they might. They make power substations. If there's even a chance that a lot of their assets will be damaged, they will definitely want to know about it."

"Until then we can try to determine if this werewolf thing is viral. Maybe understanding it will help stop it," Liz said, nibbling on a piece of bacon. "That's something people will listen to. Every government in the western hemisphere must be panicked about the attacks. If we can offer help understanding the cause, at least some of them have to listen."

"After breakfast we'll get cleaned up and head into town to get you some clothes," Trevor said, picking up his plate and bringing it to the sink. "In the meantime I'll call my friend Erik. I'll see if he can overnight one of those CellScopes his startup makes so we can do some blood work. He works with a network of doctors, so if we upload the data Erik can probably have it analyzed pretty quickly."

"All of that's helpful, but we still need to decide on a long-term plan," Blair said, wiping his mouth with a napkin and dropping the crumpled ball onto his plate. He couldn't believe he was about to say this, "I've given this a lot of thought, and I think we need to return to Peru. Every answer we need is in that pyramid. Maybe even a way to stop the werewolves *and* this ancient enemy."

"That place is still a death trap," Liz said, standing to bring her plate to the sink where Trevor had begun washing dishes. "We'd still have to deal with Mohn."

"I know," Blair said, bringing his own plate. "But it's the last thing they'd expect, right? We'll have surprise on our side, plus the use of the new abilities we've been learning. Ahiga will help too, if we can find him."

"You two want to go up against a fortified Mohn installation?" Trevor asked, shutting off the water and wiping his hands on a dishrag. "Liz is right. That's suicide unless you get a whole lot more firepower than we have right now."

"I think we should focus on learning what we can about the

virus," Liz said. "If it is a virus. That and whether or not we can prove that a solar event is coming. That doesn't necessarily tell us what we need to do, but it's something we have control over right now. We can at least get some answers, and then hopefully a solution will present itself."

"That's pretty much all you guys," Blair said, suppressing a sigh. "There's not much I'll be able to contribute without access to the temple itself. I guess I'll start compiling information on the attacks. At least we can figure out how quickly this is spreading and get some idea of what areas are affected." It wasn't the most valuable research, but it could prove useful. Doing that was better than sitting around.

"That could be important," Trevor agreed, dropping the rag and heading toward the hallway. "I'm going to go call Erik."

Trevor and Liz filed out of the room, voices fading down the hall. Blair sat at the table for several minutes, allowing the magnitude of the situation to wash over him. It was all so much to take in. He was lost and didn't mind admitting it. The answer was the same as it had been every time he'd been overwhelmed in his life. Find something he could do that would move him toward his goal; then do it. When it was done, do something else. Complete enough small tasks and eventually he would reach that goal.

Unfortunately, for that method to work, he needed to know what his goal actually was. What did he want? Wake the Mother? Then what? The uncertainty was horrible. He simply didn't know enough to make an informed decision.

If only Ahiga were here. Blair was finally ready to listen to the old man.

52

WE HAVE THEM

Jordan unbuckled his pistol and dropped the sidearm atop the hastily erected desk, dropping onto the cot without bothering to kick off his boots. The sound of the rapidly expanding military base thrummed through the thin plastic wall, troops drilling overpowered by the whine of rotors as a helicopter landed. He didn't care. That wasn't going to keep him from sleeping.

Exhaustion didn't even begin to describe the malaise that had crept into his body over the last few days. It had dulled his reaction time enough that he'd finally decided getting a few hours of sleep was all right. The world was unlikely to self-destruct any more than it already had in the next four hours.

A timid knock sounded at the door. For fuck's sake, he'd only been out of Ops for five minutes.

"What?" he roared, the single word imbued with all the hell he was about to bring down on the head of whomever had chosen this particular moment to bother him. He hoped it would be enough to scare them into coming back later. No such luck.

"Jordan?" a soft female voice called.

He forced himself into sitting position and reached over to yank the door open; then he dropped back onto the cot. "What do you want, Sheila?"

He'd grown to like the feisty scientist. There was more steel in her than almost every soldier in his command. Not even the Director seemed to intimidate her. Sure, her ire was focused on him more often than not, but her honest criticism was brutally refreshing.

She entered his tiny quarters, closing the door with a soft scraping and dropping into the folding chair next to the cot. "I'm sorry to bother you, but I needed to speak to you alone, and this is the first time I've seen you outside of the CIC."

"It's Ops," he rumbled, not opening his eyes.

"What?"

"It's Ops, not CIC," he said, massaging his temples with his index fingers. "A CIC is found on a ship."

"Okay, Ops," Sheila corrected herself. The chair creaked as her weight shifted. She was silent for a moment. That got his attention. Sheila wasn't one to hedge. She spoke her mind and didn't care who heard.

Jordan opened his eyes and sat up, giving her a worried look.

"What's going on, Sheila? You still upset about Steve?" he asked, the thought needling at something in the back of his mind. Something didn't feel quite right about how that situation ended, but he couldn't put his finger on what was wrong. Not precisely. The memory was fuzzy somehow.

"I checked NPR this morning," she said, ignoring his question. Her hair was tousled from the wind, her overalls caked with two or three days worth of grime. "The attacks are everywhere. People are posting videos. It's all over the news."

"Yeah," Jordan admitted with a defeated sigh. "It's past the point of containment. There are reports of attacks all over the southwest, from Texas to California. Even a couple in Europe. I'm not really sure what we're going to do now. Our only real hope is finding Smith, but I'm not sure even that would help."

"It might. I'm not a geneticist, so I don't know," Sheila said, pursing her lips. "That's not why I brought it up, though. I think the attacks are building toward something."

"Building toward what?" he asked, running a hand over a face that felt like sandpaper. He was good about removing the stubble, but even that effort had slipped over the last few days.

"You remember me telling you about the Galactic Procession?" she asked, withdrawing a dusty handkerchief and blowing her nose. She looked like hell, now that he thought about it.

"Yeah, you thought the pyramid was programmed to come back at a certain time, but you weren't sure why," he said. He was still skeptical about that, but Sheila was damned smart and he was learning to trust her opinion.

"I'm more sure than ever, and I think I finally know why. There is a lot of sun symbology in the inner chamber. I think it corresponds to a calendar. If I'm right, the symbols show the sun changing somehow," Sheila explained. She stuffed the handkerchief back in her pocket. "That makes a lot of sense. We know that climate has varied dramatically throughout the past. In fact we've only been in the current epoch for about twelve millennia."

"That's about how old you said the sediment covering the pyramid was, right?" he asked. He could see where she was going with this, and he was positive he didn't like it.

"Exactly," she said, straightening in the chair. A ghost of her fire returned. "Thirteen thousand years ago, Egypt was more grassland than desert. The Andes, where we're standing right now, was a field of glaciers. Sea levels were three hundred feet lower. The world was a radically different place. Then it all changed in a blink of an eye. The previous epoch, the Pleistocene, lasted for two and a half million years."

It was a lot to take in. He mulled over her words for long seconds before replying. "So what, you think this ancient culture predicted the change? What does that have to do with what's going on now?"

"The Pleistocene wasn't just one long ice age. There were warmer periods and cooler periods. It changed many, many times. I think the pyramid came back now because we're about to go through another one of those changes," Sheila explained.

Jordan tried to process it. Either he was more exhausted than he thought, or he was missing something. "So they predicted global warming and decided to get ready for it?"

"Something like that, yeah. If the previous epoch is any indication, it went from cold to colder. I'm betting that this epoch, our epoch, will go from warm to hot," she mused, raising a hand to stifle a cough. Her skin had gone pale. Apparently he wasn't the only exhausted one. "But believe it or not, that's not why I came to see you —well, not the only reason."

"Then why?" he asked.

"Jordan, as I understand it, you were here at the exact instant the pyramid appeared," she said, expression suggesting he should infer something obvious from her words.

"So?"

"So how the hell did Mohn Corp. know that the pyramid was coming back? If they knew that, then what do they know about what's coming?" she asked.

The words kicked him in the gut, and he grunted at the near physical blow. She raised an excellent point. He'd wondered since the day they'd found this place how Mohn had known, but he'd missed the obvious. What else did they know? If Sheila was right and some big change was coming, they probably knew about it. The Director probably knew about it. And he hadn't said a damn thing, not to the senior-most officer on-site.

Jordan tensed as his radio chirped. He hadn't taken it from his belt when he'd lain down. A few calming breaths later, he plucked it from his side and spoke. "Go ahead."

"Commander Jordan, we've got a hit," came the excited voice of a communications analyst. Sooner or later he'd have to learn their names.

"I'm going to need more than that," he growled with a bit more heat than he'd intended.

"Sir, do you remember the attack on the Peruvian coast? The one where Subject Alpha was spotted?" the voice said enthusiastically.

"Yeah," he grunted, tugging at the neck of his tank top. The tight black fabric clung to him like a second skin, which wasn't an accident. Tight clothing made it harder for an opponent to get a grip.

"We traced a phone call from where the attack took place. It was made to a residence in California. The same number just called in a report to HELIOS," the analyst explained. Jordan was familiar with the division. It was a shell company Mohn used to fund scientific research at several of the top universities.

"What was the gist of the report?" he asked, straightening. The analyst might be on to something.

"Dr. Gregg claims that a sunspot has been growing for the last six weeks. Preliminary research confirmed the findings. He believes it could cause a global event."

"Have you notified the Director?" Jordan asked, rising to his feet.

"Not yet. We weren't sure if it was worth bothering him," the analyst said, a note of unease entering his voice.

"It is. Prepare a full report on this Dr. Gregg. Find out who he knows in Peru that might have called him. Also, I want an assault team prepped," Jordan ordered. He picked up his sidearm and buckled it around his thigh. "Then radio the Director and tell him that I need to speak to him immediately."

53

CELLSCOPE

L iz jumped as the computer began chirping an odd melody. She staggered backward in a panic before she recognized it as an incoming *Skype* call. Trevor's computer chair tumbled to the floor, the tan carpet thankfully muffling the clatter. She took a deep breath and then righted the chair. Liz reached for the mouse and tapped the little blue icon. It was a 510 number, and the contact had a picture of a smiling man in his mid thirties. Even though she'd been expecting the call her heart still galloped.

"Hello?" she said, sinking back into the chair. A video feed sprang to life, taking up most of the screen. It showed the man from the pictures, dark haired with an enthusiastic smile. He wore a bright blue t-shirt with the word *CellScope* emblazoned across the chest in white.

"Hi, Liz?" he asked, cocking his head to the side. In the background she could see several people moving between desks in a spacious office. The man continued before she could respond. "I'm Erik. Trevor said you were expecting my call."

"Uh yeah, that's me," she answered, giving a shy smile. She knew it was shy, because the chat program showed a miniature feed of her in the corner. Sometimes she hated technology. What was wrong with using a phone?

"Did you get my package?" Erik asked. A short blond woman entered the corner of the screen. She offered Erik a sandwich wrapped in white paper with a red *Jimmy John's* logo. Erik nodded his thanks before turning back to face her.

"Yes, it arrived this morning. Trevor had to head out on an errand, but he set it up before he left," she replied. Liz glanced at the far side of the table where the odd device lay. It was roughly the size of a loaf of bread, with a tray on top where the user could insert a microscope slide. A black plastic housing had been built into the blocky base, which held Trevor's iPhone. The name CellScope definitely made sense.

"Great," Erik answered, his smile infectious. "Trevor says you need a blood sample analyzed. He says it could be an entirely new disease. Have you taken the sample yet?"

"Yes, I have several of them," she said, moving her hand to a row of covered slides she'd laid out near the base of the CellScope.

"Insert the first slide. Then tap the CellScope app. Once the slide comes into focus, the camera will automatically begin recording," Erik explained with the practiced ease of someone who'd delivered the same speech hundreds of times. "It will record for forty-five seconds. Then it will stop and upload the video to our server. You don't have to do anything."

"Okay, I'm inserting the first slide now," she said, picking up her own sample and sliding it into the CellScope with a satisfying click. She tapped the blue and white app icon, and a moment later the camera came into focus. She stared intently as it began to record.

She knew enough about biology to recognize the pile of red blood cells, each shaped like a donut with a depressed center. That part was normal. What wasn't were the lime-green veins running through each cell. It was a vibrant neon, unlike anything she'd seen or heard of outside the *X-Files*.

A moment later the red recording light clicked off and a progress indicator began filling up. It raced along, chiming when it finished.

"Ahh, there we go," Erik said, glancing at something off-screen. His eyes moved back and forth, gaze intent. "Give me just a sec. I'm reviewing the video now. I'm mostly used to reviewing ear images, so it might take a minute."

He was silent for several tense moments and then turned in her direction. The enthusiasm was forced now, a thin veneer over perhaps nervousness. "Liz, where did you get this sample?"

She thought hard over what Trevor had told her. He trusted Erik and had told her she could too, but that didn't make talking about their situation any easier. She closed her eyes, bracing herself. "I drew the vial of blood from myself this morning."

Erik glanced off-screen and then back at her. He seemed to weigh his words very carefully before speaking.

"Liz, I'll be honest. I've never seen anything like this. I'm not qualified to diagnose it. I'm not sure any more than a handful of people in the world are," he said, the veneer gone. It had been replaced by sober candor.

"That's fair. What *can* you tell me about it?" she asked. Her hands had begun to tremble.

"Well, let's see," Erik began. He trailed off, squinting as he read something. "I can at least give you my observations. Red blood cells carry oxygen to the entire body. The green striations are only grafted to red blood cells, so whatever they're doing has to be related to that mechanism. They carry something to every part of the body that requires oxygen."

"That's pretty much everywhere, isn't it? All the muscles, and the brain?" Liz asked. She wished she had a stronger foundation in biology, but at least she understood the basics.

"That's right," Erik confirmed. He paused and then continued. "Between time index thirty-four and thirty-seven, the striations move to another red blood cell. Whatever this thing is spreads like a virus. Have you noticed any symptoms?"

Liz barked out a harsh laugh that threatened to turn into tears. "Yes, I've definitely noticed symptoms."

Erik was silent for a long moment. "I don't want to press if you're not comfortable talking about it. Were there other samples you wanted me to review?"

"We have three more," she said, wiping a hand across her eyes. It came away wet.

"Why don't you go ahead and send them? I don't need to stay on the phone for that. I'll analyze them and send your brother an email with my observations," he said, tone empathetic.

"Thank you, Erik," Liz replied. She wasn't sure what else she could add.

"It's my pleasure. Even if I didn't owe Trevor, what we're looking at is fascinating. I'll have an answer shortly," he said. He reached off-screen, and the video feed disconnected.

Liz picked up the second slide in a trembling hand, mechanically inserting it into the CellScope. She wasn't sure what she'd expected to find, but she'd known guys like Erik when she'd been getting her master's. Brilliant and ready to change the world. If he was confused by this, that couldn't be a good sign.

The house's front door opened, and voices drifted up the hallway as footsteps approached.

"So I'm thinking we can use the GPS on my smartphone to track how fast you're moving." Trevor's voice preceded him down the hall. He was clearly excited. That lifted some of the darkness, drawing a faint smile from Liz. Leave it to her brother to find the silver lining. "I don't know how accurate it is, but that will give us a ballpark on your top speed. Things like that will be really important, especially if you find yourself in a fight."

Blair and Trevor shuffled into the office, Trevor wearing a pair of khaki shorts and an XKCD shirt that said, *Stand back, I'm going to try science.* His copper hair and wire-frame glasses gave him a scholarly look, though she knew that was misleading. He loved to claim he was as much redneck as he was scientist.

Blair's trip to the mall had apparently been fruitful, because he now sported a black North Face shirt that complemented his heavily muscled frame. A pair of tight-fitting blue jeans and a pair of hiking boots completed the outfit. He'd also let his stubble go and now bore a thin beard along the jawline. It gave him a rugged look, one she definitely liked on him.

"Hey Liz," Trevor said, dropping into the room's second chair. He spun it to face her, plopping his feet up on the corner of the desk. "Did Erik call?"

"Yeah, I just spoke with him," she said, feeding the third slide into the CellScope. The second slide had been Blair's blood. This one was another vial of hers, one she'd exposed to the moon for several hours last night. "He looked at the first sample. I've got the video if you want to review it."

Trevor tapped the iPhone's screen, swiping until he found the Photos app. He scrolled through the list until he found the video she'd sent Erik. Then he tapped it once. The strange blood cells filled the screen. He gave low whistle. "Ho-lee crap."

Blair leaned over his shoulder, staring down at the phone's screen. "This is good news, right? I mean, we were expecting our blood to be different, and now we know for sure that it is. It means that this isn't some mystic mumbo jumbo. There's a scientific explanation for what's happened to us."

"I guess so," Liz replied, without any real enthusiasm. Processing all this was going to take some time.

"What else did Erik say?" Trevor asked once he'd finished watching the video.

"He pointed out that these are red blood cells. Since they carry oxygen, whatever that green stuff is must be tied to the same process," she explained. Liz picked up the fourth sample. This was one of Blair's that had also been exposed to the moonlight.

"That makes a certain amount of sense," Trevor mused. Then his eyes lit up. "You said that the ancient werewolf guy said that this virus acted like chlorophyll, right? What if the green mutation conducts energy? That could explain how you use moonlight to change, or blur, or whatever else you can do. It's your fuel in the same way plants utilize the sun."

"I thought of that," Liz said, proud that she'd thought of something science-related before her brother. "The first and second samples were taken directly from Blair and I, just regular blood. I left the third and fourth out under the moon for three hours last night. If I'm right the virus will be more advanced in those samples."

"That's brilliant," Blair said, gawking at her like she'd grown a third eye. Did he really think that little of her abilities? She wasn't sure whether to be offended or pleased with the compliment.

"Erik said he'd email us back with the results. Given how quickly he looked at the first one, I doubt it will take him very long," she replied, crossing her arms and giving Blair a self-satisfied smile. He might have started this whole thing, but she'd done more than he had to help them understand what had happened. "Guess maybe all that woo-woo stuff you guys tease me for believing might not be so far-fetched after all."

54

SILVER NITRATE

Trevor maneuvered the eyedropper over the slide, carefully squeezing the black ball until a tiny drop of silver nitrate fell onto the blood sample. The liquid spread instantly, giving the entire slide an odd sheen. He set the dropper aside and then closed the slide, popping it into the tray near the top of the CellScope.

Erik's findings had been incredible. He'd shown that the samples exposed to moonlight had more advanced instances of the virus, and he had theorized that the samples themselves probably contained some source of energy absorbed from the light. That had prompted Trevor to set up his experiment.

"Is it ready yet?" Liz asked, poking her head into the office. He'd made her and Blair wait in the kitchen until he was ready. Trevor didn't often give presentations, but when he did, he admitted privately to being a bit of a showman.

"All right, all right. You two can come in," he said, waving his sister forward. She came in, dropping into the chair next to him.

Blair trailed after, arms folded across his chest. He moved to lean against the wall by the door, sour and silent. He'd been that way since he'd watched a news report this morning. The attacks had spread across the southwest, and isolated incidents had made it all the way to Canada. Trevor got that Blair blamed himself for everything. It was understandable, since technically it *was* his fault. Not that anyone could have done any better had they been in his position.

"So what are we looking at?" Liz asked, nodding at the video Trevor had up on the computer.

"Erik sent me the results of his tests. According to him, the samples exposed to moonlight have a more advanced instance of the virus. The green striations are more vibrant, and larger. Erik thinks they may contain some sort of energy, which is what prompted me to set this up," Trevor explained. He tapped the play button, which showed the same red donut-shaped blood cells but with larger green swathes coating most of them. "This is Blair's sample, the one exposed to moonlight. Watch what happens after I add silver nitrate."

Trevor brought up the CellScope website, logging in as Erik had shown him. He navigated to recent exams and brought up the video that had just loaded.

"My God," Blair said, unfolding his arms and taking a step toward the computer. "The green is just gone. It looks completely normal. This happened after you added silver?"

"We've all heard legends of werewolves, and other than the moon, the most common theme is silver," Trevor explained. He brought up a web browser that showed a Wikipedia entry on silver. "I saw a documentary on Nova a few years back. Silver was used by wealthy nobles as a blood purifier. It wasn't just superstition. It actually removes toxins from the bloodstream. So I started to wonder. What if the energy in your blood can be leeched out with silver? That could explain why legends say it's lethal to werewolves."

"That's good to know," Liz said, though her tone revealed that she disagreed. "How does that help us? I mean, it's good to know our limitations, but how does figuring out how to kill ourselves help?"

"Because it isn't just about killing yourself," Trevor shot back. He propped an elbow on the desk, staring smugly at his sister. "Polio can kill you, but if you dilute the dose enough, it becomes..."

"A vaccination..." Blair finished. He ran a hand through his hair. "Even if it doesn't make us immune to silver, it could bleed the energy from our systems. If we start going berserk, we could just take a hit of silver nitrate."

"Think about how much it could save me in home repairs," Trevor said. Liz shot him a venomous glance.

She reached for the little brown bottle, examining it closely before looking up at him again. "So I'd need to get it directly into my bloodstream. That would mean an injection. Do you have a syringe?"

Trevor nodded.

"Then I want to give this a try. I'll take five milligrams tonight, just before the moon comes up," Liz said. Her tone was even and her back ramrod straight, but Trevor could see the fear hiding in her eyes. He said nothing. He was proud of her for facing it. He wasn't certain he could do the same in her place.

"We need to talk about the attacks and how quickly they're spreading," Blair said. He'd moved back to his position against the wall near the door, as if leaving himself room to escape.

Trevor swiveled the chair to face him. The statement seemed to have cost Blair something, but his stance was resolved. Both he and Liz were clearly tired of running. They urgently needed to take a stand, to do something to combat their circumstances. He admired that about them, though he wasn't sure what they could do outside of a futile gesture of defiance.

"Okay," Liz said slowly. She set the bottle down and looked at Blair. "We know they're spreading rapidly. Too rapidly to stop."

"That's right," Blair said, heaving a sigh. "There's nothing any military or government in the world is going to be able to do. This will keep spreading. Look how far it's come in just the last month. In another couple it will surge across every continent. Werewolves will be everywhere, and the few survivors will be huddling indoors, trying to stay alive."

"So what do *we* do about it?" Trevor asked. He was a part of this now, regardless of what he wanted.

"I've given it a lot of thought. No more running. It's time to wake the Mother," Blair said, tone thick with resolve.

There was no hesitation. It was the most confident Trevor had seen him, and in that moment Trevor understood Liz's attraction to the man.

Blair continued. "She's the key to all of this. She can explain how and why she created this virus and what we're here to fight. She may even be able to stop the spread somehow."

"We'd still have to deal with Mohn," Liz countered, shaking her head. Trevor privately agreed, though he didn't voice his concern. It would be suicide. "Nothing about them has changed. If they're using the pyramid as a base of operation, we'd need to fight our way in. How are we going to do that?"

"We come up with a plan. We're werewolves. I can move faster than the human eye can track. You can melt into the shadows," Blair replied, fists clenching. "Trevor has more guns than the friggin' marines. We find Ahiga and learn everything he can teach us. Then we sneak into the pyramid and find a way to wake the Mother. I know it won't be easy, but we have to try something. Trevor, where do you come down on this?"

"Mohn has a nasty reputation," Trevor began, buying time to consider as he cleaned his glasses on his shirt. "They'll have an array of trained personnel, state-of-the-art weaponry, and military precision. They'll be entrenched and ready for any conventional assault. That said, I doubt they have any real idea what werewolves can do. If we go in quiet, we might have a chance. I'm willing to risk it. Liz?"

"I don't like it, but I can't offer any alternatives. Either we watch the world burn, or we do something stupid like send a doctor, a teacher, and an astronomer to fight heavily armed soldiers. It's a bad choice, but I'm game if you two are," she said.

"All right," Blair replied, standing a bit straighter. "Now we just need to find a way to get there. Trevor, I'm assuming you'll want to bring your weapons. That rules out conventional flights, even if Liz or I could get past airport security with Mohn watching for us."

"I have a friend with a cargo plane," Trevor offered. He didn't like the idea, but it was probably the only option. "He flies down to Mexico to bring back shipments of marijuana. I can probably convince him to fly us. He owes me."

55

THIS IS A .45

"**T**his is a forty-five," Trevor explained, picking up a heavy black pistol from the row of weapons on the table along the wall of the garage. He offered it grip first, and Blair accepted it. "Feel the weight. You never want to try firing that with just one hand. You won't break your wrist or anything, but your accuracy will be shit."

Heed him, Ka-Dun. These weapons are potent. Their use requires no energy. They are the perfect supplement to your abilities.

"How far away can my target be?" Blair asked, sighting down the barrel.

"For a beginner? I wouldn't aim for anything further away than fifteen yards. This is a close-range weapon. If you want something with more range, there are a couple other options," Trevor explained, picking up a rifle from the table. It had a polished wooden stock and a long black barrel. It was the bigger and nastier cousin to the sort of rifle he'd seen hunters use. "This is a .338. If you're using the scope, you'll probably be accurate up to about two hundred yards. Further, if you're good. It's got a hell of a kick though, so expect a bruised shoulder if you fire more than a shot or two."

"How do you load it?" Blair asked.

Trevor slid back a bolt on the right side of the gun. "You slide your rounds in here. It can hold up to six. Bring the slide back to cycle to the next round. Here, sight at the target on the garage door there. That's it. Rifles like this are great for hunting or even limited sniping. If you've got cover and can keep moving, they'll let you take down an enemy without ever giving them a chance to hit back."

Blair sighted down the scope at the target some thirty feet away. He could make out the grains of ink on the target. This thing would be great at range, though he had no idea how accurate he'd be when firing. His suite of werewolf powers didn't seem to offer anything that might help.

"Honestly, I don't think either weapon is really suited to you, though. You remember when Liz attacked me the other night?" Trevor asked, with an amused smile. What kind of man laughed at a life-threatening werewolf attack? The kind crazy enough to help them.

"Kind of tough to forget," Blair replied sardonically. He handed back the rifle. Trevor accepted it and added it back to the line of weapons.

"I used this to defend myself," Trevor said, picking up the shotgun at the end of the row. Like the rifle, it had a wooden stock, but the barrel was wider and there was no scope. "This is a Remington twelve-gauge shotgun, sometimes called a room sweeper. It's a close-range weapon with a lot of stopping power. You can take a man off his feet with this, and all you have to do is aim in their general direction. The downside is accuracy. You're good in a room this size, but if someone is much further away, you're likely to miss. This rifle holds six rounds though, so at least you get more than one shot to correct your aim."

He handed the shotgun to Blair, who planted the butt against his shoulder and aimed at the target again. "It's much lighter than the .338. This is definitely the one that feels most natural so far."

"If you had to get good with one rifle, this would be my recommendation. You can find ammo just about anywhere, and the learning curve isn't very steep," Trevor explained. He picked up a revolver from the table. "If you need something smaller, this is the pistol of choice. It's a .357, the little brother to the gun Dirty Harry used. The ammo is also easy to find, and it's very much point and shoot. It's got a kick, but it's manageable. It will core a man, though it won't knock him from his feet. You'd want the forty-five for that." He handed the pistol to Blair, who traded him back the shotgun.

"So what would you use if you had to pick?" Blair asked. Why did an astronomer need so many guns? Trevor was such a mass of contradictions.

"If I'm in close quarters, I want to knock an opponent down, so I'd use a forty-five. That gives me the time to line up a kill shot," Trevor explained matter-of-factly, as if he'd already given this a lot of thought. "For a rifle, I'd keep the .338. It requires more skill than a shotgun, but it's got much better range, and you can still use it up close if you're good. There is a more powerful rifle, but I haven't gotten it out. It's a Barrett fifty-caliber sniper rifle. You can core a tank from over a mile, but the gun weighs almost forty pounds. It's bulky and difficult to move and set up. Definitely not something I'd want to travel with, but if I was fighting a foe with superior firepower, that's the gun I'd want. Of course, the rounds are five bucks a pop, so if they didn't kill me, the bill probably would."

The door leading to the house swung open, revealing Liz in a blue blouse and a tight pair of jeans. Blair had no idea when Trevor had found the time to fix the door. He'd cleaned up the plaster as well, though the ceiling still bore the scars of the werewolf attack.

"I've taken a dose of the silver nitrate. It made me feel queasy for a minute, but other than that I haven't noticed anything," Liz said as she entered the garage. Blair tried not to stare at the curves the blouse hinted at. "Have you heard back from your friend with the plane? The sooner we leave, the better. I just finished watching footage of a werewolf tearing up a theater in La Jolla. They're talking about martial law."

"Not yet," Trevor replied, setting the shotgun back on the table and gesturing for Blair to hand him the .357. "He'll get back to us by the tomorrow morning, I'm sure. I doubt he'll have an issue with—"

Blair stopped listening. He heard something in the distance. An all-too-familiar *whup-whup-whup* that brought him back to Peru. "There's a helicopter approaching."

"I wouldn't worry much about it. We're pretty close to the flight path between downtown San Diego and Los Angeles. Military helicopters go by all the time," Trevor said, turning his attention back to the guns. "I've got a few more weapons to show you. Then we can get packed up."

"Wait," Blair said, straining to identify what he was hearing. "There's more than one helicopter. Maybe three or four. They're coming from different directions."

"Should we lock ourselves in the gun safe?" Liz asked, gripping Blair's arm.

"No, we'd be trapped. It's the first place Mohn would look," Trevor said. He ducked into the gun safe and emerged with a rifle easily as tall as he was. That must be the Barrett. It looked a lot like the .338 but was much larger and made of flat black metal. The barrel and stock were scored in dozens of places. This thing had been around the block. "I'm going to prepare a distraction. Blair, get our stuff into the Rover."

"The Rover?" Blair asked, grabbing the shotgun. "Won't they just gun us down if they have helicopters?"

"I didn't say it was a good plan, but if we stay here, the ground team will wipe us out. If we're lucky, I'll get a couple shots off with the Barrett to give them something to think about. Liz, can you get out there and scout with that invisibility trick you do? We need to know what we're dealing with," Trevor said, strapping an empty holster to his right thigh and sliding the .45 home.

"All right," Liz said, peering out the garage's only window. "It's dark out there now. I'll see what I can find. If you guys make a break for it, I'll link up with you."

Blair grabbed several packed duffel bags near the garage door and started stuffing them into the back of the Rover.

"We're relying on you, Liz. See if you can identify a leader. Then let us know as soon as possible," Trevor instructed. The approaching helicopters were deafening.

"I'll be back as soon as I can," Liz said. The shadows flowed around her, clinging to her limbs like black tar. Within moments she was just...gone.

"Blair, follow me into the house, and keep your head down. They let us know they're coming, so I'm betting they're coming in hot," Trevor said, striding up the hallway, toward the kitchen. Blair tossed the last duffel into the Rover and followed.

Trevor crouched behind the island in the kitchen, keeping the thick counter on one side and the island on the other. Blair dropped down next to him, wondering how much cover that would provide. Better than nothing, he supposed.

"There will probably be an initial burst of fire to soften us up," Trevor explained. "Then they'll deploy tactical teams. We can't be here when that happens, so as soon as the initial fire ends, you and I bolt through that back door. You got it?"

"Got it." Blair shot back. He was damn glad Liz had chosen San Diego. They'd be lost without Trevor.

"Incoming," Trevor bellowed.

56

WORLD OF HURT

The kitchen exploded, windows shattering inward in a deadly hail of glass and wood. Flecks of plaster, bits of tile, and other fragments of Trevor's life blasted in every direction as bullets screamed by. They were more pressure than actual sound, and sharp pain flared in both ears with every blast. He kept his head down, covering his ears with his hands while he waited for the chaos to end. The whole thing lasted an eternity, though he doubted more than five or six seconds passed between the time the guns began their awful whirring and the time the death stopped.

His house had been gutted. Every window had been shattered. Fist-sized bullet holes scarred every wall. Stuffing fountained out of several tears in the couch, like tendrils from some cottony octopus. Thousands of hours gone in an eye blink. But he was still alive. If he wanted to stay that way, it was time to move. He used the Savage .338 rifle as a crutch to heave himself to his feet, but he let it clatter to the ground as he sprinted for the gaping hole once occupied by his sliding glass door. It would slow him down too much, and he doubted he'd have time to line up a shot.

Instead he yanked the H&K .45 from his thigh holster. The soldiers about to invade his house would be wearing Kevlar at the very least, so it wouldn't kill them. That couldn't be helped. Nothing he had was going to down them in one shot, but then he didn't really need to kill them. He just had to knock them down. Blair could handle the rest.

"Blair, bring your big friend out to play. We're going to need him," he shouted, leaping through the wreckage where the doorframe to the back patio had met the walkway circling around the side of the house. He didn't wait to see if Blair followed. Either he would, or he was dead, werewolf or not. Trevor couldn't help in either case, so he just kept moving.

Part of him felt crazy for running into the kitchen and then outside only to loop back toward the garage. He knew it was necessary, though. Mohn would definitely use thermal imaging, so they'd known exactly where in the house to focus their fire. If Trevor and Blair had been in the garage the vehicles would have been jeopardized, and he needed both the Mustang and the Rover if his plan was going to work.

He ran low along the side of the house, pausing behind the tall wooden fence that separated the walkway from the driveway. It was a good thing. Two soldiers in black body armor were rappelling into the street on the other side. Their lips were moving, but the words were sucked away in the gale created by the helicopters. Both bore combat rifles he wasn't familiar with. The guns were bulky and resembled MP5s but were sleeker and had slightly longer barrels. The weapons probably contained a lot of stopping power. Exactly the sort of weapon you'd want if fighting a werewolf.

Trevor dropped a hand to his right thigh, drawing his .45. He moved quietly toward the gate, more from habit than need. If he was quick, he might be able to get the drop on them. He paused when he reached it, peering between two of the slats. The pair of soldiers hustled up the driveway with grim precision, moving swiftly for his position. They didn't seem aware of his presence.

He waited until he could hear them on the other side of the gate and then started firing. Four rapid cracks, all at chest level. There was an agonized yell from the other side of the gate. Trevor kicked it open, the heavy wood slamming into the second soldier. It knocked the woman backward and off balance, but she still had time to raise her rifle. It swung into alignment with Trevor's face.

Something roared behind him, taxing his already damaged hearing. The soldier's knee and upper thigh ruptured, spilling her toward Trevor. The woman's rifle sprayed a trio of rounds into the driveway, spurting concrete shrapnel from the craters they created. Then Trevor's .45 swung around for an easy shot. He steeled himself, squeezing a round into the back of the woman's head. He was unprepared for the gore, gagging at the sight. He'd hunted and skinned animals, but this was different. He'd just killed a human being in close quarters.

Blair's hulking form emerged from the shadows behind him, eerily silent despite his size. He cradled the shotgun, barrel still leaking a wisp of smoke. His voice was guttural and low. Trevor was terrified, if he was being honest. "There are two more soldiers in the house, and two just entered the backyard. Those two sound strange. Heavier than the others," Blair said.

"Great," Trevor growled, scooping up the soldier's modified MP5 as he hauled open the garage door. The din swallowed the clatter as the door revealed the inside of the garage. It had been savaged by gunfire, like the rest of the house, but the gun safe had stopped many of the shots.

The Rover had taken a round through the windshield but looked otherwise untouched. Trevor breathed a sigh of relief as he saw the Mustang, miraculously intact. Two years he'd labored on that thing.

He darted to the Rover's rear driver-side door, the sound of the helicopters and gunfire abating slightly as he entered the garage. Trevor holstered his pistol and then tapped the clicker on his keys to unlock the door. He jerked it open, depositing his newly acquired rifle on the floor. It probably still had a full clip, minus the burst into the driveway.

He glanced at the gun safe. The plan was crazy, but it might work. He turned to the hulking shadow next to him that had entered the garage. "Blair, you need to hold them off for about sixty seconds. Can you do that?" Trevor yelled the words, but he wasn't sure they were audible over the fight outside.

"I'll do what I can," Blair roared back. The sound came from low in his chest, reverberating through the air around him. His eyes narrowed, and he handed the shotgun to Trevor. "I'll need my claws for this."

"Just keep them off balance for a few seconds. You can pick out the sound of a car engine in all this, right?" Trevor shouted, cupping one hand to his mouth as he set the shotgun in the back of the Rover.

Blair nodded.

"Good. When you hear the Mustang start up, get back here as soon as you can. I want you to get into the Rover's driver seat and haul ass out of here. They can't find Liz out there, so she's fine. We, on the other hand, are in a world of hurt."

Blair looked confused for a moment as if he wanted to ask why, but he swallowed the words. He glanced up at the night sky where the helicopters lurked. Then he turned back to give Trevor a nod. Good. There wasn't time to answer questions.

Then Blair blurred into the darkness, disappearing into the backyard. The gut-thumping sound of automatic fire split the night, bright flashes in the backyard visible through the new holes Mohn had decorated his house with. Trevor slammed the Rover's door and sprinted for the gun safe. This had better work.

57

ON THE HUNT

Liz leapt silently atop a boulder on the hillside behind Trevor's house, drawing shadow around her like one might clutch a jacket on a cold night. She studied the two men in their bulky midnight armor as they whirred and clicked their way toward the yard. They looked like something out of a Terminator movie, scent and heartbeat both muffled by the metallic shells. Each bore a rifle she didn't want to be on the receiving end of, but if she played this right, they'd never see her until it was too late.

Yes, Ka-Ken. Strike and melt into the shadows. Such has always been the way of the wolf.

The urgent staccato of automatic weapons fire echoed through the valley, no doubt terrifying Trevor's distant neighbors. Instead of lights going on, though, the few she could see were switching off. People didn't want to be involved in violence of this scale. She did, however, spy a few people peeking through windows. One more way her new senses could prove useful.

Focus, Ka-Ken. There is death to attend to. Mother's will, your pack will be safe. The male is strong, as is your blood kin. They must hold until we can assist them. Kill these two; then go.

"So you aren't going to try making me kill them anymore?" Liz asked, low and under her breath. Did she even need to speak? This thing could hear her thoughts.

No longer, Ka-Ken. You have made your will known. I will acquiesce, though if the energy sickness comes again, your kin will not be safe.

"I'll remember that," she mouthed, making no sound.

Liz leapt from the rock, bounding silently through the shadows. She avoided the large shrubs or any patch of dirt. The impact could make noise or send up a cloud of dust, betraying her presence even in the darkness. How did she know that?

We are one, Ka-Ken. I grant the gift of memory. Through me, you bear the wisdom of ages.

Liz only half-listened, already focused on her target. One of the armored suits crouched in the shadow of a large boulder, mostly invisible except to her eyes. Its rifle was aimed at the house, and two boxy missiles jutted from a box on its left shoulder. She didn't know what kind of hell they could unleash, but it was best if she never found out.

Let me guide your hand. Move as I move. I will teach you.

Liz relinquished control. She would trust the beast, at least until it gave her reason not to. Her body glided forward, circling behind the rock until she was one with its shadow. She lurked mere inches from her prey, yet it was unaware. She uncoiled like a spring, one arm wrapping around the soldier's neck in an implacable grip. The other splayed her fingers outward, claws aligned like the teeth of some vicious saw. Her hand jabbed forward with incredible strength, piercing the soldier's armor and driving into his spine just below the neck. Hot, squishy blood covered her fingers.

Just like that, the soldier was dead. She eased the body noiselessly to the ground as they melted back into the shadows. Liz's abilities both awed and terrified her. These armored suits were so new she wasn't even sure the military had them, but she'd dropped one with almost no effort. And there were hundreds of werewolves just like her out there now? It was chilling.

The other soldier had finally noticed his companion's body. He paused, scanning the darkness. This one moved more carefully than the last. He seemed aware she was in the shadows somewhere, gaze never resting as he slowly walked the barrel of that massive rifle through her vicinity. Would the same trick work again? One way to find out.

Liz crept through the shadows, circling the armored soldier. He had his back to a large shrub, legs slightly bent and ready to move. She could still get the drop on him, but the bush would prevent her from attacking him from behind. He'd hear her moving in the bush before she reached him, giving him a chance to react.

So a frontal assault, then? she thought. The beast undoubtedly had a plan.

Of course, Ka-Ken. This one feels our full fury.

She pounced, leaping thirty feet and coming down atop the armor. Their combined weight flattened the bush and sent them tumbling. Liz recovered first. She flipped up, knees pinning the soldier's blocky shoulders as her claws wrapped around his helmet. She gave a roar and pulled with every ounce of her new strength. The metal groaned, but it didn't pull free.

Then she was tumbling backward as the soldier's legs wrapped around her neck. He used the incredible strength in his armor to hurl her against a neighboring boulder. The rock shattered, and she dropped to the ground, the wind knocked from her.

The soldier flipped to his feet, a trio of wicked-looking blades springing from each gauntlet. He lunged forward, stabbing once, twice, a third time into her back. She felt organs rupture. That had been a lung popping. She collapsed to the ground in a shower of blood. Her insides were filled with hot glass.

Yet the healing had already begun. Liz scythed her legs around, knocking the soldier from his feet. She grabbed his calf, hurling his helmeted head into the same boulder she'd just rebounded off of. The armor gave a shower of sparks, but amazingly it held. Liz lunged forward, seizing him around the chest in a one-armed bear hug. She used the claws on her free hand to pry at the fissure between the helmet and the shoulder. Slowly, inch by agonizing inch, she twisted it open to reveal a man in silver sunglasses, with a goatee.

The familiar staccato sounds of a weapon sounded behind her. Pain flared in her back and leg as bullets punched through her. She staggered forward, dropping her quarry and disappearing into the darkness. She was bleeding badly. How much more could she heal before she ran out of energy?

Your strength wanes. Leave these fools and rejoin your pack. They will be in need of your aid. We are the protectors, Ka-Ken. The males are lost without us, children before the storm.

To leave the fight galled her. She burned with the need to kill the man she'd just fought. He was vulnerable without that helmet. Yet she had to find Trevor and Blair. She scanned the area around his house. A haze of smoke from the near constant spurts of gunfire pooled around the still-functional lights on the back porch. The haze lent the house a muted odor like that of a funeral shroud.

She had to get down there.

58

MIND RIDE

Wonder and terror mixed in equal parts surged through Blair. The indefinable wave crashed over him, jarring but incredible. He was more. Greater. A vast array of instincts overlaid his senses, a set of tools honed through hundreds of generations. He knew how to fight. How to kill. He became one with the beast for the first time, mingling his consciousness with that of the strange presence he had resisted for so long.

Blair blurred, whipping down the pathway next to the shattered house. His passage kicked up a wind that rustled rose bushes and gravel, thankfully drowned out by the whirring rotors of the helicopters and the occasional bark of gunfire. He couldn't disappear like Liz did, but he stuck to the shadows with the grace of a practiced predator. Prey no longer. That distinction was important because it took away the fear. He would kill these soldiers, not run before them like a startled rabbit.

He dropped into a low crouch, sifting through heartbeats in the thick cacophony. Two in the house. Two more approaching from beyond the fence, somewhere out in the darkness. The latter were strangely muffled somehow, though neither he nor the beast understood why. It didn't matter. They were still distant. That gave him at least a little time.

Blair blurred into the air, time slowing as he leapt through the space that the window over the kitchen sink had once occupied. He twisted his furry body, bringing his legs around so he could land in a crouch on the linoleum. A soldier stood within arm's reach, mouth open comically as his eyes widened. The soldier made the next move in slow motion, the barrel of his rifle inching down toward Blair's face as if the air had become thick jelly.

The man probably had thousands of hours of training, and he bore the physique of a devoted athlete. Blair's hand shot out, seizing the soldier's neck and slamming the man's head into the refrigerator with a sickening crunch and a splatter of warm blood. A hot rush of need surged through Blair, fueled by the surety that feeding would increase his strength. That could come later. There wasn't time.

Blair jerked the corpse away from the refrigerator, positioning it between him and the second soldier. This one was slightly shorter, with wide blue eyes and a smattering of freckles. Her rifle spun into position, coughing a trio of rounds in his direction. They impacted against the corpse's Kevlar vest, sending vibrations up his arm.

A contemptuous growl rolled from his throat as Blair slowed time even further. The fourth bullet left the muzzle in a hot flash of burning powder, two inches of brass moving toward him like a rock tossed by a toddler. Blair's free hand shot out, cupping the bullet in his palm. It was uncomfortably warm, but he only held it for an instant. Then Blair hurled the bullet in an underhanded throw.

It caught the woman in the knee with nearly the same velocity it possessed when fired, shattering bone and cartilage and spilling her to the kitchen floor. Blair tossed the corpse of her companion atop her, kicking her rifle away from her as he prepared to feast on the helpless soldier.

Light flooded into the kitchen from the backyard. Blair shielded his eyes with an arm as he squinted out. He crouched low, nostrils flaring as he sought the data his eyes couldn't provide. The strangely muffled heartbeats were close now, four of them. The way the lights moved made what he was seeing clear. There were four of them, each affixed to one of the figures advancing into the backyard.

One of those figures took a further step forward, raising an arm. The lights vanished, plunging the yard into near darkness. Blair could still see his opponents clearly under the light of the moon. Each wore a bulky armored suit straight from Heinlein's *Starship Troopers*.

Clearly the leader, the figure with the raised arm was a bit taller than the other soldiers. His faceplate locked on Blair. Then a familiar voice boomed from some sort of amplifier. "This needs to end, Professor Smith. We've already caused too much collateral damage, and I know you don't want that. It's time to return to Peru. This only has to be as difficult as you want to make it."

Blair would know that voice anywhere. Commander Jordan. A torrent of emotion raged through him. Yet curiously the one he'd most expected was absent. Fear.

"I know you're just doing your job," Blair roared back, flexing his claws and taking a step closer to the window's shattered frame. "You don't have all the facts, though. Werewolves were created for a reason. Something bad is coming, Jordan. Leave now, or the lot of you are going home in body bags."

"I like you, Smith. I don't have any doubt that more of my men will go home in a box if we keep this up. Thing is, we've got you covered from the air, and I have even more backup on the way. There's nowhere to run. I'm holding all the cards. Be reasonable. Why don't you surrender, and we'll head down to Peru and talk about it with the Director? If you have facts we need to know, then share them," Jordan said, tone hardening as he moved the rifle resting against his shoulder into both hands. "You don't want to make us come in there, Professor. I respect you. I don't want to embarrass you in front of your new girlfriend. Liz, right? That's her name, isn't it? Liz Gregg, a medical doctor you infected."

Blair's resolve hardened. Jordan had brought her into this intentionally, hoping to goad him into rash action. A part of him very nearly obliged, wanting to leap out the window, heedless of the danger. The rest of him reined in. He didn't suppress the fury, but neither did he give in to it.

"I respect you too, Jordan. You're just trying to do the right thing, but 'thing is,' you're inadvertently threatening the human race's survival. I know you aren't going to walk away, so let's get this over with." He said, pausing to give a low, deep howl. It reverberated through the night with all the power and fury he could muster. A war cry, fierce and undeniable.

Blair blurred, twisting through the window with feral grace. Motes of debris danced lazily through the air, spinning crazily under the weight of the rotor-driven wind. He landed next to the soldier on the far right, by the squat palm tree in the corner of Trevor's yard. Posture was hard to read through the rigid suits, but this soldier was the most relaxed of the lot, clearly waiting for what he considered to be cornered prey. It was a fatal mistake.

A fierce bolt of clean blue energy arced from Blair's hand, coruscating around the figure's helmet. Blair had no true understanding of what he was doing, but he trusted the beast as it guided his actions. Only a very small part of him was surprised as he slipped past the man's defenses and into his mind. Blair *was* the soldier. He could feel the man's thoughts and memories, his horror at being a bystander in the passenger seat of his mind. It was a horror Blair understood intimately. He experienced a moment of guilt at inflicting such helplessness on another but tossed aside the regret.

The soldier spun to face his companions, rifle unleashing a hail of slugs even as the caps to the launcher tubes popped open. All four burst into the yard on fiery contrails, still faster than a baseball pitch even with Blair slowing time. The closest suit took the brunt of the damage, missiles blasting it into the closest companion. That actually worked in the second suit's favor, providing a measure of protection from the blast. The pair landed in a heap, billowing smoke from the missiles mostly obscuring Blair's view.

Only Jordan was able to react in time, somehow launching himself backward and landing in a roll as the detonation hurled his armored form through the fence and into the field beyond. Somehow Blair had expected it.

The poor soldier Blair mind-rode shrieked impotently in the chambers of his own head, horrified by his attack on his own companions. Blair reached up with both hands, forcing the man to key in the code that removed the helmet. Then Blair released him. He returned to his own body, blinking rapidly at the sudden shift in perception as time returned to its normal flow. The horrified soldier hadn't reacted yet. Perfect. Blair seized the armored shoulders in both hands, lunging for the man's throat. He tore it out in a wash of hot blood.

A sharp hiss triggered a surge of alarm, the instinctual reaction one has to a coiled serpent. Blair's conscious mind took a moment to catch up, and he went cold when he identified the sound. It was the same sound his victim's missiles had made when fired. Blair tried to spin, tried to blur, tried to do anything. It was too late. Four missiles streaked in his direction, and he was helpless as they found their target. Him.

The first pair detonated against the unfortunate power armor Blair still gripped, but the latter found their mark. The first caught him in the leg and unleashed a wave of fire and pain. A second caught him in the shoulder. The combined explosion picked him up like a terrier, hurling him across the yard and through the fence in a rough parody of what he'd just done to Jordan. Bones cracked with the impact, and the scent of his own burned flesh competed with white-hot agony for his attention. He lay there broken, unable to even contemplate rising.

We have reached the end of our power, Ka-Dun. I can aid you no further. I must sleep.

Blair couldn't make his body work. It was simply too broken. He struggled with everything he was, everything he had become. All that effort, and he barely managed to roll onto his stomach. It wasn't much, but at least he would die facing his killer.

Jordan's armored form strode boldly through the hellish yard, passing through flaming bits of debris where the palm tree had once stood. He aimed a wickedly large rifle at Blair's face.

"I'm sorry it had to come to this, Smith. Your DNA is needed in Peru. Know that it brings me no pleasure to end your life. I'd prefer to capture you, but you're just too dangerous to live," Jordan said, surprisingly somber. The statement was much more honest than he'd have expected from the man. It sounded...respectful.

Jordan raised the rifle, finger tightening on the trigger. Blair closed his eyes, ready for what would come next. He'd done his best.

59

FINAL HOUR

A higa's final hour had begun. He knew this was so, knew it with a calm certainty that elicited mild surprise from himself. The moment provided another glimpse of the Mother's wisdom, and he recalled a conversation he hadn't understood in his youth. The Mother had explained to her pupils that the day might come when they needed to sacrifice themselves, to give their lives in exchange for a necessary outcome.

At the time he'd argued vehemently against such a course. Champions were so long lived that they were effectively immortal. Given that, survival at any cost made sense, for surely their worth to the world was greater than anything that might be purchased with their deaths. Only now did he finally understand the truth of her words. Some goals were worth the cost.

Blair must reach the Mother, no matter the cost. Ahiga closed his eyes, touching the minds of the coyote pack he'd gathered. Dozens of feral minds were united in purpose, each coyote cunning and silent as they prowled the night. They were less powerful than wolves, smaller and not so bold. Yet they were what he had.

Harry the men with guns. Nip. Then fall back to the shadows. Keep them from following the whelp and his pack.

Howls and yips came from all directions as the coyotes leapt to obey. Like wolves and foxes they were social animals, and they were thrilled at the inclusion in so large a pack. It gave them a purpose greater than before, a unity they'd likely never experienced and would never experience again. Though, Mother willing, perhaps they might now that the champions had returned.

The pack flowed down the hillside, bursting into Trevor's yard through scorched gaps in the fence. The tiny creatures leapt at the men in their powerful armor, nipping and dancing away. They did the same to a group in the front yard who were prepared to storm the house. The pack could do nothing about the helicopters, but at least the men who reached the ground would be confused and slowed. It would buy time for Ahiga to do the real work.

He blurred down the ridge, wind tearing at shrubs and kicking up dust as time slowed. He leapt over the fence and rolled to his feet in the charred wreckage of what had been a lush garden just hours before. Of the four men clad in strange armor, two still fought. Both were focused on Blair's shattered and broken body lying in a heap near the smoldering remains of a palm tree. Neither was aware of his presence.

Ahiga dipped low as he sprinted, grabbing the closest foe by an ankle with both hands. He swung the man around in a powerful arc, increasing the blur for a split second to increase his momentum. Then he flung the man with all the considerable might he could bring to bear, flinging him toward the closest helicopter. The confused warrior accelerated wildly through the air as Ahiga released his blur. Sporadic gunfire drowned out a harsh scream. Then he impacted with the pane of glass at the front of the vehicle, peppering the pilots with shrapnel and the mass of the soldier's own armored form.

The helicopter tilted drunkenly, dipping low before it descended from sight to the front of the house. Moments later a fireball mushroomed into the sky. The remaining helicopters gained altitude, scattering like startled birds as their weapons silenced. Recovery wouldn't take long, but at least the explosion gave them pause. The soldiers knew they were vulnerable now.

The remaining soldier spun to face Ahiga so swiftly that *he* could have been blurring. Once, Ahiga would have easily dodged such an attack, but he'd grown old and weak during his slumber. Burning so much energy so quickly taxed him mightily, and he lacked the strength to blur away from the rifle as the ugly black barrel came up. He staggered away, rolling out of the path of the bullets as they barked from the muzzle in little puffs of flame. One tore through his shoulder, pulverizing bone and shredding flesh. It burned like the sun, but he forced the pain down.

He staggered to his feet, weighing his options. The whelp was paramount. So Ahiga made his choice. He gestured at the mangled body, forcing much of his remaining strength toward the whelp in a crackling arc of silver light. That energy wouldn't be enough to fully heal him, but it would return him to consciousness and allow him to flee.

The choice cost Ahiga dearly. Black blades, each wickedly sharp and as long as Ahiga's forearm, snapped from the soldier's wrists as he tossed aside the rifle. The blades lashed out in a pair of vicious strikes. The first carved scarlet furrows into Ahiga's chest, sending him stumbling backward to one knee. He caught the second, wrapping both hands around the armored wrist. He used the man's momentum against him, throwing himself to the ground and flinging the soldier through the remains of the fence and into the shrubby hillside beyond.

"Flee, whelp. I will delay them," he roared, flipping back to his feet. Already he ached from the fire of a dozen tiny wounds, but he must persevere just a little longer.

To his shock, the whelp used a sending, something he'd thought beyond the inexperienced champion. Ahiga felt the whelp's gratitude for the rescue and his shame for rebuffing Ahiga's teachings back in Acapulco. Also determination. The whelp would escape. He would find the Mother. He would set this right. Ahiga swelled with pride and relief. The whelp accepted his responsibility. The world had a chance.

There was movement at the edge of his vision, two men in the house, each training weapons on him. A coyote leapt from the shadows, ruining the first soldier's aim even as his gun belted a hail of death. The shots went wide, ricocheting off one of the fallen suits of armor. The second soldier fired uninterrupted, but Ahiga was ready. He blurred, just for a moment.

The motion carried him to the roof, affording him a vantage of the combat. Would that he could walk the shadows like a female. He felt exposed up here despite his crouching in the haze unleashed by the strange warriors and their never-ending hail of death. Such wishes were futile, of course. He must work with what he had.

Ahiga watched as the whelp sprang to his feet and bolted into the house, disappearing from view. Ahiga shifted his gaze to the soldiers massing in the front yard. The loss of the helicopter and the sudden attacks by coyotes had forced them to be cautious, but already they were regrouping.

Movement from the yard. Ahiga turned back to see the last suit of black armor leap to its feet and sprint toward the house, where the whelp had disappeared. The man in that suit was the gravest threat. He must be stopped.

Ahiga fell from the sky like a bird of prey, tackling the armored soldier and sending them both into a rolling tangle of limbs. This opponent was faster than the others, cleverer and more willing to adapt. He must be their leader. Their champion stabbed down with those wicked blades, pinning Ahiga's foot to the ground. He rammed the other set of claws into Ahiga's groin, flooding his manhood with shards of fiery agony.

Ahiga battled past the pain, for hesitation was death. He needed to buy Blair more time. He could not set down his heavy burden, not just yet. Ahiga wrapped his opponent in a tight embrace, ignoring his wounds as he summoned the energy for a blur.

The silvery energy moved sluggishly, mostly gone after his gift to speed Blair's healing. Yet enough remained for what he intended. He blurred away from the combat, carrying the soldier up the hillside. He bounded over boulders and around shrubs, eating up the distance and carrying the primary threat far from the whelp.

His opponent quickly realized what was happening. He struggled to free himself from Ahiga's grip, but Ahiga refused to let the man free. So the man scissored his legs, tripping Ahiga and sending the pair sprawling to the ground.

This time the soldier was the first to recover. He rolled to his feet, leaping immediately upon Ahiga's back. Metal claws plunged into his back again and again, shredding his organs and draining what little strength remained.

He knew he was dying, but there was one more task to complete. Ahiga must show Blair what he was to fight against. He must impart one final gift of knowledge to prepare him for the trials to come.

Ahiga closed his eyes, abandoning the combat. He sent to Blair with all his remaining strength, inviting the whelp to mindshare. It was his final act, but if it succeeded, he could go to death's embrace comforted because he'd made amends for his mistakes.

60

NOW

Blair staggered forward, bursting through the kitchen and down the hall toward the garage. He kept his feet, but it was a near thing. Trevor's Mustang idled in the garage, the white paint job gleaming under the halogen light that had somehow survived the apocalypse the rest of the house had succumbed to.

Trevor crouched next to the open driver-side door, a large brick in one hand. He looked up sharply as Blair entered the garage. "About damn time. Get in the Rover. I need you to drive. I'm going to send the Mustang into the street to draw their fire. Once they focus on it, I'll man the Barrett through the moonroof. You get us the hell out of here, and I'll keep the helicopters off our asses."

Blair hobbled toward the vehicle with a nod, agony burning through his right leg with every step. Whatever Ahiga had done to help him heal had gotten him moving, but his body had still suffered catastrophic damage he lacked the strength to fix. The beast remained silent, and for the first time Blair missed its presence.

He slid into the driver's seat, noting that the keys were already in the ignition. Blair turned the key, foot firmly on the brake as the engine roared to life. The garage door began to rise. He turned to see Trevor's crouched form rising from the Mustang. The muscle car shot down the driveway, toward the highway in the distance, leaving dark rubber streaks as it picked up speed. The smell of burned rubber mingled with gunpowder, blood, and dust.

Trevor sprinted toward the Rover, diving through the still-open door into the back seat. He yanked it shut behind him, grabbing the stock of the huge Barrett and pushing the barrel through the moonroof as he leaned against the back of the passenger seat. "Wait for them to take the bait."

Take it, they did. The Mustang roared forward, already threatening to career off the driveway and down the rocky hillside. It never had the chance. Two opposing streams of bright tracer rounds lit up the night. They converged on the car with chilling accuracy, coring the engine block and turning the car into a pillar of flame.

"Now," Trevor snarled.

Blair didn't need to be told twice. He romped on the gas, and the Rover rumbled out of the garage. The instant they cleared it, Trevor pushed his torso through the moonroof. Blair struggled to keep the vehicle steady, knowing that would affect the accuracy of the Barrett. He needn't have bothered.

The gun roared as they raced past the smoldering remains of the Mustang. Blair winced at the deafening boom, pressing hard on the accelerator as they reached a straight section of driveway. His eyes flicked to the rearview mirror as he picked up movement. A helicopter canted crazily, slamming into the house in a shower of flame and metal.

"God damn it," Trevor snarled, ducking back into the vehicle. His hands moved with practiced precision, ejecting the spent cartridge and slotting in another one. "I should have fucking known. Not bad enough they blow up my dream car and shoot up my house, but I have to finish the job."

Then he was out the moonroof again, apparently lining up another shot. Blair focused on the road, swerving to the left as a coyote leapt out of the way. They were everywhere, it seemed, ruling the darkness as they terrified soldiers. Bless Ahiga for the distraction.

"Speed the fuck up. The last two helicopters are closing!" Trevor shouted from above.

Blair obliged. The tires smoked as the Rover fishtailed up the last of the driveway and onto the highway's rough asphalt. He floored it, silently thanking a god he didn't believe in that no other cars were on the road. He almost had a heart attack when the passenger door opened.

It shut immediately after, and just like that, Liz's naked and bloody form huddled in the seat next to him. She was shivering violently, and he doubted it was from the cold.

"You okay?" he asked and then winced as the Barrett roared again.

"Shit," came Trevor's voice. He slithered back into the Rover to reload. "Missed. Try to keep to a straight—oh shit—Liz, where the hell did you come from?"

"Saw you guys leaving," she panted. Blair focused on the road, gliding smoothly into the fast lane. Then the world began to fade. The vehicle slowed just like if he were in a blur, but he lacked the strength to do that even if he'd wanted to. Jesus Christ, what now?

Blair, my time is nearly gone. Share your mind with me. There is much you must know before I can rest.

The voice was unmistakably Ahiga's, though it sounded distant and weaker than the other times he'd communicated telepathically. Blair instantly knew the reason why. Ahiga was dying. Blair had only one choice, even if it meant allowing the Rover to crash. He must learn what Ahiga could teach. He accepted the older werewolf's probing touch, lowering his defenses and opening his mind.

61

THE DEATHLESS

The world disappeared. Blair found himself in darkness, save for a roaring fire in a ring of rocks. It was surrounded by several tree stumps, each low enough to serve as a comfortable seat. A figure sat on the far side of the fire, silver hair pulled back into a simple ponytail. The weathered lines of Ahiga's face were somehow deeper in the firelight, etched into unmistakable resignation.

"Come. Sit. There is much to discuss and little time in which to do so," the old man rumbled, gesturing to a neighboring stump. Blair sat, accepting the reality of this place, though he didn't understand it.

"Where are we?" he asked, glancing around at the sea of darkness surrounding the small island of light.

"We are in a construct of my mind, a place between us where we can communicate much more rapidly than speech allows. Only a few moments pass for your body, though it will seem much longer here," Ahiga explained, a comforting smile slipping into place. "In the world of men, I lay dying, yet here I have time to tell you what I must."

Ahiga's death was Blair's fault, and he knew it. Where would they be now if he hadn't been so stubborn? He should have listened, but instead he had fled in the other direction and refused to take up the responsibility only he could perform.

"I am so sorry, Ahiga, about before when you met with us in Acapulco. I was scared and didn't know who to trust," Blair admitted, hating how pitiful the excuse sounded. He sat on the stump the old man had indicated. The heat from the flames warmed him despite his knowing they weren't real.

"The mistake was mine. I expected you to show me the respect an elder deserved and in my arrogance forgot that you knew nothing of my world or its ways. You were adrift in an ocean of change, seeking only to keep from drowning," Ahiga said. A pipe appeared in his hand, already giving rise to a single wisp of pungent blue smoke. Marijuana. "I have gone about this badly, but I would not speak of past mistakes. Our time is short. Let us turn to important things."

"I have so many questions," Blair said, closing his eyes as he considered. If time was limited, he might only get a question or two. What were the most important answers he could receive? "Tell me about the ancient enemy. Who are they? What form will they take? How can they be fought?"

"I cannot explain in the time remaining. I must show you. Are you ready?" Ahiga asked, smile fading. His face grew pained.

"I am ready," Blair said with a tight nod.

His perspective changed.

Ahiga was a child, playing at the banks of a river. A little girl splashed and laughed nearby, his sister Nori. She wore white swaddling that Blair didn't recognize, but it seemed normal for the children.

Behind him stood a row of huts made from woven grass, similar to ones Blair knew from the Miwok tribes of California. The village seemed peaceful, dozens of dark-skinned people living their lives. Mothers suckled babes. Grandfathers carved spear shafts. Children ran and laughed. It was a world completely unfamiliar to Blair, one he expected no one had seen for many millennia.

A figure staggered from the nearby pine trees, a woman with dirty hair and a torn dress similar to those of the villagers. She weaved drunkenly toward his sister. Blair watched curiously, wondering if he should seek help.

He turned to yell back to his parents but stopped when he heard a low hiss behind him.

The strange woman fell on Nori, knocking her on her back in the shallow water. She seized his sister's face, leaning close in a horrifying parody of a kiss. Nori screamed as the woman bit her neck and then began to chew. Ahiga stumbled backward, fleeing for the safety of the village. But there was no safety. More and more figures emerged from the trees, some with gaping wounds no man could survive. The dead walked, just as the Singer's stories claimed they would.

He ran fast and low into the forest, fleet as a deer. How long he ran, he didn't know, but Ahiga didn't stop until he was far from that place of death. Only then did he realize he was alone.

Blair's consciousness returned to the fire. Ahiga wept openly. Blair fought for words to comfort the old man but could find nothing that might dull the ache of that horrible scene. "Those were your memories, weren't they?"

"Yes, my own childhood. The first time I encountered the ancient enemy. The deathless. They killed most of my people. I, alone, was saved by a champion, though not for many more moons. I fled before the deathless, always pursued as they sought to add me to their number," he explained, making no move to clear away the tears. "After the champion slew them, I begged for the culling, praying that I would rise to protect people that could not defend themselves, people like my family."

"Those monsters, the ones you showed me," Blair began, unsure if Ahiga would understand what he had to say next. "We have a word for them, the one I mentioned in the hotel back in Acapulco. We call them zombies. The walking dead. There are movies, books, and even a whole subculture of people preparing for an imaginary zombie apocalypse. How is that possible? How could we have 'guessed' at the nature of an enemy you say hasn't been seen in nearly thirteen thousand years?"

"That is the Mother's doing," Ahiga explained, puffing on the dark wooden pipe as the fire dried the last of his tears. "It was she who created what you call the 'virus.' She understood humans to their core, the bits that make us what we are. You name this DNA. Genetics. One of the tools she used to prepare humanity was the addition of memory. She ensured that your people would remember the ancient enemy, even if only through myths or stories. That way, when the enemy appears, your people will know their weaknesses and stand a greater chance of survival."

Blair was stunned by the revelation. The idea of passing knowledge through human DNA seemed so fantastic. It was an ingenious way to ensure preservation of knowledge. Wherever people propagated, the knowledge of this ancient enemy would survive.

"The zombie craze is a relatively new thing. It's really only hit its stride in the last few years, though they've been making movies since the sixties. Why now? Why did our people suddenly start to remember this?" he asked, though he was fairly sure he knew the answer.

"The Mother created triggers for many of the changes she wrought, including the return of her Ark. They were all tied to the sun. When the old age ended and the new began, the sun changed. This process began two or three generations ago and only now accelerates," Ahiga explained, enjoying another long pull from the pipe. "More changes are coming. The most staggering will be upon us soon. This is the crux of your answer, about who the ancient enemy is and what the danger to your world will be. There is more I must show you."

Blair's perception changed again.

He hovered over modern day San Diego, just high enough to see people moving about the streets. The sun flared behind him, growing impossibly bright. Then the sky was aflame. It was as if the aurora borealis had somehow come to Southern California.

Below him, chaos erupted. Figures burst from buildings, attacking those around them. One became two; two became many. Zombies were tearing apart the people below as the sky burned. It spread, more and more of them rampaging across the city. Most moved in a slow shuffle, though more than a few sprinted toward victims. The fast zombies from more recent movies.

Blair's perception zoomed out to space, and he observed the whole planet at once. These outbreaks occurred everywhere, all at once. Zombies rampaged across the planet, increasing their numbers through slaughter. As he watched, lights everywhere winked out, the guttering candle of humanity's technology fading to darkness. People couldn't communicate, couldn't warn each other or band together. They were helpless in the face of an implacable enemy.

"My God," Blair breathed, returning suddenly to the fire. "The apocalypse you keep talking about. It's the zombie apocalypse. And werewolves were created to protect people from them. That's why you wanted us to slaughter as many people as possible, to increase our numbers and cut down on the number of zombies. Ruthless, but I finally understand."

"It was the best way," Ahiga said, eyes flashing with a shadow of his anger from back in Acapulco. "But I understand why you were loathe to embrace it. You did not understand the ancient enemy. You still don't. What I showed you, this zombie apocalypse, as you call it, this is merely the beginning. My guess at what the first day might be like. There is far worse to come."

"Worse? What comes next?" Blair asked, aghast. The flames seemed to grow brighter.

"I lack the time to reveal all. Focus on your task, rather, and worry not for tomorrow. You must seek out the Mother. She helped birth the deathless. She can give you the knowledge and weapons to fight them. Will you seek her out?" he asked, eyes pinning Blair in place. The urgency weighed tons.

"I promise, Ahiga. I will wake the Mother, somehow."

"Excellent," Ahiga said, wide smile spreading as he puffed again from his pipe. "I will not live to redeem my failure, but if you undertake this task, the disgrace staining my memory will be washed away. I will be redeemed."

"You saw the men who attacked tonight, Mohn Corp. They hold the pyramid, and their forces are likely to be stronger there than they were here," Blair said, summoning a pipe of his own. He hadn't smoked marijuana since college. "Can you tell me anything that might give me an edge? Any special powers I can use to get past them?"

"You need allies," Ahiga replied, gesturing with his pipe. "These come in two forms. You may recruit other werewolves. Most will recognize your strength, and if you tell them of the Mother's plight, they will aid you. You can also summon a pack of wolves or foxes, just as I did with the coyotes tonight."

"Will that work on dogs?" he asked, taking an experimental puff from his pipe. It tasted like smoke, giving him a light, heady feeling.

"I believe so, but I must warn you. These dogs you mention, they are an abomination. One that will enrage the Mother," Ahiga sighed, shaking his head. "Yet I believe you are correct. You can call them to your aid, and they will come. If such a tool must be used, then use it."

"What about the differences between males and females," Blair began. "Why are we different? Why—"

"My time grows short, whelp. Death wraps me in her embrace. I must leave you," he said, but the insult had a fondness to it. Ahiga's form became translucent. "Gather your allies. Free the Mother. She will aid you in what comes next."

Just like that, Blair was back in the car, struggling to right the wheel before he collided with the center divider.

62

PERMANENT VACATION

Jordan strode through flaming wreckage, kicking aside a sharp-edged hunk of rotor that blocked his path. The air around him was choked with ash and grit, but the suit's environmental scrubbers protected him. Of course they also made it hotter than hell, and his entire body was slick with sweat.

The adrenaline had faded, but the suit had injected him with some sort of chemical cocktail to stem the tide of his injuries. They left him fuzzy, but that seemed a small price to pay in exchange for keeping upright. Jordan shook his head. His mind was wandering.

He scanned the wreckage until he found a pair of legs jutting out from under what appeared to be a large section of the helicopter's console, most of the dials shattered and worthless. He seized it in both armored hands, heaving with the suit's considerable strength. The move flung the console off the prone figure, its armor dented and scored from the combat.

The helmet had been nearly ripped away, revealing Yuri's familiar face. His goatee had been burned away, and his flesh was raw pink, but one of his eyes was focused on Jordan. "Time for raise. And vacation."

Jordan smiled inside his suit, offering a hand to the beefy Russian.

The man took it, and together they pulled him from the wreckage. He was able to stand, though he clearly favored his right leg.

"Can't help you with the raise, but after this fiasco I have a feeling we're about to get a permanent vacation," Jordan said, reaching up to tap the release code into his helmet. It popped open with a hiss, and he removed it. The night air was cooler than he had expected, given the conflagration raging on the house's remains just a few dozen yards away.

"Not our fault," Yuri said, coughing weakly.

"No, but that hardly matters. Why don't you limp over to the other survivors? Extraction is already inbound. I need to call the Director," Jordan said. He waited for Yuri to begin moving toward the terrifyingly small cluster of survivors before moving in the opposite direction himself.

Several of the men were scanning the darkness with flashlights, and he couldn't blame them. Coyotes had come out of nowhere, and more than one soldier had lost a tendon. A few had even had throats ripped out.

Jordan strode far enough away that he wouldn't be overheard. Not that there was much risk of that. Anyone not in power armor must be at least partially deafened from the combat. Thankfully, Jordan's own hearing had been preserved. He could still hear the occasional cry of bats high above, now that the combat was over.

He pulled his smartphone from a secure compartment and dialed the Director. It rang once before the screen resolved into a face like granite. The Director's eyes were hard. He already knew.

"Alpha escaped. Eleven casualties. Two suits destroyed, one more barely operational," Jordan explained with clinical detachment. He'd known some of those faces, but this was war, and in war you compartmentalized emotions or you broke.

"Acknowledged," the Director replied. His features were impassive, and although his eyes smoldered, Jordan wasn't positive it was anger he read there. Frustration maybe? The Director continued. "I've arranged a flight to Panama. Pick up a suit and tie when you arrive. You and I have been called to account. The old man wants a face-to-face."

"Awful long way to fly us for an execution. Why Panama?" Jordan asked.

"Every senior department head has been summoned, but none of us have been told why," the Director said. He shook his head, clearly frustrated. "I do know that your op has been terminated. We've given up on fighting the werewolves, but I have no idea what the contingency plan is or what the old man has planned. Knowing him, it will be something none of us expect. You and I may even survive this debacle. Then again, we might not. Either way, get your ass on a plane."

"Yes, sir," Jordan said. The screen went black. Jordan was too tired to be curious. If they were going to crucify him for his actions, so be it. At least he'd face it on his feet.

63

GARLAND

The strange little man blinked out at them from a thick, bristly beard, like some lawn gnome with a hangover. He stood next to a small cargo plane that could have been lifted straight out of a bad '80s movie. The paint was peeling, and there was actual duct tape in more than one place. The thing fit the airfield, which was nearly deserted save for several similarly sized planes at a few of the other hangars.

"So let me see if I get this. You want to fly to Peru, where all those attacks started, so you can wake up some Egyptian hottie who can tell us how to stop the world from ending?" Garland said, setting the brown paper bag on the Tarmac with a clink, the same clink magnums of beer made. It wasn't even 10 a.m.

Blair hadn't the faintest idea what to make of the man. His bushy hair hadn't been touched by a brush since Metallica had rocked the mullet, a mullet this guy had never given up. The beard grew like a hedge ignored for a decade and he wore a faded black t-shirt with what might have once read *Poison*. It was hard to say with so much of it worn away. His jeans hung uncomfortably low and bore dark stains in more than one place.

All of that, Blair could handle. What he couldn't was the stench.

This man was the foulest thing Blair had ever encountered, and having new senses only made that worse. Unsurprisingly, Liz looked ready to gag too. At least they were suffering together, though he doubted Trevor was escaping the experience entirely. Still, the man was his friend, so he must have found a way to tolerate the funk.

"Yeah, that's pretty much it. You fly us to Peru, and we try and stop this thing," Trevor replied with a shrug and a sheepish grin.

"How much are you paying me for this adventure?" Garland asked, eyeing the bag of beer longingly.

"Uh," Trevor said.

"You can't even fucking pay me?" Garland asked, goggling at Trevor as if he'd just been told the world was about to end. Which he had, now that Blair thought about it.

"Maybe when we get back, but I can't really take a side trip to an ATM. We need to leave right now," Trevor said. He seemed genuinely embarrassed. "I'm sorry, Garland. I know this is a big ask. I'll make it up to you."

"Did you bring your own weed?" Garland asked with a sigh of defeat.

"They blew up my house, Garland. The whole fucking thing."

"I have to smoke you guys out too? That really sucks, Trev," he replied, though with no real heat. Blair suspected he was just happy to have people to smoke with. The lawn gnome clapped Trevor on the shoulder. "You know I like you, but I gotta eat. I can't afford to front the gas down to Peru. Can't run a business that way, you know?"

"Garland, I'm going to go out on a limb here and guess you've tried a few drugs before," Liz interjected, giving Garland a smile that might have been a little friendlier than strictly warranted.

"Drugs? I've got some opium if you want. We can smoke that once we're up," he shot back, warming at Liz's attention. "Goes great with a little beer. Just the right mix of mellow and mellower."

"Have you ever done ayahuasca?" she asked, pitching it low like a secret.

"Nah, that shit's almost impossible to get ahold of. You have to know a shaman and..."

"I know a shaman, Garland. If you take us down to Cajamarca, I'll get you ayahuasca. You can even do it with a real shaman," she offered. His eyes lit up as though he were Indiana Jones being told where to find the Holy Grail.

"All right, I'll cover gas. But I want one more thing, or it's no deal," he said cagily, though bits of a smile threatened to surface.

"What's that?" Trevor asked, wary but looking hopeful. He folded his arms across his chest, shifting his weight as a plane taxied in the distance behind him.

"Your hot sister has to ride up front with me." He grinned, giving Liz an obvious wink.

Trevor turned to his sister. She closed her eyes in weary resignation and then gave a tight nod. Blair couldn't blame her. It was going to be a very long flight for them, but it would be longest for Liz. She was definitely taking one for the team.

"Sure, Liz would love to sit up front with you. You can tell her all those stories about when we worked at Computers for Everyone together," Trevor said. They all laughed, except for Liz. She was not amused, as evidenced by her sour expression. "We've got some stuff to load up. Listen, we're not going to get inspected, are we? They're, umm, not street legal."

"Man, if they inspected me before I flew out, they'd have impounded Henrietta and dumped me in Guantanamo," Garland said, slapping the side of the dilapidated aircraft with a metallic thud. He grabbed the handle of an oval door, yanking the metal open with a groan of protest. "Stow your stuff in the back, and take seats close to the front. That will help balance the load. Liz, why don't you help me do preflight? I'm sure they can handle it."

Liz gave a shrug and a sheepish smile in Blair's direction. "At least it gets me out of work, I guess. Have fun carrying luggage."

Garland gestured chivalrously at the door, and Liz ducked inside, heading for the cockpit. Trevor nodded back to the luggage they'd piled on the Tarmac. Fortunately, Trevor had stowed two green nylon packs in his Rover for camping. They'd used them to haul what little they'd salvaged. Next to the packs was a pair of long blanket-wrapped bundles containing the few guns Trevor had managed to rescue before they'd made their escape.

Blair waited for Garland and Liz to disappear inside the plane before he broke the silence. "How reliable is this guy?"

"Garland? Incredibly. I know he looks like a roadie who never left the '80s, but he's a hell of a pilot. He's flown under the influence of every drug you can imagine so many times that it's all instinct now," Trevor said, bending to heft one of the packs.

"Where do you know him from?" Blair asked, genuinely curious. The association was a strange one.

"We were both techs at a computer store back in the mid-nineties. I'd just started school and spent all my time smoking weed and playing video games at the store after hours," he explained, picking up the lighter of the two gun bundles. Blair hefted the heavier with almost no effort. "Garland was the 'old man' back then. He knew all sorts of things the other techs didn't. We all learned from him. Not everything computer related. He used to do lines of white powder off his hand in the back of the shop. I still don't think he realizes we all knew. Anyway, he fixed computers all day long and was high the entire time. Piloting is the same for him."

"You've vouched for him. That's enough for me. Besides, if you're wrong, it's not like we'll be around to complain," Blair said, hefting the remaining pack in his free hand. They started for the plane. "Sounds like you've got a hell of a lot of stories. You're a fascinating guy. I'm glad we met, and not just because you've saved our asses repeatedly."

Trevor gave him a wide-eyed look and then a sudden grin. "Honestly? This is the most exciting thing that's ever happened to me. There's no way I would have missed this. If the world's going to end, I want to be in on the group that tries to stop it."

"I wouldn't have it any other way," Blair said, ducking inside the plane. The dimly lit room smelled of sweat and stale smoke. He dropped the guns and the pack in the rear corner next to a pair of battered bucket seats. "Listen, we haven't had a chance to talk about the Mohn attack." He glanced into the cockpit where Liz and Garland sat. The faint sounds of their conversation drifted back.

"I figured we'd discuss that together once we're in the air," Trevor said, dropping his own packs. He slid into one of the seats. "No sense doing it now just to have to explain it to Liz later."

"It's not Liz I'm worried about. I saw something horrible, Trevor. I'm not sure how Garland will react," he said, settling into the seat next to Trevor. The stuffing in the cushions had been compressed into what felt like concrete, and the cracked leather smelled like Garland. "Can we trust him with everything? Or do we want to keep some things back?"

"I think we can trust him, but now you've got me worried," Trevor said. He took the seat across from Blair. "What the hell happened back there that you haven't told me?"

"We didn't escape on our own," Blair admitted. He buckled the frayed seatbelt. "Ahiga showed up. He saved my ass from Jordan, the commander of Mohn's forces back at the pyramid. It was Ahiga that took down the first helicopter, and he's the reason those coyotes attacked. He held Mohn off long enough for us to get away. They killed him for it."

"That's shitty, Blair, but not 'keep it from Garland because he might freak out' shitty," Trevor said, clearly expecting more.

"As he died, he initiated something he called a mindshare. He showed me things. Trevor, he showed me the end of the world," Blair said, seizing Trevor's gaze. "The ancient enemy we mentioned? They're zombies, Trevor. The virus was engineered, just like the werewolf virus. Only it creates zombies. Zombies just like the ones you've seen in movies. The ones on *The Walking Dead*."

"Holy. Shit," was all Trevor had.

"Here's the thing. This is going to happen when the virus gets enough energy to 'wake up.' It gets its energy from the sun. Ahiga says there will be a massive solar event and that it will happen soon. He described a CME, Trevor, just the sort of thing you warned us about. When it hits, anyone suffering from HIV is going to die, but they aren't going to stay dead," Blair explained.

"My God," Trevor said, blood draining from his freckled face. "So the zombie apocalypse is going to start right after most of the world loses power? All those contingency plans. Theories about people using social media to spread the word if it ever happened. None of that will work."

"That's why what we're about to do is so important," Blair said, inwardly cringing at how long he'd fought waking the Mother. How many people could have been saved if he'd gone back sooner? "Every town, every city...they're all going to be cut off from each other. Some people will live, those with guns and in remote areas. But the rest are in real trouble unless they have help. Unless werewolves can somehow stop the zombies. To do that, we need to wake the woman who set this all in motion."

64

DESPERATE MEASURES

Jordan was decidedly uncomfortable in a suit. It wasn't that the charcoal pants didn't fit or that the matching jacket was too confining. The suit had been expertly tailored for his broad frame and had probably cost more than his mortgage payment. What bothered him was the lack of proper pockets. No place for a weapon or anything other than a pair of keys and maybe his wallet. It was the uniform of a businessman, not a soldier.

Yet as he stepped into the elegant ballroom, he knew it had been the correct choice. The Director had been right. Jordan glided down the impractically plush carpet, starting up the wide marble steps to the Plaza's second floor. At least the place was air-conditioned. Panama was humid, and it was hotter than shit out there. The last thing he wanted was a sweat stain.

Jordan crested the stairs and headed to a pair of tall doors on the right. They were cut from some sort of dark-brown wood, not stained oak. Mahogany, maybe? What kind of trees did they even have down here?

A pair of men in black suits flanked the doors. Each had the tell-tale bulge under the arm of his jacket. They pulled the doors open as he approached, nodding for him to enter. Jordan swept past them and into the conference room, trying to keep his confidence. He'd never been to a meeting like this. Had anyone?

The room contained about sixty chairs arranged in a giant horseshoe. A row of narrow tables followed the line of chairs, most of which were empty. Light from the setting sun streamed through the tall windows lining the western wall. Perhaps two dozen men stood in small clusters throughout the room. Every last one wore a suit.

"Jordan, over here," the Director's familiar voice called. He stood in a tight knot of greying men who probably controlled more power and wealth than most nations. Jordan recognized only one, and his legs turned to jelly. That was Leif Mohn himself, the old man. The founder. He shared Jordan's height but looked much more at home in his immaculately pressed suit. His hair had been perfectly styled, so blond it was almost white. It gave the man an indeterminate age, which only fueled the rumors. He'd been CEO since at least the mid-'80s, but he could be anywhere from his late forties to his early sixties.

Most of the men drifted away as Jordan approached, leaving only the Director and Mohn. Jordan kept his shoulders squared, posture stiff. He wasn't going to be intimidated. He'd done everything a man could be expected to do, but the situation had grown beyond one person. This wasn't his fault.

"Mr. Mohn, I'd like you to meet one of our best operatives. This is Commander Jordan, the man who led the first team into the pyramid," the Director said, gesturing at Jordan as he stepped up to the pair.

"He's also the man who let Subject Alpha wipe out a village, then elude him again in San Diego," Mohn growled. He ignored Jordan's proffered hand, staring icily with those grey eyes. "You may have directly ushered in the end of the human race. You realize that, right?"

"Me? Who sent me in with too little intel and even less firepower? I'm betting it was you that signed that order," Jordan shot back, struggling to keep a leash on himself. He failed. "You weren't there. You didn't watch friends die. You weren't asked to fight mythological, almost un-killable creatures with no intel on their capabilities. We did the best we could, but we were outclassed. Even if we'd caught Subject Alpha, there's no guarantee that would tell us anything. So keep your fucking opinions to yourself. You don't like the job I'm doing? Maybe you should come out of that goddamned ivory tower once in a while, and do it your goddamned self."

Jordan didn't give the man time to respond, stalking away and taking a seat near the far edge of the U. He studiously ignored both Mohn and the Director. He was done being a punching bag, done apologizing for failures he couldn't control. If they wanted his resignation, they could have it.

"That was one hell of a stunt," the Director said, settling into the chair next to Jordan. "I've never seen anyone stand up to Mohn before, not even the board. He rules them like a tyrant."

"How did he take it?" Jordan asked sullenly. Lashing out had felt good, though he knew there'd be a price. There always was.

"He smiled," the Director said, adjusting his glasses. "That's something we almost never see, so I'd say you made an impression."

"He was happy I was insubordinate?" Jordan asked, finally turning to face the Director. His salt-and-pepper hair was immaculate, suit pressed to perfection. But Jordan could also see exhaustion.

"I didn't say that. I said he smiled," the Director replied, shaking his head as if Jordan were truly dense. "The last time that happened, a multibillion-dollar corporation went bankrupt, and there was a trail of bodies from Iraq to Venezuela. You want my opinion? The only thing that might keep you alive after that show is a world-ending werewolf apocalypse. Thankfully we happen to have one of those. I told him you're the best. We just can't afford to lose you right now. So I guess if you had to fly off the handle, your timing was impeccable."

The lights flickered on and off three times in rapid succession, indicating everyone should take a seat. He'd never seen so many powerful people scurry before. The few women still managed to make it look graceful, a testament to how high they'd risen in what was unfortunately very much a man's world. People at this level held on to old ideas *hard*. Sexism was alive and well in the lofty halls of power.

"Ladies and gentlemen," a man's British voice called from the back of the room, "please find your seats. Each of you will find a tablet on the table before you. All relevant research and statistics have been loaded in the Mohn Crisis Management app. Feel free to follow along with the presentation. Be aware that a vote will be taken afterwards."

"A vote on what?" Jordan whispered, leaning toward the Director.

"I don't know. They called us last night and said to get everyone here. People came from as far away as London. I've never seen this sort of urgency before. Whatever it is, I think we're about to find out," he replied, crossing his arms and slouching in his chair. Bad posture was probably the most overt show of defiance he was willing to make. The Director didn't reach for the iPad, so Jordan followed his lead. He could study whatever it contained later. He wanted to stay focused on whatever theatrics the board had come up with.

The lights dimmed, and a multicolored world map sprung up on a massive screen in front of the U, perhaps forty feet across. Jordan hadn't even realized they made screens that large. Then the presentation began to play. A pin appeared in Peru, labeled *first incident*. As a calendar advanced on the upper-right-hand corner of the screen, more pins began to appear. The whole thing took maybe forty-five seconds, beginning with January 7 and ending on March 4. Two months and a sea of tags covered South and Central America, as well as Mexico. A crosshatch also covered the southwestern United States with outbreaks appearing sporadically throughout the rest of the country.

Europe, India, and Asia had their share as well. Africa was curiously empty, with only two outbreaks. Both were labeled *contained*, leaving the continent completely free of the werewolf menace. That didn't make any sense. The military forces in Africa weren't equipped to deal with werewolves, which should have torn through large population centers. Yet they hadn't. What was Africa doing that the rest of the world wasn't?

"As you can see, now is not a good time to be a citizen of the Americas, and soon the same will be true of the rest of the world," the polished British voice explained. "This is what the world will look like in another sixty days."

More pins began to fall, much more quickly now. South America became a sea of them. Then Mexico. The United States made it thirty days before it too was completely covered. Canada began to fall. At the same time, Europe was overrun. Asia and India fared better but were still over eighty percent covered. Africa had sporadic pockets of red as well. Jordan wondered who'd come up with these numbers.

The lights came up. A man in an electric wheelchair zoomed smoothly to the center of the U, commanding everyone's attention. "Ladies and gentlemen, the world is coming to an end. We simply cannot contain the outbreak. Conventional warfare is useless. Our enemy can hide among us, completely undetectable until they strike. Even our top-tier teams have lost engagement after engagement."

Eyes shifted to Jordan. He glared back defiantly, daring someone to say something. No one did.

"All of this is dire, but it doesn't mean the world has to end for *us*. Our illustrious CEO has created an oasis of technology, a place where we can gather in comfort and strength," the Brit explained. Then he rose from the wheelchair, a few people gasping in surprise. More than one looked angry at the subterfuge. "That chair was my prison for nearly a decade. Now I can not only walk but also run far more quickly than I could in my younger years, all because of the technology *we* control. The new world is coming regardless of what we want. The only question is, will we be consumed by it...or will we rule it?"

A short, hairy man with dark skin and smoldering eyes stood. He had a faint French accent. "Your presentation is quite impressive, but what exactly are you proposing? You mentioned a vote but have yet to elaborate."

"A valid question, Mr. Rutger," the Brit retorted smoothly. He walked to the hairy man's seat. "I am proposing that the board move all assets and all relevant personnel to Syracuse. Most of our research and development is done there, and it is remote, making it the ideal location to start over."

Jordan had heard enough. These people had unleashed a plague on the world, and now they were tucking tail and running, abandoning everyone. Nearly seven billion people. He wasn't going to stand for this. He found himself on his feet, hands balling into fists. "So you're just giving up, then? You're letting it all go to shit. The people on your special list get saved, and everyone else dies. That's what I'm hearing, right?"

"Yes, Mr. Jordan. That is precisely what you're hearing," the Brit gave back with a smug smile. "The world is ending. That is a tragedy without equal, but this company is in no position to change that fact. We did try, as you know better than anyone. Had you succeeded, things might have been different, but now we need to face reality. A reality you had a direct hand in crafting, I might add."

"And what do you plan to do about the pyramid?" Jordan said, voice carrying even though he hadn't shouted. "What happens if these werewolves get in there and wake up the woman we found? We can't even begin to imagine what she might be able to do. Will you be safe in your little oasis then?"

That gave the man pause. He cocked his head, gaze sweeping the room. "The commander raises an excellent point. Leaving that place to the enemy could have catastrophic consequences. It must be dealt with—permanently. The board should authorize one of our nuclear assets to be detonated at the site. In the meantime we will increase our contingent of troops there to ensure we hold it until it can be destroyed."

"You're going to irradiate Peru?" Jordan asked, even though he knew he was ending his career by speaking further. They might have forgiven his temerity because he pointed out a threat, but that granted only so much leniency, leniency he'd just exceeded.

"Yes, Mr. Jordan. We will irradiate the single largest threat to the world, which happens to be located in Peru. Far away from any population centers. The damage will be minimal. And you, yourself, suggested the threat needed to be dealt with. Do you have a better suggestion? A permanent garrison, perhaps?" he asked, scorn ripping into Jordan. The whole room shared the hostility, all save for the Director. "Correct me if I'm wrong, but the goal of war is to destroy the enemy's ability to wage it, isn't it? Didn't you just tell us this pyramid could be their greatest weapon?"

"I don't have a better plan, sir," Jordan said, deflating. The man was right. What else could they do? They had to prevent that pyramid from falling into enemy hands.

"Then you'll have whatever you need to hold the site until our full tactical response is ready to be delivered," the man said. Then he turned back to the whole council. "That is, assuming the board is willing to vote on such an action. Is anyone willing to make a motion?"

"Not just yet," the Director's clear voice rang out as he rose to his feet. He gazed around the room, defiant and regal. "I believe we need all the facts before making any decisions. What we do here could shape the future of our entire species."

"A reasonable request," the Brit said, clasping his hands behind his back. "Ask your questions, Director Phillips."

"This company had a response team waiting when the pyramid appeared. How did we know it was going to?" the Director asked, leaning on the desk with both hands as his gaze all but burned into the Brit.

"I'm afraid we're not at liberty to discuss that, even with the board..." the Brit began. He trailed off as Leif Mohn rose from the table.

The old man circled the table, coming to stand next to the Brit. He stared calmly at the Director. "I sealed those records personally, but Mark's question is valid. As of right now, I'm unsealing them. It's time you all had the truth."

Jordan didn't know what shocked him more, Mohn's candor or the fact that Director Phillips had a first name.

65

OBJECT ONE

Jordan wasn't any sort of orator, but even he recognized when he was in the presence of a master. Mohn's words had stunned the audience, shocked some of the most powerful people in the world. He'd dangled information that many had probably spent years trying to acquire, and he seemed to be asking nothing in return. It was without a doubt an ambush of some sort. Jordan had walked into enough to recognize the signs.

"This," Mohn said, tapping a button on his tablet and turning to face the gigantic screen, "is Gobekli Tepe, in what is now Turkey. The ruins were constructed in the tenth millennium BC. This is nearly five millennia before ancient Egypt or Mesopotamia, long before archeologists claim we discovered agriculture, which would have been required to create such a vast complex."

He paused to allow them to study the screen, which showed a number of simple stone monuments. Many had to weigh multiple tons, and construction must have taken decades.

"The entire complex was buried roughly two thousand years after it was created," Mohn continued, drawing most of the room's eyes back to him. "We don't know why, but that act is part of what preserved the ruins long enough for us to discover them."

Mohn tapped the screen of his tablet again, and the giant screen showed a new image, this one far more recognizable. "All of us have seen this one, many in person. The Sphinx. College textbooks will tell you it was built during the fourth dynasty of ancient Egypt, by Pharaoh Khafre, the man who built the second of the three Great Pyramids. There are two problems with this theory. First, Khafre never claimed credit. Pharaohs loved to claim credit, and a structure like this would have been recorded all over the annals he created. It wasn't."

The old man paused dramatically, delivering a wolfish smile. "That's not the only problem with the theory. Any modern geologist will tell you that the Sphinx and its entire enclosure appear to have suffered thousands of years of water erosion. Egypt hasn't seen enough rain to cause that since at least ten thousand BC."

"Is this history lesson going anywhere?" a woman's voice rang out, clear and melodic. The room's attention fixed on a statuesque woman in a simple black dress.

"Yes, Marlene, it is," Mohn said, eyes narrowing slightly. He stalked over to the table and set his tablet down in front of the woman. "The point of both stories is simple. Mankind's understanding of our past is incomplete. There are entire cultures we know nothing about, cultures that have disappeared entirely. The pyramid that appeared in Peru belongs to a culture that predates even those."

He turned from her and returned to the spot near the Brit. Then he turned again to face the room. "My grandfather knew this. He devoted his life to finding evidence of this culture. In the 1920s he found it. Tell me, ladies and gentlemen, how many of you believe in magic?"

Polite chuckles sounded through the room. Jordan was awed. Mohn held the emotions of the people here in the palms of his hands, sculpting them like an expert craftsman might a block of stone.

"A few of you have heard rumors of Object Three and the recent tests we've run on it," Mohn said, unbuttoning the top button of his white dress shirt. He withdrew a simple golden pendant with a scarlet gem in the center. Even at this distance, Jordan recognized the stylized Eye of Ra. "This is Object One, the evidence my grandfather found. It looks innocuous enough, doesn't it? At the time my grandfather found it, the object was anything but. The ruby glowed with its own inner light, and the pendant was reputed to bestow a number of abilities. Abilities my grandfather verified."

Whispers rustled through the room, but Mohn held up a hand to forestall them. "I know what you're thinking. If such objects exist, why has the existence of magic been disproved in every test, every magician proved to be a charlatan of some form or another? Let's suppose you are an ancient culture with technology not unlike what we have today.

"Your technology is based on solar power. Not just any solar power, but a specific wavelength of light emitted by the sun. This wavelength comes and goes in millennia-long cycles," Mohn explained, allowing the chain to swing back and forth. All eyes were on the pendant. "Your astronomers warn that the energy your entire culture is based on will soon fade. It will be gone for thirteen thousand years, during which none of your fabulous technology will operate."

Jordan's jaw dropped as he began to understand. The pyramid suddenly made sense.

"If you were the rulers of this hypothetical culture, might you consider building Arks to preserve your way of life? Much like biblical Noah? Places where your culture could survive until the energy you depended upon returned," Mohn said, a predatory smile slipping into place. He knew he had them. "When I first came into possession of this pendant, it still possessed power. I watched that power drain away as I used it until it was nothing but a dormant hunk of metal. Then, one day in 1987, I woke up to find the ruby glowing faintly again.

"The next day, I took the wealth my grandfather had bequeathed me, and I founded this company," Mohn continued, striding toward the wide bay windows. The setting sun bathed the carpet on that side of the room. "I did it because I realized that the power this ancient culture had depended on for so long was returning, that our sun was changing. I set up HELIOS to monitor it. I built a global empire to gather archeological data."

He held up the amulet, and it shone in the sunlight, gleaming richly in a way normal gold could never match. After several seconds the ruby began to glow. "Each of you helped me in this process. Aided Mohn Corp. in finding pieces of the puzzle. No single one of you understood our true purpose or what it was we faced, but all of you were participating in a war you didn't even know existed."

He lowered the amulet, tucking it into his pocket and crossing back to the space next to the slack-jawed Brit. "Before we call this vote, I will lay out the facts very simply. I learned that a catastrophe was coming, and that Arks like the pyramid in Peru will begin to return. I don't know how many there are, only where the first would be. I also know that our sun is about to emit the largest coronal mass ejection in known history. This wave will devastate the world's power grid. Only those very close to the equator will be unaffected, a green zone, if you will.

"Every satellite orbiting our world will be destroyed, except for the twelve that Mohn has launched in the last three years," Mohn explained, expression now grave. "We will be blind and confused, naked before the onslaught of an enemy we cannot understand. I didn't understand the nature of this enemy until the first werewolf attack, but we all understand it now. Mankind has only us to shield it, something we can only do if we husband our resources and strike from a position of strength. That can only occur if we retreat temporarily, hiding our existence in our Syracuse facility. There we will watch and plan, saving who and what we can of our world.

"Ladies and gentlemen, I call for a vote. Will we be the saviors of mankind, or will we squander our strength in a vain attempt to stave off the inevitable?" he roared, looking every inch the conquering king. The applause was thunderous.

66

FIGHT FOR ALPHA

The whine of the propellers softened to a lower pitch as the plane dropped from cloud cover, weaving a tight arc toward the Tarmac below. The windows were instantly spattered with rain as the storm buffeted them about. Liz hated small planes to begin with, but they were even worse during a storm.

She leaned forward in the seat to get a better look at the city below. She'd spent two weeks in Cajamarca, taking an advanced Spanish class, and she still remembered how hard adjusting to the altitude had been. Cajamarca was at almost nine thousand feet, as high as Half Dome, back home in Yosemite.

A sea of tightly packed buildings surrounded the airport, mostly obscured by the rain. Here and there, the steeple of a church jutted over the rest of the buildings. The locals took their religion seriously and had for centuries. It took Liz several moments to realize what was wrong. The streets were largely empty. No people. Very few cars, and none of them moving. This place was deserted. A city of over two hundred thousand people.

"Ahh shit," Garland muttered, tapping at the fuel gauge. The red needle had been hovering a bit above the *E*, but his tapping knocked it down below. "Sometimes it sticks. Henrietta likes to play games with me."

"We've got enough to land, right?" Liz asked, bracing herself against the console with one hand, and the chair with the other. She knew this thing was a death trap.

"Oh, sure. We'll be fine. I could probably coast in with no fuel at this point," he said, taking a swig from the dregs of the forty he'd been working on for the last hour. He offered her a swig and then shrugged when she shook her head. "We'll come around in one more turn to put us on a straight shot down that runway. Probably a little slick from the rain, but it's designed for much larger aircraft. We've got all the time in the world to slow down."

The plane tilted sharply, moving Liz's window so it was almost parallel with the ground. She fought off vertigo as her knuckles went white. She felt metal bend under her hand as her fingers sank into it. Oops. The plane righted itself, and then it began to drop sharply in elevation.

"Make sure you're buckled up back there," Garland yelled over his shoulder. He gave Liz a friendly smile and waggled his eyebrows. "Gonna be a bumpy landing, but I promise we'll be just fine. Still, if you want to give me a kiss for luck, I won't turn it down."

Liz just gave him a deadpan stare. Adjusting to the smell had taken hours, though at some point she'd stopped noticing it. The bad jokes and mostly incoherent stories had been much harder to deal with. To his credit, Garland hadn't tried anything more than light flirting, but she had newfound respect for her brother. Working with this guy must have been excruciating.

"Here we go," he said, eyes finally focused on the rapidly approaching runway. He brought the nose up at the last moment, allowing the rear wheels to touch down first. The plane fishtailed wildly, but somehow Garland fought the motion and kept it in a mostly straight line.

Then the front wheels were down. The whole plane shook as it rattled down the runway, but an eternity later the plane shuddered to a halt. Garland unbuckled his seat belt and polished off the bottle. He cracked open his window and hurled it out into the rain, where it shattered.

"Woooo," he yelled, giving Liz a maniacal grin. "Hell of a ride. Told you we'd make it. Now let's see about finding that shaman of yours."

An eerie howl sliced through the wind, low and deep. Then another. It became a chorus, coming from all directions. Some howls distant, some alarmingly close. Liz resisted the urge to add her voice to the chorus, unbuckling her seat belt and ducking through the cockpit's narrow door into the cargo area.

Blair and Trevor had already left their seats and were shouldering packs. Trevor knelt next to a blanket-wrapped bundle and removed his Remington, glancing up at her as she entered. "Looks like our entrance drew some attention. Don't suppose one of you can give the werewolf howl-ee handshake to call them off?"

"If anyone can do that, it will be Liz. Werewolves are a matriarchy. There's a reason females are larger and stronger," Blair said, moving for the door. He turned the wide metal handle, and the door opened with a heavy thunk. The wind immediately swept a sheet of water inside.

Great. So not only had she been consigned to throwing her life away trying to rescue this Mother she'd never even met, but now she was also expected to lead this lunacy.

"I'll do what I can, but we aren't exactly given a manual when we're, uh, recruited," she said, following Blair out into the rain. She hopped to the Tarmac, shivering as the rain sluiced over her. She'd never even considered the need for a jacket when leaving San Diego.

Trevor hopped down after her, tugging on a green Yosemite cap to shield his face from the rain. He turned to face the plane, cradling his shotgun as Garland's bushy face appeared in the doorway.

"New plan," the pilot said, cracking a nervous grin. "I'm gonna wait here. I've got two cases of beer, and I figure that will last me about three days. If you can make it back in that time, you've got a ride back to the states. If not, Henrietta and I are going home."

"What about your ayahuasca?" Liz asked, shielding her face with an arm. It didn't help much.

"You didn't tell me I had to be an extra in *The Howling* if I wanted to get it," Garland replied. He pulled the door most of the way closed. "I might be crazy, but I ain't stupid." The door jerked closed with a thunk.

"Guess we're on our own," Blair said. His hair was already plastered to his head, and water dribbled from his chin. "The howls have stopped. My guess is we're about to meet the welcoming committee."

He was right. Beyond the keening wind and the splatter of raindrops, Liz heard feet. A lot of feet. Shapes began to emerge from the rain, a wide cluster maybe a hundred yards away, near the fence bordering the Tarmac. Most of the shapes were four legged, a variety of dogs in all shapes and sizes. Three were two legged, the largest a midnight-furred female.

She paused for a moment to study them and then arched her neck in a howl that rolled over them like thunder. It was unmistakably a challenge. The small blond female behind her and a grey-furred male remained still as the midnight approached at a slow walk.

"Guess that's my cue," Liz said, slipping out of her shirt and shucking out of her jeans. She'd lost enough clothing to the change. This time she was going to strip first.

Liz let her bra fall to the ground, shivering in the rain as she removed her panties. She was conscious of Blair's eyes all but burning into her, though her brother looked studiously away. She suppressed a brief twinge of embarrassment, taking a step toward her apparent rival as she began to shift.

It came quickly now, a welcome warmth that pushed away the chill as fur erupted from her skin. In the space of three steps, she was half again as tall as she had been. She strode confidently toward the midnight until the gap between them had closed to perhaps twenty feet.

"Why have you come to my city, little girl?" the female called in Spanish, voice a low rumble. She flexed her claws, hackles raised.

Liz considered her answer carefully. If Blair was right about the whole matriarchy thing, then she was supposed to act like an alpha female. That meant showing no fear and a great deal of testosterone-driven bluster if action movies and frat boys were any guide.

"That's my business," she roared back, flexing her own claws. She took a step closer. "You can either get out of my way and leave me to it, or I can humiliate you in front of your pack."

That did it. The midnight's nostrils flared. Then she began a lumbering run toward Liz. The move surprised Liz, but not because it made any tactical sense. She was used to Blair's blurring and Mohn's troops firing missiles. This seemed almost quaint by comparison.

She is strong, Ka-Ken, but not nearly so strong as you. Her lineage is further removed from the Mother, your progeny's progeny. Her mastery of our skills is wanting. Use that to defeat her.

The female leapt into the air, coming down at Liz in a mass of claws and fangs. Liz vanished, pulling the shadows close as she rolled to the right. The midnight came down in the spot Liz had occupied, spinning as she tasted the air with her nostrils. Her eyes scanned ceaselessly, but they found nothing.

Liz waited until her opponent's back was exposed and then lunged from the shadows. She wrapped an arm around the female's throat, plunging the claws of her other hand into the small of the female's back. She let the beast guide her, slicing muscle until her hand settled around the lower spine. Then she snapped it with a crack that echoed across the Tarmac.

The female fell limply to the asphalt, paralyzed from the waist down. It was a calculated move, nonlethal but humiliating and a swift end to the fight. The gamble was that her opponent would be able to heal from it. If they were going to rescue the Mother, they needed allies, not more corpses.

The midnight surprised her, sweeping an arm around and seizing Liz's ankle. The next thing she knew, she was on her back. Her opponent's wet, furry body crashed down atop her. Fangs savaged her shoulder, drawing a cry of pain. Fury surged through her. She could have killed her opponent. This would end. Now.

Liz seized the midnight's head in both hands, jerking it away from her. She held the jaws apart and used her legs to launch herself and the midnight into the air. She had superior mobility and used it to great effect, landing on the midnight's back as they came down hard on the Tarmac.

"Yield, or I'll tear out your goddamn throat," she hissed, meaning every word. Her opponent went limp.

Liz rose and took a step back. She flexed her right shoulder, which was already beginning to heal. The midnight hobbled to her knees and turned to face Liz. She kept her head down. "You've bested me. Control of the pack is yours."

"I don't want your pack," Liz shot back. The pain was fading, but the dull ache had soured her mood. "Give us a place to stay, and we'll be out of the city tomorrow."

"Where are you going?" the midnight asked, peering up at her with amber eyes that mirrored Liz's own. She rose shakily to her feet. Apparently the spinal injury had healed.

"We must wake the Mother, the woman who gave birth to our entire species," Liz growled. She looked around, taking in the faces of everyone around her. There was a mixture of awe...and fear, especially in the midnight's companions.

67

I KNOW SPANISH

lair's tenth-grade Spanish was no match for the dark-furred female's outburst, but he recognized the tone. This was a challenge, pure and simple. Winner takes all.

It is so, Ka-Dun. Females are ever the pack leaders. We males are shapers and advisors, gifting them with our wisdom. We guide and reason, but the rule is theirs.

The gender roles were reversed from Western society, but they made perfect sense. The reversal provided a natural set of checks and balances. He wondered if the virus's creator had intended that. Of course she had.

He was shocked at the speed and brutality of the combat. There was very little finesse, just raw power as Liz-wolf casually stepped into the shadows and then emerged to rip out her opponent's spine. Her poor opponent put up a little resistance after that, but the auburn werewolf batted her down as though she were a kitten tussling with a mountain lion.

Just like that, it was over. The black-furred werewolf assumed a submissive pose, and the two shared a brief conversation, again in Spanish. Blair understood exactly one word—donde. Where. He assumed the black-furred woman was asking their destination, but that was the limit of his frustratingly inadequate knowledge.

The two werewolves who'd arrived with their beaten leader began to approach. The first was a small blond female, still a head and shoulders larger than Blair but almost a foot shorter than Liz. She was hesitant and kept her distance. The male's fur was similar to Blair's, but where Blair's was silver the newcomer's was more of a smoky grey.

The grey made a wide circle around Liz and her defeated opponent, clearly picking a path in Blair's direction. A small army of dogs trotted in his wake, complete with everything from a Chihuahua to a pair of Rottweilers. Blair could dimly sense their minds, though he made no move to engage them. That might be construed as hostile. Instead he too moved in a wide arc, meeting the newcomer forty or fifty feet from Liz.

Blair brushed the sodden hair from his face, thankful that he no longer wore glasses. There was no way he'd have been able to see in this rain. Instead, the downpour was merely annoying. He peered up at the grey male, surprised by how little intimidation he felt. Here he was, in human form, a little shy of six feet, confronted with a seven-foot werewolf with a good two hundred pounds on him.

It is natural, Ka-Dun. Your lineage is pure. You are the Mother's direct progeny. None stand higher. This one is a pale shadow, four or five generations removed from your own. Even now he trembles in awe and fear at your strength. Such is both right and proper, a measure of your higher birth.

That might have been the most the beast had ever spoken, so Blair lent the words great weight. A werewolf's pedigree must be of utmost importance in determining status. It probably also determined relative strength, if the fight between Liz and the black-furred female was any indication.

"Me llamo Adolpho," the grey rumbled, giving a slight bow. A white terrier hurried forward to sniff Blair's foot.

A fresh surge of frustration heated Blair despite the chill of the air. He was going to have a very difficult time functioning here without speaking the language.

Take the tongue from this one's mind, Ka-Dun.

Blair's jaw fell open as the implications hit him. *I can learn Spanish from his mind?*

Just so. Give me control, and I will guide you.

So Blair did. Invisible and intangible but no less real, a tendril of humming energy stretched from his mind. It caressed the grey's mind. At first the male stiffened, fists balling as he looked about him as if in search of an assailant. Then he relaxed. Blair's probe slipped through the grey's permeable defenses and into his mind. Up to that point he was more or less in control and understood completely what was happening.

Then Blair's will exploded into hundreds of tendrils. Thousands. They slithered past colorful memories, latching onto some while ignoring others. The densest collection plunged deep into the man's past, revealing images of classrooms and first steps. The places and moments he'd likely learned most of the language he now used.

Each tendril sent pulses of light flowing back into Blair, faster than he could track or comprehend. They came faster and faster, a burning heat inside his skull. He scrunched his eyes shut, sagging to his knees as he cradled his head in both hands. He had no idea how much time had passed when he found himself panting in the rain.

Blair looked up to find the grey, Adolpho, in a nearly identical pose. He too had fallen to his knees. He peered up at Blair with frightened, watery eyes. "What did you do to me?"

"I, uh...Are we speaking Spanish?" Blair asked lamely, staggering to his feet. Adolpho followed, just as shakily.

"Yes, it's the only language I know," he replied. Some of the earlier warmth had left his voice.

Blair was being an asshole. He'd just violated the man's mind without asking, something Ahiga had implied was taboo among werewolves. Blair offered a hand. "I'm sorry about whatever just happened. I'm still learning about our abilities. My name is Blair."

Adolpho's furry hand engulfed Blair's, but the handshake was gentle enough. "I understand. Every day, the beast teaches me something new. It was only recently I learned to command my pack."

The mention seemed to open a floodgate, and dogs of every size approached, tails wagging as they sniffed at Blair. He couldn't help but laugh. He hadn't owned a dog since he'd been a kid, but he'd always had a soft spot for them.

"That's amazing," he said, kneeling to scratch behind the ears of a golden retriever. "How do you do it?"

"I just...do." Adolpho shrugged. He dropped to a knee, putting his face closer to Blair's. "The beast tells me that you are strong, that you are near to the Mother, and I should obey you."

"Mine said pretty much the same thing. It also suggested I could learn Spanish, so that's why...well, sorry again. About invading your mind without asking," Blair said. The scent of wet dog was overpowering, but rather than finding it repulsive, he found it comforting.

"It is, as I understand it, your right to do so," Adolpho shrugged. Then he shifted, shrinking down to a mousy man just over five feet tall. He had wide hazel eyes and a tangle of dark hair, which the rain quickly plastered to his scalp.

One of the dogs, the small white terrier, pulled over a backpack and deposited it at Adolpho's feet. The mousy man reached inside and pulled out a bright yellow poncho that he quickly shrugged into. It probably didn't keep him warm, but it kept the rain off and covered his nakedness.

"Handy, having a clothes caddy," Blair said, unable to suppress a smile.

"So who are your friends? The red female is the strongest I've ever seen," Adolpho asked, gesturing toward them.

Blair turned to find that both Liz and the black-furred female had returned to human form. The female was a tall brunette, just over six feet. She too had donned a poncho, and was offering one to Liz. She pulled it on gratefully, though it left most of her creamy legs exposed. The blond werewolf finally approached, shifting as she did.

By the time she reached the other two women, she was a short, tanned Brazilian with blond hair that spilled down to the small of her back. She was gorgeous, walking with the sensual grace of a dancer. The Brazilian crouched next to the pack where the ponchos had originated and withdrew one. Her next words caught Blair completely by surprise.

"Hello, Liz," she said, smiling up at the tall redhead. She pulled the poncho over her shoulders and stood up. "It's been a long time. You look well. I guess we both do."

Blair turned back to Adolpho. "The woman is Liz, though I'm sure you just heard that. Looks like your friend already knows her."

"That's Cyntia," Adolpho said, nodding toward the blond woman. "She used to be dumpy and shy, but after she changed...well, you know better than anyone what it does to our bodies."

"Yeah, I can see that," Blair said, giving the man a conspiratorial grin. The mousy man shared it.

"So who is the scary-looking man with the rifle back by the airplane? He doesn't smell like a wolf," Adolpho said. He was peering at Trevor, though the earlier smell of alarm had faded. Trevor, on the other hand, still smelled wary.

"That's Trevor, Liz's brother. He's just as scary as he looks, werewolf or not," Blair explained. He began to walk toward Liz and gestured for Trevor to do the same.

Trevor sized the situation up for a moment longer. Then he slung his rifle over his shoulder and picked up his pack. He trotted over, reaching Liz and her new companions about the same time Blair and Adolpho did.

"Blair, Trevor, this is Elmira and her pack. The blond woman is Cyntia, but I haven't met the man with Blair yet," she said, pointing to each person in turn.

"Adolpho," Blair supplied, nodding in his direction.

"You must be Trevor," Cyntia said, beaming a smile in Trevor's direction. Blair had seen a lot of crushes in his time, and this was one of the worst. Cyntia apparently already knew Trevor. However, judging from the confused look on his face, he had no idea who she was.

"Yeah, and you are?" he asked, rubbing at his goatee with one hand as he peered down at her over his glasses. His hat had kept them mostly dry, but they were starting to fog up.

"I'm a friend of Liz's," she said, offering Trevor her hand. He took it, and her smile widened. "We used to study together, and sometimes we'd go out to clubs."

Liz smiled at the two of them, evidently pleased by the interaction. "Cyntia Facebook stalked you, Trevor. She made me promise to bring you down to Brazil so we could go dancing."

Trevor turned scarlet, even in the rain. Cyntia just managed to look horrified, dropping her gaze and Trevor's hand. Blair suppressed a laugh. It felt good. The interaction was the most normal he'd seen in days, despite the epic werewolf combat just minutes before.

"I, uh, hate to be a bad guest," Trevor said, turning toward Elmira. He was still blushing but obviously pretending he wasn't. "My smartphone doesn't work here, and I really need to check my email. It's very, very important. Do you guys have Internet access?"

"Yes, back at our home." Elmira nodded, the gesture more regal than any made by her companions. "Please, come with us. We will give you shelter and food, and you can tell us more about this *Mother* you seek to rescue. You will have our aid if you wish it."

68

HOPE

B ridget itched. She could feel it between her shoulders, on her calves, along her scalp. It had begun days ago, and though she was denied any way of knowing the time, she sensed that night had fallen. She felt the moon, even inside this cell.

It had made her strong, stronger than she'd have believed possible. Bridget no longer feared the manacles. She could snap them, high tech compression bands or no. She could also tear the sealed door from her little white prison, bursting into the hallway and surprising the guards.

So why didn't she? Bridget itched for battle, for the blood of those who'd imprisoned her. The feeling was primal, bestial, and yet it felt so natural. Was that a part of her transformation? What had she become?

She didn't know. Bridget resumed her pacing, careful to keep her most prized possession hidden under the humiliating white gown with the open back. The book Sheila had sent was the only reason she was still sane, the only thing to occupy her mind through weeks or maybe months of captivity.

She'd poured over the glyphs for hours every day, studying patterns and making guesses. Sometime after the first few days, the language had begun to coalesce, and she finally had a working translation. If only she'd had a pen to record her findings. For now such knowledge had to live in her head, though very soon it would be useful.

She paused her pacing, grabbing her belly with a sharp groan. She leaned against the wall with her free hand, sweat breaking out on her brow. This was the second time today, and the third in the last two days. It would pass in a few moments. At least, it had before.

Agony faded to a dull ache, and Bridget gave a sigh of relief. What was happening to her? The pain was getting worse, and the episodes were longer, albeit still just a few seconds.

Ka-Ken, you must feed. Soon the energy will overwhelm you, and I will be forced to assume control. That will be messy, as I will be driven to kill indiscriminately. It will be easier if you select a target, perhaps one of the warriors outside your cell.

"Kill?" she murmured. Other than the night she'd first shifted, she'd had little experience with the beast and certainly hadn't killed anyone. The prospect horrified her, yet there was also a part of her that found it exciting. She *wanted* to kill, to take her anger out on a target. "What if no one comes in? Will I go mad or burn up or something?"

No, Ka-Ken. When the energy overwhelms you, I will shatter this cage like kindling. The warriors outside will be the first to die, though certainly not the last. I will tear through this camp like a whirlwind, bringing death to those who dare imprison us.

"How long do I have?" Bridget asked. This could be perfect. She wanted out badly, but she was no killer. Not yet, anyway. The beast could do it for her, get revenge for Steve's death and her imprisonment all in one blow.

Another moonrise, no more. Then I will be forced to assume control.

"Can you get me inside the pyramid?" she asked. She wasn't sure what she could do there, but now that she understood the language, she could study the writings in the inner chamber. Who knew what that could reveal or allow her to do?

I sense your need. You will not be able to wake the Mother, but you can draw on energy from the Ark. If you must fight these warriors, your best chance of victory is battling them there. When we escape I will draw them there and then cede control back to you.

Knowing the alien consciousness that lurked in her head could read her thoughts was bizarre. Yet she treasured it. The beast had been her only companion over the last few weeks, and after she'd recovered from her initial fear, she'd spent long hours learning from it. She'd gained a much better understanding of exactly what the werewolves were and more of what they were capable of. She was just scratching the surface of that understanding.

Someone approaches, Ka-Ken.

The beast was right. She heard footsteps approaching, up the hall. Too measured to be Sheila. But who else would visit her? More soldiers? That made no sense, not unless they'd thought of something else they wanted from her.

The door gave its customary hiss, admitting a familiar black-clad man built like a mountainside. Jordan had a sidearm belted around his waist but was otherwise unarmed. The soldiers who'd been allowed in the room thus far all bore wicked-looking rifles. Yet he didn't smell afraid. Of course, a rock was more likely to be afraid than he was. He probably frightened death.

The close-cropped stubble along his scalp had given way to a knot of curly blond. It softened his appearance, though only by a hair. It was a good look for him.

"Hello, Bridget. I was hoping we could talk for a few minutes," he began, reaching into a pocket and withdrawing a white piece of paper that had been folded in half. "I've come with a message from Sheila, among other things. She seems to think this will mean something to you and said you could pass a response back through me. She'd have come herself, but the Director has forbidden her access."

He passed the paper to Bridget, who took it hesitantly. It was difficult not to scramble backward from the man. She still remembered when he and his team had taken her down after she'd shifted. Utterly without mercy.

Bridget examined the paper. She expected more glyphs from the inner chamber, perhaps some bit that Sheila was struggling with. To her shock, she saw a line of Egyptian hieroglyphs. They took her back almost a decade, to the days when she and Sheila had passed messages back and forth using such notes.

He does not know this message's true nature. The day will come soon when you will be free. I will help you.

That was only a rough translation, of course. Hieroglyphs were less precise than that. But they had a spin on them that Bridget and Sheila had cooked up, a way to tweak the basic meaning of a glyph to include more modern context. They had created the system back in college as a kind of prank. She'd never expected them to use it again.

"Tell her I'll need some time to consider this but that most of the message is clear to me," Bridget said, handing the paper back. They'd never let her keep it. "Was there another reason you came?"

"Yes," Jordan said, nodding at the camera. "For starters I wanted you to know that the camera is off for the duration of this discussion. I'll catch hell for it, but I'm past caring."

"So anything we say is private. Why risk the Director's wrath? This seems a lot like aiding the enemy, and I can't imagine they'll go easy on you," she said.

"It *is* aiding the enemy," Jordan agreed. He sighed heavily. "At this point I'm not so sure that's a bad thing. Sheila is convinced some sort of apocalypse is coming. I faced Professor Smith in San Diego recently, and he said much the same, that the werewolves are our only chance."

"You saw Blair?" Bridget asked, trying not to sound too eager. A surge of elation passed through her. He was alive, and Mohn didn't have him. Otherwise Jordan would have said captured, not faced.

"He's alive and well. And has some damn-scary friends," Jordan said, cracking the first genuine smile Bridget had ever seen him give. "My team came home empty handed. He got away, but I'm almost positive he's coming here."

"To wake the Mother," Bridget said. She could hug Jordan, though she doubted he'd react well to that. "He's always been resourceful. I'm sure he'll make it back here somehow, and I doubt you'll be able to keep him out of the pyramid. He'll find a way."

"I have a feeling you're right," Jordan admitted. He didn't look terribly concerned. "When he comes, we'll do everything we can to stop him. You know that, right? He was seriously wounded in San Diego. He might not survive an attempt on the pyramid. Especially not with all the ordnance that Mohn has moved in. We're prepared for war, Bridget. And I'm the guy they've put in charge of the battle. I can't let him get to the Mother. I know you and Sheila disagree with that, but I've been given a job and I have to do it."

"So you never question orders, then?" she asked, wielding the accusation with the expert skill she'd learned first dating Blair and later, Steve.

"I'm here, aren't I?" Jordan growled, though she wasn't sure if he was angry at her or with himself. "I don't know if stopping Blair is the best decision, but that's the job I've been tasked with, and I'll do it to the best of my abilities. Mohn isn't some soulless corporation. We believe we're doing the right thing. Sheila has me questioning things, but if we're in the wrong here, it's through ignorance, not malice."

"Then why are you here?" Bridget asked. Then she hurriedly raised a hand to forestall him. "Not that I'm not grateful. I haven't had any company in weeks. It's just that if you're so determined to stop Blair, and you know I want the same thing he does...well, I guess I just don't understand your motivation."

"I promised Sheila I'd deliver that note," Jordan explained, darting a nervous glance at the door. "Beyond that? I think you've been given a raw deal. I like you, Bridget. You're smart and capable and you get results. You were just in the wrong place at the wrong time, and now you're suffering for it. Me? I think you can be trusted, and I think it's the worst kind of idiocy to lock you away. I've seen what female werewolves can do. You could shred this place like paper if you really wanted out."

"You'd be smart to kill me," she said, shocked by her own honesty. But Jordan was being honest. Didn't she owe him the same? "You know I'll help Blair if given the chance. So if you think I can break out of this place, doesn't that make me a threat?"

"Absolutely," Jordan admitted, smiling again. It looked good on him, and it almost gave her hope that they could be friends. "But I'm drawing a line in the sand. I've had to compromise on some pretty core issues since working for Mohn. This isn't an area I'm willing to budge in. Like I said, I like you, Bridget. I hope we don't end up on opposite sides of this. That could be messy."

69

FIRST WAVE

The ancient wooden chair creaked alarmingly as Trevor lowered himself into it. He banged a knee tucking it under the narrow desk, stifling a curse at the sudden pain. Calling the 'office' a closet would have been generous back in the states. Harry Potter had more room under the stairs at the Dursleys'.

The center of the desk bowed under one of the massive CRT monitors that had been phased out nearly a decade ago. Stacks of unpaid bills flanked it, and a huge black tower competed for space with his legs under the desk. Trevor stabbed the power button on the bulky machine, the noisy fan firing up like a jet engine as the thing whirred to life.

"You are a dangerous man, Trevor," a voice purred from behind in heavily accented English. The floor creaked, and a soft hand rested on Trevor's shoulder. "Liz used to tell me stories about you."

Conflicting emotions bounced about in his head like marbles in a blender. On the one hand, he was preoccupied with the end of the world. He needed to know if the sunspot had burst yet. The CME's first wave could already have happened, and if that was the case, they had no more than two days before the second knocked out most of the world's power.

On the other, it had been a very long time since Trevor had enjoyed the touch of a woman, particularly one as gorgeous as Cyntia. He knew almost nothing about her, though she seemed to know a great deal about him. The Windows '98 logo appeared on the computer screen as the system booted, and he took the opportunity to face Cyntia.

"Dangerous to a six pack of Guinness and an unlucky trout, maybe," he said, giving her a wry smile. He wasn't very adept at flirting.

Cyntia was gorgeous, in the same way a tiger could be called gorgeous. Short, voluptuous, blond, and dark skinned. Yet, like a tiger's, her beauty was somehow calculated, lulling a man into a stupor just before she struck. She gave a throaty laugh as if he'd just said the funniest thing she'd ever heard.

"There are pictures of you with guns on Facebook. Pictures of you hunting large beasts. Even if that were not so, I saw you on that Tarmac. I would not have wanted to fight you," she purred, resting on the arm of the chair. He was all too conscious of her leg pressing against his arm. "Were there more room, I'd sit on your lap, and you could scratch behind my ears."

A very awkward situation began to arise. Trevor glanced down at his crotch and then past Cyntia to the living room, where Blair and Adolpho were chatting. He looked up at Cyntia with his best grin. "If there was enough room, maybe I'd let you."

The desktop finally appeared, giving Trevor an easy escape from the fire filling his cheeks. He scanned the sea of scattered icons, horrified by the mess. Eventually he found the little blue *E*. Not his favorite browser, but it would work. He opened it, waiting far too long for it to load. When it did, he browsed to Gmail and opened his account.

"You're very tense," Cyntia murmured, hands kneading his shoulders. It was heaven. "What are you looking for?"

"Nothing, I hope," he muttered back.

The browser was agonizingly slow, but eventually his email occupied the screen. He scrolled through advertisements and a few joke emails, praying he wouldn't see anything from David. Oh shit. About midway down the page was an email with the subject *First Wave*. His heart sank. It was from yesterday morning.

"You just tensed even more. Whatever it is cannot be so bad," Cyntia murmured. She was really good, but even her magic hands were not going to take his mind off this.

Trevor clicked the email, holding his breath as the screen loaded. It was brief and to the point. *First wave detected. Based on initial readings, this is the largest CME in recorded history. Have warned Washington, but gotten no response. Second wave within 48 hours.*

"Cyntia, we need to get everyone together. We're in deep shit," Trevor said, turning to face her. She seemed to pick up on his anxiety, rising from the arm of the chair.

"I'll tell Adolpho and Elmira you wish their attention," she said, squeezing past him and back into the living room. He was fairly certain the squeezing had nothing to do with the cramped quarters, but far be it from him to complain.

He trailed after her, into a room cracked and faded from too many years of use. There were a few white spots where pictures had probably lived, but the place was bare now. He didn't want to know the circumstances that had led to the werewolves taking this apartment. He seriously doubted they were the original owners.

Adolpho and Blair were involved in a rapid exchange of Spanish that flew completely over Trevor's head. Blair sat on a ripped recliner, while Adolpho occupied the edge of the couch closest to it. Trevor settled onto the far side of the couch, its cushions long since compressed into flat squares about two shades less comfortable than concrete.

Cyntia disappeared into the bedroom, appearing a moment later with Liz and Elmira in tow. Trevor followed Liz's gaze, which landed on Blair as she entered the room. She gave a slight smile, and he knew her well enough to know why. She liked the guy. The idea of them together made him happy. They were both good people, and he had the feeling Blair would treat her right. He didn't think either would admit it, but there was definitely a spark there. Sooner or later they'd slow down long enough to act on it.

"Cyntia says you have urgent news," Elmira growled as she stalked to a brown recliner. She sat delicately, a queen granting audience to her court.

In contrast, Liz plopped down on the couch next to Trevor, elbowing him in the gut. "Has it happened?"

"We'll get there. Blair, maybe you should start by explaining why we're in Peru. Otherwise what I'm about to share won't make a whole lot of sense," Trevor offered, turning to the anthropologist. Blair gave a short nod and licked his lips before speaking.

"I was the first person to be turned to a werewolf," he began, gaze roaming about those assembled. "It happened in an ancient pyramid that we just recently discovered. This pyramid was left behind by a culture we don't even have myths about. They predicted a coming apocalypse, something that would wipe out mankind. They created us to serve as champions, to hold back an ancient enemy, and to save those we can.

The room was silent, all eyes on Blair. Trevor gauged their reactions carefully. There was no disbelief, only curiosity. Cyntia didn't even have that. She crossed the room silently, settling on the arm of the couch next to him. She rested a hand possessively on his shoulder. He wasn't really sure how to react, so he didn't.

"The person who prepared all this is called the Mother. As far as we know, she's the first werewolf, the literal mother for our entire species," Blair explained.

"Is? Not was?" Elmira interrupted, hands gripping the arms of her chair as she leaned forward. Her eyes glittered with an intensity Trevor expected from CEOs or judges.

"Yes, *is*. She's still in the pyramid, in some sort of stasis chamber that's kept her alive for many thousands of years. Possibly tens of thousands. That's why we came," Blair explained, his hand finding Liz's. That drew a smile from Trevor. "We're going to wake her before this apocalypse arrives. She might be the only hope of mankind's survival."

"This ancient enemy," Elmira said, eyes narrowing. "What are they, and why have they not revealed themselves?" That she seemed to accept the Mother's stasis surprised Trevor, though in light of them all becoming werewolves, perhaps that was to be expected.

"The dead will walk. They'll attack every last living thing, killing us all if they aren't stopped," Blair said, eyes daring anyone to laugh.

"Zombies?" Adolpho said with a snort.

"We'd have said the same thing about werewolves not so long ago," Cyntia retorted, hand tightening on Trevor's shoulder. "The world is not the same. If we exist, why not zombies?"

"The question still remains," Elmira broke in. "Why has this ancient enemy not appeared?"

"That's where it gets even stranger," Liz interjected, releasing Blair's hand as she spoke. "The zombies are created from a virus, a virus all of us know. HIV. Apparently it's lain dormant for thousands of years but has become active again over the last few generations. Soon a solar event will occur that will activate this virus. When it does, every last person with HIV will die. Their corpses will rise as zombies, tearing apart cities across the globe."

The room was silent save for the ticking of the wall clock. Elmira merely stared at Liz, expression unreadable.

"This is all very difficult to accept, even with everything that has happened," Adolpho said, completing the first sentence in English that they'd heard from him. He seemed skeptical but also wary of offending them.

"Trust me, I know how crazy it sounds," Trevor broke in. He was uniquely suited to understand their reaction, having come late to the whole 'the world is going to end' party. "It sounds like the plot of some low-budget movie, right? But it's true. That's why I called everyone together. The solar event Liz mentioned has begun. It's called a coronal mass ejection, and it's going to wipe out power to most of the planet when it hits. I received word that the first wave occurred yesterday, around 11 a.m. Pacific standard time. That's the weaker wave, the baby one before the real threat arrives. We have somewhere between twenty-four and forty-eight hours before the end of the world as we know it. Maybe less."

"Let us assume you are correct," Elmira said, eyes distrustful. She brushed a lock of midnight hair from her face. "What is it you wish of us? What can we do to stop this terrible calamity?'

"You can help us wake the Mother," Liz said. She made it sound so simple.

"If this ancient enemy has yet to appear, why do you need our help?" Elmira asked, gaze weighing Liz. "Why not simply wake her yourself? You've demonstrated incredible strength and fantastic powers. Far more than any of us."

"There's a catch," Liz said with a heavy sigh. Trevor noticed her grip tighten on Blair's hand. Did she even realize she was doing that? Her tone was resolved. "The pyramid is held by a private army. They have state-of-the-art military hardware, no shortage of soldiers, and a strong desire to keep us from waking the Mother."

"We'll almost certainly take casualties getting in," Trevor announced. It was only fair that they knew what they were getting involved in.

"And this Mother will help us fight this ancient enemy?" Elmira asked, looking pointedly first at Liz and Blair. She paid almost no attention to Trevor. Werewolf racism? He suppressed a smile.

"She has all the answers. She created us and knows all about this ancient enemy," Blair explained. He seemed more confident than when they'd met, though it had only been a few days. "You've seen that some werewolves are stronger than others. I believe that's based on the strength of your virus, which is in turn related to how far from the source you are. If I'm right about that, the Mother will be much, much stronger than we can begin to imagine. She can teach us abilities we can't possibly predict. We need her."

"If this Mother is our creator, then I would see her free," Cyntia said, her leg pressed against his arm on the edge of the couch. Her sudden interest was more than a little odd, but it was difficult to question the attentions of a gorgeous woman.

"It sounds like we have little choice. If we do not help, we're defenseless when these zombies arrive," Adolpho said, also directing his argument at Elmira.

"Then it is settled," Elmira said, rising gracefully from her recliner. "We will help you rescue this Mother, though our own lives may be forfeit. We will need to obtain vehicles and sufficient weaponry. How soon do you wish to leave?"

"How far is it to the pyramid?" Trevor asked.

"About four hours," Liz said.

"We leave now, then. Let us hope we are not too late," Elmira said.

70

IT'S TIME

Blair crept up the last few feet of the ridge, dropping prone and pulling himself through the dirt until he was next to Trevor. The Barrett sniper rifle had been set up on a bipod, thick scope angled at the camp that now sprawled around the pyramid. How had they built it so quickly?

Blair willed a bit of energy to enhance his vision. The camp leapt into sharp focus, the gibbous moon illuminating the valley as brightly as the sun could. The soldiers had created semi-permanent structures, and at least several dozen troops moved between them. More probably slept inside. There were eight jeeps parked near the center of camp, guarded by a pair of soldiers wearing the power armor the soldiers in San Diego had worn. More would probably appear like wasps from a kicked nest if they were discovered.

"Do you see those cables?" Trevor whispered. A row of thick black tubes snaked from the three-story building near the center of camp and into the pyramid. "That's probably how they're keeping the place lit and under surveillance. Cut that and the whole place goes dark, giving you the advantage once you're inside. If you're quick, you can probably reach this central chamber of yours before the people inside even know what's going on."

"I'll remember that," Blair said, filing it away for later. The frigid wind howled up the ridge and ruffled his hair. His teeth chattered audibly, but he resisted the urge to shift. That would take energy, and he wanted to husband his strength. "How many soldiers do you think are in those bunkers?"

"It doesn't matter," Trevor said, raising his voice to compete with the wind. "If you're discovered and those troops come into play, it's over. They've got enough ordnance down there to wipe us all out. We'll do some damage, but they'll overwhelm us."

"Lovely. That means our only choice is waking the Mother and hoping she can help. Otherwise this is going to be a real short rescue," Blair said, glancing back at the others. They waited a little way down the ridge, a tight knot of dark forms blending with the scattered rocks. The group was surrounded by over a dozen smaller shadows, the larger dogs who'd accompanied Adolpho.

Liz was nowhere to be found, of course. She'd attempted to teach the other females her trick with the shadows, but they hadn't taken as readily to it. Either they were still mastering the ability, or they were just not as comfortable using it as Liz was.

"You're not going to make it inside without being seen," Trevor said, rifle scope slowly scanning the camp. "You can probably make it to the outer buildings, but the pyramid is well lit and out in the open. You might be able to blur inside, but there's a good chance you'll be seen. Maybe you can send the girls in? They can use that shadow trick."

"That doesn't help," Blair called back as he continued to scan the camp. "I have to be the one. Only I can wake the Mother, and I'm not even sure what I have to do to accomplish it. They've got to get me inside. I've got an idea about that, though."

"Idea?" Came Liz-wolf's low, guttural voice. She couldn't be more than a foot or two away, but Blair saw nothing. Smelled nothing. Damn, that was creepy.

"You remember I told you that Ahiga did a mindshare with me at the end?" Blair asked, turning to face the patch of night her voice had originated from. "I saw his memories. One of them was crossing the border into San Diego. He was right there, and we never knew it. A guy in a 'Niners shirt, right ahead of us in line. He changed his face, his scent, everything."

"That's brilliant," Trevor said, finally looking up from the scope. He had a dark-green hat on, with a clip that attached it to the collar of his jacket and kept it from blowing away. "You can pick off one of the soldiers and take his place."

"I can take care of that part," Liz said, an ominous growl thrumming deep within her chest. "I'll take Elmira with me. Cyntia and Adolpho can stay here with Trevor. If things go south, your attack should catch them off guard so we can get away. Blair, blur your way down to that patch of boulders there, behind that big mound of dirt. Once we have the uniform, we'll bring it to you, and the three of us can head down to wake the Mother."

How comfortable she was giving orders amazed Blair. And how comfortable the group seemed taking them. No one questioned Liz, accepting her leadership as a matter of course. Was that some supernatural werewolf trick, or just good sense?

"I'll take a vantage on this ridge," Trevor said, pointing at the base of the cliff below. "I'm going to send Adolpho and Cyntia down there to the base, in the shadows. You werewolf types can scale that cliff, so if you do make it out in a hurry, you can come back this way. I doubt Mohn will expect that. We'll keep it clear until you can reach it."

"I'll inform the others," Liz rumbled, her form suddenly appearing as she loped down the ridge.

"I'll come to terms with the whole werewolf thing, but I will never get used to how she does that," Trevor said, shaking his head.

Blair shrugged out of his jacket and removed his shirt and pants. By the time he had his underwear off, he knew he must be turning blue.

"I'm going to make for those rocks," Blair said, voice deepening as he shifted. His senses sharpened still further. Most notably, he detected the scents of the soldiers below. They reeked of complacency, though a few bore the sharp tang of wariness. Those would be the ones who'd actually fought a werewolf and knew exactly what they were facing.

"Good luck, Blair. If we don't survive, I just wanted to say you've become a real friend, man," Trevor said, clasping Blair's forearm. "Even if you do look like Chewbacca and shed all over my Rover."

Blair gave a low chuckle that was, thankfully, masked by the wind. Then he released his friend's hand, crouching atop the ridge-line. "You're a hell of a guy, Trevor. And you know what? Garland isn't the only one who thinks your sister's hot." Then he blurred, hopping from boulder to boulder as he picked a path down the mountainside. The feat would have paralyzed him with fear a couple months ago, but now he found it exhilarating. He knew his limits now, and this trek was trivial.

He landed in a small puff of dirt, turning to gaze back up the mountainside several hundred meters above. Trevor was shaking his head but looked like he was laughing. Blair grinned like an idiot. Maybe it was the adrenaline or just the fact that he was finally doing something, but he'd never felt more alive, more confident.

He peered over the lip of the dirt mound he'd sheltered behind. The camp was quiet save for a few soldiers moving between structures. They moved with purpose, heads bent to whatever tasks they'd been assigned. That boded well. They weren't paying much attention. Blair shifted his gaze to the pyramid, scanning the narrow entrance. A pair of guards waited outside, bored but alert.

"Hot sister, huh?" Liz rumbled, materializing from the shadows next to him. She was close enough to have taken his throat had she wanted to. That made her wolfish grin all the more unsettling.

"You heard that?" Blair said, trying not to appear disturbed by her sudden appearance.

"No, Trevor totally ratted you out," Liz said, giving a decidedly ominous giggle. Elmira appeared next to her, ending the moment. Liz turned to her. "Follow me. We'll head to the western edge of camp and pick off a soldier, ideally someone who looks like they have some rank. I'll carry the body back. You cover me."

Elmira's fur blended into the night even without the shadows.

Only her amber eyes gave her away. "Let us move swiftly. I do not like being so close to this many enemies. If we are discovered, it will go badly for us."

The pair disappeared, leaving Blair with nothing but time. He glanced back up the ridge. Locating the barrel of Trevor's rifle took several moments, and Blair only achieved that because he had heightened senses and knew where to look. It was the only sign of Trevor's location, which would prove very valuable if things went awry. He dropped his gaze to the base of the cliff, scanning for Adolpho and Cyntia.

Adolpho crouched behind a boulder, shielding him from nearby buildings. Blair wished he'd had time to teach Adolpho a few more things, especially the ability to blur. Maybe if he survived the coming battle. From the sound of it, he'd be needed for the imminent apocalypse. His pack was still trapped up on the ridge. They could circle down eventually, but that would take a while.

Cyntia appeared to have mastered the shadows, because there was no sign of her. He felt better having her guard Adolpho and Trevor. Females were truly frightening, weak blood or no. If the three of them could avoid detection, they'd make a hell of a distraction if, and when, Blair was trying to exit the pyramid with the Mother.

He turned his attention to the closest building, a flash of movement having pulled his gaze. A single black-clad soldier had stepped into the shadows, unzipped his fly, and begun to relieve himself against a rock. It was a monumentally poor decision. Fanged death materialized from the shadows, clamping a furry hand around his mouth to smother his scream. In one sharp jerk, his neck snapped. Then both werewolf and soldier disappeared into the shadows. Liz could extend her cloak to others? That was new.

Blair held his breath, praying no one would notice the soldier's disappearance. Long moments later Liz and Elmira appeared at the base of the mound. He scrambled down to crouch next to them, waiting as Liz stripped the man's clothing.

"I'm not sure how well it will fit. He's taller than you," she said in a low voice as she unbuckled his belt and yanked his pants free.

"I can reshape my body to be the right height," Blair said, certain he could do it even as he uttered the words. The beast spoke to him less of late, but he also had more thoughts that were not his own.

We have truly merged, Ka-Dun. I will always be separate, but less so the longer we are together.

Blair began pulling on the uniform, shifting back to human form as he did. The pants were definitely too long and the shirt too narrow for his newly muscled shoulders. He concentrated, drawing on the beast's knowledge as he willed his body to change. His legs grew longer, and his shoulders narrowed, enough that the uniform fit tolerably well. Then he studied the dead soldier's face, willing his cheeks and nose to match. The process was painful, but they snapped into the desired position.

"How do I look?" he asked, turning to face the hulking werewolves.

"That's amazing," Elmira said. It was the first time Blair had seen a shocked expression on a werewolf's face.

"If that doesn't fool them, I don't know what will," Liz said. She turned to face the pyramid. "Just walk slowly to the entrance. We'll be right next to you the entire time."

71

INFILTRATED

Jordan ducked out of Ops and into the brisk night air. It was a welcome relief after he'd spent hours poring over reports in the stuffy confines of the hastily erected building. Mohn had given him everything he'd asked for, a full company of soldiers, all the proper ordnance, and ten suits of the new X-12 power armor. It was enough firepower to topple a government, but would it be enough to keep this place safe from a sea of rampaging were-wolves? Maybe in the short term. About half of the material was already on-site, and the rest would arrive over the next few days.

"Commander," Yuri's synthesized voice called from his X-12. He stood some thirty feet away, breaking from his patrol to trot over to Jordan. He'd really taken to the armor and wore it almost every-where. "Have you heard Mohn scuttlebutt? Is mothballing every site except this one."

Jordan was surprised word had already made it to the line troops, but then, rumors always moved faster than command anticipated they would. He fell into step with the Russian. "You didn't hear it from me, but we've lost the war. Mohn is pulling back to Syracuse, setting up their own little kingdom."

"What about us?" Yuri asked, unreadable beneath his faceplate.

"We're the last line of defense. If the werewolves wake the woman inside, Command believes she'll unleash devastation that will make what we're currently facing look like a bad Monday at the office," Jordan confided. They wound around a hastily constructed Quonset hut housing one of the new divisions.

"Smells like stalling tactic, Commander," Yuri said, giving Jordan a sidelong look. "What's real play?"

"They're going to nuke the pyramid. The package arrives in two days. All we have to do is hold off until..." He trailed off, staring at the pyramid.

"Sir?" Yuri asked, turning to see what Jordan was staring at.

"I gave strict instructions that no one was to be given access to the pyramid," he said, pointing at a soldier being challenged by the guards. "Who the fuck is that, and why are they trying to gain access?"

"Will check," Yuri said, taking a step closer to the pyramid. "Gate Guard One, is Yuri. Request confirmation. Who is visitor?"

There was no immediate answer. The figure was admitted to the pyramid, disappearing into the tunnel as both guards returned to a state of relaxed vigilance.

"Don't like this. Why no answering?" Yuri asked.

"Because that wasn't a soldier they just admitted. I want you to assemble every X-12 as quietly as possible," Jordan ordered, cursing himself for only stationing two guards at the entrance. He didn't know what trick Smith had just pulled, but he knew without a doubt it was Smith. He must have fooled the man's eyes, somehow. "We'll rendezvous at the tunnel entrance in five minutes. Go."

Yuri was already moving, sprinting toward the barracks. Jordan trotted toward the new armory, where the suits were housed. He'd be needed in this fight. "Ops, this is Jordan. Notify the guards inside the central chamber that they're about to have company."

"Roger that, sir," an unfamiliar voice answered. They'd shuffled quite a few personnel, and he'd had no time to learn their names.

Jordan strode through the black plastic door, making for the stall containing his power armor. The little setup really was ingenious.

Each piece of armor was attached to robotic arms along the inner walls of the stall. There was just enough room for a person to squeeze inside. He did so, stabbing a red button near eye level. It flared to life, and the stall began to whir.

The robotic arms aligned each piece of armor, snapping them together first around his legs and then his chest. He extended his arms, allowing the stall to do its work. The helmet came last, settling over his head and snapping into place with a sharp hiss as it sealed the environment within.

The new HUD R&D had installed came to life, giving him a wealth of information. Battery charge was at eighty-seven percent. All four missiles were loaded. No damage had been detected, although a small yellow alert near the bottom of the screen claimed that the seal on the right knee was in need of maintenance.

Jordan stepped from the stall, moving for the rack of rifles on the far wall. He drew one of the J-9s, the latest weapon Mohn had sent. It fired high velocity .338 rounds, something command called a Black Lotus. They weren't as devastating as the .50 calibers, but he could squeeze off thirty to a clip with minimal recoil, and anything he hit generally stayed down.

Soldiers began filing in behind him, moving into their assigned stalls with practiced precision. He strode past them, exiting the bunker and waiting outside, where he had a better view of the pyramid. There was nothing to see, at least not outside. If he wanted better intel, he'd have to ask Ops for a direct feed. The request might distract them at a critical moment, so he waited impatiently for the squad to assemble.

They emerged one after another, filing into two neat rows of four behind him. Yuri's X-12 already waited at the tunnel entrance. Jordan turned to the squad. "Let's move like we have a purpose, people. We get in and take down the intruders, no matter the cost. Collateral damage is authorized. Do whatever it takes to eliminate the enemy."

72

JEDI MIND TRICKS

"Halt, soldier," one of the guards barked, snapping his rifle to his shoulder. The barrel was aimed at Blair's chest. The second soldier mirrored the motion. "You know you're not supposed to be here. What the hell are you doing away from your post?"

Blair briefly considered his options. If he tried to lie his way past the guards, they would see through his bluff almost immediately. If he killed them, the rest of the camp would be on him in seconds.

"Wait," the second soldier said suspiciously, taking a step closer and aiming his rifle at Blair's chest. "Is that blood on your uniform?"

Blair had only a moment to act before things spiraled out of control. But what to do?

Force your will upon them, Ka-Dun. Make them accept your words. I will guide you.

Blair took a deep breath and just went with it.

"That's the blood of the last grunt who gave me this kind of lip," Blair growled, forcing authority he didn't feel. He stepped up to the first soldier's barrel, allowing the weapon to poke him in the chest. Energy moved within him, infusing his next words with *something*. He knew the name of exactly one officer here, and he hoped it was the right one. "Commander Jordan ordered me down to the central chamber to inspect the cabling. We've lost two monitors, and he doesn't like the blind spot. You're going to let me past, and you aren't going to give me any more grief about it. Understood?"

"Yes, sir," both men assented in unison, lowering their rifles as they snapped to attention. They stepped aside, clearing a path into the pyramid.

Blair blinked for a moment. Could it have been that easy? Guess he was due for a break. He hoped his luck would hold for the rest of the trip down.

He advanced past them, down the tunnel that, given how tight the corners were, he guessed may have been bored into the rock with a laser. His heart thundered as he strode away half expecting them to turn and shout at him to stop. They didn't. He made it to the massive doors, which stood open to the night. The black cables snaked past them, and he briefly considered severing them. Not yet.

Blair entered the pyramid for the first time since his brief taste of death. This was a wholly different experience. When he gazed at the hieroglyphs covering the walls, he understood them as if he were reading English. If only he had the time for study. What knowledge must they contain?

"Did you just Jedi mind trick those guards?" Liz rumbled from the shadows, softly to avoid being detected by the cameras or the guards he'd just bluffed. "Wait till Trevor hears about this. He's going to crack up."

"We weren't the droids they were looking for," Blair said, forcing a smile.

Blair wished he shared her enthusiasm. Now that he was finally confronted with the reality of the situation, he was terrified. What sort of opposition would they face reaching the Mother? It couldn't be as easy as what they'd encountered thus far. Would they be able to escape? Could he even wake the Mother at all? So many unknowns.

They continued down the corridor, eventually reaching the spot where he and Bridget had paused to study the glyphs that very first day. He stared up at the beautifully scripted wall, understanding it in a way he couldn't possibly have then. It was so clear. The tide of undead washing across the world. The champions standing against them. Citizens coming willingly to their deaths because they knew there must be champions to save the rest of them.

Even this place was described, an Ark. Not *the* Ark. *An* Ark, one of many. This place held so many secrets, but he'd bought understanding at the cost of an even more precious commodity. Time. He just didn't have it. Blair hurried forward, aware of Elmira's form flitting from shadow to shadow. There was no sign of Liz.

He made his way deeper, eventually reaching the final slope that led into the central chamber. He remembered Steve's shattered husk, the broken remains of a great man. He remembered long hours with Bridget, her presence inspiring the same lust it always had, despite her betrayal. Most of all, he remembered dying, just a few hundred steps from where he stood now. Would he die again today, this time more permanently?

"Listen," Elmira hissed, flitting to the shadow next to one of the statues lining the corridor. "Do you hear that? Up above. The way we came."

Blair listened. He heard a clatter of metal boots on stone. A lot of boots. Too many for him to make out their number. Those boots were still distant, but they were getting closer. That had to be an armed response. Soldiers would be here soon. He dropped to one knee, reaching for the cables. "They know we're here. Liz, I'm going to cut the power. We're out of time."

"Do it. I'll get down to the central chamber and scout their position. Blair, do that mindshare thing with Elmira and me," Liz commanded, still shrouded in shadows. "Once we know what we're dealing with, we'll formulate a better plan."

73

FREE

B ridget awoke with a gasp, scrambling backward as she wildly studied her surroundings. She'd been dreaming about a different world, one covered in ice and snow. The pieces melted through her fingers, leaving nothing but ephemeral images. She lay against the wall of her cell, nightgown soaked through with sweat.

A hurried set of footsteps and the rapid heartbeat they belonged to ran down the corridor outside. They stopped outside of her cell, which opened with a hiss and revealed Sheila's wide brown eyes. She wore an ill-fitting soldier's uniform, complete with a matte-black helmet.

"We have to get you out of here," she panted, chest heaving. She darted a glance behind her and then turned back to Bridget. "If you can break your restraints, now is the time. I spiked some coffee and gave it to the gate guards. We have maybe five or ten minutes before someone notices something."

"Sheila, what are you doing? They'll kill you for helping me," Bridget replied, rising to her feet as gracefully as the restraints would allow her to.

"Only if they can catch me," she said, leaning on the doorframe as she caught her breath. "Jordan let slip that Blair is coming, and given the fact that every soldier is grabbing a gun, I'm guessing he's arrived. I'm hoping you can get me up to the ridge above camp, then come back and help him do whatever he needs to do."

"Of course, Sheila. Stand back," Bridget said, closing her eyes. She summoned all the fury, all the helplessness she'd experienced these past weeks. It was finally time to fight back.

She opened the cage, allowing the beast free rein. It came surging forward, but instead of repressing her conscious mind, the beast's mingled with hers. They were one blended being, united in their need to escape this place, to right the injustices that had been inflicted on them.

Bridget sucked in a deep breath and let out a howl that shook the walls. It grew deeper as she changed, muscles writhing as fur burst from her body. By the time the howl ended, the transformation was complete. She stood hunched in the cell, her back and shoulders pressed against the comically low roof.

The restraints had grown to accommodate her larger form, but no matter how strong they were, they had a breaking point. Bridget strained, pulling her wrists apart with as much strength as she could muster. Her arms burned with exertion for long seconds. Then the restraints gave way in a shower of broken metal. She repeated the process with her ankles, stepping into the hallway to join Sheila.

"Let's go. Run for the ridge. I'll be behind you, in the shadows. If anything tries to stop you, I will deal with it," she snarled.

74

UNEXPECTED ALLIES

Trevor watched in horror as floodlights burst to life throughout the camp. Eight armored figures sprinted for the tunnel leading into the pyramid. They moved with military precision, in two columns of four. He remembered them from San Diego. How could he forget? He, Liz, and Blair had been forced to run then, and they'd only had to deal with four. Now there were twice as many and who knew what defenses inside the pyramid. They boiled out of the camp as though they were ants scrambling from a struck anthill, moving to encircle the pyramid's western face, where the entrance lay. This whole op was going to hell very quickly.

He moved his scope to the closest building, the one just beyond Adolpho and Cyntia's hiding spot. A figure burst out, but unlike the others, she darted *away* from the pyramid, toward the cliff. She kept shooting glances over her shoulder, scrambling across the rocky ground with the sort of desperation reserved for those who know their lives depend on running.

"No, no, no," Trevor murmured, dropping the scope and surveying the area around the fugitive. His fears were confirmed. At least two dozen soldiers had taken notice. Their training wouldn't allow them to ignore someone fleeing during a combat op. They'd be compelled to investigate. If the person had simply walked away calmly, she might have had a chance.

The Mohn soldiers took up the hunt like a pack of hounds, fanning out as they moved in her direction. Trevor's jaw dropped as a patch of darkness sprouted claws, rending the soldier at the rear of the group. Trevor glanced down at Cyntia's hiding spot, but she was still there. Another female werewolf had joined the fight, but he had no idea who she was.

Adolpho broke from cover, pointing at the soldiers and barking something that the wind snatched away. A half dozen shapes loped through the darkness, those dogs that had managed to find their way down to him. There were far fewer than he'd arrived with, maybe five or six. The soldiers reacted instantly, several dropping to firing positions behind rocks as they brought their weapons to bear.

The layered staccato of multiple rifles split the night as bullets pinged and whined below. Some found their targets, and three of the dogs dropped. One of the survivors, a burly Rottweiler, tackled one of the soldiers who'd fired. The pair went down in a tangle of limbs.

Other soldiers were stopping now, lining up shots as they adjusted to multiple opponents. The stranger materialized behind one of them, tearing out his throat before disappearing again. Trevor had a better look this time and could clearly see silver fur. Blair was the only silver werewolf that he knew of, but this was clearly a female.

The fugitive continued her mad dash, bounding over rocks as she made her way to the base of the ridge. That gave Trevor a moment of pause. There was no way the person could have climbed it unaided, not without the help of a werewolf or a jet pack. She must be working with the strange new werewolf.

He compartmentalized the situation, settling his cheek against the rifle as he peered through the scope again. Enemy of my enemy and all that. What mattered right now was downing those soldiers so his people could live. He found his first target, a tall man taking shelter behind a boulder. He ducked from cover and loosed a volley from his assault rifle. Trevor couldn't see the man's target, so he had no idea if the shots hit.

He cleared his mind, settling the crosshairs over the man's throat. Then he stroked the trigger. A thunderous crack echoed across the valley as the man's head evaporated into gory mist. Trevor glanced up from the scope, surveying the battle for more targets. There was an abundance of them. The last few dogs had already gone down.

Cyntia had apparently melted into the shadows with the newcomer, which left Adolpho and the fugitive. The fugitive had been smart enough to take cover between the large boulders at the base of the ridge, leaving Adolpho as the only viable target for almost twenty soldiers.

A withering hail of bullets lanced into him, knocking him back like a hurricane would a plastic bag. He rolled behind a boulder, probably buying himself time to heal. Then Cyntia appeared, disemboweling one soldier and then immediately slashing the throat of another. The silver seemed to take that as her cue, and she leapt from the darkness and into a trio of soldiers.

That still left over a dozen, with overlapping fields of fire. They lit Adolpho up, peppering the grey with a withering storm of bullets. He tried desperately to hide behind the rocks, but there was simply nowhere to go. Werewolf or not, his body was still flesh and blood, and Trevor watched in horror as Adolpho fell limply to the ground. The hail didn't slacken, more and more bullets sending up gouts of blood and gore as they tore the body apart.

Trevor closed his eyes and took a deep breath. He couldn't help Adolpho, but he could avenge him. He opened his eyes and found another target. Then another. Reload, aim, kill. He picked off four more before he ran out of targets. Cyntia and the silver crouched next to Adolpho's corpse, talking.

The silver put a hand on Cyntia's shoulder and then sprinted for the base of the ridge. She scooped up the fugitive like a toddler and began to bound up the steep hillside like a mountain goat on speed. Cyntia stayed with Adolpho for long moments before she followed.

Trevor rose to his feet and took a step back from the cliff. He rested a hand on his .45 and waited as calmly as he could. Not long after, the silver bounded over the lip of the ridge, landing heavily several feet away. She set the fugitive down. The woman had short brown hair and was wearing a Mohn uniform. Her face was pale and drawn, and she seemed to fight for breath, though he wasn't sure if that was from exertion, fear, or altitude sickness. Maybe all of them.

"Who are you?" Trevor asked, pointedly ignoring the silver. He was totally *not* terrified of the nine-foot werewolf just a few feet away.

"My name is Sheila. I'm part of the team that's been studying this place. We're the ones who started this whole thing, who unleashed the werewolves," she gasped, clutching at her chest. She looked like she might keel over at any moment, pausing to breathe in several more sharp lungfuls of cool night before she continued. "You don't seem all that surprised by the sight of a werewolf. You're here with Blair, aren't you?"

"You know Blair?" Trevor asked, removing his hand from his weapon. "Yes, I'm with him. He just took a team into the pyramid."

"Oh, thank God," she gasped, leaning heavily against the granite. She turned to face the silver. "We may actually have a chance. You should get down there and help him."

"Not until I'm sure you're safe," the silver rumbled, fixing Trevor with a baleful stare.

"If you threaten him, I will rip out your heart and eat it," Cyntia rumbled, stepping from the shadows just a few feet from Trevor.

"We don't have time for this," he said, stabbing a finger at the pyramid. "Blair and Liz are down there. They're going to need what-ever help we can provide. Both of you furry types should get your asses down there and help. I promise Sheila will be safe. She looks like death, and she probably needs to get to lower elevation, or she might get pulmonary edema. I'll get her back to the car where she can rest. Is everyone happy with that?"

The silver nodded grudgingly. Cyntia looked like she might argue, but when the silver bounded over the cliff and down the ridge, she trailed after. That left him with Sheila.

"So I'm guessing you know all about our impending zombie

friends?" he asked, relaxing enough to turn back to the camp. He didn't trust her yet, but if she couldn't breathe, she wasn't much of a threat. Besides, if she was on the level, Blair might need her help deciphering everything in the pyramid. Assuming they'd live.

"Zombies?" she asked, obviously confused.

"I'll explain on the way. Let's go," he said, wrapping an arm around her shoulder and helping her down the path back to the car.

75

CASUALTIES

L iz draped the shadows around her, prowling the darkness as she loped down the corridor and into what could only be the central chamber. She paused at the entryway, surveying the room before her. Several chrome stand lamps provided a modicum of illumination. She assumed they must run on some sort of batteries, because they'd apparently survived Blair cutting the power.

The lights revealed five obelisks, one in each corner and a larger one in the center. They'd clearly been constructed by the same culture that had built this place, and they clashed sharply with the more recent additions. A pair of bulky black turrets atop tripods sat on opposite sides of the room. Each had a wicked-looking barrel and a small red dot that ceaselessly scanned the darkness for targets. They passed right over her seemingly without notice.

The hall opposite the doorway she stood in had the most obvious modifications. A wide semicircle of concrete had been erected, with a narrow steel door set in the center. Four slits had been left in the stonework, probably to allow people to fire out at targets without exposing themselves.

On either side of the stonework stood a guard in the same armor she'd fought in San Diego. They too watched the darkness for targets, the faceless masks they wore probably allowing them to see in darkness, somehow. Their vigilance was hardly surprising. Dousing the lights had no doubt alerted them.

Liz considered the situation. Blair had to survive to reach the Mother, no matter the cost. Then, if they were very lucky, the Mother would help them deal with Mohn. If not, all of this would be for nothing. The pyramid only had one exit, so everything Mohn could bring to bear was about to come down on them like an avalanche.

They had to get inside before reinforcements arrived. They'd have to deal with the turrets, kill the armored guards, and then break down that steel door. It was a tall order whether they were werewolves or not.

Liz, can you hear me? Blair's voice echoed in her mind.

"I can hear you," she whispered, almost soundlessly. "Can you see what I'm seeing?"

I can, Blair's disembodied voice said. *Let me deal with the turrets. When the guards come for me, you and Elmira deal with the guards and get that door down.*

"Got it," she murmured, moving silently down the ramp into the chamber. She circled to the far side, maybe twenty feet from the armored guard on the right. She could be on him in a heartbeat as soon as Blair had the man's attention.

Liz held her breath as she realized she needed to pee. That almost drew a hysterical laugh. It was just so incongruous to the situation. But she gritted her teeth and waited. She didn't have to wait long.

Blair's silver form appeared in the doorway for just an instant before he blurred to the middle of the room, near the central obelisk. He was directly between the pair of turrets. She wanted to drag him into the shadows but resisted the urge as both turrets swiveled in his direction. They moved more quickly than the guards, though each armored form had begun to react as well.

Her heart leapt into her throat as the turrets began to chatter. A stream of brass shells ejected from the top of each as bright gouts of flame erupted from each muzzle. The rounds streaked toward Blair faster than the eye could follow. He moved even more quickly, blurring away in a roll that carried him to the far side of the obelisk. That would shelter him from the guards, at least.

What he'd set in motion took a moment to register. Blair had been directly between the turrets. Once he'd moved, the rounds they had fired continued forward and into the turret on the opposite side of the room. Both boxy contraptions exploded into sparks as they were knocked onto their sides, severely damaged from the friendly fire.

She turned her attention back to the guards, who'd already begun a flanking maneuver to get a line of sight to Blair's hiding place. Liz had a perfect view of the closest guard's back, and she used it to devastating effect. She leapt forward, tackling the armor to the ground with a screech of metal. She slammed the helmet against the marble floor as hard as she could once, twice, and then a third time. The faceplate cracked but didn't shatter. Damn, these things were tough.

Before she could do more, her opponent reacted, twisting his body to get an arm free. He extended his metal claws, scything them through the tendon of her right leg as he bucked his entire body. The move sent her toppling to the floor and allowed him to roll away. He came to his feet, pausing for a split second to eye the rifle he'd dropped when she tackled him. She knew he'd never make it, and he seemed to reach the same conclusion, cracked faceplate swiveling back to her.

She rose to her feet, baring her fangs and willing the injury to heal as she rested her weight on her good leg. The soldier didn't give her time, launching himself at her with both sets of claws. She caught his arms, but he came down on her with all his weight. Her bad leg gave way, and they fell to the marble, both straining for the upper hand.

Liz twisted suddenly, rolling on top of her opponent. She brought her face down in a vicious head butt, finally shattering the faceplate. The man within was in his early thirties. He had a thick black goatee and silver sunglasses. It was the same man she'd fought in San Diego. He snarled up at her. "Is time to die, little wolf."

She had just enough time to think he was overconfident before she realized her mistake. With her body atop his, she made a perfect target for the slits set into the man-made bunker Mohn had constructed. Automatic weapons' fire thundered through the room as pain blossomed all over her body. Liz scrambled off her opponent with a shriek, rolling back into the shadows in desperate flight.

Be calm, Ka-Dun. These wounds will heal, though more slowly than you might wish. Had you not injected yourself with poisonous silver, it would happen more quickly, but we cannot change the past.

Great, an 'I told you so' from a voice in her head. Liz gritted her teeth and limped to the base of an obelisk as she sized up the room. Elmira was wrestling with the other armored soldier. One of her arms hung limply at her side, but she used the other to grab her opponent's armored arm and hurl his body into the door. The impact made a sizable dent, but the door had clearly been made to withstand worse.

Elmira leapt on the soldier, pinning him to the ground with her good arm as she savaged the armor around his neck with her fangs. It was an intelligent move because it put her in a blind spot the weapon slits couldn't reach. Unfortunately Elmira didn't seem to have taken Liz's opponent into account. The man with the goatee rolled to his feet. His armor rocked backward as four missiles streaked from the boxy launcher atop his shoulder.

They corkscrewed into Elmira's back, all four detonating in a wave of light and sound that blinded Liz as it launched her backward. Her ears rang painfully as she shook her head and tried to get back to her feet. The explosion filled the room with smoke and debris, but she could still make out the destruction.

Two of the obelisks were nothing but rubble now, and Mohn's bunker was scored and battered, though the door still held. There wasn't enough left of Elmira to identify her, and Liz realized with cold certainty that Elmira was dead. The blast had also caught her opponent, who was struggling weakly near one of the intact obelisks.

Rage overcame Liz. She ignored her wounds, charging across the room and toward the downed guard with the Russian accent. She planted her wounded leg atop his back, ignoring the pain as she ground his chest against the floor. Then she seized his leg with both hands and ripped. It came off with a metallic pop and a spray of blood.

The man gave an agonized shriek and started thrashing wildly, but Liz leaned heavily atop him. She kept him pinned as she prepared to deliver the killing blow.

76

WAKING THE MOTHER

Blair came to his feet behind one of the obelisks, surveying the room in horror. This place was of incalculable worth, with both historical and practical value. Mohn had just destroyed it with automatic weapons' fire and frigging missiles. Much of the room had been reduced to rubble, yet the bunker the soldiers had erected was still a barrier.

Elmira was gone. Of that, he was sure. Even if he hadn't seen the explosion, he could no longer feel his link to her mind. Liz was still there, a ball of rage as she leapt atop the sole surviving guard and ripped off the poor man's leg. That instant, Blair recognized Yuri. He felt a twinge of pity, but it was only a twinge. The werewolves hadn't chosen this war. Mohn had.

He turned his focus back to the bunker. How the hell was he going to get inside? A pair of grey-green eyes peered out through one of the gun slits, falling on Liz. Blair blurred, accelerating both body and mind. In an instant those eyes could be replaced by a gun, so he had to strike now.

A spike of pure will shot across the intervening space, glowing with faint blue light as it struck the owner of the grey-green eyes.

Then Blair *was* that woman, Corporal Yasmin, a twenty-six-year-old who'd joined Mohn for the money after a stint in the Marines.

With her eyes, Blair surveyed the inside of the bunker, taking in the other three soldiers. All three bore familiar-looking rifles, each barrel inches away from the slits cut into the stone. None of them said anything as Blair stepped behind them. He calmly pressed the barrel of Yasmin's rifle to the skull of the nearest soldier and fired.

The man went down in a spray of blood, and before either surviving soldier could react, she fired again. This time she sent a hail of bullets, which lanced into both targets. The second was knocked from his feet, and Blair continued firing until both stopped moving. Then he walked Yasmin to the dented bunker door and threw back the metal bar holding it closed.

He pushed it open and dropped his rifle, stepping into the central chamber. He felt a dim surge of fear from Yasmin's trapped consciousness as she saw Liz's bloodied form just a few feet away. Liz-wolf's fangs flashed, and the auburn wolf was on Yasmin. Blair fled her mind and returned to his own.

Blair lumbered into a run, shaking away the vertigo from so rapidly changing his perspective. He sprinted past Liz, trying not to watch as she tore Yasmin apart. He sprinted through the doorway and into the bunker, not bothering to close the door after him. He had no idea if it would serve as any kind of barrier when Mohn's reinforcements arrived, and there were only a precious few seconds left.

He lurched to a halt as he entered the sarcophagus chamber, gasping as he had his first real view of the room's majesty. He'd been dying when he last saw it, unable to fully appreciate the marvel of it all. Seven clear sarcophagi radiated from the center of the room like spokes on a wheel. They were covered in an array of gemstones, rubies and emeralds and diamonds. Pulses of light flowed between each at irregular intervals, flowing from gem to gem on invisible pathways.

The walls were a pristine white, covered in a sea of flowing silver glyphs that rearranged as he watched. The substance was similar to marble but with its own inner light. It provided soft illumination that pulsed in time to a heartbeat. The heartbeat of the Mother, he'd be willing to bet.

He crossed the room to stand next to the only occupied sarcophagus. The room was beautiful, but it all paled in comparison to the woman within.

The woman was slender and petite, perhaps five feet tall. She looked tiny in the massive sarcophagus, which probably could have held a full-sized female werewolf. She lay on a bed of her own silver hair, waist long and lustrous despite millennia of stasis. She had delicate features that made her appear childlike, though she might very well have been the oldest living person in the world.

Her clothing was exquisite, like nothing he'd ever seen. She wore a clean white wrap around her breasts and a matching skirt that fell to her thighs, each embroidered with silver runes. Her neck, wrists, and ankles were all adorned with a variety of jewelry. Each piece was made of gold, most containing rubies or diamonds, though there were a few emeralds as well. Were those gems significant? The colors matched the sarcophagus. Any one would make a man rich.

"Moment of truth," he muttered, wondering exactly how to wake her. He should have asked Ahiga when he'd had the chance. Surely the old man would have said something unless the method was blindingly obvious.

There are a pairs of rubies near the center of the rejuvenator. They are the largest gems. Do you see them?

He did. Each was fifty or sixty karats, possibly the largest of their kind in the world. They were so large that placing his hands on them didn't quite cover the gems.

"Now what?" he asked.

Close your eyes and use your will to probe the rejuvenator as if it were the mind of another. Once you've touched it, you will understand.

Blair suppressed the lingering fears about Mohn's impending arrival. He gave himself completely to the task, focusing his will and *pushing* into the sarcophagus. There was a moment of resistance. Then he tumbled through, into another place.

He stood in an empty room similar to the Mother's chamber, but the walls were lined with gemstones and veins of gold. It looked like the control nexus of a starship from some space opera. He glanced around wondering exactly what he was supposed to do now.

"Who are you?" came a melodic voice from behind him. He spun to find the woman from the sarcophagus, standing before him. She was breathtaking. The Mother in all her glory, or her consciousness anyway.

Piercing green eyes studied him as she repeated the question. "Who are you? What has become of Ahiga?"

He wondered idly how it was he could understand her language, but with their minds touching perhaps she'd already learned English. Or he'd learned whatever she was speaking.

"I'm, uh, Blair," he answered lamely. What did one say to the progenitor of an entire culture, a woman tens of thousands of years old? "Ahiga is dead. He died protecting me and sent me in his place to wake you."

"Has the enemy returned, then? Are we too late?" she asked, eyes widening in alarm. She took a step closer.

"Not yet, but their return is imminent. I don't know if you understand astronomy the same way we do, but the sun has sent out a coronal mass ejection, the thing we believe will wake the enemy. It could happen in the next hour, or in a day. Two at most." He answered as honestly as he could, trying not to gawk at the woman before him.

The Mother looked relieved, posture relaxing as she took another step closer. She was close enough to touch now, or whatever would pass for touching here. "Then all is not lost. Still, time is short. I must know of this new world. Will you mindshare with me?"

"I—what does that entail, exactly?" he asked, remembering the mindshare with Ahiga. That had been brief because the old man was dying. Would this be similar?

"I would taste your memories. All of them. Walk the footsteps of your life, seeing all you have seen," she explained, stretching forth a delicate hand. It hovered near his cheek. "In exchange, I will grant you a portion of my own memory, a fragment of it. Ask one question, and if it is in my power to show you, then I will."

"What is this place? How did you build it? Why?" Blair asked, all in a jumble.

"That is three questions," she said, giving him a tolerant smile. "The answers are complicated, but I will show you my discovery of the First Ark many, many millennia ago. Lower your defenses. Share your mind with me."

"Okay," he said, steeling himself as her hand brushed his face. There was an immense heat that began where her fingers brushed his skin, and surged through his entire body like a bolt of lightening. He could feel her rummaging through his thoughts like so many folders in a file cabinet, sifting and weighing as she learned about his world.

Then the world winked out. He was elsewhere, as he'd been with Ahiga. But there was no campfire, no looming darkness. He was inside her memories, seeing what she had seen. A glimpse of the world as it had been in another age.

77

THE FIRST ARK

Seeing through the Mother's eyes was a fascinating experience. It was a bit like controlling Yasmin had been, except he could do nothing but observe. The Mother huddled in a small gully with several other figures, shivering beneath layers of crudely stitched fur. Fat flakes of snow fell from the sky, and judging from the thick dusting the figures wore, he assumed they'd been there for at least a little while.

"How much longer will that take? We cannot be here when night falls, or we will leave nothing but our own corpses for our pursuers," a short, stocky man growled. He had thick, bristly black hair and a beard to match. His eyes were set deep into his skull, beneath a heavy brow, and he cradled a flint-tipped spear in one hand.

The man he'd spoken to looked up calmly with grey eyes. His hair was also dark, though it was more brown than black. His beard was shorter but just as tangled as the other man's. He held a pair of rocks in his hands, one a small striker and the other something that made Blair gawk. That was a core.

Blair had spent a summer learning primitive survival skills back in high school. They'd used the same Stone Age technology as the Cro-Magnon of France, and Blair had spent maddening afternoons attempting to create workable stone axe blades from cores much like the one this man held. Based on the technique he employed, Blair could at least guess the rough moment in history when this memory had occurred. Somewhere between twenty and twenty-two thousand years ago, during one of the world's harshest glaciations.

The man's quick, sure strikes made a mockery of Blair's pathetic attempts, quickly shaping the stone into a sharp wedge that would no doubt be affixed to the four-foot yew shaft propped against the rock face next to him. "If Set and his followers catch us and we are unarmed, then we will be just as dead. My last blade was lost saving *your* life, Sobek."

Both names tickled at the back of Blair's mind. They were familiar, but he wasn't sure where he'd heard them.

"Patience. We have time yet," the Mother said. Having words issue from a throat Blair had no control over was so odd.

"Precious little of it. They've dogged us for many days now. I still do not understand why Set is so persistent," another woman said, rising from a bundle of furs piled between two rocks. She towered over the Mother's comparatively tiny form, long red hair bound with a simple leather cord. She too carried a spear. "Osiris, you are chieftain now. We will follow where you lead, but Sobek is not wrong."

"I know, Sekhmet," he said, without looking up to meet her gaze. "That is why you will head to the top of the ridge and see if we are still pursued. Silently, like a cave lion."

If Blair had a mouth, he'd be gawking openly. Sekhmet. Osiris. Sobek. The names were soberingly familiar. All three were figures in the Egyptian pantheon.

The redhead scrambled up the hillside in near silence, kicking loose little drifts of snow as she ascended. She was out of sight in seconds, moving with the grace of a life-long hunter.

"You know as well as I that our pursuers have not given up. What did you not wish her to hear?" Sobek rumbled. He folded his arms and stared a challenge at Osiris.

Osiris didn't answer, didn't address the challenge in any way. He turned to the Mother, staring her directly in the eyes. Blair's natural inclination was to look away from that haunted gaze, but of course he couldn't. He was merely an observer here.

"Isis, you speak for the spirits. The Valley of Hidden Voices is close. Will the spirits protect us if we enter?" Osiris asked, striking a final flake from his new blade and then affixing it into a notch cut in the top of the spear shaft. He applied a thick amber-like substance to it and then wrapped the shaft in a leather strip.

"You cannot mean to enter," Sobek hissed, eyes narrowing as he took a step toward Osiris.

Osiris uncoiled like a viper, the tip of his new spear resting against Sobek's throat before the smaller man could react. "I am chieftain now, Sobek. Not your rival. Not your far brother. Your chief. You will abide by my decision, or we will take your meat to sustain the tribe."

"I am sorry, Osiris," Sobek said, shrinking away from the newly made stone blade. Blair remembered just how sharp they could be. "But surely there is another way. If we go there, we will be damned. No one returns from the Valley of Hidden Voices. It is cursed."

"Yes," Osiris said, pulling his weapon from Sobek's throat. He began wrapping furs around himself, clearly preparing to depart. "Isis, I would hear your words on this."

He turned to address the Mother. Isis, the fabled wife of Osiris. She spoke. "The spirits will offer us no protection. If we enter the valley, we do so at great peril."

"If we do not, then we are all dead," Osiris snapped. He seemed to be on the verge of saying more, but Sekhmet's silent form dropped into the camp.

"They pursue us still. They will be upon this place not long after the sun sleeps," she said. She studied Osiris's preparations for departure. Then she began gathering her own furs.

"All of you need to decide right now if I am truly your chief," Osiris said. He straightened, gaze roaming their assembled faces.

"We go where you go," Sekhmet said simply.

Isis answered by reaching up and squeezing Osiris's arm. Blair could feel the cool flesh. He could feel his own heart beating, or rather Isis's heart beating.

"You are my chieftain," Sobek snarled. He seized the last of his furs and threw it about his shoulders. "If you wish to doom us with this madness, that is your right."

The long, low trumpet of a horn split the gathering dusk, from a mile or two away. That silenced the assembled group. They moved into a loping run as one, departing the gully and winding their way between two hills. How long they ran, Blair wasn't sure. Since the experience was a memory, he had the sense that some details were skipped.

Clarity returned when the assembled group reached the crest of a tall hill. Isis turned in a wide circle, looking out over a frozen waste-land in a way that provided Blair with a wealth of information. There were no mountains to speak of, just a few hills and the occasional glacier. If his observations were right, these people had originated somewhere in France, and they were heading northwest. That could put them somewhere in modern-day England, though he was by no means certain of his conclusion.

"Spirits below," Sekhmet breathed. She raised a trembling finger, and Isis's gaze followed it.

A familiar pyramid stood in the valley below, ringed on three sides by glaciers. It was conspicuously free of both snow and ice, which probably accounted for the clear discomfort evidenced by Isis and her companions. They had a right to be superstitious.

Osiris began picking his way down the icy slope without a word. The others followed, with Isis bringing up the rear. Blair could sense her emotions, the memory of intense fear she'd experienced from her first sight of the pyramid. He didn't blame her. She'd probably never seen a structure more complex than a crude debris hut, but now she was confronted with something that, in her mind, could only have been created by a god.

They reached the valley floor swiftly and headed toward the pyra-mid. As the last light of the sun fled the sky, the moon cut a hole in the clouds. It provided enough light to see, but the dim light made the pyramid even more foreboding. Blair wasn't entirely certain he wanted to see what would come next.

Osiris had stopped near the mouth of the pyramid's entrance, which was identical to the one he'd walked through just minutes before, back in modern-day Peru. These Arks appeared to be identical, at least on the surface.

Sobek and Sekhmet drew up short next to Osiris as Isis forced herself forward. The young shaman finally drew even with the others, but Blair could feel her desire to run. She nearly did when the shadows at the mouth of the tunnel stirred and a figure emerged.

It was roughly the same height as Isis but much broader of shoulder and had a heavy brow that overshadowed its eyes. Thick, dark eyebrows gave it a brutish look, and Blair realized with shock what he was seeing. Isis and her companions were modern-day Homo Sapiens. The figure that had emerged from the Ark was not. This was a Homo Neanderthalensis, commonly known as the Neanderthal.

Modern history taught that they'd gone extinct roughly forty thousand years ago, which was quite a bit earlier than what he assumed he was seeing. Either science was wrong, or this memory took place further into the past than he'd believed.

The Neanderthal approached slowly, raising a hand to beckon them forward. Its other hand clutched a golden staff that shone in the moonlight. The head of the staff bore a large ankh, a clearly Egyptian symbol despite the fact that this memory predated Egypt by fifteen millennia or more.

Osiris was the first to move, taking several steps closer. He clutched his spear tightly, keeping himself between the Neanderthal and his companions. "Greetings, Old One. Your kind is rare. I have not seen one such as you since I was a child."

The Neanderthal said nothing, instead taking several steps back into the pyramid and beckoning for the others to follow him. Osiris did so, and the others followed.

78

TOO LATE

"Fan out and set up a kill zone," Jordan barked. Both squads of armor trotted down the last corridor, leaping off the sides of the ramp as they entered the central chamber.

By the time he reached the doorway, his troops had already assumed defensive positions in a rough line to either side of the opening. Their weapons swept the room as the soldiers looked for any opposition. There was none.

The room had been on the losing side of a war. Ancient stone was gouged and broken. Two of the massive obelisks had been shattered. He knew Sheila's heart would break if she saw the devastation. This place would never be the same.

Bodies littered the room. Most were his men, two armored guards and Yasmin's blood-soaked body. Jordan crouched next to the closest form, one of the armored guards, minus a leg. It was Yuri. In theory, the armor would have self-sealed the wound, so he was possibly still alive. "Evans, carry Yuri to the surface. Get the chopper warmed up, and get him to Panama. Understood?"

"Yes, sir," Evans said, shouldering his rifle. He knelt, scooping up Yuri's mangled armor. He trotted back up the ramp, heading for the surface. The move didn't make tactical sense. It removed one of his soldiers from a combat situation. But Jordan was done throwing away lives. Yuri deserved a chance.

He turned his attention back to the scene before him, trying to piece together the battle that had occurred.

One of the corpses was a badly mangled monstrosity with black fur. Her body was shattered, bones jutting out at odd angles and huge rents marring her flesh. Sightless eyes stared vacantly at the ceiling, and she was missing three limbs.

At the far side of the room lay the entryway to the bunker. The door stood open, which could only have happened from the inside. Ice filled his belly. Somehow Smith had tricked the soldiers into opening the door. A bright white light pulsed from within the battered bunker. Jordan wondered if it had done that the last time he was here. Or had Smith already entered and started whatever process would wake that woman?

There was no sign of opposition, but all his men were down. The werewolves had won the skirmish, and if that was the case, there was only one place for them to go.

"Teams of two, cross the chamber and rush that room. Kill anything moving inside," Jordan ordered, still scanning the central chamber as his men moved to obey. Something wasn't right here. This was too easy.

He crossed the room slowly. He was about midway when the first pair of soldiers reached the doorway to the bunker. Something roared from the darkness, huge and terrible. It came at them sideways, just like it had back in the cornfield. A silver female tore into one of the men behind Jordan, shredding armor like tissue and tearing out his throat. He'd expected auburn, the color of Smith's new accomplice, Liz Gregg.

The last thing he'd expected was for Bridget to show up. Even knowing she could have broken free of her cell at any time, his mind just couldn't wrap around the fact that she was here now. How had she known about Smith's arrival? He felt a brief twinge of guilt for

Adams, the soldier she'd just killed. He could have done something to neutralize Bridget, but he had left her where she was, knowing she was a threat.

Jordan was still processing the attack when another form flashed from the darkness, this one completely unfamiliar. A blond female picked up Cortez and hurled the man face first into the central obelisk, where he landed with a crunch of stone and metal. How many targets were they dealing with? It didn't matter. What did was stopping Smith from getting inside that room.

"Form a defensive perimeter around the bunker. Ureksav, Brody, get inside and terminate anything that isn't us. The rest of us will keep them off you," Jordan barked, already sprinting toward the bunker.

The trouble with fighting these damn werewolves was that they could vanish at will. How the hell could he fight an opponent that he couldn't track?

He walked his rifle over the darkness, placing his back against the bunker's battle-scored edifice. The rest of his men took up similar positions as Ureksav and Brody squeezed through the door.

The silver werewolf lunged from the darkness again, this time armed with a rifle taken from one of his fallen men. She pressed the barrel against the back of a helmet, stroking the trigger before anyone could offer warning. The man's head exploded through his faceplate. His now headless body collapsed to the ground, leaving the werewolf open.

Jordan and two other men lined up shots, filling the air with high-pitched whines as their bullets tore at the darkness. Bridget let out a yelp as she rolled back into the shadows, the kind a dog made when it had been hurt. There was no way to know how badly she'd been wounded, of course. Or really if she had been at all, since she might be able to heal any wounds they could deal. It was so hard to know how much punishment a werewolf could take before they could bring it down.

He needed a way to flush her and her companions out. What did they want in this situation? Him and his men dead, obviously. But there was more to it than that. She was protecting Blair, giving him time to finish his work. "Everyone inside the bunker. Now!"

79

EMBARASSING ACCIDENT

Blair experienced a moment of vertigo. Then he was back within the strange control room construct, a sort of psychic waiting room. The mental construct hadn't changed. He stood exactly as he had before, as did the Mother. Or Isis, if he were to use her real name. She stood before him, eyes smoldering with fury.

"Seven. Billion. People," she said, voice quivering with what rage. "Do you know what you've done? You are like locusts, infesting every continent. Seeding the world for the ancient enemy's return. The deathless will slaughter your people, giving them billions of willing slaves. Our world will burn, and there is nothing I can do to stop it. Yet even that is not the greatest crime.

"You have destroyed the great pack itself. It is bad enough that you hunted wolves to near extinction," she roared, eyes flashing. "You've twisted their DNA, creating cruel mockeries. These *dogs* your people have bred. They are a sad remembrance of the majestic creatures that stood with us against the ancient enemy in ages past. We have great need of the pack, but you moderns have eradicated them. It is as if your kind knowingly sought the worst ways in which to ensure your own destruction."

"I couldn't possibly—" Blair began.

"Silence," the Mother thundered. Blair tried to get a word in, but her gaze silenced him more than her words had. "You are fortunate that I do not burn your mind to a cinder for your own crimes. Had you woken me when Ahiga first asked, he might still be alive. We might have had months to prepare, instead of hours. Yet you waited. Waited until it was too late.

"Then there is the matter of the Ark itself. You have destroyed two of the control rods and severely damaged another. You witnessed my memories. You know this place is older than even I can understand, yet the damage you have wrought has turned it into nothing more than a stone monument," she hissed, leaning in close enough that he could feel the heat radiating from her. "We lie naked before the storm. Our champions are scattered and leaderless, their numbers too few. Ahiga is dead. The Ark is in ruins. The enemy is upon us, and he is legion. Why even wake me at all? Why not let me go to my end in ignorance?"

"You know what? Fuck you. You don't get to take this out on me," Blair snapped, leaning in until his nose nearly touched hers. After all that he had sacrificed, all that he had been through, she blamed him. "I didn't ask for this. I knew nothing about your world or about this ancient enemy. I've been chased, shot at, and nearly killed more times than I can count. I've seen friends killed. Hell, *I've* killed friends. All because of *you*. Because of the preparations you left. Lady, I get that you're pissed off, but this is not my fault. I woke you up so you could help us deal with this ancient enemy. Can you do that? Because if not, you're wasting my time."

"You have the temerity to lecture *me*, little whelp?" she hissed, those emerald eyes growing dangerous. "I will deal with the pitiful wretches that assail your pack. When I am done, I will return, and we will speak of your insolence. Spend the time learning humility, for if you speak to me that way again, I will tear out your spine and hang your skull atop this place as a warning to fools everywhere."

The world exploded into a billion tiny pieces. Blair staggered backward, suddenly back within the sarcophagus room. He caught himself against the wall, weakened by whatever he'd just experienced. The rejuvenator began to hum. Then that hum grew to a whine. The rejuvenator shimmered, and the Mother's body began to rise, passing through the translucent material until she rested on the surface.

She flipped to her feet, shifting in midair. The process was unbelievably rapid, occurring in an eye blink. She stood, nine feet of silver fur and infinite rage.

A pair of armored men pounded their way into the room, drawing her gaze. She blurred toward them just like he would have done but far, far faster. The move shook him to the core, because it completely changed the rules as he understood them. Apparently Isis could use the powers of both sexes.

She seized both suits by the head, dashing them together like a pair of melons. She dropped the now headless corpses and turned to face him.

"We will speak when the slaughter is finished. Remember what I have said," she roared, and her hot, fetid breath washed over him. "Humility, little whelp, your life depends on it."

Blair wasn't proud of what happened next. Warm wetness spread around his crotch as his bladder released itself of its own accord. Yep, she had, quite literally, made him wet his pants.

80

THE MOTHER

L iz staggered away from the armored soldier, clutching at the new wound in her side. The arm spurs were sharp enough to sever limbs, though thankfully she'd danced away before he'd been able to puncture anything vital. She knew she was at the edge of her abilities, chest heaving as she bled from a multitude of wounds.

Gathering the shadows was like hefting boulders. She staggered into the darkness, collapsing against one of the undamaged obelisks. She was exhausted. Maybe she should just lie down. No, Blair still needed time, and as long as she could buy that, she couldn't stop fighting.

"Let me handle this," a voice growled from the shadows next to her. That must be the silver werewolf who'd shown up out of nowhere, just in time to delay the soldiers seeking to stop Blair. Without her, Liz would already be dead. "You're in bad shape. If they get a clean shot at you, I don't think you'll survive."

"You're not doing much better," Liz panted, nodding toward the severed arm across the room. A new one had grown back, but it still hung limply at the silver's side. "I don't think either one of us is going to make it out of this, but it doesn't matter. We have to give Blair the time he needs."

"To wake the Mother, I know. I'm Bridget, by the way. I was on Blair's team. He might have mentioned me," the woman said, rising shakily to her feet. The hope in her voice drew a surprising surge of jealousy. Was this Blair's girlfriend?

"I'm Liz. He never mentioned you, but he didn't really talk about the team," she said, grunting as she regained her feet. "We've been dodging Mohn for weeks with hardly a moment to catch our breaths."

Bridget's disappointment was brief, quickly buried under a mask of purpose. Her amber eyes glowed. "We need to attack again, keep them all from getting inside that bunker."

Liz was too tired to answer with more than a slight nod. Bridget melted back into the shadows, and Liz did the same. The effort left her lightheaded, and she had to clutch the obelisk or risk falling. A roar sounded from the far side of the room as Bridget's silver form barreled into an armored soldier. She grabbed an arm, yanking with all her might. It came loose with a tortured shriek of metal that battled the agonized shriek of its owner.

An answering hail of fire came from the several suits remaining, now inside the bunker and using the firing slits. One appeared in the doorway long enough to launch its missiles. Bridget dragged the still-screaming soldier in front of her, using his body to block the explosion. His scream cut off abruptly, replaced by one of Bridget's as she was launched backward and into the wall. She tumbled to the ground and didn't rise.

Liz tried to hobble back into the fight, but the moment she released the obelisk, her balance failed. She sprawled onto the ground in a heap. She struggled feebly but was forced to admit that further action was beyond her. She was done with this fight, regardless of her wishes.

Two soldiers moved in her direction, red dots seeking a target as they scanned the ground near her. She was about to die, and Bridget didn't look like she was faring much better. They'd done everything they could against tremendous odds. She should have been proud of that, but all she wanted to do was sleep.

Stone and metal burst apart in a shower of debris as the bunker simply ceased to exist. Several armored figures were part of that debris, slamming into obelisks or the wall with bone-shattering force. Something massive and beautiful came striding out of the cloud of dust, a silver female perhaps a foot taller than Bridget.

Four armored soldiers were still moving, all wounded but obviously still in the fight. The silver could only be the Mother, and she ricocheted between them faster than the eye could follow, cutting down first one and then another. It was the same ability Blair used, the one he'd claimed only men could do. How was that possible?

The third managed to pepper her with missiles, which detonated in a now familiar explosion of shrapnel and debris. The Mother roared with fury, seemingly unaffected by the blast. She blurred through the cloud of smoke, grabbing the soldier by the neck and dashing his faceplate against the wall so many times that nothing recognizable was left.

One soldier remained. His missile tubes were empty, and he'd apparently realized his rifle was useless, because he tossed it away in a clatter. "Come on, you bitch. You might kill me, but I'm going down swinging."

"You," the Mother thundered, taking a step toward the audacious soldier. "You are the leader of these fools, the one responsible for damaging the Ark. For hunting the pathetic whelp who waits within my chamber. You have accelerated the doom of our world, helping to usher in an age of darkness."

She blurred forward, seizing the soldier's wrists in one of her massive hands. She hoisted him into the air, until his face was even with her own. She delivered a wicked head butt, shattering his visor and revealing a hard face framed by blond hair. Commander Jordan. "Your price goes beyond death. First, you will know the damage you have wrought. Allow me to show you."

The Mother peered deep into his eyes for long moments. Then

Jordan began to scream. It went on and on until it finally trailed off into a whimper. "I—I didn't know. Dear God, what have we done?"

"You have been judged, Commander Aaron Jordan. I find you lacking," she growled. Her jaws opened, enveloping the man's throat. She bit down in a spray of blood and metal, savaging his flesh with the brutality of a predator. Then she discarded his body as though it were a fast food wrapper, forgotten just as easily.

She turned toward Liz, striding across the floor until she towered over her. "Be at ease, little sister. I will destroy this offal, and then I will return. If you possess the strength, tend to your sisters. Know that there will be a redress for the wrongs done to you."

Then the Mother blurred, disappearing up the tunnel to the surface.

81

MOTHER'S WRATH

The Mother called upon the watchful eye of Zopolote to extend her senses. Scores of hearts beat frantically outside the mouth of the Ark's exit, a sea of ignorant rabble come to silence a voice they could neither understand nor contain. Her voice.

Not since the days when she'd helped deliver such terrible power to the deathless had she felt this kind of fury. Millennia of planning were washed away by the foolish decisions of a handful. Why had Ahiga not woken her the moment the Ark had activated? Why creep out to see this new world, endangering everything?

He'd been such a curious boy, and that had not changed when he came to manhood. His actions here should bring no surprise. Yet she felt the sting of it keenly. This young one, Blair, had some excuse for his behavior. He'd grown up in a decadent world without the horrors her people had faced. But for Ahiga, there could be no forgiveness. His dalliance had cost them everything.

The Mother blurred from the mouth of the tunnel, leaping skyward. She soared into the air, weightless for an endless moment. Then she plummeted into the ranks of her enemies, like a star. They brought their curious weapons to bear, these guns. Such weapons allowed the unblooded to think of themselves as warriors, but the weapons conveyed neither discipline nor skill.

She danced among them, tearing out throats and ripping off limbs. At first the multitude rushed toward her. They fired their weapons, wounding only their allies as she flowed around each attack. More and more fell, cut down as she glided through their ranks.

The Mother lost count of the number she'd slaughtered, instead focusing on the thrill of the hunt and the taste of hot blood and warm flesh. On and on she killed, leaving a sea of bodies in her wake.

Then they broke, scrambling in all directions for the imagined safety of the hills. She shattered their illusions, teaching the fools the folly of their actions. She blurred from target to target, slaughtering with all the fury she could muster. All her anger, her frustration. All her disappointment, her despair. She channeled them into death, burning them away as she killed.

After a time, her pace slowed. There were very few foes now, scattering into the night like rabbits before the wolf. Yet she could see far more keenly under the moon than they realized. They could not hide. They were too slow to run. The few remaining would-be warriors stank of fear and panic. They were broken, yet she gave them no mercy. They had to die, every last one. Not just for their sins, but because more champions would be needed. More were always needed when the deathless came.

She leapt atop the southern slope of the Ark, scanning the horizon. Four figures had reached a narrow trail leading to a ridge above. She would deal with them first. Two more hobbled away from the lip of a ridge that had been covered in ice during the Mother's time.

One was dressed in the same uniforms as the rest of the soldiers. The other, she recognized from Blair's memories. Trevor, their ally and a respectable warrior for this age. He would need to be culled eventually, but not this night. He would be accorded much honor when his time came, not be part of such a tasteless slaughter.

She blurred to the bottom of the trail the four frightened rabbits fled down, peering up at the nearest soldier. The man had dropped his rifle and smelled sharply of urine. She blurred again, disemboweling the wretch. Before his body could fall, she did the same to the second and then the third. The fourth had turned before she took his throat.

The Mother scanned the area around the Ark. Incredibly that had been the last foe. She'd slaughtered them all, every last unblooded mongrel. Relief flooded her. The Ark was again hers, despite the tremendous cost. Now it was time to return and see what could be salvaged, both of the Ark and of her new Ka-Dun.

82

ANSWERS

Blair emerged from the tunnel in time to hear Jordan's final scream, slack-jawed as the Mother ripped out the Commander's throat. She savaged the armor like it was cloth, wrenching away a mouthful of flesh and metal. Jordan's sudden death crashed into Blair, knocking him to his knees. He could only stare.

For what felt like months, Jordan had been a bogeyman dogging his every step. The Terminator sent to track him down. Bare minutes ago that very man was converging on their position with an unstoppable army. Blair had been certain the werewolves were going to die, though no one had given voice to that belief. Yet now the man that had driven them to despair had, himself, been killed. Effortlessly.

The Mother paused near Liz, speaking in a tone decidedly friendlier than the one he'd received. Then she blurred back to the surface. He almost felt bad for the Mohn soldiers. How long would they last? Three minutes? Five, maybe? He only hoped that she'd leave Trevor alone. Not that he could stop her if she decided to take his life. He doubted all of them together and in top form could do that.

"Liz, are you all right?" Cyntia's thick Brazilian accent came from just a few feet away. She materialized in human form, unabashedly naked. The woman crouched next to Liz, cradling her head with a surprising tenderness.

"Well, my intestines were blown all over the walls," Liz wheezed, not attempting to rise. "I think I'll live, though."

"Not sure I can say the same," Blair said. He put his back to the obelisk near Liz and Cyntia, sliding down into a sitting position. He was too tired to appreciate that both women were naked. "Pretty sure I may have pissed her off, and I don't think that's going to do anything good to my life expectancy."

"If she comes after you, she'll have to go through me first," came an unexpected voice. He looked up to find Bridget before him, also naked. She was covered in blood and soot, her hair matted to the side of her face.

"You know," he said, feeling a little light headed, "this is starting to look like the intro to a bad porn film."

Bridget sat heavily a few feet away, rolling her eyes as she did. "I'm too tired to slap you."

"I'll do it as soon as I can get up," Liz called weakly.

A chorus of screams began in the distance. The Mother had begun her grisly work.

"I almost feel bad for them," Blair said, staring at the tunnel that led to the surface.

"I don't," Cyntia said, tone sour. "They deserve what they get for killing Adolpho and Elmira."

"Oh, God. I'm so sorry," Liz said, lifting her head from Cyntia's lap. Cyntia forced it gently back down.

"We are at war. Death happens, and I must become accustomed to it," Cyntia replied, lapsing into a sullen silence.

"Bridget, what happened to Steve and Sheila?" Blair asked because he wanted to change the subject and because he was genuinely curious.

"Steve...didn't make it," Bridget said, avoiding his gaze. She looked back after a moment. "Sheila is fine. It was her that got me out of where Mohn was holding me. She's with your friend. Trevor, he said his name was."

The screams above were less frequent and more distant. Tension thickened. No one mentioned the reason why. The Mother would be returning soon.

"She's alive. That's wonderful news," Blair said. It was a bright spot among all the horrors they'd faced. He caught Liz's eye. She was watching him curiously. "Sheila was part of my research team. She's also one of my closest friends."

Everyone turned toward the tunnel as if some silent signal had been given. No one dared speak. The terror of a single question silenced them. What would the Mother do when she returned?

Then she was there. The Mother stepped from the shadows near the central obelisk, just a few feet from their little circle. She'd returned to her human form, so innocuous at first glance. That illusion faded the moment anyone met her ancient gaze. Not only had she not torn her clothing during her transformation, but also the strange garments were completely clean. Not so much as a single spec of dirt or blood disgraced her image.

"The dawning of the next age is upon us," the Mother said, looking to Liz. She didn't even glance at Blair. "Our sun changes, beginning the next phase of the cycle. It will remain this way for years beyond counting, fueling the strength of the deathless. Even now they rise among every people across this world. You must be prepared to face them."

"I'm in no shape to walk, much less fight," Liz said, though not forcefully enough to suggest a challenge. Blair doubted anyone else was stupid enough to speak to the Mother the way he had.

"Impertinent for one so young. I like your spirit," the Mother said, with a wolfish grin. She settled into a cross-legged position not far from Liz and Cyntia. "Your pack needs time to recuperate. Let us use that time wisely. You must have a great many questions. Ask, and I will answer as I can."

"I think Blair should be the one to ask the questions," Liz said, nodding in his direction. Her gaze held a respect that made him sit up straighter. "He's the one who discovered this place and learned your language, the one who risked everything to make it back here. I think you owe *him* answers, not me."

"You'd defer to this male?" the Mother asked, eyebrows rising. Then she gave a slight smile, one she shared with all of them. "This truly is a different time. Your ways are strange, but in this I will honor them. Ask your questions, Ka-Dun. Hear them answered."

"Your memories. That was you discovering an Ark, wasn't it? One somewhere in Europe," he asked, keeping his tone as humble as possible. He was talking to a survivor from a past age, one who could answer so many questions about the origin of man. Assuming she didn't kill him out of hand.

"I did. My people were being exterminated by a rival tribe. We fled and had no choice but to seek shelter in the Valley of Hidden Voices, a place our shamans had long said was cursed. There we found the Ark, as you saw. We were ushered inside, where I learned the secrets of the place," the Mother explained. She heaved a heavy sigh. "I lack the time to tell you the full story, but it was there that I made my greatest mistake. I helped craft the evil that would become the deathless."

"Why?" Blair asked, aghast.

"To save the man I love, the man from my memories. Osiris," she explained.

Bridget gave a low squawk of recognition, eyes like saucers as she met Blair's gaze. He nodded at her and then turned back to the Mother. "What are the Arks?"

"I do not believe anyone can fully answer that question. We do not know how old they are, or who built them originally. But each contains a vast store of knowledge and incredible power," the Mother said. She began toying with a lock of her hair. The gesture was childlike, completely out of place on what was, for all intents and purposes, a goddess.

Then she rose abruptly, glancing at the tunnel. "Do you feel that? It begins."

Blair did feel it, a tingling that washed over his entire body. It could only be one thing. "It's the second wave. Our world is ending."

EPILOGUE

"Well, I guess they succeeded," Trevor said, still processing the slaughter in the valley below. A silver werewolf who moved faster than Blair and hugged the shadows even more tightly than Liz flowed between soldiers. Wherever she passed, people died. Some tried to fight, but it didn't save them.

"She's terrifying," Sheila said, leaning heavily on the rock she was using as a seat. Even under the thin moonlight, she looked paler by the minute. "That is the most terrifying thing I have ever seen. Those men don't have a chance. Trevor, what if she comes after us?"

He considered the question for several moments. "Then we die. There's no way we can outrun her, and we certainly can't fight."

"Out of sight, out of mind. I'm ready to head down to that car you were talking about," Sheila suggested, a pleading note creeping into her tone.

"You aren't getting an argument from me," Trevor agreed. No sense in drawing this Mother's attention. He picked up his Barrett, offering his free hand to Sheila. He doubted she'd be able to make the walk by herself, especially in the dark. "Here, take my arm. I'll guide you. It's not very far, just a few hundred yards. We'll be there in no time."

Sheila nodded gratefully but saved her breath for walking. Picking their way down the mountainside in the dark was agonizingly slow, but it was still better than the alternative. Long minutes later they finally reached the little dirt track Liz had jokingly called a road. The battered pair of pickup trucks waited in the moonlight. Despite how tiny the vehicles were, compared with their testosterone-fueled American equivalents, they were almost as wide as the path.

"There you go," Trevor said, helping Sheila into the passenger seat of the closest truck. She gave a relieved sigh as she settled into the torn seat. Maybe it was the light coming from the cab of the truck, but she looked whiter than any sheet.

"Thank you, Trevor. I couldn't have done that on my own on a good day, and this is not my best day ever," she said, panting rapidly. He felt the altitude himself, but he was in pretty good shape.

"Wait, do you see that?" Her attention had turned to the southern horizon. Her eyes widened.

Trevor spun to see what she was looking at. "My God. It's started."

Yellow and scarlet ribbons of fire veined across the sky, spiderwebbing their way closer with incredible speed. It was like the Aurora Borealis on an indescribably massive scale but much, much more dangerous. They were nowhere near the poles, so they would miss the brunt of the radiation, but electronics the world over were about to be destroyed.

Sheila began to thrash and shake. It looked like some sort of epileptic seizure. Crap. She might bite off her own tongue and bleed out if he didn't get something between her teeth. He glanced around until he spotted a dead branch from a scrubby bush. That should work. He picked it up, breaking off both sides until he held an eight-inch length.

He leaned on Sheila's lap, pinning her as best he could while he tried to force the stick into her mouth. She thrashed wildly, making the task incredibly difficult. "Come on, Sheila, don't fight me. This is for your own good."

Sheila began coughing. White goop oozed from her mouth. What the hell was that? A gob landed on his arm, and he gagged in disgust.

Then Sheila struck like a snake, seizing his hand in her mouth. She bit down hard, ripping off a hunk of flesh between his thumb and forefinger. He jerked away from her, pulling a length of gauze from his cargo pants. The sky bathed them in a hellish undulating glow, brighter than full noon, though the color was off. Everything was too white.

"What the goddamned fuck, Sheila?" Trevor growled. His hand was on fire.

Sheila staggered jerkily to her feet, lumbering in his direction. Her eyes were milky white, arms outstretched. She looked just like a...*fucking zombie*. Trevor acted with reflexes honed in preparation for just this occasion. He ripped his combat knife from its sheath around his calf, dancing on the balls of his feet as Sheila closed.

As soon as she was close enough, he grabbed her arm, jerking her toward him. She tripped, falling heavily to the ground. Then he was on her, jabbing the knife into her skull. He twisted it, jerking the blade free and staggering back. She flopped to the ground and twitched once before she lay still.

He punched the hood of the pickup. Sudden rage flooded him. This couldn't be happening. Not to him, of all people. He'd spent years preparing for something like this. "Are you fucking serious?" he shouted to the universe. "The zombie apocalypse starts, and I get bitten in the *first thirty seconds*? Really?"

Trevor's hand began to tremble. He held it up near the light inside the truck's cab. Black veins had already begun crawling up his wrist.

Note to the Reader

Wow, that was a pretty messed up cliffhanger. Trust me, I didn't want to leave it there but the novel is already 130,000 words and my editor threatened to hurt me if I didn't cut it here.

Sign up to the mailing list to receive a free copy of the **The First Ark**, which explains where the Mother comes from and how the zombie virus was created. Once you're done, check out **No Mere Zombie: Deathless Book 2!**

Want more info on the series, character artwork and other goodies? Check out my website at chrisfoxwrites.com.

If you'd like to visit us on Facebook you can find us at https://www.facebook.com/chrisfoxwrites

Made in the USA
Lexington, KY
19 August 2019